"Hailey. Listen to [barcode] **as he spoke. "You** **Middle East right now.**

"But— "

"It's not safe. Your brother didn't want you in danger."

She heard the plea in his voice. "But mission work is dangerous. Clay knew that. I know it, too."

"I don't care how prepared you think you are, you can't go there alone."

She touched his shoulder, surprised at the tension she felt under her hand. "I won't be alone. I'll have others with me. And, of course, I'll have God."

His shocked gaze locked with hers. "The Lord can't protect you from roadside bombs."

Looking into Wolf's angry expression, Hailey knew words wouldn't get through to him now. But maybe a firsthand account would.

"Come to church with me this afternoon," she said. "A couple who are permanently based in the Middle East are visiting," she explained.

"You're not going to listen to another word I say unless I agree to this, are you?"

"Nope."

"You are one hard-headed woman, Hailey O'Brien." His tone held a hint of admiration.

"So I've been told, Captain Wolfson."

A SOLDIER'S HOMECOMING

RENEE RYAN
AND
MINDY OBENHAUS

2 Uplifting Stories

Homecoming Hero and *Falling for the Hometown Hero*

LOVE INSPIRED
INSPIRATIONAL ROMANCE

LOVE INSPIRED®

INSPIRATIONAL ROMANCE

ISBN-13: 978-1-335-43061-8

Recycling programs
for this product may
not exist in your area.

A Soldier's Homecoming

Love Inspired
22 Adelaide St. West, 41st Floor
Toronto, Ontario M5H 4E3, Canada
www.LoveInspired.com

Printed in U.S.A.

CONTENTS

Renee Ryan grew up in a Florida beach town where she learned to surf, sort of. With a degree from Florida State University, she explored career opportunities at a Florida theme park and a modeling agency and even taught high school economics. She currently lives with her husband in Wisconsin, and many have mistaken their overweight cat for a small bear. You may contact Renee at reneeryan.com, on Facebook or on Twitter, @reneeryanbooks.

Books by Renee Ryan

Love Inspired

Thunder Ridge

Surprise Christmas Family
The Sheriff's Promise
Opening His Holiday Heart

Village Green

Claiming the Doctor's Heart
The Doctor's Christmas Wish

Love Inspired Trade

The Widows of Champagne

Love Inspired Historical

Charity House

The Marshal Takes a Bride
Hannah's Beau

Visit the Author Profile page at LoveInspired.com for more titles.

HOMECOMING HERO

Renee Ryan

Come to me, all you who are weary and burdened, and I will give you rest.

—*Matthew* 11:28

To First Lieutenant Erik J. Anthes.
I'm humbled by your continued dedication to
our country. Thank you for your service, my friend.
May God keep you safe and in His arms always.

Chapter One

U.S. Army Captain Ty Wolfson stared at his friend's childhood home in stunned silence. He'd been so focused on getting off post he hadn't considered what he might find once he arrived in Savannah. The possibility that he'd be standing in front of a two-hundred-year-old house in the heatrt of the historic district hadn't crossed his mind.

Not once.

But here Wolf stood, confronting generations of tradition, wrapped up neatly in what the historical marker deemed O'Brien House.

As he read the story of the O'Brien family history, guilt twisted painfully in his gut. It should be Clay preparing to climb up these steps. Not Wolf. Not like this, under these terrible circumstances.

And yet…he *would* walk inside that house. To fulfill the promise he'd made to Clay on that Iraqi roadside.

Determined to accomplish the difficult task before him, Wolf started forward, but a jolt of sorrow knifed through him. The feeling was so strong, so visceral he had to stop and swallow several times to get the emotion under control.

Breathing hard, he lowered his gaze to the grainy photograph he'd kept with him for the last six months. The sight of Clay's little sister grinning back at him made Wolf's heartbeat quicken with anxiety.

Dressed in a traditional graduation gown with the requisite mortarboard scrunched on top of her head, Hailey O'Brien looked far too young, and far too innocent to have set such a dangerous course for her life.

Whatever it took, Wolf would stop her. He owed that much to Clay. And the friendship they'd shared in Iraq.

Blinking the grit out of his eyes, he stuffed the photograph back in his pocket and studied Clay's childhood home a moment longer. He knew he was stalling, but he needed a chance to take it all in.

The three-story brick mansion filled an entire city block. Each floor boasted rows of tall, double-glass doorways leading onto cast-iron balconies. A fence in the same ornate design ran along the perimeter of the manicured lawn, encircling tall trees and large bushes that reached halfway to the second floor.

With his gaze tracking the adjacent streets, Wolf experienced a sense of claustrophobia. There were too many trees in this part of town and the houses were too close together. He'd lived too long in the desert not to feel pinned in now.

Shivering, he blew into his cupped palms. The temperature had dropped to a sharp, bitter cold that turned his breath to frost. Clay had prepared him for the heat, with his constant griping about the Savannah humidity. But he'd said nothing about this bone-rattling cold that made Wolf's leg ache more than usual.

A light mist swirled in the gray, depressing air. The perfect accompaniment for all the regrets he harbored in his heart. Duty was all he had left. Duty and this one goal, the fulfillment of his promise to a fallen friend.

"Might as well get this over with," he muttered.

Gritting his teeth, Wolf set out across the street. He hid the pain in his left leg behind an even gait and stone-cold determination.

After three sharp raps of the ornate knocker the door swung open. Wolf jerked in surprise. With her dark hair, big green eyes and curvy figure, Hailey O'Brien was not the teenager he'd prepared for in his mind. She was a woman—a throat-clogging, heart-stopping, *beautiful* woman.

He knew he was staring. How could he not? Clay's sister was nothing like the fuzzy graduation picture her brother had kept on the dash of their Humvee and Wolf now had in his pocket.

Wolf tried to speak. Even managed to open his mouth, but memories got in the way and he pressed his lips tightly together. His head filled with contrasting images of Clay kicking around a soccer ball with some local kids outside the forward operating base. Clay blinking up at him on the Iraqi roadside as he was bleeding out.

Clay issuing the request that had brought Wolf to this house today…

You gotta keep Hailey out of the Sandpit, Wolf-man. No mission work. Not here. Promise me you'll stop her.

Wolf hadn't hesitated in his response. *I won't let you down.*

The memory of his own words pushed Wolf into action. "Are you Hailey O'Brien?"

She nodded. Slowly. And it finally registered that she'd been standing there speechless, just like him. Even now, she simply stared at him with her beautiful, unguarded, attentive eyes. Waiting. Watching.

"I…" Wolf cleared his throat. "I was a friend of your brother's."

Instant pain filled her gaze and the wall went up. Wolf hadn't expected that.

"You knew Clay?" she asked at last, her voice deeper and throatier than he'd expected.

"I did. He asked me to—" Wolf cut off his words midsentence, realizing he couldn't blurt out why he was here without some sort of buildup. "That is, I was with him when he died." Which wasn't what he'd meant to say, either.

She blinked. "You were?"

"Yes."

She blinked again. And then…

One lone tear slid down her cheek.

Great beginning, Wolf, you made the poor woman cry.

With concentrated effort, he softened his voice. "My name is Ty. Ty Wolfson."

"Wolf." Her shoulders snapped back. "Yes, of course. I should have…expected this."

"You know me?"

She nodded. "My brother mentioned you in his e-mails."

Wolf didn't know what to do with that information, so he redirected the conversation. "Is this a bad time?" He shifted his gaze, only just noticing the purse strapped around her shoulder and the coat slung over her arm. "You look ready to go out."

"Oh. I... No." She drew her bottom lip between her teeth. "I mean, I am heading out, but it can wait."

Okay, good. He had her attention again. Now, if he could get his tongue to work properly he might be able to finish what he'd come here to do. Then he could return to his temporary housing on post and give in to his exhaustion. The forty-eight-hour journey out of Iraq was catching up with him.

"What I have to say won't take long," he promised. Not if he could help it.

"Oh. *Oh.* I'm so sorry. I'm being rude, making you stand out there in the cold." She gave him a quick, tense smile. "Please. Come in. I don't know what I was thinking."

Wolf heard the genuine remorse in her words, saw the guilt in her eyes and felt bad for upsetting her. "No worries. I didn't give you any warning I was coming. I'm sure this is a shock."

Her smile turned a little watery, but she stepped aside to make room for him to pass.

Frowning at the fancy rug just inside the doorway, Wolf stomped off the week-old Iraqi desert still clinging to his boots and moved forward. The smell of furniture polish and old money had him hesitating. But only for a moment.

Shoulders back, he followed Hailey down a portrait-filled hallway. He tried to look anywhere but at Clay's sister. Easier said than done, especially considering the confines of the tiny corridor. Each step she took was dignified and regal, the perfect blend of confidence and class that came from a life spent in country clubs and expensive schools.

Wolf shouldn't be watching her so closely. It reeked of betrayal to his friend.

Forcing back a spurt of guilt, he focused his gaze on the wall of pictures. They were hung in a haphazard pattern that made an odd sort of sense. Some of the photographs were in large frames, some small. Some were yellowed with age, others much newer. But all had the common theme of family, stability and normalcy, things Wolf had never experienced in his thirty years of life.

His guard instantly went up.

Good thing, too, because in the next moment Hailey led him into a large room with fancy tables, ornate chairs and more photographs. Lots and lots of photographs.

He could handle the obvious wealth reflected in the expensive furnishings. But *this,* this shadowy sense of homecoming, left Wolf wanting things he couldn't form into coherent thoughts.

There was something about this room that put him on edge. The comfort that radiated out of every corner was a visible reminder of everything Wolf had missed out on as a child.

Great. Nothing like being the big stinkin' fish out of water in an already tense situation.

Hailey set her purse and coat on a chair, then turned back to face him. "Please, have a seat, uh… Lieutenant?"

"Captain," he corrected automatically, looking for a suitable place to sit. "It's Captain now."

Unable to settle, Wolf avoided the fragile-looking furniture and strode through the room with clipped, restless strides.

Now that he was here, facing Clay's sister at last, he didn't know how to begin.

At the beginning? The end? Somewhere in between?

Hands clasped in front of her, Hailey eyed the soldier pacing through the original parlor of O'Brien House, all the while trying to keep hold of her composure. Unfortunately, Captain Wolfson's nervousness was wearing off on her. Clearly he had something important to say, but he wasn't having much success in getting the words past his lips.

So she waited.

And watched.

He couldn't stand still for more than a few seconds at a time. His fingers tapped out a chaotic rhythm on his thigh. Her toes caught the uneasy cadence, until she realized what she was doing and stopped. Clay had been jumpy like this the first time he'd returned home from Iraq.

Clay. *Oh, Clay.*

Her heart lurched at the mere thought of her brother. Tears stung the backs of her eyes. How she missed him. She'd been so proud of his role in the Army, awed by his dedication, and inspired by his descriptions of the strides the military was making in Iraq. But then God had taken him home. And Hailey had been forced to examine her own life. She hadn't liked what she'd discovered about herself.

But that was in the past. She was a different woman now, with more conviction. Where Clay had set out to bring peace to the Middle East, she would do what was necessary to bring hope.

Lord, help me to honor my brother's sacrifice with my mission work. Let him not have died in vain.

Feeling stronger, resolved, she focused once more on Captain Wolfson. He looked at home in his Army camouflage and tan combat boots. What Clay used to call his BDUs.

As she waited for the captain to speak, Hailey silently congratulated herself on maintaining her composure. When she'd opened the door to him earlier she'd almost lost it.

During that terrible, heart-stopping declaration that he'd been with Clay when he'd died the tears had pressed against her lids. Only one had escaped. She'd held the rest back. That's what mattered. As her mother had always said, an O'Brien woman kept her poise under *all* circumstances.

Oh, but it hurt to look at this man pacing through her home like a caged panther. With his dark hair, ice-blue eyes and direct gaze, Captain Wolfson was far too much like her brother.

Except...he was nothing like Clay. Hard. Yes, that was the word that came to mind as she gazed up at him. No. Not hard. Sorrowful. Wounded. A man with regrets.

She could stand the suspense no longer. "You said you have something important to tell me?"

He jerked at her voice and then his hand shot out, as though he was reaching for something. His weapon? Clay had reacted the same way whenever a loud noise surprised him.

"I'm sorry, Captain." She spoke softer this time. "I didn't mean to startle you."

"It's okay." He closed his hand into a tight fist. "I'm just a little low on sleep."

Possibly. But she doubted that was the cause of his jumpiness. She rose slowly, careful not to make any sudden movements. "You have something to tell me about Clay?"

"Yes. But sit back down." He gestured to the chair she'd just abandoned. "Please."

"If you'll join me."

He looked at several pieces of furniture, narrowing his eyes as he went.

Understanding dawned. "Clay didn't like this room, either." She allowed herself a short laugh. "He said it was too girly."

Wolf smiled at that. It was a quick, almost indiscernible lift of his lips, but a smile all the same. Unfortunately, the gesture made him seem somehow…sadder.

Shoulders set, he lowered himself to the love seat facing her. She could practically hear his thoughts colliding into one another as he leaned forward and captured her gaze with his. "You should know that Clay died honorably."

It was her turn to smile, grateful for those simple, straightforward words affirming what she already knew. "I'm glad to hear it."

"You're not surprised."

"Clay was an honorable man."

"*That* he was."

An uncomfortable silence fell over them.

Hailey swallowed. "Was that what you came to tell me?"

"No." He broke eye contact, but not before she saw the agony in his gaze.

This conversation was hard on him, that much was clear. Well, it was equally difficult for her. She still missed her brother. Desperately. He'd been the last of her living relatives. After six full months, she often found herself waking in the middle of the night with tears running down her cheeks.

But as bad as she felt over her loss, this man had watched Clay die.

Without thinking too hard about what she was doing, Hailey moved to a spot next to him on the love seat and took one of his hands in hers. When he didn't pull away, she squeezed gently. Her meeting at the church was no longer important. Giving this man comfort mattered more. Maybe, in the process, she would find a moment of peace, as well.

For several seconds, Captain Wolfson sat deathly still next to her, staring at their joined hands with his brows scrunched together. Confusion? Frustration? She couldn't read his emotions anymore.

And then a dreadful thought occurred to her. "Did something happen to Clay that the military hasn't told me? Something…classified?"

"No." He sucked in a harsh breath. "*No*. His death was senseless, but not unusual. Our Humvee hit a roadside bomb. Clay lived a few minutes longer than the other three soldiers with us."

The other three? Counting Clay and Captain Wolfson that made five men in the truck. "Are you saying you were the only one who made it out alive?"

"Yes." The word came out softer than a whisper. And so sorrowful.

Hailey clasped his hand a little harder. "I'm sorry."

He squeezed back, then lifted his gaze to meet hers. She gasped at what she saw in his eyes. Pain. Grief. And something else. Guilt, maybe? Was he suffering from survivor's guilt? She'd heard about the terrible emotion, but had never truly understood it.

Until now.

Lord, how do I help this man?

She wasn't trained for something like this. It was more than she could handle.

Just as despair nearly overtook her, Wolf's face cleared of all expression and he tugged his hand free. "Clay made one final request before he died."

A sense of dread whipped through her. She didn't want to hear the rest. Captain Wolfson had the unrelenting look of a man filled with resolve, the kind of determination a person got when he had to do *or say* something awful.

As afraid as she was to hear the rest, she had to ask, had to know. "What was my brother's last request?"

"He asked me to stop you from going to the Middle East."

Hailey shifted uncomfortably in her seat. "But…that doesn't make any sense."

In fact, the very idea was absurd.

Captain Wolfson rolled his shoulders, his gaze never fully releasing hers. "He was adamant."

"You must have misunderstood. My becoming a missionary was Clay's idea."

"Not in the end." He spoke the words in a hard, ruthless tone while his eyes—those sad, grief-stricken eyes—flared with raw emotion.

Hailey wished she didn't see the misery in him, didn't understand it and want to soothe it away. So she focused on what she knew for certain. "You're mistaken. Clay's e-mails said otherwise. I saved them all, including the one where he first encouraged me to start the application process."

"Yeah, well, he changed his mind." Wolf's tone hardened even more than before. "When he was bleeding out on the desert floor."

Hailey recoiled. "How can you say something so awful, so...*graphic?*"

"Because you're not listening to me." He rose abruptly, towering over her with his massive size. He looked every bit the warrior now, a man who had seen and done awful things.

Odd, but she wasn't afraid of him. Only confused. His words and attitude didn't match any of what Clay had said to her. "It's... I mean, I..."

"Hailey. Listen to me." His voice shook as he dropped to one knee. The gesture brought his gaze at eye level with hers. "Clay was right to send me. You can't travel to the Middle East right now."

"But—"

"*Listen* to me. It's not safe. Your brother didn't want you in danger."

She heard the plea in his voice, saw the conviction in his bunched shoulders. "But, Captain Wolfson, mission work is dangerous. Clay knew that. *I* know it, too."

"I don't care how prepared you think you are, you can't go in there alone."

She touched his shoulder, surprised at the tension she felt under her hand. "I won't be alone. I'll have others with me. And, of course, I'll have God."

"*God?*" His shocked gaze locked with hers. "The Lord can't protect you from IEDs."

She sighed at his vehemence, not to mention his very real anger at God. She had to make him understand the

Truth. "If it's His will, He can. Besides, you're missing the point."

"No. You are."

Looking into Wolf's angry expression, Hailey knew words wouldn't get through to him now. But maybe a firsthand account would.

"Come to church with me this afternoon," she said.

He looked at her as if she'd gone insane.

"We're having a reception for some visiting missionaries," she explained quickly. "Including a couple who are permanently based in the Middle East."

He opened his mouth, probably to protest, but she raised her hand to stop him from interrupting her. "No. Wait. Don't say anything yet. I want to make a deal with you first."

His eyes narrowed. "What sort of deal?"

"If you promise to listen to the Mulligans' story without judgment, then I'll promise to listen to your arguments with the same mind-set."

He looked at her for an endless moment. As each second passed, frustration filled his gaze. But then he shook his head at her and said, "You're not going to listen to another word I say unless I agree to this, are you?"

"Nope."

"You are one hardheaded woman, Hailey O'Brien." His tone held a hint of admiration.

"So I've been told, Captain Wolfson."

A moment of solidarity passed between them. And something else. Something pleasant, but not altogether comfortable. "So you'll come with me today?"

"Do I have a choice?"

"Not if you want me to listen to the rest of your arguments."

He smiled at her then, with the kind of stomach-twisting grin that turned his blue, blue eyes to a deep midnight. He no longer reminded her of Clay. In fact, the man was far too handsome for his own good. Hailey had to remind herself why he was here. He wanted to stop her from going to the Middle East.

"All right. You win this round, Hailey. For the next, let's say, two hours." He glanced at his watch. "I'm all yours."

I'm all yours. Hailey's heart kicked hard against her ribs. *I'm. All. Yours.*

Three simple words, spoken in such a matter-of-fact tone. But Hailey knew the battle was far from over.

Captain Wolfson had made a promise to her dying brother. He didn't seem like a man who would relent easily.

Of course, what he didn't know was that she'd made her own promise. To the Lord.

Chapter Two

Hailey stepped onto the front porch ahead of Captain Wolfson. Although she could feel his intense gaze on her, she managed to click the lock in place on the first try.

Gathering her composure, she turned to face him directly.

Their gazes locked, held. And held some more.

Her pulse did a little cha-cha before settling into a heavy, thick *thump...thump...thump.*

Something deep inside her, the part she'd ignored since Clay's death, recognized this man as a kindred spirit. Was it solidarity from a mutual loss? Or something more disturbing?

Either way, it wasn't supposed to be like this. She wasn't supposed to be emotionally involved with a man after only a half-hour acquaintance.

Yet, here she stood, blinking at him without a word coming to mind. As the silence lengthened, the cold, wet air encircled them, creating an illusion that they were the only two people left in the world.

She wasn't attracted to the man. Was she? No. He

wasn't her type. She preferred artistic intellectuals who wore wire-framed glasses. Not big, strong, elemental warriors.

"Where are you parked?" she asked, pleased at her even tone. If her mother was still alive she'd be proud of Hailey. After all, O'Brien women always kept control of a situation, no matter how unusual, unexpected or emotionally charged.

"I'm three blocks that way." He angled his head to her left.

She lifted her eyebrows, fully aware that the city's layout didn't afford adequate parking. "You actually found an open spot on the street?"

"Yeah. Total cakewalk." He gave her a wry grin. "If you consider three passes down eight different streets easy."

Hailey heard a trace of humor underneath the frustration in his voice. He didn't seem angry about the inconvenience of finding a parking space, only mildly annoyed. That said a lot about his character.

Her brother's friend was a patient man, even when he was clearly exhausted.

She found herself intrigued by him all over again.

Hailey, no. Not your type. Remember why he sought you out today.

"Captain Wolfson—"

"Ty." One side of his mouth kicked up. "My name is Ty."

Oh, why, *why* did he have to turn appealing now, when she was working so hard to put him in the role of opponent?

A breathy sigh slipped out of her before she could stop it. "Ty, I—"

"Or...you can call me Wolf."

Wolf. Right. That's what Clay had called him. She could see why, too. His eyes were just like a wolf's. Stark, emotionless, guarded. Maybe even a little scary.

"Who's afraid of the Big, Bad Wolf?"

He sighed, looking slightly disappointed in her. Clearly, he'd heard that one before.

Why had she said it, anyway? Maybe it was because his grin had made her feel like Little Red Riding Hood skipping unwittingly into the beast's trap.

She'd been wrong in her earlier assessment of the man. He wasn't elemental.

He was dangerous.

And when it came to men, Hailey O'Brien did not *do* dangerous. Ever.

It was important she remember that little factoid about herself. "All jokes aside, I think Wolf suits you best."

He lifted a shoulder. "Call me whatever you like."

"Well then, *Wolf,* do you want to ride with me?"

"No." He looked over his shoulder in the direction he'd indicated earlier. "I have my own wheels."

His answer was quick. A little too quick. "How can I be sure you'll show?"

"Because I said I would."

She recognized her mistake at once. Even without Clay's e-mails to attest to his character, the rough honesty and deep code of ethics Wolf lived by were obvious in his direct gaze and straightforward manner.

"I'm sorry." She broke eye contact, resisting an urge to dig her toe in the knothole at her foot. "I didn't mean to insult you."

"Apology accepted."

Before he could speak again, she rattled off the address for Faith Community Church.

He nodded. "I know the one."

Again, he surprised her. "You do?"

He didn't reply at first, merely stared at her. A battle seemed to wage behind his eyes before he said, "Hailey, this isn't my first trip to Savannah. I was at Fort Stewart six months before I was deployed to Iraq this last time."

"But Clay's e-mails said you two met in Iraq."

"We did. We became friends—" He stopped, shut his mouth, swallowed hard and then started again. "We became *friends* when I got transferred to his platoon twelve months ago."

She reached out to touch his arm but he shifted away and then started down the front steps ahead of her. Without turning around, he waited for her to join him.

Play it safe, use your head and never, never make a decision out of emotion. Those had been the rules the old Hailey had lived by before Clay died.

The *new* Hailey was a full-grown, twenty-six-year-old woman who lived by a different set of standards. She took risks. Lots of them. Well, not yet. But she would soon. When she boarded a plane to Iraq. Or Afghanistan. Or wherever the mission board sent her.

Deciding to start being brave right now, Hailey marched down the stairs, head held high, and faced Wolf. "I'll see you at the church in fifteen?"

"Just so we're clear," he began. "I'll meet your missionaries. I'll listen to their stories, but then you have to let me say what I came to tell you. All of it. Without interruption."

"That's the plan."

"Good. We understand one another." He turned to leave without speaking another word.

Oh, but she'd caught the grim expression on his face. And the unrelenting tilt of his chin. On the surface, the man looked like a hard, physical specimen ruled by his own prowess. But Captain Wolfson was no knuckle-dragger. He was intelligent, determined and loyal.

He was not going to come around to her way of thinking easily.

Sighing, Hailey watched him head down the side-walk. Only then did she notice his slight limp. Had he been injured during the attack?

It was possible. After all, he'd been blown up by an IED. The muscles in her stomach twitched at the thought.

Lord, why have You brought this man into my life? Why now?

With effort, she folded her confusion deep inside her and headed toward her own car.

Twenty minutes later, Hailey steered into the parking lot of Faith Community Church of Savannah. A feeling of home washed over her.

Like most modern churches, FCC was a functional collection of brick, glass and steel. But despite its lack of worldly grandeur, Hailey always met the Lord here. Even during the dark days following Clay's death, she'd found comfort. And peace. Not from the building, but from her church family.

It was her turn to give back to others in need. A spurt of excitement twisted along her spine. She would no longer be on the sidelines, waiting her turn. Soon, she would be in the heart of the action.

Smiling, she exited her car at the same moment a

motorcycle roared into the empty spot beside her. The snarl of the engine had her jumping back. Her hand flew to her throat and she flattened herself against her car.

Loud, obnoxious, danger-on-two-wheels—what sort of insane, *crazy* person rode a steel beast like that?

As soon as the question came to her, she noticed that the person climbing off the bike wore BDUs and tan army boots. Even before he removed his helmet, she knew whose face she'd see.

Didn't she already recognize the powerful set of Wolf's shoulders and the way he favored his left leg?

There was something so familiar about the man, something that made her feel both safe and uneasy at the same time.

Maybe it was because he reminded her of Clay.

Or…maybe not.

She took in a steadying breath and sighed. She might tell herself she liked the artistic type, she might even believe it in her head, but Captain Wolfson was a *man*. A warrior. A bona fide hero in BDUs.

It was hard not to be attracted to him.

Her twenty-six years of safe existence hadn't prepared her for someone like him, someone who made her question everything she'd ever known about herself and the very real need in the world around her.

Wasn't that the point of her decision to become a missionary? To live out her faith among people? After all, what good did a formal education and countless Bible studies do if she didn't put her knowledge to use in the real world?

And this man, the one pulling off a *motorcycle* helmet, was here to stop her from taking the next step in her Christian walk.

Fat chance.

Convicted all over again, she waited for Wolf to join her on the sidewalk that led to the front of the main church building.

They walked in silence.

Despite her best intentions, Hailey kept sending him covert glances from below her lashes. She was aware of the man with a sharp-edged clarity that was downright disturbing. "You won't regret joining me this afternoon."

He made a noncommittal sound deep in his throat.

Ho-kay, so he was going to play it *that* way?

"I thought you promised an open mind?" she said, failing to keep her annoyance out of her voice.

"It's open." He tapped his left temple. "Wide open." He sounded sincere. But then he gave her a grin that could only be described as…wolfish.

Oh, boy.

Thankfully, she caught sight of a familiar face heading their way. Relief spread through her. "Look, there's J.T." She lifted her hand in greeting.

"Who's J.T.?" Wolf asked, his voice wary.

"Our mission's pastor."

"Right."

Hailey wasn't sure what she heard in Wolf's voice, but he didn't sound convinced.

His next words confirmed her suspicion. "He doesn't look like any pastor I've met before."

Hailey eyed J.T., trying to see him from a newcomer's point of view. "That's because he looks younger than he really is. Don't be fooled, he's in his thirties."

"It's not his age." Wolf narrowed his eyes. "It's something…else."

There was such gravity in his voice that Hailey felt the need to reassure him. "J.T.'s a good guy. You'll like him." She played her ace. "Clay did. They were friends. *Good* friends."

Before Wolf could respond J.T. pulled her into a tight hug. "Hellooooo, beautiful."

Wolf had thought he'd seen everything. He'd survived fifteen brutal years with a mean, alcoholic father. He'd lived on his own for the next fifteen after that. He'd faced insurgents, enemy fire and an IED. But he'd never confronted anything—or anyone—like Hailey's pastor.

Man of God or not, the guy was overly friendly with Clay's sister. In fact, *Pastor* J.T. hugged Hailey a little too long, with far too much enthusiasm.

Inappropriate. That's the word that came to mind as the two finally untangled from each other's arms.

When J.T. kept his hands on Hailey's shoulders, a white-hot ball of emotion roiled in Wolf's stomach. He ignored the sensation and detached himself emotionally from the situation. He was a master at compartmentalizing. It was a gift.

Besides, what did it matter whether he approved of the relationship between Hailey and her pastor?

It was none of his business, emphasis on *none*.

"J.T.," she said, "I have someone I'd like you to meet." Hailey shifted out of the pastor's reach—which was good—and turned those compelling green eyes onto Wolf. Not so good.

His breath tightened in his throat and that ball of emotion rolling around in his stomach tied into a tight knot.

So much for detachment.

"Wolf, this is J. T. Wagner, our mission's pastor."

Despite his instant dislike of the guy, Wolf shook J.T.'s hand. With his surfer-dude, spiky, sun-streaked hair, ratty cargo pants and rock-star T-shirt, J.T. looked like a grown man masquerading as a teenager.

Something wasn't right.

Other than a diamond stud in his left earlobe, the pastor wore no jewelry. Not even a wedding ring.

Yeah, Wolf had checked.

After another moment of inspection, Wolf realized why the picture didn't fit completely. Despite the civilian clothing, J.T. had military written all over him. It was in his stance and the way he moved.

A former soldier turned pastor. Talk about a walking, talking nightmare for a man who didn't want to discuss the military or what had happened in Iraq or anything to do with the good Lord.

Wolf had to give the guy points, though. J.T. didn't flinch under his scrutiny.

Hailey cleared her throat. "J.T., Wolf was a friend of Clay's. They were together in Iraq."

J.T. nodded at Wolf, and a moment of camaraderie passed between them. Wolf didn't know what to do with that. He'd decided to dislike the man, on principle if nothing else. But he realized that wasn't going to be as easy as he'd first thought.

"How long have you been home, soldier?"

"Since this morning."

J.T. cocked his head. "Did they have a welcome-home parade at Cottrell Field?"

Wolf rolled his shoulders uncomfortably. "I chose not to attend."

He'd told himself it was because he'd been focused

on getting to Hailey and fulfilling his duty. But his reasons were more complicated than that.

Without Clay and the others marching by his side, Wolf didn't deserve a welcome-home celebration.

Had he seen that bump in the road, had he paid more attention to that sick feeling in the pit of his stomach that day, all four of his fallen friends would be here today.

He—

Hailey touched his sleeve, her soft voice breaking through his thoughts. "You didn't look for Clay's tree?"

"No." He hoped she'd leave it at that.

It wasn't that he hadn't tried to pay homage to his friend. But when he'd pulled alongside the long row of evergreens, one planted for each fallen soldier of the Third Infantry Division, Wolf had lost the stomach for it. Literally.

Disgusted with himself, for his self-indulgence as much as his weakness, he'd climbed back on his motorcycle and had headed straight to Savannah.

"You really are determined," Hailey said, shaking her head in resignation.

Wolf stared into her eyes, silently communicating his resolve. "I made a promise to a friend. I—"

A loud whoop of feminine shouts cut off the rest of his words. "Hailey, Hailey. There you are."

A group of teenage girls swarmed her, giggling and laughing at such a shrill decibel Wolf wanted to cover his ears with his hands.

"Come on, Hail. The program's about to start." One girl after the other tugged on her, buzzing around her like bees to a flower. "You promised to sit with us."

Hailey looked at Wolf with a question in her eyes,

"Go on. I'll find you later."

She hesitated, looking uneasy at the thought of leaving him behind. "Are you sure?"

"No worries, *Hail*." He winked at her. "I'll be right behind you."

She sighed. "If you're sure."

"Positive."

After a final glance over her shoulder, she turned her full attention on the giggling girls. Three steps and her demeanor changed. She turned into one of them. She laughed and smiled and…was that a skip? Did the woman literally have a skip in her step?

A surge of unexpected anger had him gasping for a decent gulp of air.

Did she have any idea what her life would be like once she arrived in the Middle East? Did she not understand the dangers she was about to face, merely because she was an American *and* a woman?

She couldn't possibly be prepared for the culture shock. Most soldiers weren't, and they had training.

If nothing else, Wolf had to make her understand what she was getting herself into.

Not until Hailey disappeared inside a larger crowd did Wolf remember the man standing beside him.

He turned his head, only to discover that J.T. was watching Hailey, as well. The man's eyes were filled with an emotion that had nothing to do with friendship.

Were the two dating?

Was it any of Wolf's business?

Yeah, as a matter of fact, it *was*.

He'd promised Clay he'd keep Hailey safe. And safe meant safe. From *all* threats. That included the kind that came wrapped inside surfer-dude pastors.

Wolf nearly growled.

J.T. visibly pulled his gaze away from Hailey and re-focused on him again. "So you were a friend of Clay's."

The words were spoken as a statement, an attempt perhaps to open up friendly conversation.

Wolf wasn't in the mood. "I was with him when he died."

"That's tough, man." Understanding flared in J.T.'s gaze and something else, something tragic. "I…" He shook his head. "There aren't words."

Wolf recognized the haunted look in the other man's eyes. It was the same Molotov cocktail of nasty memories mixed with guilt he'd seen in his own mirror. "No. There aren't."

J.T. rocked back on his heels and then stuffed his hands into his pockets. He blinked once, twice. By the third try his expression cleared and the carefree pastor was back. "Welcome to FCC, soldier." He slapped Wolf on the back. "Now come with me. You can tell me about yourself while we head inside."

Yeah, as if that was going to happen.

Feeling trapped, he matched J.T. step for step. Something in the pastor's manner warned Wolf to brace for impact.

What had started out as a long day was about to get longer.

Chapter Three

All Wolf wanted to do was climb back on his bike and ride. It didn't matter where. As long as it was anywhere but here. He still had most of his forty-eight hours of leave left. He could go a lot of places in that amount of time, even within the hundred-and-fifty-mile limit they'd given all returning soldiers.

At least J.T. had quit with the probing questions and Hailey had stopped looking at him with all that distrust in her eyes. Like she feared he was going to bolt at any second.

Okay, yeah. He wanted to take off. But he'd made a promise to Clay's sister.

He wouldn't break his word.

Pulling in a tight breath, he settled back against the metal chair Hailey had saved for him. He managed to sit through the Mulligans' introduction before the fidgeting set in. He contained his twitching to a light drumming of his fingers on his thigh. But as the missionaries continued talking, nothing could stop the hard ball of dread clogging in Wolf's throat.

Open mind, Wolf. You promised Hailey an open mind.

He took another breath. Slow and easy.

"It's not numbers we're after," Harold Mulligan said. "It's hearts." The man paused, and then slid his gaze over the crowd with deliberate slowness.

Wolf took the opportunity to study the missionary. The man was just what he'd expected. Tall, scarecrow thin, middle-aged with sandy-blond hair and fervent eyes.

"No obstacles are too big for God," Harold continued, pulling his wife closer to his side with an affectionate little tug. "Patty and I go where the Lord leads us."

Patty smiled up at her husband. The woman could be anybody's mother, thanks to her plump figure, curly helmet hair and polyester pants.

Harold cleared his throat. "Patty and I are on a faith journey that will impact eternity."

Wolf blinked at that last sentence, only now realizing what was making him so antsy. Mr. Mulligan wasn't saying anything of substance. He was speaking in fancy rhetoric—one lofty, Christian cliché after another.

Yet, throughout the room, heads bobbed in agreement to each hollow statement.

Had Wolf missed something here?

"We're doing important Kingdom work," Patty added with just enough gravity to earn her…wait for it…another round of head bobbing from the crowd.

Wolf shifted, gritted his teeth. Swallowed hard.

Open mind, dude. Get your mind open.

"Our goal is simple," she said. "We want to expand God's Kingdom to unreached places."

Yet. Another. Platitude.

Wolf couldn't take much more.

Thankfully, Mrs. Mulligan turned her attention to

the open laptop on the table in front of her. "It's best if you see the people we've met for yourself."

One keystroke later and a PowerPoint presentation popped up on the screen behind her. In the perfect splash of added drama, a contemporary praise song blared through the computer's speakers.

For five solid minutes, photographs of men with haunted eyes and missing teeth, women holding impossibly small babies and children with lost appendages slid by on the big screen.

Unable to look away, unable to bear the sight of those sorrowful kids, Wolf's stomach clenched. It was one thing for the men and women of the U.S. military to put themselves in harm's way. That was their job, what they'd signed up to do in the recruitment office.

But the Iraqi children couldn't choose for themselves. They had no control. And IEDs didn't discriminate.

Wolf shifted in his seat.

Why did the missionaries have to show all those blown-up kids, he wondered?

Oh, yeah, right. He knew why.

This was propaganda. At its finest.

Even still, it was impossible to remain unmoved. Wolf swallowed a lump in his throat the size of a cannonball and proceeded to drum his fingers on his thigh. Faster. Harder. His foot joined the erratic routine.

Those kids. There's too many to protect. It's an impossible task.

The music hit a crescendo and Wolf glanced over at Hailey.

She was wiping at her eyes and sniffling. Her conviction was palpable, her passion for the wounded kids evident in the slump of her shoulders when one of their pictures hit the screen.

His job just got harder.

As though sensing his eyes on her, she glanced over at him. Helpless despair was etched on her face.

Wolf knew the feeling.

She gave him a wobbly smile. He smiled back, but he was pretty sure the gesture made him look less than enthusiastic.

Sighing, she reached out and covered his hand with hers, squeezed gently then let go. The light contact, though short, had a soothing effect on him—enough to make him relax against the back of his chair and focus once more on the missionaries' testimony.

All right, he admitted it. The Mulligans might speak in Christian clichés, but their hearts seemed to be in the right place. Wolf still wasn't comfortable with their presentation. It wasn't what they were saying that bothered him so much. It was what they *weren't* saying.

Not once did they mention the dangers that came with their posting in an "undisclosed location" of the Middle East. And didn't that say it all?

They didn't speak of insurgents or the bounties on Christian ministers' heads. They didn't allude to IEDs, except in the subtext—obviously the blown-up children got that way somehow. Bottom line, the Mulligans were giving only one side of the story.

Confused, Wolf searched out J.T. He spotted the pastor lounging against the door frame in the back of the room. His gaze was glued to the screen, his attention completely engaged.

What was wrong with the guy? Surely he saw the flaws in the Mulligans' presentation.

The missionaries made it sound as if living in the Middle East was some sort of fun-filled adventure, with the added benefit of helping people along the way. Oh, sure, the wife spoke of her loneliness and missing her church friends, but she said nothing—not one word—about burkas or the deep-rooted hatred for Americans.

And nobody in the room but Wolf seemed to notice the glaring omissions.

Lambs to the slaughter.

He couldn't take it any longer. "I have to get out of here."

Hailey's eyes widened. "But you promised," she murmured. "You said you would stay and listen to the whole presentation."

"I'll be back. I just need a moment. I need…" *Air.*

"I—" She cut herself off and then gave him a short nod. "Okay."

The woman was certainly playing nice. Wolf appreciated that, until she gave him "the look." The one people sent him in airports and other public places. That insulting mix of hero worship, horror and sympathy.

Wolf hadn't expected that from Hailey.

Oddly disappointed, he rose and stalked toward the back of the room. He had a bead on that bright red exit sign and nothing was going to stop him from leaving.

He stepped out of the room without incident. Unfortunately, he was able to enjoy only three minutes of freedom before J.T. had the bad manners to join him.

Well, all right. *Good.* Wolf had a few things he wanted to say to the pastor.

"What's up, Wolf?"

Straight to the point. This was Wolf's kind of conversation. "Those people in there. They aren't telling the whole story."

"What are they missing?" J.T. sounded clearly confused.

"Don't tell me you really send people onto the mission field that unprepared." Talk about blind faith. Even Joshua had dispatched spies into the Holy Land before engaging in battle.

"What do you mean by unprepared, *exactly?*"

All right. Maybe Wolf was wrong. Maybe he'd jumped to conclusions. Maybe the real presentation happened later. "What sort of training do you give your missionaries before they leave the country?"

"Training? Oh, you mean preparation." J.T. nodded in understanding. "Not to worry, Wolf. We don't send anyone into a foreign country without putting them through an extensive application process."

Application process? Sounded sketchy to him. "What does that involve, *exactly?*"

Clearly unhappy with Wolf's sarcasm, J.T.'s lips flattened. "The usual stuff."

Right. "Let's pretend I don't know what that is."

J.T. spoke slowly, patiently, as if he were talking to an imbecile. Which they both knew Wolf was not. "We make sure they have a heart for God and a love of His Word. That they understand their job is to plant seeds through relationships. You know, that sort of *stuff.*"

Now Wolf was insulted. "What about general knowledge of the region, the terrain, the culture? What about basic survival skills?"

J.T. looked at him oddly. "We have classes. They learn how to speak to the unchurched and how to build relationships through common ground." He was so cool, so in control.

So full of it.

"What about when things go wrong? Are they prepared for that?" Wolf frowned. "I know all about the random kidnappings and ransoms and…worse."

"There are always safety issues," J.T. admitted. "But we aren't naive *or* stupid. We don't send our people into the field alone. There's always a seasoned missionary from that region who guides them along the way, a person who knows the terrain and the culture and, yes." He held up a hand to stave off Wolf's argument. "That includes teaching them which areas are safe and which ones to avoid."

"What do you mean by 'seasoned'? As in a former soldier, or a cop or even someone who knows how to defend himself properly, someone who hasn't spent his entire life in country clubs?"

"Ah, I get it now." J.T. nodded sagely. "You're worried about Hailey going to the Middle East."

"Ya think?" Wolf wiped a hand across his mouth, determined to keep his temper in check. "The question is, why aren't you more concerned? I know you're former military, so don't bother denying it."

"Hadn't planned on it."

"Were you ever in Iraq?"

"I was there." J.T.'s voice came out flat, unemotional. *Hard.* "Three times. Afghanistan, six."

Nine deployments to the Middle East? Not possible. For regular Army, anyway. Which meant only one thing. J.T. had been Special Forces.

Now the guy's behavior really confused Wolf. "If you've been over there that many times, you gotta know how dangerous it is to send someone like Hailey into the region unprepared."

J.T. remained silent. Wolf could almost see the thoughts running through his head. The sorting, sifting, measuring.

Wolf waited, mainly because he could tell that whatever conclusion J.T. was coming to, the guy wasn't happy about it.

About time.

"Okay, Wolf, maybe you're right. What Hailey and the others on her team are gearing up to do is beyond our usual scope here at Faith Community Church." The admission came hard, if his tight lips and stiff tone were anything to go by.

Wolf let out a relieved breath of air. "So you'll help me discourage Hailey from going to the Middle East."

"No."

And they were right back where they'd started.

"But you just said I was right."

"I said *maybe* you're right."

Semantics? The guy was arguing over word choice?

"There are some things we have to leave up to God," J.T. added, his tone full of conviction. "We have to trust that His plans are bigger than ours and that His timing is always perfect."

"Now *you're* talking in platitudes?" Wolf expected better from a former Green Beret. At least a little more realism.

"Not platitudes. Truth. We haven't lost a missionary yet. Not on my watch."

Before Wolf could challenge him on *that* shortsighted rationalization, J.T. went back to thinking. He scratched his chin, but this time not a single emotion crossed his face.

At last he dropped his hand to his side. "I admit you

make a good point. Sending missionaries into long-term assignments might require more than the usual preparation."

"Might?"

J.T.'s eyes narrowed in thoughtful consideration. "We could start with a series of classes on basic survival techniques and see where that leads us."

Okay. They were getting closer to the same page.

"That's not a bad idea," Wolf admitted reluctantly. *Very* reluctantly. After all, what J.T. suggested didn't solve Wolf's immediate problem—keeping Hailey out of the Middle East.

"And I think you'd be the perfect person to teach the class."

"Me?" Wolf's heart stopped a beat, and in that single instant he experienced all the pain, guilt and regret of the past six months.

He could not, would not—no, no, no—teach any class inside a church. It was hard enough to be here today. He could *not* walk into this building on a regular basis.

He wasn't that much of a hypocrite.

"You're the pastor, J.T. Shouldn't you teach the class?"

J.T. dismissed the suggestion with a flick of his wrist. "An active-duty soldier would be better." His lips curved at a shrewd angle. "And it might be just what you need, too."

"What's that supposed to mean?" Although, Wolf wasn't sure he wanted to know.

"It would be a chance for you to give back. And who knows, serving others might help you with your guilt."

Wolf's shoulders stiffened. "Who said anything about guilt?"

J.T. simply blinked at him, his gaze saying, *It's right there, soldier. In your eyes.*

Wolf looked away from all that wisdom and understanding. He didn't want an ally. Or a friend. His friends were dead.

And Wolf's guilt was something he had to bear alone, every day, over and over. No amount of church-going or talking or serving others would erase his failure on that Iraqi roadside.

But maybe—just maybe—teaching a survival class to a room full of out-of-touch idealists could serve the one goal Wolf might actually be able to achieve.

If he did his job correctly, with just the right spin, he could prove to Hailey how unprepared she was for a trip to the Sandpit.

"All right, J.T. I'll teach your class on basic survival skills, but only if Hailey signs up."

"She will. I guarantee it." J.T.'s grin turned smug. "All I have to do is use my influence on her."

Yeah, that's what Wolf was afraid of.

Hailey glanced over her shoulder, craning her neck in the direction of the door Wolf had disappeared through. He'd been gone a long time. J.T., too.

What were they doing? What were they discussing? Her?

And wasn't that the most self-centered thought she'd had all day?

Shaking her head, she concentrated once more on the pictures in front of her. The image of a young boy caught her attention. According to Patty Mulligan, he'd been blown up by an IED. And had lost both his legs.

Hailey squeezed her eyes shut, trying not to see her

own brother similarly wounded. Or worse, broken and dying on a lonely desert road.

Oh, Clay.

She didn't hear Wolf return until he slipped into the seat next to her and whispered, "What did I miss?"

Her eyes flew open, but she couldn't allow herself to look at the man who had been with her dying brother. What must he have seen? How bad had it been?

Did she really want to know?

"You missed more pictures, a few stories," she mumbled, not quite looking at him, but not quite ignoring him, either.

"Ah."

She started to shift her gaze back to the screen, but something in Wolf's tone had her turning her full attention back to him.

Her heart skipped a beat. And then another.

Wolf looked…he looked…happy? No, not happy. Pleased. Captain Wolfson was pleased with himself.

Uh-oh.

He smiled, then. A big, carefree grin that made him appear more than a little dangerous. She quickly looked away from all that charm, highly disappointed at the effort it took her to do so.

At last the Mulligans' presentation came to an end.

Again, Wolf leaned over and spoke in her ear. "Well, that was certainly interesting."

Again she didn't like his tone. Nor was she overly fond of the way her body instinctively leaned toward his.

She snapped her shoulders back and sat up straighter. "What's that supposed to mean?"

"What?" One of his eyebrows traveled slowly toward his hairline. "I can't remark on the speech?"

Funny how his answer put her further on edge. "You know you didn't mean that as a compliment."

He shrugged, neither denying nor confirming her accusation.

Enigma. That's what the man was turning out to be. Brooding one minute. Tortured over some distant memory another. Smiling the next. He was full of secret pain and silent regrets. Oh, and charm. Can't forget the charm.

Hailey didn't like the way her heart yearned to peel away the hard layers to get to the real man, the one she glimpsed when he smiled, the person who needed her compassion and understanding.

What was wrong with her? Shouldn't her mind be solely on her upcoming mission work for the Lord? Especially here. Now.

J.T. rescued her by choosing that moment to address the room.

Hailey leaned forward, determined to pay avid attention to whatever her friend had to say.

Wolf started to speak again. She shushed him.

"Did you just shush me?"

"Yes," she hissed.

He chuckled softly.

J.T. thanked the Mulligans for their presentation, and then added, "Our guests will be available for the next hour to answer any of your informal questions. But before we break away, I want to let you know about a class I'm thinking about offering."

J.T. made eye contact with Wolf.

Wolf nodded in response.

"What was that about?" Hailey asked.

Wolf shushed her.

Well. Nervy. The man had some kind of nerve.

"It's been brought to my attention," J.T. continued, "that the church might want to offer a six-week training course in basic survival skills to anyone going on a mission trip."

An excited buzz rose in the room.

"Show of hands. Any interest in something like that?"

Dozens of arms shot into the air.

"Excellent. Look for an e-mail in the coming days," J.T. said before dismissing the group for a short break until the next missionaries took the stage.

Something felt off about what had just happened. Hailey blinked at Wolf. He smirked back.

"Wait a minute." She looked hard at Wolf, turned her gaze to J.T. then swiveled back to Wolf again. "Are you teaching the new classes?" Her heart clunked against her ribs at the thought.

"Maybe." He grinned. "Okay, yes."

"Because…"

"It's a good idea?"

She narrowed her eyes. "Why do I think your involvement in this is anything but simple and straightforward?"

"Because you have a suspicious mind?"

"Not before I met you," she muttered.

Chuckling again, he rose and offered her his hand.

She paused, but then realized she was being rude. She accepted his assistance with her trademark graciousness.

When their palms pressed tightly together, a quick spark of…of…*something* skidded up her spine. Flustered, she pulled her hand free. "Let's, uh, let's go…go meet the Mulligans."

Had she just stuttered? Really?

"Sorry, Hail." He looked down at his watch, swayed as he did so. "Your two hours were up ten minutes ago. I'm gone." He turned on his heel, making a beeline for the exit.

She followed him into the hallway. "You're walking away? Just like that? What about our agreement? Isn't it my turn to listen to you?"

"I'd love to stay." He tunneled an unsteady hand through his hair. "But it's been a long journey home. At the moment I don't have much talk left in me."

Of course. Wolf had only just arrived in Savannah. Today. "You must be exhausted."

"You have no idea."

She should insist he leave and get some sleep, right now, but she couldn't let him go with so much unsettled between them. "Let's have dinner together Friday night."

"Are you asking me out?" He looked surprised, but not altogether unhappy at the prospect.

"No." *Was she?* "Okay, yes. I want to talk about—" she lowered her eyes "—Clay." Which was true, just not the complete truth.

There was something else going on between her and this bold warrior, something that had nothing to do with her brother. Something that was distinctly theirs. But she didn't know how to voice any of that.

It was probably best not to try.

"Please, Wolf, I want to know more about my brother's life in Iraq." She sighed. "You're my only connection to him now. You…" Her words trailed off.

He touched her cheek softly. "All right, Hailey. Friday night works for me. I'll pick you up at seven."

She instantly remembered the motorcycle he'd roared in on. *"No."* She took a calming breath. "I mean. I, uh, I'll cook."

Which could end up being far worse. She was a notoriously bad cook. B-A-D. Bad.

Wolf didn't need to know that, though. She had three days to pick up a few basic culinary skills.

If she failed? Well, there was always takeout.

Chapter Four

Wolf was back in Iraq, on the road outside Baghdad. Clay had taken the driver's seat, as usual, even though Wolf had argued the point until he'd lost his voice.

The bump up ahead hadn't moved since the last time they'd taken this route. But it had grown larger, monstrous. The IED underneath the debris was impossible to miss. Yet Clay nosed the truck straight for the bomb.

"Look out!" Wolf shouted, his voice hollow in his ears.

Moving in slow motion, Clay turned to look at him. His features were distorted, his movements uneven. "Don't worry, Wolf-man, everything's under control."

But it wasn't.

The Humvee dipped, then lurched forward.

Wolf reached out to grip the dashboard. He came up empty.

His breathing quickened into hard, angry puffs. The acrid smell of death surrounded him. He swiped at his forehead.

Bang!

Bang, bang, bang.

Enemy fire. Coming at them fast.

Wolf ducked. The Humvee started its roll.

He grabbed for Clay, but he missed and hit the ground hard. The impact knocked the breath out of him.

He dragged in choking gulps of air.

Another round of gunfire exploded through the air.

Wolf reached for Clay again. This time he caught him. Clay shrugged him off. "Not me. Hailey." His face turned a dingy gray below the blood-smeared cheeks. "Promise me, Wolf-man, promise you'll save my sister."

"I will," Wolf vowed. "No matter what."

The rapid-fire shots came again. Faster. Louder. *Bang, bang, bang.*

Wolf looked frantically around him. His vision refused to focus. "Medic," he shouted. "We need a medic."

"Wolf."

The oddly familiar voice came at him from a distance, like an unwanted echo inside his head.

Bang. Bang.

"Wolf."

He peered into the darkness that had fallen over the desert. The landscape blurred in front of him.

"Wolf, come on, man." The voice came at him again. "I know you're in there. I heard you call out."

Wolf pushed to his hands and knees.

The ground turned slick under his sweating palms. Slowly the room came into focus. His mind cleared, inch by brutal inch.

Right. *Right.* He was home. Back in the States. In one of the apartments on post. And he'd had The Dream again.

Bang, bang, bang.

Wolf flinched, resisting the urge to take cover.

"Wolf!"

He rolled his shoulders forward, recognizing the low-pitched baritone at last. What was J. T. Wagner doing here?

Shaking off the lingering despair that always came with The Dream, Wolf shoved to a standing position. He moved too quickly and lost his balance. He grabbed for the desk, miscalculated, knocked over a glass, which proceeded to shatter into a thousand little pieces.

"You all right in there?" J.T. called.

"Yeah, yeah, hold on. Just hold on." Wolf ached everywhere, but forced his feet to move. "I'm coming."

He made two tight fists with his hands, breathed in slowly. Exhaled. Repeated the process until he was back in control.

Barefoot, he maneuvered carefully around the broken glass and headed toward the door.

With each step anger warred with confusion. What did Hailey's pastor want with him? And why hadn't the man used the modern convenience known as a cell phone? If J.T. could find out where Wolf lived, he could have gotten his phone number just as easily.

Wolf kicked aside the duffel bag he had yet to unpack and yanked open the door. "What?"

Unfazed by the rude greeting, J.T. skimmed his gaze over Wolf's rumpled form. "You look terrible."

No kidding. The weight of The Dream was still on his chest, like a living, breathing monster determined to drag him back to that day on the Iraqi roadside. Back to… Back to…

He pressed the tips of his fingers against the bridge of his nose. "What time is it?"

"1730."

Five-thirty? In the afternoon? "And the…uh, day?"

"Thursday."

Not good. So. Not. Good. He trooped to the lone window in the room and tossed back the curtains. The afternoon light assaulted him, the pain a physical reminder that he was alive. *Alive,* while Clay and the others were dead.

Wolf's eyes slowly adjusted, enough to see that the sun was making its descent toward the horizon.

Grimacing, he gripped the curtain tightly inside his fist, then let go. Darkness returned to the room, blinding him as effectively as the light had. "Guess I was more wiped than I thought."

Making an odd sound in his throat, J.T. flicked on the overhead light. "How long did you sleep?"

Wolf wiped the back of his hand across his eyes. "Twenty, maybe twenty-one hours."

"Ah."

Confused by this visit, Wolf turned to face J.T. The guy had moved a few steps deeper into the apartment. Apartment being a loose term for the seven-hundred-square-foot dump. The room was made up of cinder blocks, linoleum, a metal desk and a twin bed. But as dismal as the tiny space was, it was twice the size of the room he'd had in Iraq.

J.T.'s gaze drifted around the perimeter. "I take it you haven't had time to find a permanent place to live."

"Not yet." Wolf hoped J.T. was through with the questions. It was none of his business why Wolf had chosen to bunk in a barren apartment reserved for enlisted men and women.

"If you need help finding a place to live," J.T. offered, "I have a lot of contacts in the area."

"I'm good."

"Okay." J.T. leaned calmly against the wall next to the door. A delusion. There was nothing casual about the guy.

"Why are you here?" Wolf asked.

J.T. didn't move away from the wall. He just kept… leaning. The guy did a lot of leaning. Strange that Wolf hadn't noticed that before.

"I thought we could talk about the survival classes you're going to teach at the church."

Yeah, right. Like that couldn't have been done over the phone. "Nothing more?"

J.T. didn't move, not an inch, but Wolf could see the man morphing into a pastor right before his eyes. Here it came…

"That's up to you."

Wolf sighed. Looked like FCC's young pastor had a new project. "I don't have anything I need to discuss."

"Whatever you say, but I've been where you are, Wolf, and I think—" J.T. stopped himself midsentence and started over. "Well, anyway, I spoke with the senior pastor about your class this morning. He gave me the go-ahead."

Wolf waited for the rest. J.T. hadn't made the twenty-mile trek to Fort Stewart to tell him something he could have relayed in a text message.

Pretending only a mild interest in his surroundings, J.T. inched his way around a camouflage backpack, the unpacked duffel bag and various piles of gear.

For the first time, Wolf noticed the slight catch in the guy's steps.

How had he missed that?

"If the classes go well we might consider turning them into an ongoing series."

"That's nice," Wolf said, his voice tight. J.T. was clearly working his way around the conversation the same way he'd picked his way through the apartment.

"It would be a great ministry opportunity for a soldier."

And there it was. The guy's real agenda.

Wolf shook his head, his uncompromising glare relaying the message *No, no. Not me.* Not *me.* He already had a "ministry opportunity." And her name was Hailey O'Brien.

That was the one good thing about The Dream. Whenever it came, he always woke up more determined to carry out his promise.

"No pressure, Wolf," J.T. clarified as he perched on a corner of the metal desk. "For now, let's focus on your first class. I'd like to set it up for next Wednesday."

That soon? "Any specifics you want me to cover?"

"I'll let you decide."

Oh, J.T. was good, tossing the responsibility back at Wolf, making him engage in the task from the get-go. No pressure? Yeah, right.

An awkward silence fell between them. Wolf refused to be the first one to speak.

A mistake. J.T. steered the conversation in a personal direction. "What's your story, Wolf?"

No way were they going there. "I was wondering the same thing about you." Wolf shoved his hands into his pockets. "Why'd you leave the military?"

J.T. shrugged, oh so casually, but Wolf noted the closed-off look that filled his expression. Denial. Yep, he recognized that one immediately.

"I was called into ministry."

Wolf didn't buy it. "A soldier doesn't decide to leave the Army one day and become a minister the next," he challenged, suddenly very interested in what the good pastor had to say next.

"You're right. My decision didn't come overnight." He readjusted his position. The new placement of his leg looked almost unnatural. "Long story short, I'm a better pastor than I was a soldier."

Which raised a lot of unanswered questions. Like the fact that J.T. was sitting here. With Wolf. At Fort Stewart.

"How'd you get on post?"

The guy broke eye contact. "I drove."

"You know that's not what I meant."

J.T. sighed. "I was given a medical discharge two years ago." With slow, purposeful movements, he lifted the left leg of his cargo pants. The ratty hem traveled past a shiny, *metal* ankle and stopped midway up a plastic calf.

A prosthetic. Wolf drew in a sharp breath.

That kind of injury could easily turn a man bitter. Wolf had seen it happen often enough. But J.T. hadn't let his disability hold him back. Instead, he'd gone into ministry.

What kind of faith did that take?

More than Wolf would ever have.

An unexpected wave of awe and respect filled him. Despite losing a leg in combat, J.T. had a certainty that radiated from him. He knew his purpose in life.

Wolf didn't have convictions like that. Not anymore. Despite his recent promotion to captain, he didn't have any real direction, either.

He realized now, as he stared at the certainty in J.T.'s gaze, that he'd lost more than his friends that day on the Iraqi roadside. He'd lost his faith. And no matter how many Army chaplains quoted Romans 8:28 to him, Wolf didn't believe God worked all things for the good to those who loved Him. Not anymore.

J.T. dropped his pant leg back into place and put on his pastor face. "My turn for a few questions."

Wolf nodded. J.T. was a brother in arms, one who'd had the courage to reveal his career-altering injury. Wolf owed him the same courtesy. "All right."

"Why did you seek out Hailey as soon as you arrived back in the States?"

Wolf forced down the litany of emotions the question awakened and focused only on words. Words he could do. "I made a promise to Clay, right before he died."

"You were in the Humvee with him, right?"

"Yeah." The heaviness in his gut, in his throat, in his very soul, threatened to choke him. The only way to control the unwanted sensation was to focus on the conversation. Except…

Clay should be the one talking to J.T. right now.

God had taken the wrong man that day.

Did the Lord make those kinds of mistakes? Was Wolf really supposed to be here? Or was he supposed to be—

"Go on. What did Clay ask you to do?"

Wolf swallowed. "He asked me to keep Hailey out of the Sandpit."

"But that doesn't make any sense," J.T. said. "Her becoming a missionary was Clay's idea."

"Hailey said the same thing." Word for word, in fact.

Apparently she'd discussed her decision with J.T. In detail.

Which did *not* sit well with Wolf.

"Hailey let me read Clay's e-mails," J.T. continued. "They were inspiring and very convincing. I don't understand why he would change his mind so drastically."

Wolf knew why.

"Because of the way he died. In his last moments of life, he had an epiphany. He didn't want Hailey anywhere near IEDs."

"Even if what you say is true, what makes you think you'll change her mind?"

"Because I *have* to."

"You might not like what I'm about to say, but, Wolf, if the Lord wants Hailey in the Middle East, she'll end up there, no matter what you say or do to prevent her from going."

Wolf's stomach rolled at the thought. "I don't believe that." He blew out a hard breath. "I *can't*."

"I realize that." The disappointment in J.T. was tangible, but thankfully he didn't continue arguing his point of view. "So, you want to go over the details of your class now, or later, say early next week?"

Happy to focus on the new topic, Wolf searched for some shoes other than combat boots. "Now works for me." He found a pair of worn-out leather flip-flops sitting under the bed. "As long as we can talk over a burger."

At the moment, Wolf could use a little junk food. The Dream, not to mention the sparkling conversation he'd just suffered through with J.T., had left an empty feeling in the pit of his stomach.

"I'm starving," he added for good measure, just in case J.T. thought he was stalling.

"Me, too." J.T. opened the door and waved Wolf past. "After you, soldier."

Maybe J.T. would turn out to be a friend. A real friend. Then again—Wolf remembered how the man's eyes turned soft whenever the conversation turned to Hailey— maybe not.

At precisely 7:00 p.m., Hailey opened her front door and froze. She had to work to keep a sharp thrill from skidding up her spine. But, *wow,* Wolf cleaned up nicely.

He'd chosen to wear civilian clothes, which made him look approachable, and yet still very tough. The guy was one hundred percent alpha male. All power and grace and soldier-boy charm.

For a moment, she could do nothing but stare. He didn't seem to mind, so she took her time studying him.

His ensemble was simple. Jeans, a light blue polo shirt and a chocolate-brown leather jacket. His clean-shaven jaw and chiseled features made him look as if he'd just walked off a Hollywood movie set. But the pain-filled eyes made him look lonely. And maybe just a little bit lost. Wounded, even.

Yes, there was a reason why she'd searched Google for terms like *battle fatigue* and *survivor's guilt*.

Somewhere during her research she'd had a revelation. The Lord hadn't brought this man to her doorstep to help Hailey with her grief. But the other way around.

She was supposed to help *him*. But first she had to get her mouth working properly.

He broke the silence for her. "Hi."

"Hi, yourself." Oh, brilliant response. And wasn't she using all three of her degrees to their fullest?

Of course, he wasn't helping matters with his intense eyes and stiff shoulders.

Finding it hard to catch her breath, she lowered her gaze to the colorful array of wildflowers he held in his hand. "Are those for me?"

"They are."

What a sweet gesture. And an insight into his true nature. Wolf was a good guy, both considerate and thoughtful.

He gave her a lopsided grin. The man really was hazardous when he looked at her like that. And she couldn't stop staring at him. She was suddenly thinking of fairy-tale endings and Prince Charming on a white horse and...

What was wrong with her?

Hailey considered herself an academic, a thinker rather than a feeler. She was not the fanciful sort. She had a plan for her life, one that had no room for an active-duty soldier with a killer smile.

He thrust the flowers awkwardly toward her.

"Oh, uh, thanks."

She took the bouquet from him with a slight tremble. Their fingers touched. It was just a brush of knuckles, a mere whisper really, but her heart fluttered against her ribs.

"Please, come in." Holding on to a sigh—barely—she stepped aside for him to pass. "Dinner is almost ready."

The pleasant scent of sandalwood and spices followed him as he swept into the foyer. The heels of his combat boots skimmed across the hardwood floors. For a big man, he was exceptionally light on his feet.

But then he stopped abruptly and she nearly collided into him. "Oh."

She lost her balance.

"Careful." His hands gripped her shoulders gently, holding her until she was steady again.

"So." He lifted a single eyebrow. "Where, exactly, am I going?"

This time she did sigh. She'd forgotten he didn't know the house. He seemed so at home. Maybe it was that confident stride of his, or that take-charge attitude. Or maybe it was just wishful thinking. "Follow me."

Resisting the urge to look over her shoulder, she led him into the kitchen. She'd set two places on the antique table in the bay window alcove.

He eyed the settings with obvious misgivings. "Fancy."

"It's the O'Brien family china and crystal. I always bring it out for special occasions." She smiled up at him. "I thought this qualified."

"That's, uh, nice."

She'd lost him. He'd put up that invisible barrier between them, the one that communicated things like "keep your distance" and "back off" and, her least favorite, "not interested."

She took a deep breath and let it out slowly. "Or we could eat out on the deck. Paper plates. Plastic cups. At this time of year we might have to contend with the cold, but there won't be any bugs."

"I don't mind cold."

"The porch it is."

Within moments, she had them settled at the table on the deck. The outdoor lights provided plenty of light. The sounds of traffic and laughing filled the air.

They ate in silence, which wasn't as bad as Hailey would have predicted. She liked looking at Wolf. Despite his fidgeting, a sense of peace filled her when she was in his presence.

As she'd warned, the temperature had dropped below fifty, which translated to bone-chilling cold to Hailey's way of thinking. Wolf didn't seem to notice, so she huddled inside her sweater and endured. He took his time eating, seeming to savor each bite.

Yet the tight angle of his shoulders told her he wasn't completely relaxed. Every few minutes he would run his gaze from left to right, right to left, instinctively checking for danger.

"How's the food?" she asked.

"Awesome." He shut his eyes and breathed deeply. "It's been a long time since anyone cooked for me."

Guilt, that's what made her set her own fork down. "I didn't make dinner."

He lifted his eyes to meet hers and she could see the barrier going up again. And just when they were making progress.

"You have your own chef." It wasn't a question, rather an accusation, as though he didn't have much use for pampered women.

She bristled. "Of course not. I don't have servants waiting on me hand and foot, if that's what you're implying."

His skepticism radiated in the air between them. "You clean this place all by yourself?"

From the disbelieving look on his face, she knew he wouldn't understand why she employed Mama Dee. Aside from the fact that Hailey allowed the historical society to use O'Brien House for special events and tours—and thus each room had to be spotless at all times—Mama Dee needed the money. She was a single mother with five kids under the age of fifteen.

"I know what you're thinking, Wolf, but I don't order out every evening. Tonight, well—" she lifted a shoulder "—I wanted to make sure you had something special to eat."

Shock, disbelief, wariness, they were all there in his gaze. "You wanted me to have something special to eat?"

"I did." She twisted her napkin in her hands. "My cooking skills aren't at a level where I could have pulled that off."

"I don't know what to say." Now he just looked shocked.

And she felt awkward.

Determined to lighten the mood, Hailey closed her hand over his. "You don't have to say anything."

"Yes, I do." He rotated his wrist until their palms met. He squeezed, held tight for a moment too long then released her hand. "Thank you for going to so much trouble. I'm grateful. But, Hailey, I'm a simple guy with simple tastes. I'd have eaten a PB and J with equal enthusiasm."

Happy the tension had lifted, she spoke without considering her words. "I'll keep that in mind next time."

"Next time." He smiled. "I like the sound of that."

"Me, too."

They stared at each other, neither speaking, neither moving. The way he looked at her with all that intensity and raw emotion in his gaze nearly did her in. "Tell me what your dream meal would entail."

He leaned back in his chair and, oh, yes, *finally,* his shoulders relaxed. "You promise you won't laugh?"

"Of course I won't."

"Pizza. The greasier the better. There aren't a lot of Italian restaurants in Iraq."

"No." She let out a short laugh. "I don't suppose—"

The squeal of tires sent Wolf jumping out of his chair. He spun around, looking frantically around him. Right to left. Left to right. He flexed his fingers then made a tight fist. His eyes had a wild look in them, yet he was very, very aware. Ultra-alert. Only after he took a few deep breaths, and then several more, did he start pacing the length of the deck.

Back and forth. Back and forth. When he started on a third pass, Hailey took charge. "Let's go inside. You can tell me about Clay over dessert."

Chapter Five

Shadows chased one another around in the kitchen, layering an eerie, desolate mood over what had started out as a promising evening. Despite the many deep breaths he took, Wolf's pulse refused to slow to a normal rate. Unease from the squealing tires still nagged at him. He drummed his fingers against his thigh and waited for Hailey to speak. To smile. To do…something.

She could at least turn on a light. But instead of reaching for the switch, she moved through the room, igniting candles along the way. The golden glow cast a romantic mood.

Had she done that on purpose?

Or was she trying to calm him with the soft lighting?

Either way, a strange, sweet feeling melted through him, permeating the steely place deep in his core no one had ever breached. Wolf had been alone so long he thought he'd gotten used to the solitude, maybe even craved it on some deep, unhealthy level.

But something in him had shifted. And now he wanted more out of life than merely existing from one day to the next. He sensed Hailey was the key to this change.

Which was too bad for him.

She was Clay's sister, aka off-limits.

It didn't matter that her presence soothed Wolf in a way nothing had since that day on the Iraqi roadside. It didn't matter that she'd known exactly what he needed when that car had startled him. What *mattered* was why he had come here tonight. Because of his promise to Clay.

He could almost hear his friend saying, *This is not a date, Wolf-man. Not. A. Date.*

Struggling to keep his mind on his real task, Wolf looked everywhere but at the beautiful woman in the kitchen with him. He was making a considerable dent in cataloging the items in the room—antique table, china, fancy stoneware, various pots and pans—when Hailey finished lighting the candles and turned to face him directly.

Their gazes locked and the air clogged in his throat.

He forced out a slow, careful breath.

Hailey O'Brien was a stunning woman, even in a simple pair of jeans and a sweater. Wolf knew he would find an expensive designer label somewhere near the waistband of those perfect-fitting jeans. And that pretty blue sweater had definitely cost more than he made in a month.

The woman had style, with the expensive taste to match, which only managed to punctuate all the reasons why she couldn't go to the Middle East as a missionary.

Feeling restless again, Wolf looked away from those mesmerizing green eyes locked with his. His gaze landed on a photograph secured to the refrigerator by two heart-shaped magnets. He squinted through the threads of golden candlelight. A man and woman stood arm in arm in front of a Christmas tree. Wolf stepped closer and realized he was staring at a relatively recent snapshot of Hailey and Clay.

They were both dressed in formal black, wearing their perfect smiles and classic good looks as comfortably as Wolf wore his BDUs.

"That's from two Christmases ago," Hailey said in a soft voice from behind him. "Right before his first deployment."

Wolf nodded, but remained silent. What could he say, anyway? *I'm sorry? Did you have a good time that night?*

"We used to throw a Christmas party every year," she continued. "It was a family tradition my parents started before either of us were born."

Family tradition. Those two words were everything Hailey stood for and Wolf did not. Consequently, his mind spun around one unrelenting realization.

The Lord had taken the wrong man that day.

Clay had had a reason to live, a purpose outside the Army. Wolf had neither. No family. No wife. Not even a girlfriend. And he certainly didn't have a sister determined to head into a dangerous war zone for her pie-in-the-sky ideals.

Which reminded him…

Hailey wanted to talk about her brother. Wolf wanted to talk about the Middle East. He'd do both with one conversation.

But not in this house. There were too many reminders of Clay surrounding them.

"It's still early." He faced Hailey straight on. He told

himself he needed to be able to see her expression, to read what was going on inside that beautiful head of hers, but the real reason was he couldn't look at Clay anymore. Not even in a photograph from two Christmases ago. "Let's go for a ride."

"A ride?" She took two deliberate steps away from him. "On…on your motorcycle?"

Her voice shook just enough to make Wolf forget about important conversations and painful memories and well, *everything,* except calming her concern. "No, Hailey," he said in a soothing tone. "I drove my car."

"You did?" Was that disappointment in her voice? Interesting.

"You want to ride on my bike?" Wolf couldn't have been more surprised.

Or more pleased.

The idea of Hailey sitting behind him, hanging on to his waist, trusting him to keep her safe around hairpin turns, brought forth all sorts of warm, fuzzy feelings. Disconcerting for a guy who didn't do warm or fuzzy. Ever.

Not. A. Date. Why couldn't he remember that?

"Well, actually…" A line of concentration dug a groove across her forehead. "I do."

She had a million doubts in her eyes, but she didn't back down.

Brave girl.

"You're sure about that?"

She gave him a careless lift of her shoulder. "A short spin around the block might be fun."

Oh, yeah, it'd be fun. He'd make sure of it. "How about next time? When we go for pizza?"

At the suggestion, everything about her seemed to relax. "That works for me."

Worked for him, too. And if he had his way, he would ignore his misgivings and make sure their "short spin around the block" *was* a date.

But tonight, he had a more pressing matter to address. One he wanted finished between them. Tonight. "Let's get out of here."

"Okay. I just need to get my coat and then we can go." She hurried out of the room.

"I'll take care of the candles and meet you on the front porch," he called after her.

"Sounds good," she tossed over her shoulder.

Wolf couldn't stop a grin from forming. The night was suddenly looking up. But then he remembered what lay ahead and his smile vanished. Flattening his lips into a grim line, he snuffed out the candles. With each puff of air he mentally clicked off the reasons Hailey couldn't go to the Middle East.

Insurgents.

Unstable governments.

IEDs.

Roadside bombs.

He no longer needed to remind himself this wasn't a date.

Curious as to where Wolf had parked his car, Hailey let him lead her down the front steps of O'Brien House. A cool breeze blew across her face. She could smell the damp in the air.

Night had completely blanketed the city with its inky stillness, but that didn't pose a problem in this part of town. Since Savannah was best seen on foot, streetlamps had been erected at close intervals along all the sidewalks in the historic district, giving tourists enough light to see the city's famous architecture.

There was so much illumination on Hailey's street she could practically count the leaves on the azalea bushes.

Unfortunately, the lighting didn't provide any relief from the cold. She shivered.

And then Wolf halted beside a car parked directly in front of her house and she shivered again.

Shock slithered slowly down her spine, skidding to a stop at the soles of her feet.

What had she gotten herself into?

Unable to speak, her eyes tracked over what had to be the saddest excuse for a muscle car she'd ever seen.

"This is yours?" she managed to croak past the tightness in her throat, trying not to let her dismay show.

Grinning like a proud papa, Wolf ran his hand lovingly over the roof. "Hailey, meet Stella."

It was years of training from her mother that kept her mouth from hanging open. "You named your car?"

"You bet I did." He gave the hunk of metal an affectionate pat. "This little beauty has been my only constant for the last ten years." He grinned broadly. "Isn't she great?"

"Sure…"

The car Wolf adoringly referred to as *Stella* looked ready for a permanent trip to the junkyard. Hailey squinted. Were those large, dark-colored patches splattered over the hood rust marks? Dirt? A combination of the two?

"Are you sure that thing…er, Stella…is safe?"

"Have a little faith." Wolf leaned in close enough for

her to smell his spicy, masculine scent and tapped her lightly on the nose. "Stella might be in desperate need of a paint job, but the old girl is in her prime."

Hailey slid a skeptical glance over the car—hood to tail, tail to hood. "I'll have to take your word on that."

"Come on, sweetheart, where's your sense of adventure?"

"I think I left it in the house." She deliberately turned her back on the car. "Maybe I'll just head inside for a moment and look for it."

Chuckling, Wolf swung her back around with a gentle hand on her shoulder. "No way are you bailing on me now. You've come this far. Might as well go the distance." He opened the car door for her. "Go on. Climb in. Stella doesn't bite."

"I'm going to hold you to that." Heaving a dramatic sigh, she lowered herself into the passenger's seat.

The crisp smell of lemon and new-car scent surrounded her. A single glance at the car's interior and Hailey took back every negative thought she'd had about Stella.

Delighted, she rubbed her hand across the butter-soft, blue leather seats and then eyed the shiny, chrome-plated dials.

Wow!

Wolf had clearly spent considerable time and money on restoring Miss Stella's interior. Afraid to touch anything, Hailey perched on the edge of her seat, folded her hands in her lap and waited for Wolf to walk around to his side of the car.

Now that her initial Stella-shock was wearing off, something Wolf had said earlier came back to mind. The moment he settled in behind the steering wheel, she addressed the issue head-on. "You mentioned that Stella has been your only constant for the last ten years. Does that mean you don't have any family?"

"That's right." Staring straight ahead, he placed his hands on the wheel at the ten-and-two position.

The tone of his voice told her not to press the subject. She did anyway. "Not even a distant cousin?"

"No, Hailey." His hands clutched the wheel tighter. "No one. The Army's all I've got."

She recognized the emptiness in his voice, understood the bleakness it represented. The emotion was so similar to what she felt herself that her heart skipped a beat. Yet even as she empathized with Wolf, she sensed his loneliness wasn't as straightforward as hers. She feared his past held something dark, something she could never truly understand.

Should she quote Scripture to him at this point, or maybe recite words filled with God's truth about His unfailing love?

No. Something in the way Wolf held his body slightly away from her, almost isolated, didn't inspire her to introduce the fundamentals of God's love into the conversation.

Except…

What if she started by addressing the one thing they had in common? "I guess we're both alone in this world."

He made a noncommittal sound in his throat, one that clearly said the topic was closed. Without looking at her, he turned the key in the ignition and Stella roared to life.

Hailey gasped as a succession of grinding metal, snarls and rumbles whipped through the air.

Wolf pressed down on the accelerator. Stella responded with a loud, menacing growl.

Gasping again, Hailey braced her hands on the dashboard and hung on for dear life.

Stella wasn't through. She shook. She shimmied. Until, finally, "the old girl" descended into a vibrating rumble.

Needing a moment to collect herself, Hailey shut her eyes. She couldn't think past the blood rushing in her ears. Or was that terrible noise coming solely from the car?

"Ready for a sweet ride?" Wolf asked.

No! She slowly opened her eyes. *Be brave, Hailey, be brave.* "Sure."

He put Stella into gear and pressed on the gas pedal. Surprisingly, the car's engine settled into a low-pitched purr as she slid away from the curb.

After several blocks of pitch-perfect propulsion, Hailey grudgingly admitted that Miss Stella did indeed give one sweet ride.

Relaxing enough to unclench her fingers, Hailey settled back against the soft leather of the comfortable bucket seat. "Where are we going?"

"I thought we'd head out to Tybee Island."

He wanted to go to the beach? So soon after returning home? "I would think you'd be sick of sand by now."

Clay had avoided Tybee for months after his first deployment.

"I am." A grim look crossed his face. "But I haven't had nearly enough water."

Of course. "That makes sense."

"Besides." His expression lightened and he hooked

his wrist over the top of the steering wheel. "It's a pretty drive."

"You think so?" She couldn't say she particularly agreed. "The road is nothing more than a causeway that cuts through the marshes."

"Exactly."

She narrowed her eyes, confusion gathering inside her. "I don't follow."

"There isn't a lot of marshland in the desert."

"No. I suppose not." She should have realized that on her own.

After several moments of Wolf concentrating on the streets and Hailey watching him out of the corner of her eye, they broke free of Savannah.

For the next five or so miles, Hailey tried to look at the familiar scenery from Wolf's perspective. Not an easy thing to do. The marshes were just plain spooky under the silver light of the full moon. Even with the windows rolled up against the cold, the tall grasses were ripe with the smells of mold, mud and rotting fish. It was a perfect hunting ground for gators and snakes.

Hailey shivered yet again, which was really quite enough of that.

She had to admit, though, words like *Middle East* and *desert* did not come to mind as the scenery whizzed past in a blur. As a matter of fact, Miss Stella seemed to be gobbling up the road a little faster than Hailey would have thought possible.

From under her lowered lashes, she checked the speedometer. Eighty-five. *Eighty-five?*

A rush of adrenaline surged through her blood. *Breathe, Hailey. Just breathe.*

"Are we late for something?"

"No. Why?"

She pointed to the speedometer, trying not to give in to panic, but—*oh, my*—he'd just pushed their speed past ninety.

"We're going a little fast, wouldn't you say?"

He flashed her that quicksilver grin of his, the one that had her thinking of big, bad wolves. "I like fast," he declared.

Afraid to take her eyes off the road, Hailey white-knuckled her seat and stared straight ahead. Okay, yes, the causeway was a long stretch of uninterrupted highway. And there were no other cars out tonight.

But still…

Wolf must have sensed her agitation. "Are you all right?"

"Fine. Never better." She dug her fingers deeper into the soft leather of her seat, but she didn't take her eyes off the road. Blinking was simply not an option. "Having loads and loads of fun over here."

"Uh-huh."

"All right, Wolf, let's face it. There's fast and then there's fa-a-a-ast."

He chuckled, but immediately eased up on the gas pedal. "I know what I'm doing." He patted her hand. "Trust me, sweetheart."

Oh, sure. Trust him. That was just soooo easy to do when she was sitting in a muscle car with a guy named *Wolf,* traveling faster than she'd ever gone before.

The best she could do was *not* talk. And maybe watch the scenery. What little she could decipher.

She caught a flash of…something rush by on their left. She figured the quick burst of light had come from Fort Pulaski. The historic Civil War fort sat on a tiny island between the Atlantic Ocean and the Savannah River.

"You can relax your spine a little. We're nearly there," he announced.

"Praise the Lord!"

Only after he eased up on the accelerator again did she slant a glance in Wolf's direction. The bright moonlight revealed his features clearly, enough that she could see his brows scrunched in concentration. Obviously he was contemplating his next words very carefully.

"You might be interested to know I ate lunch with your pastor the other day," he said at last.

"You did?" She wondered when he'd had the time to meet Keith Goodwin, Faith Community Church's senior pastor, then remembered the e-mail she'd received this afternoon. "Oh, you mean J.T."

"We hammered out most of the details for the survival classes I'm going to teach at your church."

"That explains why he sent out a blanket announcement encouraging everyone taking a mission trip to attend. The class starts next Wednesday, right?"

"Yep." He proceeded to beat out a complicated beat on the steering wheel. "Will you be there?"

"Wouldn't miss it."

He fell silent for a moment. Thanks to the close confines of the car, she could feel the tension in him.

"Tell me why you want to be a missionary," he blurted out in a rush.

She sighed heavily. "That was certainly straight to the point."

"Maybe. But we've put off this conversation long enough. You know why I agreed to come to dinner tonight."

No, actually, she'd forgotten. She'd settled into the evening as though they were on a first date, explaining away the awkward moments to the usual getting-to-know-one-another jitters.

She wouldn't make that mistake again.

"Yes, I know why you're with me tonight." She ignored the sting of rejection building into tears behind her eyes and continued. "You think you have to convince me to stay out the Middle East."

"There's no 'think' about it." He slowed yet again, enough to swing Stella down an alley leading to beach access. He slid the car into a parking place under a low-burning streetlight and then cut the engine. "But I promised you an open mind and that's what you'll get from me."

He sounded sincere. She wasn't sure she believed him.

"Help me to understand your motivation, Hailey."

"Why?" She frowned at the shadows dancing across Stella's hood. "So you can use the information against me?"

"I wouldn't do something that low. I'm really interested in your answer. What can I say?" He gave her a crooked smile. "You intrigue me."

Glowing from the unexpected compliment, Hailey held back a gasp of pure feminine pleasure. Suddenly the interior of the car felt too small, too intimate. It was hard to think coherently with this handsome soldier sitting next to her. "Let's discuss this on the beach. I tend to think better when I'm walking."

He gave her what she was starting to consider the "Wolf" look and then reached for the door handle on his side of the car. "Whatever will make you most comfortable."

His tone sounded so rigid, the angle of his jaw looked so implacable, Hailey feared he thought she was trying to put off answering his question.

She picked at a speck of white fluff on her sleeve, wondering what he would think if he knew the real reason for her suggestion. She wasn't stalling. She was merely finding it hard to keep her mind on her goals with his masculine scent teasing her nostrils and his presence scrambling her thoughts.

But as far as her calling to become a missionary? Well, Wolf would either understand her reasons or he wouldn't. No matter what he said or did, he would *not* convince her to stay out of the Middle East.

Forcing down any last remnants of unease, Hailey summoned a brisk air of confidence and climbed out of the car.

Game on.

Chapter Six

Hailey started down the beach several feet ahead of
Wolf. The full moon cast a brilliant, silver streak of
light over the ocean, while the scent of salt water and
sand clung to the cold air. Waves broke onto the shore
in perfectly timed intervals, creating a sound track for
their walk. But with so many thoughts working around
in her brain, Hailey couldn't enjoy the scenery.

The sand squeaking under Wolf's feet alerted her to
his progress. He caught up with her just as she paused to
watch a transport ship ride the distant waves. Its large,
guiding light bobbed up and down as the vessel tracked
slowly toward the horizon.

Now that the time had come to tell her side of the
story, her heart pumped wildly against her ribs. Or was
her reaction because he was once again standing so
close…*too close?*

She slid a quick glance in his direction. He carried
himself with an unmistakable air of seriousness. His
gait was stiff and careful, as though the soft sand presented a slight challenge for him.

Again, she wondered if he'd been wounded in the

roadside bomb attack and whether or not he had a lingering injury. One that acted up in the damp beach air.

Of course, now probably wasn't the best time to ask him. She'd stalled long enough. "If I'm going to explain where I am and where I'm heading, it's important you know where I come from."

"I know where you come from." His voice matched his stiff gait. "Generations of family tradition, with the kind of long-reaching roots that didn't just start a few years ago but *centuries* ago."

He didn't sound impressed. On the contrary, his voice held a note of censure.

She stopped walking.

He did the same.

The moonlight gave her enough illumination to see his face clearly. The sharp angle of his jaw made him look harsh and unforgiving.

"You hold my upbringing against me." She all but gasped out the words.

"I'm trying not to."

A part of her appreciated his honesty, but the obvious doubt in his tone told her he wasn't having much success.

Hailey gave him a bewildered shake of her head. "Why is it wrong to come from an old family, to have solid roots?"

He twisted his stance to look out over the water, shutting her out as effectively as if he'd completely turned his back to her. "There's nothing *wrong* with it. It's just not something I have much experience with. My family wasn't exactly like yours."

Something in his tone alerted her to tread carefully. "No?"

He continued looking out over the water. "Let's just say my childhood wasn't as...secure as yours."

His softly uttered words said it all. Clearly, Wolf's

parents—one or both of them—had let him down in some terrible way. Although she didn't know the specifics, her heart took a painful dip in her chest for all that he'd suffered. And, yes, she had no doubt he'd suffered.

"I'm sorry, Wolf." What more could she say?

"I believe you are." He turned and closed the distance between them—literally and figuratively. The barriers he'd erected earlier were gone. Completely. He'd simply let them drop and was now looking at her with stormy emotion waging a war in his gaze.

Hailey felt honored that he trusted her enough to let her see all that raw pain. And yet, she was petrified she would somehow let him down. He kept so much inside him she had no idea how to proceed. Or what words to use.

Fortunately, she didn't have to say or do anything, because in the next moment he took her hand and cupped it protectively in his. She watched, fascinated, as he stroked the pad of his thumb across her knuckles. Once. Twice. Her heart did another quick flip at the same moment he twined his fingers through hers.

"Tonight isn't about me or my dysfunctional childhood," he said at last, still staring at their joined hands.

Perhaps any other time Hailey would have agreed with him. But if she'd learned anything in her countless Bible studies, it was to go in the direction God nudged her. At the moment, she felt a strong shove toward Wolf. "Maybe if you told me—"

He spoke right over her. "Go on, Hailey, help me to understand your desire to become a missionary. And don't use fancy clichés like we heard from the Mulligans. I want honesty from you."

He was so large, so intense, so...*close*. Yet fear wasn't the first emotion that ran through her. It was a strange mix of excitement and fascination. Like he'd claimed about her earlier, the man definitely intrigued her. "All right. If that's what you want."

"It is."

In silent agreement, they resumed walking, still holding hands. Even though her instincts warned her not to get too comfortable, the connection between them felt so natural, so familiar, Hailey didn't try to pull away.

"Just like you said, I come from an old Savannah family, with solid roots and a legacy that can be traced back to the seventeen hundreds. There's always been wealth and privilege in my family. But don't think that means the O'Briens have ever taken their blessings for granted. My mother in particular took her position in society very seriously. She spent her entire life dedicated to her causes. She—"

Hailey cut off her own words, a sense of loss and frustration mingling inside her. She knew she would never fill her mother's shoes. And, much to her shame, there were moments when she was glad for it. Sitting on charity boards and supplying funds for various causes had never been satisfying. Unfortunately, it had taken Clay's death to reveal that truth to her.

With a gentle tug on her hand, Wolf slowed their pace. Hailey hadn't realized she'd sped up.

"What about your father?" he asked. "Tell me about him."

Glad for the change in topic, Hailey smiled. "He was the senior partner in the law firm my great-grandfather founded. Daddy was a really good lawyer but he was an even better father. He was kind, loving, firm yet fair."

"You were fortunate, then."

"I was," she said, pausing to decipher what she heard in his tone. Bleakness? Envy? If only he would tell her more about his past. If only she could read his expression and decipher his secrets for herself. But the moon had slipped temporarily behind a cloud.

Wolf cleared his throat. "Clay mentioned your parents were killed in a plane crash."

Instant pain unfolded in her chest and threatened to crowd out the breath in her lungs. Hailey *couldn't* give in to her grief. Not in front of Wolf.

She inhaled a ragged swallow of air and said, "My father was flying the company jet. My mother was his only passenger. They were coming to a University of Georgia football game. Clay and I were waiting for them at a private airport in Athens. We were supposed to all sit together at the game. I… We…"

Before she realized what he was doing, Wolf swiveled in front of her and caught her up in his arms. "I'm sorry, Hailey. Losing both of them at the same time." He made a sympathetic sound deep in his throat. "That had to be tough, especially with parents like yours."

With Wolf's strong arms wrapped around her, Hailey gave up fighting the onslaught of emotions demanding release. Sighing, she rested her cheek on his shoulder and let the sorrow come.

After a few endless moments of gasping for air, she was able to continue. "As hard as it was to lose them, losing Clay was harder." A series of silent sobs wracked through her body. "He wasn't just my brother. He was my best friend."

Wolf's embrace tightened. "Clay was the best man I ever met."

She smiled into Wolf's muscular shoulder. The leather jacket felt cool on her cheek. "Of course he was."

Murmuring an unintelligible response, he dropped a kiss on the top of her head.

After several minutes of Hailey clinging and Wolf rubbing her back soothingly, he set her away from him. The cold, damp air slapped her in the face.

They set off down the beach again. This time, Wolf didn't take her hand. The lack of connection left her feeling isolated and alone.

"I know Clay joined the Army after your parents' plane crashed. What about you, Hailey? What did you do after they died?"

"I finished college with a degree in Latin and one in Greek. Then I earned another in Classical Literature." She kept her voice even, or as even as she could under the circumstances.

"I take it you like learning."

She shrugged. "With my parents dead and Clay in Iraq, school was my only lifeline, the only thing I knew."

"Understandable."

Why did he have to be so sweet? When he was here for all the wrong reasons? "Anyway, one of my professors told me I couldn't take classes forever, not without an end goal in mind."

"He kicked you out?"

Wolf's outrage made her smile. "Not exactly, but *she* didn't encourage me to stay, either. Since I didn't really know what I wanted to do with my life, I came home and took over my mother's charity work."

"Is that when you decided to become a missionary?"

"No." She abruptly changed direction and ambled toward the water's edge. This was where the conversation got hard.

She pulled in a sharp breath. "There was something

still missing. At Clay's urging, I joined Faith Community Church and started taking Bible studies." She dug a toe in the wet sand, kicked a ball of white foam in the air. "Within a year I could rattle off Scripture as well as any trained pastor."

Wolf drew alongside her. "That's a bad thing?"

"It was for me. I'd intellectualized my faith. Clay kept pushing me to get my hands dirty, but I didn't know what he meant. And then…" She paused until she was certain she could speak without her voice breaking. "He died."

Just saying those two horrible, awful, *painful* words, tears welled in her eyes. She held them back with a ruthless blink and turned her head to look at Wolf. Even under the muted moonlight she saw her own sorrow mirrored in his gaze.

That gave her the courage to finish with the honesty he'd requested. "Not long after his death, I realized what Clay meant. I was just playing at being a Christian."

"Doesn't seem that way to me."

"Come on, Wolf. Don't you understand? Having a heart for causes is *not* the same thing as having a heart for people. The truth is…" She choked back a sob. "I'm a fraud."

Wolf stared into Hailey's eyes. They were bright with unshed tears. He'd never seen such self-recrimination, or such conviction to change. Except, possibly, when he looked in his own mirror.

Willingly or not, Hailey had just revealed her greatest fear—that her life was meaningless and without purpose.

Wolf had lived with that particular terror himself.

He'd lost everything that day in Iraq. His brothers in arms, his best friend, even his purpose. Or rather his surety in his future with the Army.

He'd been questioning his life choices ever since. Rightfully so. But in Hailey's case, she was dead wrong. "You're no fraud. You're the real deal."

"Not yet." She swiped the back of her hand across her eyes and sniffed. "But I will be."

"Don't do this to yourself. I saw you in action the other day, with those teenage girls. You touched their lives right in front of me."

"It's not the same."

"Why? What's wrong with helping people in your own church?"

"It's not enough." She batted at a strand of hair that had fallen over her face. "Not *nearly* enough."

"Oh, I get it now." He laughed without a stitch of humor. "You think risking your life in a foreign land is the only thing that will make you a real Christian."

"I didn't say that."

"You didn't have to."

Her expression turned stormy. "You're intentionally misunderstanding me."

Not even close. "Look, Hailey, giving men and women a uniform and a gun doesn't make them soldiers. Nor will hopping on an airplane and flying to the Middle East make you a better Christian."

Her head snapped back as if he'd slapped her. "My brother thought otherwise."

A high-definition image of Clay's pale face insinuated itself into Wolf's mind. For one black moment, he was tempted to give Hailey all the gory details of her brother's death. The sights, the sounds, the terrible smell of blood that haunted Wolf in his dreams.

"No, Hailey." The effort to restrain himself had his words coming out hard and fast. "Clay didn't believe that for a second."

"He did. I have his e-mails to prove it. He died because he believed in the Army's mission. I have to honor that. I have to honor him."

The sheen of tears in her eyes gave Wolf pause. But only for a second. "How do you plan to do that? By dying for your beliefs, as well?"

"You're being intentionally obtuse." She wrapped her arms around her waist and stared out over the water. "J.T. understands my motives. Why can't you?"

Overwhelmed by an intense surge of jealousy at the mention of J.T.'s name, Wolf's jaw tightened of its own accord. He swallowed. *Hard.* Then forced his teeth to unclench. "Don't mistake a guy's romantic interest in you with understanding."

Her head whipped toward him. "It's not like that between J.T. and me."

"It's *always* like that."

She spun away from him. "I'm through with this conversation."

"Well, I'm not." He reined in his temper enough to walk calmly around her. "Despite what you think, Clay isn't looking down from heaven waiting for you to prove you're as courageous as he was. His last request was to make sure you stayed safe. I'm here to ensure that happens."

Her stubborn expression returned. The silence lengthened to an uncomfortable amount of time. In that moment, with her eyes telling him she would *not* back down, Wolf realized more arguing on his part would hurt his cause.

A smart soldier knew when to walk away, or at least when to build a different plan of attack. "How many mission trips have you gone on?"

Making a sound of dismay in her throat, she tried to maneuver around him.

He blocked her retreat. "How many?"

She lowered her gaze. "One."

"That's it?"

"It was enough," she said to his feet. "It made me hungry to do more."

Which was admirable, in its own way. Yet the question still remained. Why the leap from a short mission trip to a permanent posting in the Middle East?

"Where did you go on your *one* trip?"

"Jamaica." She slowly raised her head. "For two and a half weeks. And I'm heading to Haiti in a few weeks. I'll be there for seven days."

Wasn't that just *great*. The woman was basing a life-altering decision on practically zero field experience. The Army would never send a soldier overseas with such a gross lack of training.

"A Caribbean island is nothing like the Middle East."

"I know that."

"Do you?"

Moving quicker this time, she twisted around him and began retracing her steps back to the car.

Wolf followed hard on her heels. "Hailey—"

"Don't." She thrust her palm in the air between them. "I have the money, the time, the desire. It's not like I'm leaving anyone behind. Now that Clay is gone, I don't have...*anyone*."

The catch in her voice broke his heart. "You have your friends and your church." But even as the words slipped out of his mouth, Wolf knew how empty they sounded. Hadn't he hated hearing them all his life?

His frustration was making him careless. Why couldn't the stubborn woman see she was making a mistake?

"Hailey, I admire your passion." At her skeptical glare he added, "I do. But you won't be heading into a mission field that's been well traveled. There are bad men over there with guns, men who hate women like you."

"What do you mean women like me?"

"*Christian* women."

"That doesn't mean I shouldn't go." Her feet moved faster, kicking up large sprays of sand as she went. "Someone has to reach the desperate people living in that region. Why not me?"

He could give her a thousand reasons. He focused only on the main two. "Because you don't have the training or the experience."

"I'm getting both." She pumped her legs faster. "Step one was Jamaica. Step two is Haiti. Step three...well, God will reveal that to me in time."

Wolf easily kept up with her, even though his frustration made his steps jerky. "Hailey—"

"Stop worrying about me. When the door finally opens to the Middle East I'll be ready."

"You don't have an assignment yet?"

"No."

Well, that was new information. Maybe, just maybe, Wolf was going about this all wrong. From her own admission, Hailey wasn't scheduled to leave for the Middle East anytime soon. And she wasn't leaving for Haiti for several weeks. That gave him time to show her just how unprepared she was.

Ideas came fast now. But at the moment, he didn't bother sorting through them. He had a better idea. "Okay, Hailey, I see I'm not going to change your mind." Not tonight, anyway. "Let's call a truce."

She stopped dead in her tracks. "You're giving up?"

"Yeah, I am." He backtracked to her side. "For now."

Seconds of intense staring passed between them. Wolf experienced an uncomfortable pounding in his chest, the one that came every time he looked straight into those gorgeous, heart-stopping green eyes.

"Something tells me you aren't completely giving up on your quest," she said at last.

"A temporary truce is still a truce," he pointed out.

"In other words, I won't be getting rid of you anytime soon."

"That about sums it up."

Her gaze sparkled with a contradictory mix of resignation and…pleasure? Wasn't that interesting?

"Cheer up, sweetheart." Feeling generous, Wolf gave her the big, loopy grin that was guaranteed to make her eyes soften. "All that extra time together could turn out to be a win-win for us both."

Chapter Seven

Wednesday dawned bright and cool. It was another beautiful winter day in southern Georgia. Fort Stewart practically sparkled with sunshine and birdsong.

Far from being deceived by the idyllic scene, Wolf entered his office with a cynical heart. His soldiers weren't adjusting to life in the States as well as he'd hoped. Of course, they'd only been home a week. Maybe they just needed time. And lots of attention from their commanding officer.

Knowing the importance of what lay ahead of him, Wolf tried to keep his mind on work and *not* on Hailey. Not so easy, especially since he'd made a point of staying away from her these last five days.

There was no doubt the woman was unprepared for the hazards of missionary work. But she had to come to that conclusion on her own. With a large nudge from Wolf, of course. The series of survival classes were the perfect vehicle to steer her in the right direction.

In the meantime, Wolf needed to focus on the job the Army paid him to do. First order of business, he needed to decide what to do about the fight he'd just broken up at the PX.

He flexed both his hands in frustration. His unit was already three days into reintegration training, yet the discussions and accompanying videos designed to help soldiers adjust to life back home weren't taking.

Today's fight was not the first Wolf had come across this week. He'd also dealt with a handful of domestic disputes, never a favorite. And some of his soldiers were already showing signs of alcohol abuse. Despite their vehement denials.

Wolf leaned back in his chair and covered his eyes with his hand. There were too many soldiers with too many problems for one man to address, especially a man suffering with his own readjustment issues.

If he was going to have any chance of helping his soldiers, he had to help himself first.

Decision made, he bolted from his chair and headed out of the office without speaking to his NCO.

He'd put off this errand long enough.

Ten minutes later, Wolf sat on the bottom row of bleachers at Cottrell Field and stared at the line of trees across the empty parade grounds. This was the place where soldiers in the Third Infantry Division commemorated the best and worst of Army life.

Alone with his thoughts and far too many emotions churning in his gut, Wolf began to regret his decision to come here today. Terrible memories poked at him.

Refusing to buckle, he rested his forearms on his knees and kept his gaze locked on the long row of evergreens.

His mood threatened to turn dark and turbulent, so he forced his mind back to a happier time, back to the welcome-home ceremony he'd participated in after his first tour of duty. If he closed his eyes he could still hear the music, still feel the energy and sheer joy of being home at last. He'd led his platoon through the tunnel of trees with a large grin on his face. The explosion of cheers from his fellow soldiers' families and friends had made him feel light-headed.

In that one moment, he'd mattered, perhaps for the first time in his life. He was no longer a mistake, as his father had always claimed, no longer the boy unworthy of love, whose own mother had abandoned him at the age of ten. As an officer in the United States Army, Wolf had shed his past and found his future. His life course had been set.

Until the day Clay and the others had died. On his watch.

Struggling to absorb the reality of his failure, Wolf kept his eyes shut and slowed his breathing. In. Out. In. Out. His skin had turned ice-cold, as though there'd been a sudden change in temperature. At least his hands remained steady. He was still in control.

Snapping his eyes open, he stood.

It was time to get this over with.

With slow, determined steps he circled the perimeter of the parade grounds. His boots felt heavier than usual, but he kept moving forward, all the way to the line of trees dedicated to the fallen men and women of the Third ID.

A burst of angry energy slammed into Wolf like a punch. But he didn't stop moving. He tracked slowly down the row, reading each name scrolled on the accompanying plaques.

His steps never faltered until he approached the four shortest trees, the ones representing *his* men. His personal loss.

Images of the bombing besieged him. Flying metal. Stinging flames. His fellow soldiers' screams.

Wolf shuddered. But his eyes remained dry. He was still in control.

Logic told him he wasn't the only one who had missed the signs of the IED. But he'd been the Truck Commander. His sole job had been to hunt for danger.

Fighting back a wave of guilt, he dropped his gaze to the first plaque and read the name aloud. "Staff Sergeant Ronald Matthews."

He moved to the next tree. "Specialist Demitri Ross."

And the next. "Private First Class Kevin Ingram."

At last, he drew alongside the final plaque in the row. "First Lieutenant—" his voice hitched "—Clay O'Brien."

Clay's last words rolled through his mind. *You gotta keep Hailey out of the Sandpit....*

Wolf repeated his response. "I won't let you down."

But what if he did? What if he failed his friend?

No. Unacceptable. Hailey's life depended on Wolf winning their current stalemate.

Desperation made his heartbeat quicken. And then he did something he thought he'd never do again. He lifted up a desperate prayer to God. *Lord, help me stop Hailey from going to the Middle East. Give me the tools and the knowledge to keep her out of harm's way.*

He opened his eyes and studied Clay's tree with an unblinking stare. "Your sister, she's not what I expected.... I don't know... I can't..." His eyes filled with tears.

No. He couldn't do this. Not now. Not today. His control was slipping. He had to get out of here before it vanished completely.

He headed to his car with ground-eating strides.

The sun's ruthless midday rays nearly blinded him,

but not completely, not enough to shield the familiar figure waiting for him at the edge of the field.

"You have a bad habit of turning up at the worst possible moments," Wolf growled through clenched teeth.

"What can I say?" J.T. rolled his shoulders. "It's what I do best."

All kinds of responses came to mind, but Wolf was too drained to verbally spar with the man. "What do you want this time?"

J.T. cocked his head toward the line of trees behind Wolf. "You find Clay's tree?"

"Yeah." Wolf made a sound deep in his throat, half threat, half plea.

"Want to talk about it? It might help to share your burden with someone who's been where you are."

The guy was certainly persistent. "You'll have to excuse me." Wolf pushed past him. "I have to get back to work."

J.T. joined him step for step. "Let me buy you lunch first. Off post. There's a restaurant in Hinesville that serves the best Cuban sandwiches north of Miami."

Wolf increased his pace. "Can't. I have to spend the afternoon scaling a mountain of paperwork."

"One hour won't make a difference."

Wolf hesitated. For a fraction of a second.

J.T. took advantage. "Look, soldier, no agenda here. I just want to go over last-minute details for your class tonight."

Right. Wolf knew what J.T. was doing. The guy was building a relationship with him, instilling trust before he started in with the evangelizing. It's what Wolf would do if their situations were reversed. The realization only managed to aggravate him more. "I'm not one of your mission fields, *Reverend* Wagner."

"Didn't say you were."

Even knowing J.T.'s game, even recognizing what time spent with the man would mean, Wolf relented. "All right. I'll go, but only if you promise me one thing."

"Name it."

"No God talk."

J.T. stopped in front of a black SUV and regarded Wolf with kind, patient eyes. He didn't look like a pastor anymore, but a man who'd been through his own tragedy and was now on the other side. Wolf couldn't help but envy him that.

"I'm not here solely as a pastor."

"Oh, yeah?"

"I figure you need a friend. And maybe—" J.T. drew in a sharp breath "—so do I."

That got Wolf's attention. "Aren't you surrounded by *friends* all day long at your church?"

"You'd be surprised." J.T. unlocked the car door, swung it open but didn't climb in. "People expect a certain…shall we say…behavior out of a pastor. It's hard to be a spiritual leader and human at the same time. Know what I mean?"

Yeah, Wolf knew. As the leader of an entire unit of soldiers he had to keep a professional distance at all times. Consequently, he'd dealt with his share of loneliness through the years. J.T. might be a pastor, but he was proving to be a man with similar challenges as Wolf.

Maybe they could be friends.

Except…

There was something—or rather, *someone*—standing between them. Wolf decided to cut to the chase. "Are you interested in Hailey?"

A rush of emotions fled across J.T.'s face before he covered them with a blank stare. "I'll admit, there was a time when I thought Hailey and I might get together, but it wasn't in God's plan for either of us." He looked expectantly at Wolf, waiting perhaps for him to interrupt.

When he didn't, J.T. continued. "I've long since resigned myself to the fact that she'll never be more than a friend to me." He paused. "What about you? Are you interested in her?"

Despite the fact that Wolf had started this thread, he didn't want to answer the question. What he felt for Hailey was private. Hard to explain. And certainly none of J.T.'s business. But the guy had been candid when he could have hedged. Wolf owed him the same level of honesty. "Yeah. I am."

J.T. went dead still, but Wolf could see the guy's mind working through the new information. Eventually, his face relaxed and he said, "Okay. This is good. No, it's real good. For you both."

Instant relief flooded through Wolf, as if he'd been waiting for J.T.'s blessing. Looked like they were on the road to becoming friends after all.

Thanks to Savannah's notoriously bad traffic, Hailey arrived late to the church Wednesday night. Surprised to see so few empty seats, she slipped along the back row of chairs and sat in one of the last ones available.

Glad the class hadn't started yet, she smiled at several familiar faces. It took her a moment to realize that there was a disproportionate amount of women in the room. Clearly word had spread that a good-looking, *single* Army officer would be teaching the survival classes.

Even as Hailey argued silently with herself, she couldn't stop a possessive thought from taking hold. *Mine.*

Perfect. She was already anxious about seeing Wolf again. Now she had to contend with a new set of emotions.

The man was quite simply turning her well-planned life into one of uncertainty and raw nerves.

Pulling her bottom lip between her teeth, Hailey gathered her courage and searched for Wolf. She found him standing with J.T. at the front of the room. Heads bent at identical angles, they studied a sheet of paper Wolf held in his hand. So absorbed with the contents on the page, the rest of the room might as well not exist for either man.

Standing shoulder to shoulder, both had an undeniably masculine appeal. Hailey had to admit that J.T. was as good-looking as Wolf. But whenever she thought about pursuing something beyond friendship with the pastor she felt...nothing. Not even a flutter of interest.

But all Wolf had to do was capture her gaze and her stomach performed a somersault.

As though sensing her gaze on him, Wolf lifted his head and scanned the room. When all that intensity leveled onto her, Hailey's stomach began a series of quivering little flips.

She quickly lowered her head and discovered that her fingers were locked in a choke hold around her pen. This crazy reaction to a man she'd known less than a week was absurd.

Relaxing her grip, Hailey looked back up. But Wolf had returned his attention to the paper in his hand.

He still wore his BDUs, the handsome brute. There was something compelling about a man in uniform, especially when the man had broad shoulders, pale blue eyes and day-old stubble running along his jaw. It made a woman think of happily-ever-after and a house full of black-haired children. Dangerous territory for someone who'd lost all of her loved ones to tragedy. Deep down, Hailey couldn't really believe there was a happy ending waiting for her.

She cringed at the thought. But before she could give in to her rising concerns, J.T. walked to the center of the small stage with Wolf following closely behind. They turned to face the room as a unit, looking completely in sync with one another.

Wolf looked at her and winked. *Again* her stomach performed a rolling somersault.

What was she supposed to do with this attraction?

Clay's sage words instantly popped into her mind. *If you're not sure what to do, give it up to God.*

Yes. She would surrender this confusing dilemma to the Lord. Feeling marginally better, Hailey took a calming breath.

J.T. addressed the room. "It's always advisable to go into a foreign country as equipped as possible. Spiritual preparedness is only one of the necessary steps to effective missionary work." He scanned the room with an all-consuming glance. "You should also know how to protect yourself should the worst-case scenario occur."

A few gasps met this remark, but J.T. didn't seem to notice. He motioned Wolf forward. "This is Captain Ty Wolfson, an active-duty soldier who's agreed to teach a six-week course on basic survival skills. I know some of you are heading to Haiti in less than three weeks. We'll make sure you get the bulk of the information you need before you leave. Let's start with a word of prayer."

Everyone in the room bowed their heads, Hailey included.

"Heavenly Father," J.T. began, "I thank you for trusting Your children enough to call us into service. May the world be further evangelized for Your glory, not our own. I pray You open our hearts and minds to what Captain Wolfson has to teach us tonight. We ask all of this in Christ's name. Amen."

Hailey barely had time to raise her head before Wolf took over. "I've had a chance to review a list of all your upcoming mission trips. Since you will be heading into several different locales, I've decided to focus on basic techniques that can be used in any situation or terrain."

He caught Hailey's eye and smiled. He looked entirely too smug, as though he had a secret agenda designed solely for her.

She suppressed a shiver.

"The most important element to survival is between your ears." Wolf pointed to his head to drive home his statement. "If you use your wits and remain calm you'll have a better chance of survival in any situation."

Hailey wrote two things in her notebook: *Stay calm. Use your head.*

Good advice so far, if not a bit obvious.

"Should the worst happen and you end up alone in unknown territory…" Wolf's voice turned grave. "The key is not to panic."

Hailey added to her list. *DON'T PANIC.* She underlined the phrase three times. On the third swipe her hand shook.

"Your priorities should be shelter, water and food, in that order." Wolf strolled through the room as he launched into a description of each category. He meandered down the aisles until he stopped directly in front of Hailey.

Pen poised over her notebook, she gazed up at him. The look he gave her warned her to brace herself for what was about to come next.

She swallowed.

"Make one mistake and you're in big trouble. Make *two*—" he held the pause for effect "—and you might not survive at all."

Hailey shuddered. Not from the obvious subtext in Wolf's words, but from the intense, almost pleading look in his eyes. He wasn't merely worried about her. He was *afraid* for her.

That undisguised emotion held far more weight than mere words ever could. Wolf knew exactly what life was like in the Middle East. He was making a judgment call on firsthand knowledge. Whereas she was going on an inner tug and a handful of e-mails from Clay before he died.

Horrified to feel a strong thread of doubt take root, Hailey white-knuckled her pen.

Looking a little too pleased with himself, Wolf moved away from her.

As if on cue, J.T. lowered into the empty chair beside her. "Don't let him scare you. He's just trying to make a point."

Hailey lowered her eyes to her notebook. The words *DON'T PANIC* captured her attention. It was an excellent reminder.

"Not to worry," she whispered with renewed resolve. "I'm made of sterner stuff than either of you know."

J.T. patted her hand. "I don't doubt it."

Smiling at her, he rose from his seat and went to lean against his usual spot on the wall a few feet from the door.

Wolf wove his way back to the front of the room. "Over the next six weeks you're going to learn how to signal for help, build a fire, find shelter, gather food and water and administer basic first aid. During our last class together I'll teach you how to protect yourself when attacked, either by a four-legged predator or..." He paused again. "The two-legged kind."

A chorus of gasps wafted through the room. Seemingly oblivious, Wolf punched a button on a laptop and a PowerPoint presentation blinked across the screen behind him.

As he began a detailed instruction on various ways to use a flashlight to signal for help, Hailey's mind raced over his troubling remark about two-legged predators.

Insurgents, terrorists, it didn't matter what name they were called. They were evil men who killed in the name of their god, who cowardly strapped bombs to children and sent them to their deaths.

Am I kidding myself, Lord? Am I trying to change hearts that are unchangeable?

No. She refused to become discouraged. She had a plan, a good one that would involve working directly with Muslim women. Hailey would help educate them and hopefully, in the process, enlighten them to their worth as human beings.

Most of all, she would love them.

It all started with love. Christ's love. And despite Wolf's countless arguments otherwise, Hailey's goal was *not* unattainable. If that were true, Clay died for nothing.

She closed her eyes and tried to picture her brother in her mind. He'd sacrificed his life for his beliefs. She might be called to do the same. Was she ready for that? Was she—

"Hailey?"

She flicked open her eyes and noticed that a shadow had fallen over her paper.

"Hailey."

Heart pounding, she looked up. And straight into Wolf's concerned expression.

"Are you all right?" he asked.

"I was… I mean…" She gave him a shaky smile. "Yes, of course. I'm fine."

The sound of shuffling feet alerted her to a sudden rash of movement coming from all sides of the room. People were getting out of their seats and leaving.

"Where is everyone going?" she asked.

"We're taking a ten-minute break before we meet outside to practice signaling with flashlights."

"Oh." And just like that, her mind went blank. She had nothing else to say. Nada. Zip. Not a single word.

"Come on." He reached out his hand. "If you're especially good, I'll let you be my partner."

Okay, that comment really deserved a response, or maybe even two, and yet words *still* escaped her. Feeling foolish, Hailey silently placed her hand in Wolf's. An immediate sense of well-being filled her.

Right. Now she was tongue-tied for an entirely different set of reasons. Wolf might be a complex, driven, frustrating man, but he was also handsome, charming and appealed to everything female inside her.

Much to Hailey's dismay, and despite J.T.'s raised eyebrows, it felt perfectly natural holding Wolf's hand as they walked out of the room together.

She was still struggling to find her voice when he tugged her down the hallway and toward the back of the church.

Chapter Eight

From the corner of his eye, Wolf watched an array of emotions flutter across Hailey's face. Confusion, sadness, worry, all three were evident in her expression.

"I know what you're trying to do," she said, tilting her chin at the stubborn angle he was growing to dread.

Before responding, he opened the door leading to the empty field behind the church and motioned Hailey to exit ahead of him.

"What is it you think I'm *trying to do?*" he asked.

Nose in the air, she marched several feet forward then spun back to glare at him. "You're trying to scare me." She poked him in the chest. Hard. "Aren't you?"

Denial would be beneath them both. However, there was nothing wrong with a little procrastination. "And if I am?"

"You admit it?"

He took a moment to consider the sky. The night air had turned cold and misty, almost gloomy. Not a single star cut through the thick cloud cover. "Yeah, I admit it." He leaned in close to her ear. "But is it working? Am I scaring you, Hailey?"

A soft, scoffing breath slid past her lips. "Not in the least."

Wolf wasn't fooled by all that false bravado. Like a green soldier on his first deployment, Hailey was scared and riddled with doubts but she didn't know what to do with either emotion.

"Come on, Hailey. I saw the terror in your eyes when I mentioned predators," he said. "We both know I've got you thinking."

"Maybe so." She blinked at him, looking momentarily thrown off guard by the swift admission. "But I am *not* afraid."

"Uh-huh."

"I'm *not*." Her words came out strong enough, but she grabbed his arm as though it had become a lifeline. "I'm just irritated. Yes, that's the word. And maybe a little annoyed at your not-so-subtle attempt to scare me away from my calling."

The look in her eyes said otherwise. "Hailey, there's nothing wrong with being afraid. Fear is good. Fear is healthy. And sometimes—" he looked pointedly at the hand that was now clawing into his biceps "—fear is the only thing that will keep you alive."

"Stop trying to confuse me." Her fingers tightened still more. "Fear is not good. It's the opposite of faith."

"Tell yourself whatever helps you sleep at night. But make no mistake." He slowly unpeeled her hand from his arm, one finger at a time. "I have no intention of watching you climb on an airplane headed to the Middle East. *Ever*."

Slapping her palm against her thigh, she jerked her chin at him. The building's outdoor lighting gleamed in her eyes, making her look fiercely beautiful and yet

painfully vulnerable. He wanted to yank her into his
arms and hold her until she wasn't frightened anymore.
But that would defeat the purpose of his plan.

So he remained perfectly still and waited for her to
break the silence.

"Don't look so smug," she warned. "I *will* get my
way on this."

"I'll say the same to you."

She shook her head at him. The building's artificial
light turned her dark waves into a rippling black wa-
terfall of curls. She really was extraordinary. She took
his breath away.

"So, here we are again. At a stalemate." Her voice
rang with such frustration, his chest ached with remorse. He hated being at odds with this woman, even
if he was right and she was dead wrong.

"I'm not happy about this, either," he said.

"Then give up. Accept defeat."

"Not a chance." Despite her arguments otherwise,
he'd won this round. Hailey was having doubts, just as
he planned.

Next order of business. Wolf needed to reveal the
harsh realities of the Sandpit. In living color. The most
accessible footage was on the Internet.

But how was he going to get the stubborn woman in
front of a computer?

While he was contemplating various possibilities,
she changed the subject on him. "How are you settling
into life back in the States?"

"Slowly." He wondered if he should tell her about
his visit to Cottrell Field this morning but quickly decided against it. There was already too much tension

between them. He didn't want Clay in the middle, too. "I'm moving off post this weekend."

"But…" Her eyebrows slammed together. "I didn't realize you were living there."

"Only temporarily. I'm moving to a town house in Savannah." As soon as the words left his mouth he had his idea. "Would you help me shop for towels, kitchenware, you know, stuff like that? I could use a woman's opinion."

Especially if that woman was the green-eyed beauty staring at him now. He watched in fascination as Hailey transitioned right before his eyes from a woman of fierce resolve to one filled with age-old female secrets. The kind that hooked a man into all sorts of promises.

"Of course I'll help you," she all but purred. A slow grin spread across her face. "Under one condition."

His blood pumped slow and thick through his veins. Oh, yeah. He'd give this woman anything she asked of him. *"Anything."*

"I want a ride on your motorcycle." She raised her hand to keep him from speaking over her. "Or no deal."

He couldn't resist a smile at the sight of all that fierce determination. "Done."

Really, that had to be the easiest bargain he'd ever struck with another human being.

Saturday morning dawned clear, the blue sky completely cloudless. Hailey, however, had several other concerns on her mind that wiped out her joy over the gorgeous weather.

Frowning, she climbed out of Wolf's car and jammed her fists on her hips. "It's not that I don't appreciate Stella." She eyed the steel monster for a long moment, her annoyance melting into an odd sort of fondness. "In fact, the old girl's starting to grow on me."

"She does have her charm," Wolf agreed, patting the roof of the car with a rather unhealthy dose of affection.

What is it with him and this car? And why did it matter to Hailey so much? She couldn't possibly be jealous of a hunk of metal.

Could she?

"Nevertheless," she said, sharply ignoring the knot of unease twisting in her stomach. "I find it necessary to remind you that we had a deal. You promised me a ride on your motorcycle before we went shopping. And yet, here we are."

She made a grand sweep of her hand, making sure the arc included not only the building but the entire parking lot.

Laughing softly, he swung his arm over her shoulder and tugged her against his warm, muscular body. "Come on, Hail, lighten up. You know we can't cart around supplies on my bike."

She answered with a very unladylike snort.

"Tell you what." He drew her in a fraction closer to his chest. "You fulfill your end of the bargain and as soon as we're done here I'll fulfill mine."

Instead of shoving him away—like she should, considering his arrogant tone—Hailey snuggled deeper inside Wolf's embrace. She told herself this strange desire to be near him had nothing, *nothing,* to do with the sense of comfort and safety she felt in his arms. Nor was it because of the pleasant tingle running up her spine that came when she breathed in his masculine scent of leather, soap and spice.

No. The decision to cling to him was all about the cool breeze sweeping across the parking lot. Nothing more.

Then why did she feel so lost when he dropped his arm and headed toward the store's entrance ahead of her?

"So, uh, Wolf." Hailey trotted after him. "Remind me again why we're shopping here and not on post."

"Simple." He pulled loose a shopping cart from the long stack, his gaze riveted on a colorful display of a popular sports drink. "More variety."

"But everything's so much more expensive here," she said.

He went completely still at her remark. The only part of him moving was his blinking eyelashes.

"Wolf?"

"I can afford this store," he ground out through a clenched jaw.

Momentarily bemused by the sudden change in him, Hailey looked everywhere but at his irritated expression. How could she have predicted he'd be so touchy? Because Clay had been the same way when he'd first returned from Iraq. Seemingly inconsequential things had upset him, while others had not. There had been no predicting his reaction, not at first, not until he'd acclimated.

"Wolf, I'm sorry," she began carefully. "I didn't mean to imply that you couldn't afford this store. I was only trying to be practical. I…" She sighed. "I apologize."

He responded with a distant nod. "Okay."

It wasn't much of an acceptance. Probably because her apology hadn't sounded sincere enough. "Really, Wolf. I'm sorry."

"I know." He pushed the cart out of the way of oncoming traffic. "Try to understand, Hailey. To me, shopping in *any* store is a luxury. After a year in the desert, I just want to cruise aisles full of so many choices my head spins. And this particular store is known for its variety."

"Then what are we waiting for? Let's get to it."

They shopped for two full hours, wading up and down the aisles with no real plan. Understanding the situation better, Hailey allowed Wolf to push the cart at his pace. She also stood by patiently while he struggled over what seemed basic, straightforward decisions to her.

To him, they were dilemmas.

What color towels should he pick? Did he need four dinner plates or eight? Two skillets or one?

She could tell by the increasingly taut series of expressions on his face that each decision was getting harder for him to make.

They turned onto the small appliance aisle, and he stopped. He just stopped. Right there. In the middle of the aisle, and stood motionless, blinking rapidly, seemingly riveted by whatever he saw up ahead of him.

Desperation suddenly filled his gaze. And then…

His eyes went dead.

Hailey had lost him. Completely. And she wasn't sure how to get him back.

An ugly void of nothing filled Wolf's mind, followed by an intense rush of panic. Rage hovered so close to the edge of his control he didn't know what to do with it.

His thoughts tumbled over one another so quickly he had to grip the shopping cart ruthlessly to keep his hands from shaking.

There were too many noises surrounding him, too many colors and too many people. So…many…people.

He was having sensory overload. He recognized the signs, yet he was too detached from himself to do anything about it.

He couldn't make another decision. Not. One. More. But that wasn't the main reason his mind had become a ball of chaotic fury.

It was the ridiculous argument he'd overheard. The one still going on behind him.

He breathed in a slow, careful breath, then let it out even slower. But nothing helped. His anger increased as the woman carried on, complaining about the low thread count in the bedsheets someone had handed her. On and on she went.

Didn't she understand what a privilege it was to purchase a set of bedsheets in the first place? Didn't she know how fortunate she was to have a bed at all, much less sheets and blankets? And yet she was *still* complaining.

Wolf had to get out of here. Before he said—or did—something he couldn't take back.

"Wolf." Hailey's voice called to him from what seemed a great distance. He'd nearly forgotten she was here with him.

She placed a gentle hand on his arm. The soft touch instantly calmed him.

"Wolf, honey." Her voice washed over him in soothing ripples. "Look at me."

He rolled his gaze in her direction.

They stared at one another, both understanding that he was teetering on the edge.

"Why don't you wait for me in the car?" she suggested softly.

He shook his head, unable to focus completely on

what she was saying, but knowing he needed to do what she advised.

"Go on." She nudged him with her hip. "I'll finish up here."

"I—"

"It's all right." She cupped his cheek tenderly. "Just go to the car. I've got this."

He resisted the urge to close his eyes and lean into her hand. "I need air," he admitted.

"Oh, Wolf, it's okay." She caressed his cheek. "It's *okay.*"

Her kindness—he didn't know what to do with it. Part of him wanted to embrace it, to fall into all that goodness and affection he saw in her eyes. Another part of him wanted to run because he couldn't release the anger gnawing at him.

Lash out? Escape? Both viable options. Which meant he had a classic case of fight or flight.

Without another word he turned on his heel and started toward the front of the store. He halted after two steps.

His breathing wouldn't stop its erratic rhythm, his head swam with too many angry images but at least he had the presence of mind to remember where he was, who he was with and what they were doing.

"Here." He dug his wallet out of his back pocket and handed her a bunch of bills. "Use the cash to pay for my purchases."

She took the money without question. "I'll make this quick."

"Okay."

"Go on, Wolf. It's all right." Her eyes held such un-derstanding, it made him feel stripped to the bone. He didn't want anyone, not even Hailey, to see that deeply into his soul.

He stalked to the store's entrance at a fast pace. His chest ached. His eyes burned. But he kept his mind blank and his senses shut down, refusing to look at people, or listen to any more of their conversations.

He'd never felt this before, this all-consuming fury.

But he'd never felt this alone before, either.

Not even in those early days after his father died of alcohol poisoning. Although Wolf had been saddened by the tragic passing, there had also been a sense of relief. His father had been set free from his pain. Wolf had turned to God after that, and had discovered that his faith could get him through the worst life tossed his way.

He had never wavered in his beliefs. Until his Humvee had hit the IED.

Wolf's steps grew heavy, but he made it to Stella and planted his palm on the car's hood. Breathing slowly, methodically, he lifted his eyes to heaven. *Lord, I need Your help. I need...*

What? What did he want from a God that had abandoned him on that Iraqi roadside?

As soon as the question materialized Wolf knew. He wanted his faith back. He wanted to believe again. He wanted God to prove to him he wasn't here by mistake. That he still mattered.

And that maybe, just maybe, he was worthy of a woman like Hailey O'Brien.

Gulping for air, Wolf climbed into the car and sat behind the driver's seat. He leaned on the steering wheel and cradled his head on his forearms.

Dear Lord, I...

He didn't know what to pray for first, there were so many requests running through his mind. He knew he wanted to find a purpose beyond himself, something that meant he was more than just a guy who'd randomly survived an IED attack, while better men had died.

But, wait, he already had such a purpose. He already had a worthy goal.

At last, he knew what to pray. "Lord, I need Your help with Hailey. I need Your guidance. But if You remain silent, if You refuse Your assistance, I will stop her from her dangerous quest somehow. I *will* find a way."

No matter the cost.

Chapter Nine

Hailey found Wolf sitting alone in his car. He leaned heavily on the steering wheel, with one foot resting on Stella's floorboard and the other flat on the concrete. He hadn't noticed Hailey yet, probably because he was looking straight ahead, his eyes glazed and unfocused.

All that masculine vulnerability radiating out of him took her breath away. Tears leaked out of her eyes. She brushed them away with a quick swipe. It was so easy to forget this big, charming man had just returned from a war zone where he'd lost four of his men, including his best friend.

Searching for the right words, Hailey wheeled the overflowing shopping cart out of the way of traffic and stopped next to him.

"Wolf?"

He blinked once, twice, then swung around to face her.

The war of emotions raging in his gaze evened out at last and his expression cleared.

Wolf was back.

Heaving a sigh of relief, Hailey crouched down in

front of him. "I was worried about you," she whispered, afraid to say the words too loudly.

He placed his hands on her shoulders and something moved inside her, something good and permanent and *terrifying*. She was falling for this gorgeous, sad, courageous man, and she wasn't sure what came next.

Wolf's gaze softened. "Thank you, Hailey."

"For...for what?"

"For knowing what to do back there. For getting me out of the store before something bad happened. No one has ever cared about me like that." His blue eyes flickered with gratitude. "I owe you. I—"

He broke off, blinked. Blinked again. He had more to say. She saw it in the way the muscles jumped in his jaw, but then his gaze filled with a different sort of intent and he leaned forward.

Hailey's stomach dropped to her toes at the same moment Wolf's mouth pressed lightly against hers.

He was actually kissing her. Right there, in the middle of the busiest parking lot in Savannah. And...and... *she* was kissing him back. Rather enthusiastically, if she did say so herself.

Surprised at her behavior, Hailey lost her balance. Wolf caught her with a hand behind her back, the movement enough to break the kiss.

He smiled slowly and her stomach performed a perfect roll.

"Well," he said, still grinning.

"Well," she repeated.

"I didn't plan that."

"I... I know." She angled her head slightly away. This good-looking, flawed soldier had too much power over her, enough to make her start building dreams of happily-ever-after around him.

Was that why he'd kissed her? Had it all been part of his plan? To distract her from her goal?

"This doesn't change anything," she said with only a hint of her usual conviction. "I'm still going to the Middle East."

He knuckled a lock of her hair off her face. "I'd be disappointed if a simple kiss could change your mind that easily."

Simple? Who was he kidding? There was nothing *simple* about that kiss, and they both knew it.

"Of course." He twirled the errant strand around his finger. "I think it's only fair to warn you that I'm still going to do everything in my power to sway you to my way of thinking."

"I'd be disappointed if a simple kiss could change your mind that easily," she said, using his own words against him.

He laughed, a quick burst of humor. Finally, he looked like his old self again, enough that internal warning bells sounded the alarm in Hailey's head. "We have a lot of bags to unload," she reminded them both. "We should probably get to it."

He looked over her shoulder and grimaced. "Right." He helped her stand. "Come on. We're burning daylight."

Working in silence, they stashed the bags in the trunk. Ever the gentleman, Wolf helped Hailey into her seat before heading to his side of the car.

While he rounded the front end, she debated whether or not to bring up the incident in the store. Over the last week, she'd done considerable research about return-

ing war veterans and their unique struggles. Wolf had
some clear signs of battle fatigue, but not all of them.

According to one article, too many people pretended
nothing was wrong. But silence was often the biggest
detriment to a soldier's healing. If Wolf was going to
overcome whatever was bothering him, he *had* to talk
about it.

Sorting through several different approaches to the
conversation, Hailey waited until he shut the car door
and turned to look at her. "Ready?"

She shook her head. "No. First, I'd like you to tell
me what happened back there."

"We, uh—" he looked quickly away "—kissed?"

Yes. Oh, *yes,* they had. But that wasn't what she
meant. "Lovely as it was, I'm not talking about our kiss."

"You thought it was…*lovely?*" He didn't seem to
know what to make of that.

"No, actually, I thought it was spectacular."

"Yeah." A very masculine grin spread across his lips.
"It was."

Refusing to let him sidetrack her—which, unfortunately, he was on the verge of doing—Hailey refocused
the conversation. "I was talking about what happened
in the store."

His smile vanished, but he didn't seem as disturbed
by the question as she would have expected. In fact, he
looked like he wanted to talk. Which, according to Hailey's research, was a really, *really* good sign.

She relaxed back against her seat in relief, until she
realized he wasn't actually talking. Not yet, anyway.

Perhaps he didn't know where to start.

She decided to help him out. "Were there too many

choices in there? Was that what triggered your, um… reaction?"

His lips twisted into a frown. "Not exactly. It was that ridiculous argument I overheard."

"What argument?" she asked, more than a little confused.

"There was a woman, just behind us, or maybe one aisle over, complaining about the low thread count on the sheets." He shook his head in disgust. "She was making it sound like it was the end of the world because she couldn't find sheets soft enough for her guest room."

Hailey furrowed her brow. Why would something so innocuous shove him close to the edge? "I'm not sure I understand."

Wolf's eyes took on a hard expression. "There was such entitlement in her tone, like it was her *right* to have the softest sheets known to man, when so many people in the world don't even have a bed."

His words triggered a surprisingly strong reaction in Hailey, a mixture of shame and guilt and conviction. Her greatest fear was that she'd end up like that woman, ungrateful for the advantages in her life.

"I know I overreacted," Wolf admitted. "It's not that I begrudge people having nice things. That's what makes this country great. You know? The freedom to choose, to achieve, to go after whatever we want, whether it's good for us or not."

Finally, Hailey understood what had happened to Wolf inside the store. "You want people in this country to appreciate what we have," she ventured. "That's what got you so upset, the woman's lack of gratitude."

He shrugged. "My anger was out of proportion to the

situation. I've never been that furious in my life. Not even when my mother walked out and left me to care for my alcoholic father all by myself."

What? His mother had abandoned him? Hailey forgot all about soft sheets and sufficient gratitude. It took all her mental effort to fight off the powerful rush of anger slamming through her. The emotion was so strong she could hardly breathe.

"How old were you when she left?" she asked, her voice sounding oddly calm, considering the fury building inside her.

"Ten."

So young? "Oh, Wolf, how awful."

He looked at her oddly. "Didn't you say Clay told you about me?"

She nodded, unsure why he'd steered the conversation in that direction.

"Clay never told you about my childhood?"

"Of course not," she assured him. "He wouldn't have betrayed your confidence like that."

Instead of offering comfort, her words seemed to make him tenser. "I don't understand what you mean."

There was so much confusion in him. Didn't he realize how loyal Clay had been to their friendship? "The circumstance of your childhood wasn't Clay's secret to tell, not even to me. He kept his descriptions to your character and how it showed in everyday, ordinary events."

Like how Wolf always had time to play soccer with the local Iraqi kids, even when he was exhausted from a full day's grueling work. How he accepted the dangerous missions others didn't want to take. How he would speak with his soldiers, whenever, wherever, no matter the situation or problem.

So caught up in trying to remember the rest of what

Clay had said, Hailey barely noticed Wolf shutting down again. With very controlled movements, he slipped on his sunglasses and reached for the ignition.

"Wait." She placed her hand over his. "Did you say you had to take care of your alcoholic father? All by yourself?"

He let go of the key and sat back. "You caught that, huh?"

"But you were only ten years old." A baby, really. At that age she'd had nothing more on her mind than dance classes, swimming lessons and what candy to pick at the movies.

"I grew up fast," he said.

And suffered for it, she thought, in ways she couldn't possibly understand. A child should never have to be that responsible at such a young age. "I can't imagine how hard it must have been for you."

"You have no idea." He ran his fingertip along the steering wheel, round and round and round. "My father was a mean drunk."

Hailey hurt for the little boy he'd once been. So much her heart ached. Not only had he been forced to become an adult at the age of ten, he'd clearly been wounded by the two people he was supposed to rely on most, his parents. Yet, despite all his hardships, Wolf had turned out to be an exceptional leader, a man others trusted with their lives.

Clay had said Wolf was the best person he knew. Hailey completely agreed.

Tentatively, she reached out and touched his hand. When he didn't pull away, she curled her fingers around his.

He stared at their joined hands for a long moment. "The Army is the only real family I've ever known. But now, after the bombing—" he swallowed hard "—even that's tainted."

Unable to stop herself, Hailey pressed a tender kiss to his cheek, then fell back in her seat once again.

He touched the place where she'd kissed him, smiled briefly then dropped his hand and scowled again. "I go over the details of that day in my head, over and over again, wondering how I missed the signs of the IED."

Hailey's eyes widened at the self-recrimination in his voice. "You don't actually believe the accident was your fault?"

"Maybe I do." His words came out barely audible.

What a terrible, terrible burden to carry all these months. "Were you driving?" she asked. "Is that why you think you're to blame?"

"No." He shook his head. "Clay was behind the wheel. Like always. But, Hailey, I was the Truck Commander." He looked at her with genuine remorse in his eyes. "It was my job to be on the lookout for trouble."

She supposed that argument made an odd sort of sense—to him. But it wasn't the full story. It couldn't be. He was leaving too much out. Nothing in life was ever that black-and-white.

"If my brother was driving, like you said, doesn't that mean he missed the bomb, too? And what about the gunner?" She pictured in her mind the Humvee Clay had once shown her. "If he was standing in the turret, wouldn't he have had a fuller range of vision than either you or Clay?"

"We all missed the bomb," Wolf said quietly. "But it was my sole responsibility to see it in time."

Knowing exactly what to say, Hailey touched his shoulder. "Wolf. I don't blame you for Clay's death."

The muscles beneath her hand tensed. "Because of my negligence four good men are dead, including your brother. I stole your family from you, all because I missed something I was trained to see."

The despair in Wolf's voice shook her to the core. Now she understood why he was so determined to follow through with his promise to Clay.

"The explosion was not your fault," she insisted, gripping his shoulder in earnest. "If you need someone to blame, blame the insurgents who laid the bomb. Blame the terrorists who hate us so much they fight dirty. They are the ones who stole Clay from us. And, yes, Wolf." She leaned closer to him. "Make no mistake. We both lost our brother that day."

Making a strangled sound deep in his throat, Wolf pulled away from her and reached for the ignition again. One twist of his wrist and Stella exploded into action.

Hailey jumped back at the awful sound. Even if she wanted to continue the conversation, Wolf wouldn't be able to hear her over the roar of the engine.

What a convenient way to end the conversation.

Only after he put the car in gear did Stella's obnoxious growl settle into a loud purr.

"Once we unpack the supplies," Wolf said over the rumble, "I have a video I need to show you on my computer."

Considering the grim twist of Wolf's lips and his cold, intimidating tone, Hailey knew she didn't want to see whatever was on that video.

But she would sit through the show, for no other reason than to prove to Wolf she didn't blame him for Clay's death. Then, *maybe,* he would stop holding himself responsible, as well.

* * *

The unpacking and subsequent organizing took longer than Wolf anticipated. The sun had gone down a full hour ago. With it, the temperature had dropped at least ten more degrees. Wolf's leg ached like an angry bear.

Rubbing out a kink in his thigh, he looked over at Hailey puttering around in his kitchen. The mood had lightened between them, enough that he no longer wanted to talk—or even think—about what had happened in Iraq. He just wanted to enjoy her company.

He watched, fascinated, as she went to the sink and flipped on the faucet. After squirting dish soap in the pooling water, she tackled the task of washing a stack of plates recently freed from their packaging.

Unable to take his eyes off her, Wolf's heart took a tumble in his chest. Hailey moved with a sleek grace that captivated him. She was all poise and fluid motion and beneath her deceptively easygoing manner was the heart of a warrior. She would fight for her beliefs to the bitter end. He'd been kidding himself to think otherwise. She would also stand boldly beside those she considered her own.

Wolf wanted to be hers.

Taking a deep breath, he rocked back on his heels and tried not to disturb her while he was battling this strange mood.

Then again, why not interrupt her?

Decision made, he ambled into the kitchen.

"Are you planning to work through dinner?" he asked in what he hoped was a light tone. He couldn't tell over the drumming of his pulse in his ears.

She looked over her shoulder and smiled. "What time is it?"

Captured in that sweet gaze, he swallowed. "Just after eight."

"I didn't realize it was so late." She looked around the town house and her smile deepened. "We've certainly accomplished a lot."

"Enough for one day." He concentrated on a spot over her head, searching for anything to keep his mind off the way his heartbeat continued to pick up speed at an alarming rate. "Let's get something to eat."

"But I'm not through washing dishes."

"I say you are."

He reached around her, turned off the faucet then stepped back. She spun around with a gasp. Blinking rapidly, she looked flustered and confused and adorable. He had to fight not to pull her into his arms and kiss her.

There was something about this woman that called to the man in him. He felt incredibly normal around her. And accepted, truly accepted.

A flood of warmth captured his cold heart. Hailey O'Brien was a special woman. By refusing to hold him responsible for her brother's death, she made him want to forgive himself, to turn back to God and be a better man, the man he never thought he could be but desperately wanted to become.

She moved a step closer, piercing him with her gaze. There was curiosity in her eyes. And something else. Something that told him she was fully aware of him, fully engaged in the moment.

Needing something to do, Wolf grabbed a dish towel off the counter, took her hands in his and began drying them.

She let out a shaky sigh.

He liked that sound. It made him feel like an alpha

male, called to protect his woman from danger. And, yeah, Hailey was starting to feel like his woman.

"Are you going to kiss me again?" she asked with unmistakable excitement in her eyes.

He could get used to her looking at him like that. Grinning like the Big, Bad Wolf she'd once called him, he continued rubbing her hands. Slowly. Methodically. "It's a high possibility."

"So, um…" She cleared her throat. "Are you going to do it anytime soon?"

He tossed the towel over his shoulder, then lifted one of her hands to his lips. "I'm thinking about it."

Now she looked annoyed and maybe a little impatient. "Are you gonna think about it much longer?"

"That bother you?" he asked, knowing full well that it did.

"You bet it does." She tugged her hands free and then skimmed her fingertips across his cheek. "You have exactly five seconds to get busy, soldier. Or I'll take matters into my own hands."

He liked that idea. A lot. "How long do I have left?"

"About three seconds."

"One…" He counted slowly, fighting for patience. "Two…"

She let out a feminine huff and grabbed his shoulders. "Three."

He closed his eyes as she pressed her lips to his. Her kiss was tentative, innocent and so sweet Wolf's eyes stung behind his lids.

Just as he started enjoying himself, she pulled her head back. "There." Her tone rang with triumph.

Wolf grinned at her, realizing he hadn't felt this good in a long time. Maybe never. "Very nice."

A blush spread across her cheeks.

He leaned forward for another kiss, but then her stomach growled and he stopped his pursuit. "Hungry much?"

She gave him a wry grin. "I suppose I should warn you. I get mean when I don't eat."

He doubted that, but he played along. "Then we better get you fed." He walked over to the counter and yanked Stella's keys into his hand. "If I remember correctly, you owe me a pizza."

"I'll gladly pay up." She took the keys out of his hand and twirled them around her index finger. "But before we head out, didn't you want to show me something on your computer first?"

His good mood plummeted at the reminder. With considerable effort, he folded his emotions further inside him and took his keys back. Nothing was going to ruin this moment, especially not a series of video clips of IED explosions. "Later. Maybe after we eat."

Thankfully, she didn't argue. "Okay."

Wolf watched, mesmerized, as she twisted her hair into one of those intricate braids only women knew how to build.

"What are you doing?" he asked.

"I'm pulling my hair back so it'll fit under the helmet."

"What helmet?"

She gave him a pitying look. "The one I have to wear to ride on your motorcycle."

He shook the car keys in front of her nose. "We're taking Stella."

"Oh, no. No, no." She plucked the keys back and then tossed them into the sink of soapy water. "You promised me a ride on your motorcycle."

Wolf was already shaking his head before she finished speaking. No way was he putting her on his bike at this hour. "It's too dark outside."

"Why would riding in the dark be a problem?" She angled her head at him. "Don't you have a headlight?"

"Sure, but you won't be able to see much. Why bother?"

"Because I'll be able to tap into my other senses. Feel the wind on my face. Hear the roar of the traffic. Maybe smell the pine trees. As a matter of fact…" She drummed a finger on her chin. "Not being able to see just might make the whole experience more exciting."

It probably would, Wolf silently admitted to himself. But he wasn't giving in to her request. Riding a cycle could be dangerous. Riding at night even more so.

"Come on, Wolf."

"Absolutely not."

She gave him a sad puppy-dog look that just about broke his heart. "Please?"

"No."

"I have tricks to make you change your mind."

Okay, that sounded interesting. "Yeah? Like what?"

She opened her mouth, shut it, concentrated for a moment, then began again. "You might as well quit arguing. You will give in."

In the face of all that female confidence, Wolf knew she was right. She was going to win this one. But his pride wouldn't allow him to go down without a fight. The woman was going to have to earn her ride.

"Go ahead, sweetheart." He folded his arms across his chest. "Convince me."

Chapter Ten

Smiling in triumph, Hailey wrapped her arms around Wolf's waist and prepared to enjoy the ride. She couldn't hear much over the noise of the motorcycle's engine.

She didn't care.

She felt great. Free. And to think, she'd nearly missed out on this fabulous experience because of Wolf's stubbornness.

Thankfully, he'd given in to her request. All it had taken was a few steps in his direction, a lot of female attitude on her part and a saucy grin. The poor man had gone down without a fight.

But right now, instead of gloating—there'd be plenty of time for that—Hailey allowed herself to embrace all the wonderful sensations of the moment.

Her pulse raced in time with the roar of the engine. Her stomach flipped over and over and over again. While her eyes filled with happy tears.

This was an adventure she wouldn't soon forget.

No denying it, Hailey had lived a sheltered life. If she'd have continued existing in her safe, predictable world, she'd have missed out on today. She'd have missed out on Wolf.

Smiling broadly, she hugged him a little tighter.

Misunderstanding the gesture, he slowed down. "Sorry," he yelled over the wind. "Didn't mean to scare you."

Touched that he was that concerned about her, she shouted back, "I'm not afraid."

"Really?"

She laughed into the wind. "Speed up."

With a twist of his wrist, he did as she requested, muttering something that sounded suspiciously like, "Woman after my own heart."

Hailey sighed, ready to admit the truth at last. She wasn't falling for Wolf, she'd already fallen. It had been coming on for a while, maybe all the way back to Clay's first e-mails about his friend with the odd nickname. In some place deep within her, Hailey had been waiting for Wolf to come home to her.

And now that he was here, she was a better person for knowing him. It wasn't just his good looks that had captured her heart. It was his courage. His integrity. And, oddly enough, his devotion to her brother's last request.

Not that he'd win that particular argument, but Wolf's commitment to his promise showed what sort of man he was deep at his core.

With another twist of his wrist, he slowed the motorcycle so he could take the off-ramp that fed into Savannah's historic district.

The moment they turned onto Liberty, Hailey sighed. Her ride was drawing to an end.

Traffic was light at this time of year. That didn't

mean there weren't tourists. They passed three separate walking tours in less than five city blocks.

Determined to squeeze every ounce of pleasure out of this adventure, Hailey tried to look at the downtown from a visitor's perspective. She knew the draw was the city's rich history and unique architecture. But to her, Savannah was simply home. The only one she'd ever known.

She would miss living here when she left for the Middle East. The city had a quirkiness and charm that couldn't be found in any other place in the world. Once she became a full-time missionary, Hailey would have to leave everything and everyone she loved behind.

She fought back a frown, but couldn't stop the wave of sadness that coursed through her veins.

Wolf pulled the motorcycle to a stop in front of her house and her mood took another turn for the worse. Feeling apprehensive, she climbed off the bike and then yanked off her helmet with a little more force than necessary.

"Why don't you come inside," she said, eyeing Wolf carefully. "Once we order the pizza I'll grab my laptop and you can cue up whatever it was you wanted to show me."

Wolf looked up at her house. A shadow of unease crossed his face, but then he gave one firm nod of agreement. "Yeah, okay. It might be better to do this here. Where you're comfortable."

At his businesslike manner a shiver of foreboding passed through her. Worse, the tension was back between them. Suspecting what he planned to show her, Hailey doubted the evening would end on a high note. And that was the real shame here.

* * *

Sitting alone at Hailey's kitchen table, Wolf waited for her to return with her laptop. His hunger had all but disappeared. And with each passing second, his doubts increased.

Maybe this wasn't the best time to show Hailey the video montage he'd found on the Internet. When the idea had first occurred to him, his primary goal had been to scare her into staying home.

Now, he wasn't sure he wanted to frighten her. Not like this. But how else could he convince her of the dangers she would face in the Middle East? Reason hadn't worked. So far the survival classes hadn't done the trick. Even his well-thought-out pleas had fallen on deaf ears.

Wolf was out of ideas.

So here he sat, rubbing his aching leg, preparing to fight dirty. But what else could he do? Walk away? Not going to happen.

He tapped his knee with an impatient drumming of his fingers, wishing Hailey would return soon. The picture of her and Clay still hung on her refrigerator. The sight of all that happiness, now lost forever, was a bold reminder of why Wolf had to resort to shock tactics in order to bring Hailey into compliance with her brother's wishes.

Glancing at the photograph, it struck him once again just how different the tuxedoed Clay was from the fearless soldier Wolf remembered. The guy in the picture looked younger, more carefree, on the brink of continuing the O'Brien legacy.

Hailey looked equally charmed and ready to take her place in the world, as well. In that brief snapshot in time, the future was full of possibilities for them both.

Then Clay had gone off to war. And everything had changed.

Guilt weighed like a stone in Wolf's gut. Had Clay survived the IED instead of him, would he be the one sitting in this kitchen waiting for his sister to return? Perhaps they'd be planning Clay's next career move, Hailey's unconditional support making the choices seem endless.

What would it be like to have that kind of woman in his life, a woman who knew what loyalty and permanence meant?

Wolf had no answer to the question. The mere suggestion was beyond his comprehension. How could a man whose own mother hadn't wanted him ever understand a woman like Hailey and what it would take to make her happy?

Before he could ponder the question, Hailey returned and joined him at the table.

"We have at least thirty minutes before the pizza arrives." She slid a high-end laptop computer toward him. "It's booted up. What did you want to show me?"

Against his better judgment, Wolf held Hailey's gaze a moment too long. She wasn't exactly scowling, but her eyes were bright and full of apprehension, as though she sensed what was about to come. With all that emotion brimming in her gaze, she looked far too young to head into a war zone.

If the insurgents got hold of her, they would…they would…

Wolf shook the thought away with a fierce jerk of his head.

He hated what he was about to do, but he hated the

idea of this beautiful, untouched woman heading into danger even more.

He swallowed back the last of his misgivings and lowered his gaze to the computer.

A few keystrokes later he found the Web site he wanted. Two more clicks and the video montage was ready to go.

"Okay. We're all set." He glanced over at Hailey again. "I'm going to show you a few scenarios similar to the one where your brother died."

"Wolf, no." Panic filled her gaze. "I don't need to see how Clay died. He's with the Lord now, and that's all that matters. It's not important how he got there."

"Unfortunately, how he died *is* important." Wolf covered her hand with his. The idea of losing her to the violence of the Middle East was enough to steal his breath. "I'm sorry, Hailey, I can't let either of us forget why I sought you out in the first place."

She squeezed her eyes shut, took a deep breath and then slowly nodded. "Okay, fine. Let's just get this over with."

"It's for the best," he said, trying to convince himself as much as her.

But for the first time since Clay's death, Wolf felt the stirrings of genuine anger. Not guilt but anger, bordering on fury. Why had his friend put him in this impossible situation?

If Wolf kept Hailey out of the Middle East, she could easily end up bitter, perhaps never forgiving him for taking away her dream, as misguided as it was. On the other hand, if she did make it to the Sandpit, she could just as easily lose her life to a random act of violence. Or worse.

As bad as either scenario was, Wolf knew his duty.

With a surprisingly steady hand, he pressed the Enter key. An image from a homemade video filled the screen.

No turning back now.

Hailey held her breath as Wolf swung the computer to face her again. She braced against the emotions bubbling inside her, with little success.

Relax, relax, relax, she told herself, but she couldn't hold back the sick feeling of panic whirling in her stomach.

Wolf wasn't playing fairly.

Nevertheless, Hailey would endure this terrible moment. And then she would get through the next. And then the next, holding steady through the entire process until Wolf shut off the computer.

Blinking hard, she took in the scene playing out on the screen. A soft gasp flew from her lips.

The video Wolf had cued up had been taken from atop a military transport vehicle, one that had an upper deck large enough to hold several heavily armed soldiers.

The picture quality was terrible. And there was no audio to speak of, other than the grind of the truck's engine and some off-color bantering between the men. It was the kind of good-natured ribbing Clay and his friends used to give one another while watching University of Georgia football games.

But how could the soldiers be so carefree? Didn't they know what was about to happen?

Her heart constricted painfully in her chest. How was she going to watch these men die?

She wanted to rail at Wolf for making her sit through

this. She glanced over at him, ready to tell him what she thought of his underhanded tactics, but then she noticed the tense look on his face. He didn't want to watch this video any more than she did.

"Why are you putting us through this?" she asked, more than a little angry at him.

"Because you need to see for yourself the sort of danger you're heading into." Determination exuded out of him.

"There are other ways," she whispered.

"If I thought that were true we wouldn't be sitting here now."

Frowning, she returned her gaze to the screen and braced for the inevitable explosion.

The image was bumpier now that the highway had turned into a long stretch of uneven pavement.

One moment the soldiers were driving along, with an endless expanse of desert flanking each side of the road, the next moment...

Boom!

The camera jerked.

And then the image blurred, fading to black.

Unfortunately, the audio still worked. "Get out, get out, get out," someone yelled.

The soldiers were still alive. "Thank God," Hailey murmured.

But before she could discover their ultimate fate, Wolf reached over and clicked the Enter key again.

The image disappeared. Only to be replaced by another.

This one was from the same camera angle, but the truck moved at a snail's pace along a city street amid heavy civilian traffic.

"That's Baghdad," Wolf told her.

Hailey ignored him, her gaze riveted to the screen. Hot tears of frustration filled her eyes. Why couldn't she look away?

She didn't have long to ponder before another...

Boom!

This time, the explosion came from several yards up ahead of the military vehicle. The sound of screeching tires was all Hailey caught before Wolf clicked a button and another video began.

She sat through three more explosions before she slammed the laptop shut and glared at Wolf. "Enough."

Conviction flickered over his harsh features, but Hailey also saw the haunted look below the hard emotion. The videos had disturbed him as much as they had her.

She opened her mouth to speak, but he cut her off. "*Now* do you see how dangerous it is over there?"

The grief in him was palpable. Clearly, this hideous little exercise had backfired on him. And now he was the one most disturbed by the explosions, both guilt-ridden and filled with regret. The poor man needed redemption. What he didn't understand was the Lord had already given it to him. He just hadn't accepted it yet.

The instinct to push him down the path toward healing made Hailey speak too quickly, with little finesse. "All you managed to prove was how random the violence is over there. *In fact,* the only similarity I saw in those five videos was the haphazard nature of the explosions."

A muscle shifted in his jaw. "That wasn't my point."

Oh, she knew what his point had been. "Regardless. That's what I'm taking away from this. And so should you. The death of your men was not your fault, Wolf.

Please, hear me." She pinned him with her stare. "It wasn't your fault."

For a tense moment he just sat there, blinking at her with a glazed look in his eyes. Then he lowered his head and a shiver ran through him. It didn't take all three of Hailey's college degrees to figure out Wolf was back in the desert, grappling with painful memories.

"This isn't about me." His head snapped up and he looked fully aware of his surroundings. Too aware. "Why won't you accept how dangerous the region is?" He all but growled the question at her.

"I'm not an imbecile. I *know* it's dangerous over there. But I won't cower my way through life. Not anymore." She stood, slapped her palms on the table and glared down at him. "If I die over there, then I die. But at least I'll know I gave my life serving the Lord."

"No." Making a sound of anguish deep in his throat, Wolf rose from the table and yanked her into his arms. "You can't die. Not on my watch."

Hearing the fear in his voice, she pressed her cheek against his chest and sighed. "Oh, Wolf, don't you see? If I stay here, I'll die a slow death of the soul, from a life of superficiality and meaninglessness. Short-term trips to places like Jamaica and Haiti aren't enough. I have to make a bigger commitment."

"I don't buy that." He shoved away from her. The rush of hostility on his face chilled her to the marrow. "There is nothing in the Bible that says you have to climb on an airplane to serve the Lord. You can serve right here, in Savannah. I know of several soup kitchens and at least one homeless shelter that could use your help tomorrow, if not sooner."

Technically he was correct. But in Hailey's case

"climbing on an airplane" was the only way for her to achieve her goal, the only way to honor Clay's sacrifice.

She had to make him understand. "Wolf, please, let's sit back down and start this conversation over."

His expression darkened. "We've both said enough for one night."

He spun away from her and left the kitchen without another word.

Oh, no. He wasn't getting off that easily.

"Don't run away from me," she said. "We had too good of a time today to end on this harsh note."

He stopped, unmoving, practically frozen in mid-step. "You're right. We did have a good day together." He heaved a sigh. "But I need time to think about everything you've said. Give me that, Hailey."

She reached up to touch his back, but stopped short, her fingers hovering just shy of making a connection.

"Okay, I'll leave you alone." *For now,* she added silently to herself.

Keeping his gaze averted, he shrugged into his jacket. "I'll call you tomorrow."

In the next heartbeat, he was gone.

Chapter Eleven

He didn't call.

Not the next day, like he'd said. Or the next. Or even the next. Nearly an entire week passed without a word from Wolf. Hailey tried not to take his silence personally. After all, she'd given him a lot to think about. Nevertheless, she couldn't help wondering...

Why hadn't he called?

She felt her eyes go a little weepy as she watched him conduct the second half of their weekly survival class. He hadn't looked at her once in the last thirty minutes. In fact, he hadn't looked at her at all since she'd arrived. Coupled with his authoritative tone and systematic manner he'd adopted for tonight's lesson, Wolf might as well be a complete stranger to her.

More than a little irritated, Hailey abandoned all pretense of paying attention to his detailed explanation on how to build a fire and moved to the back of the classroom. She felt better, more in control, now that she was standing rather than sitting.

Perched against the wall, she followed Wolf with her gaze. Her heart tripped at the sight of him moving

casually through the room as he spoke. He was almost
feline in his movement, like a big jungle cat on the hunt.
As if to add to the untamed picture, he wore all black
tonight—black jeans, black shirt, black leather jacket.

Talk about fighting dirty.

Why did the man have to be that attractive, and that
appealing, when all Hailey wanted to do was ignore
him?

She deserved to be angry at him. She had that right.
Or so she told herself. But all she really felt was sad.
And maybe a little lonely.

She'd opened her heart to Wolf, and she'd thought
he'd opened his as well, at least a little. He wouldn't
have shared the story of his painful childhood if he
didn't have feelings for her. She knew him well enough
to know he was too private of a person to open his soul
to just anyone.

But she wasn't sure their relationship would ever
progress beyond an awkward friendship.

Not with his promise to Clay standing between them.

"You're scowling."

Hailey jerked at the sound of the softly spoken words,
barely audible but discernible all the same. She hadn't
heard J.T. join her. Then again, he was another one who
moved with catlike grace, despite his disability.

Sighing over the interruption, she rolled her gaze in
his direction. "I'm not scowling. I'm just paying very
close attention to the lesson."

J.T. didn't look convinced. "Okay."

"I am."

"Sure. Sure." He had the audacity to smirk. "Whatever you say, Hailey."

"J.T. I—" She slammed her mouth shut. This was

ridiculous, carrying on an argument in hushed tones. Especially when Hailey had far more important matters on her mind, like how to break through the invisible wall Wolf had erected between them.

She wanted to be left alone to think. Although...

Given his history, maybe J.T. could shed some light on Wolf's recent change in behavior.

She motioned him to follow her into the hallway.

Once they were out of earshot of the class, J.T. broke the silence first. "What's wrong, Hailey?"

His question took her by surprise. "Who said anything was wrong?"

"I know you well enough to know when something's bothering you." He gave her one of his shrewd pastor looks. "Or maybe I should say...*someone*."

By the practical no-nonsense tone of his voice, it was clear J.T. was firmly entrenched in the role of pastor. Under the circumstances, that worked for Hailey. "You're right. I am upset."

"Is it Wolf?"

She answered truthfully. "Yes."

"What has he done?"

"He's done nothing. *Nothing* at all." And wasn't that the real problem here?

That Wolf was allowing his promise to Clay to overshadow everything else between them, to the point of completely shutting Hailey out now that they'd come to yet another impasse?

Although Hailey admired Wolf's commitment to her brother, she sensed his guilt was the driving force behind his actions as much as his inner sense of integrity.

J.T. shifted next to her, the movement drawing her

eyes to his injured leg. A silent reminder of his own tragic past. "You and Wolf have been hanging out, right?"

"A little." He shoved his hands into his pockets. "We've had a few lunches together, discussed the survival classes, stuff like that."

Oh, they'd talked about more, Hailey sensed it by J.T.'s professional manner. He was in pastor-mode and wasn't going to reveal anything else on the matter.

We'll see about that.

"How much do you know about Wolf's days in Iraq?" she asked.

"Enough to know I've been where he is now." He didn't have to elaborate. Although Hailey wasn't privy to the particulars of J.T.'s time in the military, she knew he'd been blown up with his men. Just like Wolf.

Hailey knew she could dance around what she most wanted to discuss with him, or she could be direct. Since she had never been one to avoid the tough issues she pressed on. "Wolf blames himself for his men's deaths."

As soon as she blurted out the words, she realized his guilt was really the crux of the matter. If Wolf could accept the fact that he was the victim of a random act of violence rather than the cause, he would begin the healing process.

But how to get him there? Maybe J.T. had some ideas.

"By missing the signs of the IED he thinks he caused the accident," she added when she realized J.T. hadn't responded to her earlier remark.

Still maintaining his silence, he gave her a noncommittal nod, neither confirming nor denying whether this information was news to him.

"On the other hand," she continued, holding his gaze, "I don't blame him for Clay's death."

"That's good." Yet again, the pastor tone and distant manner revealed nothing of J.T.'s thoughts.

In her blazing frustration, Hailey wanted to shake the man for his lack of cooperation. She resisted. Barely. "How can I make him see the truth?"

"You can't."

That was not the answer she was looking for. "But surely there's something I can do."

J.T. shook his head. "I'm sorry, Hailey. You can give him your patience and understanding, but the rest is up to Wolf."

She slammed her fisted hands against her sides. "I hate feeling this helpless."

"Waiting is hard for all of us, but this is between Wolf and the Lord. Trust that God is already at work in him. He'll bring your soldier to healing. In His time, not yours."

As much as Hailey wanted to argue the point, she knew he was right. Like it or not, she had to wait on the Lord.

"Thanks, J.T. That's not really what I wanted to hear, but I can't deny the logic in your words."

"Not just logic, Hailey. Truth."

"Of course."

"Now that we've settled that." He offered his arm in a gallant gesture still common in the South. "Let's get you back to class so you can learn how to light a fire."

Sage words if ever she'd heard them.

Wolf noticed the exact moment Hailey and J.T. returned to the classroom. Both looked lost in their own thoughts. Whatever they'd discussed in the hallway must have been heavy stuff.

He expected Hailey to look up any minute and scowl at him, like she'd done all evening. But she quietly returned to her place against the wall and proceeded to stare at her feet.

He'd never seen her that subdued. He started to go to her, to find out what was wrong, see if he could help, but then he realized he was in the middle of teaching a class.

Fortunately, he'd covered enough for one night.

"And that's how to build a fire under the best and worst conditions." He shifted his weight back on one foot then shot a quick glance over the assembled group. "Any remarks, questions, complaints, concerns?"

Several hands shot into the air.

He smiled at the obvious enthusiasm in the room. After only two lessons, Wolf was growing to respect these people and their commitment.

They weren't misguided do-gooders with more heart than sense, like he'd first thought. They truly wanted to serve their God, for all the right reasons, and with a fiery passion that humbled him.

Their dedication made Wolf long to have his own calling. But why would the Lord use a man like him, when there were so many out there who hadn't made his colossal mistakes?

Unhappy with the direction of his thoughts, Wolf forced his mind back on task and began fielding questions.

As he spoke, his gaze shifted in Hailey's direction.

She hadn't moved from her spot on the wall, and she was still staring at her feet. She must really be upset with him. Who could blame her? He'd told her he would call and he hadn't.

Not because he'd been avoiding the hard conversation, but because he hadn't known where to *start* the conversation.

Now he regretted his indecision. He didn't like hurting Hailey. It left an empty feeling inside him.

Holding his smile in place, he focused on answering the next question about waterproof matches. "Yes," he replied. "Carrying a small box with you at all times would be wise. As to where to purchase them, any sporting goods or local hardware store should have a variety of choices. But if cost is a factor, you can make your own."

"Really?" someone asked. "How?"

Wolf glanced at the clock mounted over the doorway. He'd promised J.T. he'd have everyone out of here by 2100. It was 2102. "You'll have to wait until next week for that answer. I'll bring written instructions for everyone to take home with them."

Enthusiastic murmurs filled the room. They were actually excited about making their own matches.

This time Wolf's smile felt real as he ran his gaze over the group. "Anything else?"

No one raised their hand. Just as well. He was all talked out. "Okay, then. We're done for the night." He gathered his materials and stuffed them quickly into his bag. "Everyone have a good week."

He stepped to his left so J.T. could join him and say the final prayer of the night. But the pastor didn't move from the back of the room. Instead, he caught Wolf's gaze and said, "Why don't you close us in prayer, Captain Wolfson."

Say what?

The muscles in Wolf's back immediately stiffened.

J.T. wanted him to pray? Out loud? In front of all these people? Sweat broke out on his brow.

Was the man kidding?

Apparently not. J.T. hadn't moved off the back wall. Not one inch.

Torn between bolting and getting the job done, Wolf stood frozen in place, on the verge of panic like he'd never experienced before.

He'd faced enemy fire less terrifying than this room of eager, wide-eyed idealists waiting for him to pray for them.

He slowly bowed his head, but not before he looked desperately in Hailey's direction. She wasn't looking down anymore. And she wasn't scowling. She was smiling, *at him,* with a look of genuine encouragement in her gaze.

Feeling stronger, he closed his eyes. "Lord… I…"

He looked up again, feeling hopelessly lost. Hailey mouthed the words: *You can do it.*

He swallowed and started again. His voice stronger this time, he said, "Thank you, Lord, for this time together. I ask that You send us out this week with courage and faith. And may we honor You in everything we do…in Jesus' name. A… *Amen.*"

Low chatter and the rustle of people leaving their seats filled the air. He must have done an okay job with the prayer, even if his words had been a bit generic. At least no one had laughed, or snorted in disgust.

Needing something—*anything*—to make him feel less exposed, Wolf looked at Hailey again. She smiled at him. With the same sweet look in her eyes as before. He couldn't understand why she wasn't holding a grudge against him for not calling her.

She baffled him. But right now, as he stared at all that acceptance in her eyes, Wolf couldn't help himself. He smiled back.

That was all the encouragement she needed. She muttered something to J.T., then broke away from him and headed for the front of the room.

Wolf forced himself to remain where he was. Nonchalant. Normal. Nothing out of the ordinary here. Except...

His heartbeat had decided to kick into overdrive. And a trickle of sweat rolled down his back. Hailey O'Brien made him nervous. A completely new and terrifying sensation.

Fortunately, she wasn't the only one who wanted to talk to him. By the time she made it to the front of the room, Wolf was already surrounded by a handful of people asking him rapid-fire questions all at once.

He did his best to answer them, one by one. Patient. Smooth. In control.

Who was he kidding?

He couldn't make his mind work properly. Not with Hailey hovering just outside the circle of people, watching, waiting calmly for her turn to speak to him.

Once Wolf had answered all the questions, he turned his full attention onto Hailey.

Every muscle in his body tensed. There was something different about her tonight, a curious blend of patience and consideration.

"Hi," she said, her eyes revealing nothing.

"Hi," he said back, feeling like an awkward teenager in the throes of his first crush. The woman fascinated him in ways he hadn't begun to untangle in his mind.

He had a thousand things he wanted to say to her,

now that they were face-to-face. But just like every time he'd picked up the phone this week to call her, he was stuck without an opening line.

First and foremost, he needed to apologize for not calling her. Except…how did he do that? What could he say that wouldn't come off sounding trite?

"So, here's the thing," she began, her eyes still unreadable. "We ended things on a pretty dramatic note last time we saw one another."

"You could say that." He swallowed, determined to get his apology out before she continued with whatever else she had to say. "Look, Hailey, I'm sorry I—"

"Don't mention it." She waved a hand in disregard, cutting off his apology midsentence. "You've been busy. The important thing is that we're both here now, feeling unnecessarily awkward with one another. Let's not do this. Let's just move on, okay?"

Stunned she was going to let him off that easily, he cleared his throat. "I like that idea."

He wanted to say more but out of the corner of his eye he saw J.T. bearing down on them. Whatever the pastor had to say, Wolf didn't want to hear it right now.

"Let's get out of here," he suggested, keeping his eyes on J.T.

Following his gaze, Hailey made a soft sound of impatience in her throat. "We agree on something at last."

Even though Wolf gave J.T. a back-off glare the pastor closed the distance with clipped strides. "Just wanted to thank you for another great class, Captain." He held up his fist, knuckles facing Wolf.

Wolf forced down his impatience and pounded J.T.'s fist with his own. "Thanks."

Lowering his hand, J.T. looked from Wolf to Hailey then back again. He repeated the process two more times, a slow smile tugging at his lips on the last pass.

"What?" Wolf demanded.

"I see I'm interrupting. I'll just leave you two alone so you can speak in private."

With a surprisingly quick gait, he hustled out of the room, practically dragging the last two stragglers with him. He shut the door behind them with a decided click.

Okay. Good. Wolf was completely alone with Hailey. Here was his chance. "I really am sorry I didn't call you all week."

She regarded him with a complicated array of female emotions no man could ever hope to decipher. "Understandable. I gave you a lot to think about."

"Nevertheless," he said carefully, not sure why she was being so nice about this. "My silence was rude."

"Okay, yes, it *was* rude. But you're forgiven." Her tone held nothing but sincerity. The woman was actually letting him off the hook. No questions asked. No explanations needed.

Grace personified.

Wolf's heart dipped in his chest. But then reality set in. "Hailey, I like you," he admitted. "More than I can put into words."

"But...?"

Grimacing, he stuffed his hands into his pockets. "Who said there's a 'but'?"

"There's always a 'but' when a man starts a sentence with those three horrible words, *I like you.*" She sighed dramatically. "It's the kiss of death to any relationship."

They had a relationship?

Of course they did. But not like she meant. And not like he wanted.

"Okay, you're right. There is a 'but.' You see, no matter how much I like you, and would love to explore what comes next, we can't forget that Clay is standing between us. And probably always will."

Even if Wolf managed to keep Hailey out of the Middle East, even if she didn't grow to hate him because of it, they would never know if they were together because of their shared bond over Clay or because they truly worked as a couple.

Talk about a stalemate.

She notched her chin a fraction higher. "Then we have to get to know one another without him around."

Not possible. "How do you suggest we do that?"

"We go somewhere that doesn't remind either of us of my brother."

He snorted. "That place doesn't exist."

Her gaze turned thoughtful. Planting one hand on her hip, she tapped her chin with the other. "We just need to find a way to understand one another's position better, without your promise to Clay muddying the process."

As if he was the only stubborn one in the room. "Or your determination to honor his death complicating things, either."

"Fair enough."

She fell silent and got a faraway look in her eyes. "Perhaps instead of looking to the future, we have to go back to the past. Yes, that just might be the answer."

He hated that idea. His past was best left buried. He regretted revealing the ugly circumstances of his childhood to this woman, yet it was too late to recall the words. Besides, Wolf wasn't ready to quit on her, on them. "What did you have in mind?"

"I need to introduce you to the person I used to be.

Then you'll better understand the person I've become and why I have to go to the Middle East as planned."

Why would Wolf want to meet the old Hailey? He liked the new one just fine.

"Come on, Wolf. We have to try something."

She seemed pretty definite, like she had it all figured out in her head. Which did not instill a lot of confidence in him. On the contrary. "What sort of 'something' are we talking about here?"

"Well…" She secured her gaze on a spot just off center of his face. "I have to attend a dinner and silent auction this weekend. We're raising money for inner-city children."

Despite the noble cause, Wolf felt his shoulders bunch with tension. "Where's this event being held?"

"At the country club."

No way. He'd been to a country club once. In college, with a girl he'd been dating at the time. He couldn't remember the particulars, but he remembered feeling uncomfortable and out of place all night long. The evening had ended badly. "I don't do country clubs."

"But surely you'll make an exception this time." She touched his arm and gave him "the look," the same one that had prompted him to fire up his motorcycle against his better judgment.

The woman had a way of making him forget logic and reason.

He choked down a gulp of air.

"The dinner is the most efficient way for me to show you who I used to be."

He didn't want to know. No good could come of this. "I don't own a tux," he said, cringing at the note of desperation he heard in his voice.

"Wear your dress blues." She gave him a good, long once-over. "It's hard to resist a man in uniform."

Doomed. He was absolutely powerless in the face of all that female persuasion. "All right. I'll go." He grasped at the remaining scrap of his pride. "Under one condition."

Her lips curled into a feline smile. "Name it."

Oh, she was feeling smug now. *Let's see how long that lasts.*

"I'll brave the country club with you—" he nearly choked on the words "—if you go skydiving with me first."

She gave him a burst of strangled laughter. Her gaze darted around the room, landing everywhere but on him. "I couldn't possibly jump out of an airplane."

Of course not. Hence the suggestion. "That's my condition, Hailey." He held firm. "Take it or leave it."

She gaped at him for several seconds. "You're serious."

"I am." He gave her his best wolf grin. Yeah, he had a few tricks himself. "Not to worry, though. I'll make sure you get proper training before you have to jump out on your own."

"You want me to jump a...alone?" she squeaked. "Not hooked to someone who knows what he's doing?"

"I'll be right next to you, holding on until you pull the rip cord."

"I... I..."

"Where's that new adventurous streak of yours?" he goaded. "The one that's gonna carry you halfway across the world to a war-torn region?"

She muttered something under her breath, the words

sounding jumbled and not very nice at all. Something about a baboon and unfair tactics and…

Best not to decode the rest.

"Come on, Hailey. All you have to do is go skydiving with me—" he held a perfectly timed pause "—and then I'll brave the big, bad country club with you."

He crossed his arms in front of his chest and smiled. He had her. There would be no country club in his future.

But then she straightened her shoulders and pulled her lips into a tight little rosebud of defiance. "All right, big boy. You're on. I'll go skydiving with you."

Yeah, right.

He leaned in close to her ear, turning the screws. "Bring your sunscreen, baby, we're going to get pretty high up there. Wouldn't want you to get burned."

"Don't you worry about me, *baby*. I'll be fine. Super-duper fine." She poked him hard in the chest.

"Just make sure your dress uniform is clean by Saturday night. I want to show you off to all the fine ladies of Savannah. They love getting to know young, good-looking, *single* military officers."

He nearly choked on his own breath.

Somehow, while he'd been congratulating himself on his own brilliance, she'd done it again. The feisty little tiger had turned the tables on him.

Hailey O'Brien was turning out to be one formidable woman.

And Wolf was turning out to be a man who couldn't say no to her.

Chapter Twelve

The sound of the airplane engine reminded Hailey far too much of Stella's obnoxious growl. Perhaps that explained why she couldn't stop shaking. Or maybe she wasn't really shaking at all. It was hard to tell with the two-seater airplane vibrating like an overexcited Chihuahua.

Wolf's muscle car had nothing on this contraption.

When they'd arrived at the airfield with the jumpmaster, the exterior of the tiny airplane had looked passable enough. But then all three of them had taken their places inside and Hailey had discovered the interior, save the pilot's seat, had been gutted so that it could hold extra skydivers.

Now that they'd taken off, she glanced over the jumpmaster's head at the gaping hole on their right, the spot where a door was supposed to be.

Gulping for air, she quickly turned her head the other way. But her gaze landed on the grinning man beside her and her stomach dipped to her toes.

Wolf's expression held far too much glee. And maybe even a little bit of crazy.

Why wasn't he more concerned they were about to jump out of an airplane at thirteen thousand feet? That was over two miles above the ground.

And they were in a flying tin can, with only a few scraps of material, strapped to their backs, preventing them from falling, literally, straight to their deaths.

Hailey wasn't just scared. She was petrified.

Wolf must have read her mind, because he reached out and squeezed her hand. "Don't worry," he yelled over the airplane's roar. "I packed our chutes myself."

That gave her a measure of relief. Unfortunately, it wasn't enough.

She slammed her eyes shut, telling herself this was a large, courageous step in the right direction to becoming a woman of adventure. If she lived through this, Wolf had to go to the country club with her tonight. The two didn't seem equally scary in her mind, but apparently they were in Wolf's. It was all about perception, she supposed.

Keeping her eyes firmly shut, she ran through the instructions the jumpmaster, Ken, had drilled into her head all morning. As soon as the pilot cut the engine—and wasn't that a frightening prospect?—the three of them were supposed to climb on the wing of the airplane and fall backward so they could clear the airplane.

She was then supposed to assume a position similar to a belly flop and simply enjoy the ride for seven thousand feet. Wolf and Ken would be on either side, guiding her. When the time came, they would release her and she would pull the rip cord on her own.

This, of course, was all assuming she was still conscious. A high possibility since the temperature was at least thirty degrees colder at this altitude.

She felt a tap on her shoulder. Unhappy with the interruption, she cracked open one eye.

"Tell me that isn't a spectacular view," Wolf shouted, pointing to the ground below.

Taking a deep breath, Hailey stabbed a glance out the window. They were flying directly above the ocean, but the shoreline was in clear sight.

Okay, yes, the view was beautiful. Unfortunately, Hailey couldn't tell Wolf she agreed with him. She was too busy remembering the jumpmaster's warning about landing in the ocean. If that little disaster occurred and she didn't get out of the parachute quickly enough, the water could drag her under. To death by drowning.

And Wolf considered this fun?

The man had a death wish. Pure and simple.

Jamaica, Haiti, the Middle East, whether she spent a week or a lifetime in any of those locales, she didn't think she'd feel as concerned about her life as she did now.

The pilot cut the engine.

The sudden silence took Hailey by surprise and she nearly choked on her own gasp.

"It's go time," Wolf said cheerfully.

Lord, please, please, get me through this alive. I don't want to go splat on the ground.

"I'm ready."

She quit thinking so hard and let her training kick in. Just as Ken had instructed, she followed him onto the wing of the airplane, one terrifying step at a time.

Clinging to the metal structure, she scooted over far enough for Wolf to join them.

She didn't dare look down.

Wolf's hand closed over hers. "I'm right here with you. Every step of the way."

She gave him a shaky smile.

"We do this together," Ken reminded her.

"Right. Together." She turned her palm and pressed it flat against Wolf's. Her fear cut in half.

"On three." He squeezed her hand then let go. "One. Two."

"Three," she shouted and then leaned backward.

Her feet tumbled over her head.

She only had time for impressions after that. Wolf and Ken were still on either side of her, holding her steady. The wind slapped her in the face so hard she could barely breathe, the noise of it screaming through her ears at a deafening level.

She checked the altimeter on her wrist, shocked to see she'd already fallen three thousand feet.

Wolf tugged on her jumpsuit. She glanced in his direction. He gave her a thumbs-up.

A few more seconds passed before Wolf and Ken let her go. That was her signal to take control. She threw the rip cord and felt rather than heard the Velcro release her parachute.

She braced for a hard jerk as the parachute began filling with air, but her feet floated gently below her.

Amazed at how easy the transition had been from free fall to floating, Hailey reached for the toggles. She practiced steering by pulling on one and then the other. At last, she allowed herself to look down.

The view was amazing. Blue sky, green water, sandy beach. How could anybody witness all this beauty and not believe in God?

With her senses poised on high alert, Hailey drank in the experience. Every sight, sound and smell consumed her.

Both Wolf and Ken landed several minutes ahead of her. Wolf gathered his parachute with quick, jerky tugs, all the while searching the sky for her.

She waved at him.

He waved back and then dropped the chute so that he could make a cradle with his arms, as if he were waiting to catch her if she fell.

It was a joke, but a really sweet one with all kinds of symbolism she didn't have time to unravel.

Landing on the beach turned out to be somewhat anticlimcatic. She pulled hard on the toggles and hit the ground, feetfirst, with a soft thud.

Joy burst through her.

"I did it. I did it. I did it." Hopping from one foot to the other, she pumped her fists in the air in her own version of a happy-dance.

Wolf scooped her up into a hug that lifted her several feet in the air.

Overwhelmed with emotion, she clung to him, wrapping her arms around his neck. "That was amazing."

He set her on the ground and kissed her smack on the lips. "*You're* amazing."

They stared at each other. Both breathing hard. She wanted this man in her life. Always. But did he want to be in hers? Or was his promise to Clay the only thing keeping him here?

She hated that she didn't know the answer to that, that he might not know for sure, either.

Wolf broke eye contact first and went about systematically removing the rest of his parachute, mainly the now-empty container still strapped to his back.

Ken joined them and gave Hailey a high five. "Well

done, beautiful. One of the best first jumps I've ever witnessed."

"It was fantastic."

He helped her out of her parachute then turned to Wolf. "I need to get back to post. I have a buddy picking me up at the lighthouse. You two need a ride into town?"

Wolf shook his head. "We dropped off my car earlier this morning."

"Good enough." He smiled at Hailey and then handed her a small business card. "Let me know if you ever want to do this again. I'm only a phone call away."

She thought she heard Wolf growl. Surely she was mistaken? "Thanks, Ken," she said. "But once was enough for me."

"If you change your mind…"

She smiled. "I'll call."

"Sounds good." He walked over to Wolf, said something in a low tone. Wolf nodded. They both laughed, then Ken slapped him on the back.

"All right. See you two later." Ken headed out, waving a hand over his head in farewell.

Watching him leave with his parachute bunched in his arms, Hailey realized she was still jumping from foot to foot. "I can't seem to stand still."

"It's the adrenaline." Wolf slanted an unreadable glance in her direction. "It'll wear off soon."

She wanted it to wear off now. She hated this nagging, uncomfortable feeling, as if she were ready to jump out of her own skin. Too many emotions collided into one another. Excitement, fear, relief, joy and something else, something darker, something she couldn't quite name.

"So." She bounced toward Wolf. "What happens when the adrenaline finally wears off?"

He didn't like the question. She could see it in the way his hands paused over folding his parachute.

"You're gonna feel exhausted in a few minutes. Maybe even a little depressed. But it'll go away soon enough and then you'll be ready for your next jolt. *Jump.* I meant, jump."

No, he'd meant jolt. "That sounds almost like…like… an addiction."

He didn't respond. But the uneasy look in his eyes told her she was right.

Was Wolf hooked on adrenaline? Was that why he drove a ridiculously fast car, owned a motorcycle, jumped out of airplanes?

"Wolf? Is that why you do this?" She waved her hand in a wide arc. "For the rush?"

"No." He answered quickly, seeming very sure of himself.

"Then why?"

"It's complicated."

She waited for him to say more. But he just stared at the water. And stared. And stared.

Why wouldn't he explain himself?

Still looking out over the ocean, he discarded his parachute and then sat down, right there where he'd been standing. He drew his legs up and caged his knees inside his clasped hands.

Hailey joined him on the sand, hugging her own legs to her chest.

"I don't know why I jump out of airplanes, Hailey. I don't analyze it. I just do it."

There was more to it than that, but for now she accepted his explanation, determined not to push him. She sensed his reasons were tied to what happened to him in Iraq, but she wasn't sure. The not-knowing was the hard part.

For several minutes they sat in silence. Hailey watched the waves crash onto the shore, one on top of another, never ending, never ceasing. Like God's grace, freely offered to all who wanted it.

"If I was going to analyze my motives," Wolf said at last, "I'd probably say it's a test."

"A test?" she repeated. "For who? You?"

"No." He drew a circle in the sand with the toe of his boot. "I guess I'm testing God. I need to know if I was really meant to survive that attack, or if the Lord made a mistake. I need to know if *I* was a mistake."

Tears filled her eyes. How could such a courageous, competent man think he was a mistake, when he had so much to offer the world? "Oh, Wolf. God doesn't sit on some royal throne up in heaven, picking and choosing who lives and who dies."

He lowered his chin to his chest. "What if He does?"

She gathered her words carefully. "I don't know why the others died. Some things we'll never completely understand until we get to heaven. It was just their time. You were left behind for a reason. The Heavenly Father has a plan for your life."

"He can't use me." A devastated look flashed in his eyes. "I can't be trusted. Look what happened on that roadside."

Lord, he's not hearing me. "You can't keep blaming yourself, Wolf. It's unproductive."

He buried his face in his hands. His words were muffled, but she thought she heard him say he should have seen the bomb.

"Okay, Wolf, let's go with that. Let's say that, yes, you should have seen the bomb. Now what?"

He dropped his hands and leveled a shocked gaze on her. "What do you mean?"

"Supposing the accident was your fault. What then? Do you spend the rest of your life making amends? Or maybe you chase the next adrenaline high, until you ultimately kill yourself?"

He flattened his lips into a grim line. "I'm careful."

"Nobody's *that* careful."

He grew silent.

Oh, no. He didn't get to shut down on her now. They'd started down this road. They were going all the way. "If you're right, Wolf, and you are to blame for your men's deaths, then, I repeat, what comes next?"

"I…" He blinked, then shook his head slowly, miserably. "I don't know."

"Well, I do." In fact, she knew exactly what came next. "You forgive yourself. That's what. God has already forgiven you." She leaned forward and touched her lips gently to his cheek. "*I've* forgiven you. Now it's your turn, Wolf."

His eyes hardened. "What? You think everything's going to fall into place after I forgive myself? Is that what you're saying?" His voice held a large amount of bitterness, but Hailey also heard an unmistakable twinge of hope underneath. Just enough to make her feel they'd made progress here today.

"Not all at once. But, yes, Wolf. Everything starts to get better *after* you forgive yourself."

Chapter Thirteen

Wolf stood inside the country club, trying not to feel stiff and uncomfortable among the pretty people of Savannah. While he waited for the coat-check girl to return with his and Hailey's claim checks, he pretended not to notice the wary stares thrown his way, or the wide berth most people gave him.

Obviously, this particular country club didn't have a lot of military personnel among its membership. Like that was a big shocker.

He hid a yawn behind a slow, deep breath. His leg had started to ache hours ago, the lingering pain a constant reminder of what had happened that day in Iraq. Twice now Hailey had sent him reeling with her words of encouragement and forgiveness. She really didn't blame Wolf for her brother's death. He accepted that now, felt blessed by it.

If he was honest with himself, he'd rather be somewhere alone with Hailey, where they could talk, just the two of them. She'd be leaving for Haiti soon and he didn't want her boarding the airplane until matters were a little less volatile between them. Nevertheless, she'd been incredibly brave this morning. It was only fair he held up his end of the bargain tonight.

Compelled, he glanced over at his lovely date. She was still speaking to the elderly couple she'd introduced him to when they'd first arrived. The Pattersons seemed nice enough. He shot a smile in their direction and tried to keep his thoughts clear, but they kept circling back to the conversation he'd had with Hailey on the beach.

Now that she'd forgiven him, she wanted him to forgive himself, as if it were just a matter of changing his mind-set.

Well, forgiveness wasn't something Wolf had much experience with, not with the sort of childhood he'd endured. Survival, now *that* he understood. Wolf had lived the first fifteen years of his life in a vicious cycle of abuse and poverty. But he'd gotten out. Was it now his turn to give back?

A warm sense of destiny settled over him.

In the next moment the coat-check girl returned. He took the two slips she offered him with a smile and then turned back to his date.

His breath hitched in his chest. Hailey stood alone now, under a beacon of golden light, her smile solely for him.

He took a moment to simply enjoy the view.

The woman was all female curves in a fitted green dress. The color matched her glorious eyes. She'd piled her hair on top of her head in a messy array of curls that managed to look very elegant. At first glance her hair looked dark, almost black, but under the light Wolf could see the deep red undertones. The color reminded him of cherry cola. His new favorite drink.

"What?" Hailey cocked her head at him, her brow furrowed into a cute little frown.

He closed the distance a bit more, inhaling her perfume. He loved that spicy, floral scent that was solely hers. "I didn't say anything."

Her frown deepened. "You didn't have to. You have a strange look on your face."

He twirled one of her dark curls between his thumb and forefinger. "I was just admiring the view." He dropped his hand. "If I haven't told you already, you look beautiful tonight, Hailey. Really stunning."

And Wolf was feeling incredibly tender toward her. The sensation made his heart pound so hard his chest hurt. Which wasn't altogether a terrible sensation, just... unsettling.

"Well, I—" She visibly swallowed. "Thank you, Wolf. You look beautiful, too. I mean—" she gave a little self-conscious laugh "—you look handsome. The uniform is working for you."

He leaned in closer, catching another whiff of her precious scent. "But is it working for you?"

"Oh, yeah." Her eyes looked a little dazed. "It's really working for me."

"Then I'm glad I wore it."

They smiled at one another.

"So where do we go next?" he asked, prepared to brave the rest of the evening for Hailey's sake.

"The first room on our left." She hooked her arm through his and tugged him down yet another over-decorated hallway.

"What's in there?"

"The silent auction. Since we have over an hour before the dinner is served I figure we can see if there's anything worth bidding on tonight."

"Sure, why not?"

For the next ten minutes, they meandered through the room reserved for the silent auction. There were at least a hundred items up for sale.

There were fancy hotel stays with opening bids more than Wolf made in a month. There were weekend getaways, spa treatments, the latest electronic gadgets, lunches with dignitaries. But the one item that really grabbed Wolf's attention was the ridiculous opportunity to spend the afternoon with Uga, the famous bulldog mascot for the University of Georgia.

"Why would anyone want to pay money to spend the day with a glorified mutt," he wondered out loud, looking down the rather long line of handwritten bids. He zeroed in on the most recent number recorded. "Would you look at that, someone bid eight hundred dollars. That's insane."

"Shh." Hailey looked over her shoulder with a horrified expression on her face. "Somebody might hear you."

"Did you just shush me?" he asked, trying not to laugh. "Over a dog named U-G-A?"

She swung back around to glare at him. "Don't you dare make fun of my favorite bulldog." She actually sounded offended. "And, for your information, his name is pronounced *Ugh-ah*."

Apparently, it was up to Wolf to give the woman a reality check. All that oxygen-deprived air in the plane must have left her a little loopy. "He's a dog, Hailey."

"You might want to take note, Captain Wolfson. People around here take their college football very seriously. *And* their mascots."

"Let me guess," he said, trying to keep a straight face. "You went to the University of Georgia and now have an unhealthy fondness for smushed-faced dogs."

"Smushed-faced dogs?" Head high, she yanked a pen out of her purse. Keeping her eyes glued to his, she scribbled down a bid.

He leaned over and read the outrageous amount. "And you think I'm crazy for jumping out of airplanes?"

"It's for a good cause."

He said nothing, mainly because he liked her all worked up like this. Not that he'd tell her so. He wanted to get out of here in one piece.

Giving in to a smile, Wolf took in the room with a quick swoop. "So this is how you used to raise money for all your causes? Pawning off stuff to the rich folks of Savannah?"

She didn't answer right away, but instead looked around the room as he had done, perhaps trying to see the situation from his perspective. "A silent auction might seem like an odd way to raise money." She lowered her voice. "But some people will only give to a charity if they're getting something in return."

Yeah, he'd already figured that one out on his own. "What percentage of the night's take goes to the kids?"

She blew a tendril of hair away from her face. "All the items are donated, Wolf. The foundation gets a hundred percent of the proceeds."

Well, that was something at least.

"Don't look so disappointed," she said. "This isn't a Christian organization, but the people in attendance do care about their community."

She linked her arm through his and steered him out of the room before he could respond. "Come on, let's go take a look at the gardens. They're beautiful this time of year."

He chuckled at her transparent attempt to change the subject. "Smooth, Hailey. Very smooth."

"The money from the auction is only a portion of what we'll raise tonight," she said, once they left the room.

"How else will you get funding?"

She slid a glance at him from beneath her lowered lashes. "We place a stack of envelopes at every table."

"Envelopes?" He had no idea what that meant. "For what?"

"After the presentation the chairman of the board will get up and ask everyone to consider giving a donation directly to the foundation."

Wolf rubbed a finger over his temple, trying to relinquish the pressure of the headache building behind his eyes. The people were here, like Hailey said, and they were providing money for a good cause, yet something about the evening felt off. He couldn't figure out what.

"Wolf. No matter why the checks are written, the important point is the children win out in the end."

Okay, she had a point. A valid one. "Speaking of which, where are the kids?"

She stopped walking and stared at him. "What do you mean?"

"I haven't seen a single kid here tonight. Why not?" When he was young he would have given anything for the kind of meal they were going to serve later.

"The children can't be here tonight. It wouldn't be… it wouldn't be…" She looked at him helplessly. "Well, it wouldn't be appropriate."

"Why not?"

She gave him a shrug. But something in the gesture increased the tension in him. "Oh, I get it. They aren't good enough for this crowd." Just like he hadn't been good enough when he'd been a kid.

"No." Her hand practically clawed at his arm. "That's not what I meant at all. This entire evening is about the children, and the rec center we're going to build for them with the money we raise."

"Have you met any of the kids yourself?"

"Well, no." She dropped her head. "But I—"

He didn't wait for the rest. So this was the old Hailey. No wonder she'd been so determined to change. But had she really? She hadn't even met the kids she was supposed to be helping. He picked up his pace, not wanting to continue this discussion.

Hailey followed hard on his heels. She grabbed his arm and dragged him toward a door leading to an outdoor balcony.

The cold slapped him in the face, but she kept dragging him across the marble stones. Click, click, click, her heels struck like hammers to nails.

She stopped abruptly. The night closed in around them, like a phantom. The club's outdoor lighting provided just enough light for Wolf to see Hailey's troubled expression.

"Wolf, try to understand. This isn't a Christian organization."

"You said that already."

She started to say more but then shivered from the cold.

He unbuttoned his coat and wrapped it around her

shoulders. They stared at one another for a long, tense moment. She looked so tiny inside his jacket. Lost.

But was he looking at the old Hailey, or the new one? He hated that he didn't know for sure.

Ever since he'd walked into this place he hadn't been able to stop thinking about the life he'd lived as a child, how instead of writing checks for good causes his father had been too busy looking for his next drink. Wolf, like many inner-city kids, had alternated between scrapping for food and dodging his father's fist.

"After tonight," he said, "the people here will go back to their cozy existence where the most important problem they have to face is the thread count in their bedsheets."

He knew he sounded bitter, but he couldn't untangle the ball of tension in his gut. "They don't understand the despair that comes from wondering if there's going to be a meal tomorrow."

Not like Wolf understood it. Terrible memories bombarded him. Once, when his dad had gone on a month-long bender, Wolf had survived solely on the free lunches he'd gotten at school. The weekends had been nightmarish, but he'd lived through them.

In the end, the Army had been his ticket out.

But not every kid could take that route.

Something has to be done for the rest. The thought was so clear in his head he wondered where it had come from.

"Oh, Wolf." Hailey shifted closer to him. "This is what I've been trying to tell you ever since we met."

"Come again?"

"Don't get me wrong, these types of functions serve a purpose. But you're right. Many of the people in there are just like you described. And for the last twenty-five years of my life, I was one of them."

He heard the familiar sorrow in her voice, but tonight it sounded more like guilt than regret.

"I never got my hands dirty, Wolf, because no one ever taught me how."

"That's your excuse?"

"No. Not an excuse. An explanation of who I used to be. But everything changed for me when Clay died. He'd been planting seeds for months prior to the day of the bombing. His death gave me the final push."

Wolf admired the courage it must have taken Hailey to take that hard look at her life. But her role model had been a hardened soldier stuck in a war zone. If only Wolf could see what Clay had put in his e-mails he might have a better idea how to proceed.

"I don't want to be insulated anymore." Hailey wrapped his coat tighter around her shoulders. "I want to get to know the people I serve, personally. I want to live with them, cry with them, find joy and hope with them. I did a little of that in Jamaica. It's what I hope to do in Haiti and ultimately in the Middle East."

Admirable, yes, but again Wolf was struck with the notion that Hailey was still living with blinders on, unable to see the need right next to her. "You don't have to go to the Middle East to do what you just described."

"It's where Clay went."

Yep, now he knew for certain. Her perspective was skewed. "Your brother was sent to the Middle East. Stop romanticizing what he did over there. He was a soldier who lived in a war zone, and all that that implies. People are killed on a daily basis. Some are even tortured in brutal, unimaginable ways."

"Exactly." Her conviction all but radiated out of her. "There are innocent people who live in those war zones. People who aren't trained soldiers. Somebody has to care about them. Somebody has to show them the love of Christ. And that somebody is going to be me."

"How do you know it's supposed to be you?"

"I just do."

"That's not good enough. I want to hear specifics."

She fell silent, and then sank onto a wrought-iron bench.

Wolf sat down next to her and took her hand gently in his. "Don't you think I've been paying attention at our survival classes?"

She slid a glance in his direction. "What's that supposed to mean?"

"Your friends have taught me as much as I've taught them, maybe more. A person doesn't go on a mission trip to prove a point. She goes because she's called."

"I was called." She snatched her hand free. "To the Middle East."

Maybe she had been. Maybe. "Tell me the moment you knew for sure."

She climbed hastily to her feet, spun around and then clutched at the railing behind her. "When Clay died."

As though a light turned on in his head, Wolf knew exactly what he had to do next. He had to introduce Hailey to local people in need right here in Savannah.

If, after that, Hailey still believed she'd been called to the Middle East, then Wolf wouldn't stand in her way.

Not that he'd let her go over there unprepared. He'd do what he could to protect her, even if it required him climbing on that airplane with her. It would mean a complete change in his own lifestyle, but if that's what it took to keep her safe, then he'd do it.

Of course, there were a lot of "ifs" that still needed to be settled before life-altering decisions had to be made.

Wolf rose and joined her at the railing, stunned that he was actually thinking about giving up. No, not giving up, getting more information for them both. "What are you doing Wednesday morning?"

"Nothing that can't be rescheduled." Her brows lifted in inquiry. "Why?"

"I want to take you somewhere that might benefit us both."

"Don't you have to work?"

"Not on Wednesday." He'd already scheduled the day off in the hopes of finishing his move into the town house. Now he had a different plan in mind. "I'll pick you up at 0900."

"Where are you planning to take me?"

"Someplace where you can get your hands dirty."

Chapter Fourteen

Wolf found J.T. sitting alone in his office. The pastor was bent over a stack of papers, completely absorbed in his work.

Leaning against the doorjamb, Wolf waited a few beats then broke the silence. "Want to grab some lunch?"

J.T. didn't bother looking up. "I was wondering how long you were going to stand there staring at me."

"You knew I was here?"

Head still bent, J.T. flashed a quick smile. "You're not exactly light on your feet, soldier."

Wolf chuckled. "I'll file that information away for later."

J.T. joined in the laughter. After a moment, he tossed his pen aside and leaned back in his chair, his smile still holding. "Have a seat and tell me what's on your mind."

Wolf hesitated. He hadn't planned to have this conversation here, in the church, but J.T. must have countless resources a mouse click away in his computer. It made sense to take his friend up on his offer. Except…

J.T. might misunderstand this visit, thinking Wolf

had come for guidance rather than a simple list of home-less shelters and soup kitchens.

Feeling mildly uncomfortable, Wolf lowered himself into one of the two chairs facing J.T.'s desk. His gaze landed on a free-standing marble plaque that looked like a generic paperweight at first glance.

He read aloud the Scripture etched in black calligraphy. "I consider my life worth nothing to me, if only I may finish the race and complete the task the Lord Jesus has given me—the task of testifying the Gospel of God's grace. Acts 20:24."

"The senior pastor gave that to me on my first day here," J.T. explained. "It helps me remember that I'm investing my life in the only thing that matters, in a legacy that will live on after I'm gone."

Wolf remained silent, holding perfectly still, moving only the tip of his finger across the bold lettering.

He reread the Scripture, trying to comprehend the meaning behind J.T.'s bold remark. "Do you mean spreading the Gospel?"

"Roger that." J.T. steepled his fingers under his chin and stared at Wolf with a satisfied light in his eyes. "You've come a long way since the first time we met."

Wolf rubbed his leg absently. He supposed he had, from a certain perspective. There wasn't as much anger in him, nor as much despair. The Dream wasn't coming as often, either. He knew he owed much of his healing to Hailey. In their short acquaintance, she'd softened his hard edges and made him want to be a better man.

That wasn't to say Wolf didn't still feel lost at times. And confused. "I have a long way to go."

"We all do," J.T. agreed.

The certainty in the pastor's voice surprised Wolf. "Even you?"

"Especially me." J.T. stared off into space then gave his head a quick shake. "So, what brought on this sudden offer of lunch? You doing okay, adjusting to life back in the States?"

"I'm getting there."

Now why had he admitted that? Why hadn't he told J.T. to mind his own business? Like he had every other time the guy had probed too far into his mental state.

Fingers still braced under his chin, J.T. eyed Wolf with a look that was filled with concern yet also held deep understanding. "What can I do to help you, Captain?"

Wolf's gaze darted around the room. The use of his rank was a clear sign of respect on J.T's part, a reminder that they shared a common bond.

"Wolf?"

He drummed his fingers on the arms of the chair, still not looking directly at J.T. This wasn't the way the conversation was supposed to go. Wolf had come here to get a list of local homeless shelters. Nothing more.

You could have done that over the phone, he told himself. *Or e-mail.*

But he hadn't. He'd sought out J.T. personally, and not just to get the list. He realized that now. Somewhere along the way Wolf had grown to trust J.T., as both a friend and a pastor.

Man up, Wolf. Tell the guy what's really going on.

"Hailey thinks I need to forgive myself for my men's deaths," he blurted out. "She says the bombing wasn't my fault."

As soon as the words slipped from his mouth, he

wanted to take them back. But it was too late. The truth was out there, hanging in the room like a heavy, invisible shroud of gloom.

To his credit, J.T. didn't react. He simply continued sitting in his chair, cool, calm, completely laid-back. Oddly enough, the guy's casual posture had Wolf relaxing, too.

"What do you think? Do you agree with her?" J.T. asked.

"I…" He paused to consider the question and not just answer off the top of his head. "I want to agree with her, but I don't know if I can. The guilt." He squeezed his eyes shut a moment. "Sometimes, it's too much to bear."

A series of creaks and groans filled the air as J.T. shifted in his chair. The pastor no longer looked calm, but very, very intense. "Yet, you're here now. Talking to me. That's a good thing."

Wolf wasn't so sure.

J.T. leaned closer, just a fraction more, but enough to make Wolf sit up straighter. "Tell me why you sought me out today."

Wolf rubbed a hand over his face. "Because I'm tired of feeling like this. I'm tired of shouldering this burden alone."

"Good." J.T. nodded. "That's the first step, admitting the problem."

Wolf should feel pressured. Uncomfortable. He didn't feel either. Instead, he experienced a strange sense of peace now that he'd shared his concerns. "What do I do next?"

J.T. sat back, assuming his casual pose once again. "I'm afraid there's no magic formula. You're already serving here at the church. You're making a difference with a lot of people. That's a start."

J.T.'s words confused him. "I'm just teaching survival skills."

"Your classes are serving a purpose for the Kingdom. Keep teaching them."

"That's all?" It didn't seem enough.

"No. Serving is just the beginning. You might also want to spend time in prayer, read the Word, seek counsel from other Christians." J.T. leaned forward. "But, Wolf, nothing will help until you give this up to the Lord. Healing starts with surrender."

Surrender. Wolf balked at the concept. It went against everything he knew as a soldier. But maybe J.T. was right. Maybe he had to give this up to God, rather than agonize over details he couldn't control. The problem was, handling details was what he did best.

Look where that's gotten you.

Wolf shuddered at the thought.

"I want you to listen to me, Captain." J.T. captured Wolf's gaze with an unyielding glare. "We live in a fallen world. Life here on earth is messy."

"You think I don't know that?" he growled.

J.T. held his stare, refusing to back down. "Sometimes you can do all the right things and still get a bad outcome."

To his shame, Wolf felt the pinprick of tears behind his eyelids. He hated this feeling of helplessness. So he lashed out. "Speaking from experience, J.T.?"

The guy didn't even flinch. "Yeah, I am."

Wolf lowered his gaze, swallowed several times then forced a note of calm in his voice. "I'll take what you've said under advisement."

"Meaning you didn't hear a word I said."

"I heard you." Wolf rose.

J.T. followed suit. "You still want to go to lunch?"

No. But he was no coward. He met J.T.'s gaze and grinned. "As long as we can talk about football."

Scooting around his desk, J.T. gripped Wolf's shoulder. "I think that can be arranged. You a University of Georgia fan?"

Wolf thought about Hailey's over-the-top reaction at the silent auction. She'd been a little rabid—but kind of cute, too—when she'd lost out on her bid to spend a day with the school's mascot. "I'm becoming one."

"Good man."

They headed for the door, but Wolf stopped midway, remembering the initial reason for his visit. "Before we go, I need a list of Savannah's homeless shelters and food banks."

J.T. looked at him oddly. "Why?"

"I want to take Hailey on a date before she leaves for Haiti."

"To a homeless shelter?"

"You got a problem with that?"

For a moment, J.T. just stared at him. Then he released a quick laugh. "Not at all." He went back to his computer. Fingers on the keyboard, he asked, "You need phone numbers and addresses, too?"

"If you have them."

"Give me a sec." He moved his mouse around, left-clicked a few times, then typed something on the keyboard. The next thing Wolf heard was the sound of a printer firing up.

J.T grinned. "You're in business, soldier."

Finally, Wolf thought, something was going his way.

* * *

At precisely 0900 Wednesday morning, Hailey locked her front door. She turned and caught sight of Wolf coming up her walkway.

She studied him as he approached. He was dressed in what she was coming to recognize as his civilian uniform. Worn jeans that hung low on his lean hips, a black T-shirt that clung to his muscular chest and a leather jacket that topped off the masculine ensemble rather nicely. The guy was a walking magazine ad for an expensive men's cologne.

Her stomach quivered in reaction.

The Lord had brought Wolf into her life at the worst possible time, under the worst possible circumstances. And yet, she couldn't help but feel blessed he was here with her now.

Of course, she'd be foolish to forget he'd initially sought her out because her brother had asked him to find her. The reality, always in the back of her mind, left Hailey feeling a bit depressed.

Still, she headed down her front steps with a light heart. Drawing closer to him, she caught a whiff of spice and soap that was pure Wolf.

She smiled. "Good morning."

"Good morning." He dropped his gaze and grinned back. "I see you dressed comfortably." His smile broadened. "I always did like a woman who could follow orders."

She tried not to smile at his teasing manner. "Yeah, well, don't get used to it."

"Wouldn't dream of it." Still smiling, he pulled her arm through his and steered her toward the heart of downtown.

The sensation of being this near to him, walking arm in arm like a real couple, was incredibly appealing. Hailey found herself snuggling closer. Wolf's grip tightened, just a little, enough to communicate he was enjoying this, as well.

When they passed by his car, Hailey realized she had no idea where they were going. "We aren't taking Stella?"

"Nope. We're walking."

Determined to go with the flow and be flexible, Hailey held silent for two entire city blocks. But curiosity got the best of her midway down the third street. "Where are you taking me?"

He laughed. "I knew you wouldn't last the whole way without asking."

Was she that predictable? Or did he just know her that well? "So…?"

"We're going to the Savannah People's Mission, your town's version of a soup kitchen." He slanted a challenging look at her. "You've heard of it, right?"

"Sure I have."

Which was mostly true. Months ago, J.T. had given her a list of all the homeless shelters, soup kitchens and food banks in town. She'd read about the organizations then shoved the paper in the back of her Bible. Not because she was heartless, she told herself quickly, but because she wasn't involved with any of the ministries that would put her in a position to need their names and locations.

But now Wolf was taking her to a soup kitchen, within walking distance of her home. And, despite all her charity work in town, she'd never technically heard of it.

What did that say about her?

They rounded the corner of one of her favorite squares.

A tiny grove of camellia bushes ran along the main sidewalk. Such pretty, bold flowers, daring to bloom when others lay dormant. The winter chill couldn't keep them down.

So engrossed with their courageous beauty, it took a moment for Hailey to realize Wolf had stopped walking. She turned her head and gaped at all the people.

An impossibly long line snaked around a rectangular, nondescript building that stood adjacent to one of the historic churches open for daily tours. However, these people were not tourists. Some were dressed nicer than others, but they all had a look of defeat about them.

How had she driven by this building countless times in her life, but had never known it was a soup kitchen? "This is the Savannah People's Mission?"

Wolf hooked his thumbs through his belt loops. "You've never been here before?"

"No." And yet the mission was only a handful of blocks from her home.

Why hadn't she known it was so close? Why hadn't she *cared* enough to know?

She drew in a shaky breath.

"Let's go inside," Wolf suggested. "There's a lot to do before they open the doors for lunch."

A sudden wave of fear danced a chill up Hailey's spine and she remained frozen in place, unable to move. What if she couldn't help these people? What if they didn't accept her help?

"Come on." Wolf tugged her toward a side door. "We go in this way."

"You've been here before?"

"I came yesterday during my lunch hour."

"You did? Why?"

He lifted a shoulder. "I wanted to check it out before I brought you here."

He'd put a lot of forethought into this outing.

Gaze still locked with hers, Wolf drew her through the doorway.

The moment they stepped inside the building, a large black woman gave a whoop and yanked Wolf into a bear hug. "Two days in a row." She pulled back and beamed at him. "What a blessing you are, my boy."

Wolf shrugged. "I can't seem to stay away." He slapped his palm onto his chest. "You've captured my heart, Cora Belle."

Giggling like a young girl, the large woman waved her spoon at him then caught sight of Hailey. "And who's this pretty thing?"

"I brought you another helper. Hailey O'Brien, meet Cora Belle, the best cook in Savannah."

Laughing at Wolf's outrageous compliment, the big lady smiled at Hailey. "Any friend of this boy's is welcome in my kitchen. Besides—" she jabbed Wolf with her elbow "—I'd never send away a helping hand."

Hailey instantly liked Cora Belle, but she wasn't sure how to proceed. "I'm here to work," she offered, hoping she sounded more confident than she felt. "Just tell me what to do."

"I got plenty of hands in here." Cora Belle turned back to her stove. "Why don't you help Captain Ty and my husband set up tables in the dining room?"

That sounded like something she could do. Hailey might not be able to cook, but she could set a table with her eyes closed.

An hour later the dining hall was full of chattering people, hovering over full plates of food. Hailey had been assigned to the relatively simple task of serving the potatoes, but she still felt uncomfortable, much as Wolf had looked at the country club.

She didn't make eye contact with the people she served. She simply heaped a spoonful of potatoes on the empty plates thrust in front of her.

That made her a coward, she knew. But as much as she disliked this new insight into her character, Hailey couldn't muster the courage to lift her head.

How could she serve the Lord, when she couldn't even look His people in the eye?

Please, dear God, give me the courage....

Gulping down her trepidation, she lifted her head and connected her gaze with a woman who looked to be her same age. Something about her felt familiar, yet Hailey was sure she didn't know her.

Perhaps it was the loneliness masked behind the woman's shaky smile. Over the last six months, Hailey had experienced that emotion far too often. Maybe that was the way to go. Strike common ground, connect on a personal level.

Hailey returned the smile.

The young woman looked quickly away and moved on.

So much for making eye contact, Hailey thought.

Feeling completely out of her element, she caught sight of Wolf weaving his way from table to table.

Unlike her, he looked comfortable. He spoke to every person he came across, treating each one like a long-lost friend. He wasn't afraid to touch them, either. He clutched a few men on the shoulder, then placed a gentle hand under an elderly woman's elbow as he steered her to a seat at a table. For a man who'd experienced such an unsafe, lonely childhood, Wolf made family wherever he went. Not friends, *family*.

Hailey wondered if he realized that about himself.

Watching him work the room, she felt embarrassed by all the lofty speeches she'd given him about what it meant to serve people in need. Just like she'd always feared, she *was* a fraud.

Wolf, on the other hand, was authentic. And so at ease with everyone he met. They gravitated toward him. He was probably just as good with his soldiers as he was with the people here today. Well, of course he was. Clay had said as much in his e-mails.

Hailey hadn't realized she'd been standing there, staring at him, until a kind-faced, middle-aged woman slid in beside her. "I'll take over if you need a break. You've been serving for a full hour."

"I have?"

The woman gently pulled the spoon out of Hailey's hand. "Go on, get yourself a plate and join the others."

"Oh, I couldn't possibly take food."

"Volunteers are encouraged to eat with our guests." She bumped hips with Hailey. "Go on. Make some friends."

"Sure. I can do that." Hailey drew her lip between her teeth and moved to the back of the line.

Once she had a full plate of food, she chose a seat at a table where the young woman she'd made eye contact with earlier sat.

"Hi."

No response.

Hailey tried not to sigh. "I'm Hailey."

Still no response.

"Mind if I sit with you?"

The woman raked her with blunt appraisal. "It's a free country."

Find that common ground, Hailey told herself. *Don't give up.* "Like I said, I'm Hailey." She spoke softly. "What's your name?"

"Sara."

"Really?" Hailey filled her fork with potatoes and quickly took the bite. "My mother almost named me that."

"Why didn't she?"

"You know what?" Hailey let out a short little laugh. "I don't know."

Sara gave her a small smile, one that still had suspicion clinging to the edges.

"Do you have any kids?" Sara asked.

Unsure where this was going, Hailey shook her head. "No. I'm not married."

Sara tossed her fork down and snorted. "Like that matters."

Caught off guard by the woman's response, Hailey lowered her own fork. Less than five minutes into the conversation and she'd already managed to offend Sara.

Nevertheless, Hailey would not turn tail and run. Yet. "Do you have any children?" she asked.

An echo of a smile crossed her lips. "I have an eight-year-old daughter."

So old? Hailey did a quick calculation in her head. Unless she looked younger than she was, Sara had to have had the child when she was still a teenager.

"My daughter's in foster care right now," Sara explained. "It's been a tough year."

The shame in her eyes made it clear she did not like accepting charity.

"You don't have any family?" Hailey asked.

Sara lowered her head. "My parents disowned me when they found out I was pregnant."

Such a harsh response. If only Hailey knew what to do to help her. She didn't think money was the answer. Sara needed a long-term solution.

Hailey remembered a story in Scripture where the disciples didn't give alms to a blind man but gave him his sight instead.

What would be the equivalent here? A job, maybe?

She had all kinds of contacts in the business community. Surely one of them would hire Sara.

Unable to make any guarantees, *yet,* Hailey stayed focused on their conversation. "What's your daughter's name?"

"Sara." She gave a self-deprecating shrug. "I never did have much imagination."

Hailey reached to her, touching her sleeve with a tentative hand. "Why not name your daughter after yourself? Men do it all the time. My brother was named after my father."

"Was?"

"He died in Iraq," Hailey said. "Six months ago."

Sara's shoulders slumped forward. "I lost my boyfriend, Tyler, back in the early months of the war. He was called up before we could get married. We were waiting until he came home." Her voice filled with regret. "But he never came home."

How awful. "How'd your boyfriend die?"

Sara's lips trembled. "His Humvee hit an IED."

A gasp flew out of Hailey before she could stop it. "I'm so sorry."

I want to live with them, cry with them, find joy and

hope with them. Had Hailey really said those words to Wolf only a few nights ago? She'd been referring to people of other cultures, like the ones she would meet in Haiti next week. But here, right in front of her, God had given her someone who needed her help now. Not next week. *Now.*

"My brother died from an IED, too," she said.

A look of unity passed between her and Sara. Tragedy had struck them both, but Hailey had had money and security to soften the blow of her loss.

Sara had not been so fortunate. She'd been disowned by her family, unmarried and completely on her own. Without the official help of the military she'd been left destitute.

Hailey would help her. She just had to figure out how.

Chapter Fifteen

Wolf watched Hailey scribble on a piece of paper then hand it to the woman she'd been speaking with since sitting down. With their heads bent close together, they looked as if they were in the middle of a serious conversation.

Once again, Hailey had surprised him. She'd clearly been uncomfortable when they'd first arrived, but that hadn't stopped her from helping where she was needed. She'd moved tables, stacked plates, served food and now was in the process of doing what she did best. Impacting another person's life for the better.

"You look at that gal the way my husband used to look at me when we were first married," Cora Belle said with a dreamy glint in her eyes.

Completely unconcerned he'd been busted for staring at Hailey, Wolf laughed. "He doesn't look at you like that anymore?"

"It's different now." But as soon as she made her claim, Cora Belle waggled her fingers at her husband. He paused in the middle of wiping a table and tossed her a wink.

"It doesn't look so different to me. In fact," Wolf said, grinning, "that light is burning so strong I might have to put my sunglasses back on."

She slapped him lightly on the arm. "Oh, you."

Wolf relaxed against the wall behind him. "How long have you two been married, Cora Belle?"

"Fifty-three years come next March."

Talk about staying power. Wolf was impressed. "What's your secret?"

Before answering, the older woman smiled after her husband as he walked back into the kitchen, arms full of dirty plates. "Having the Lord in our lives is the key." She pursed her lips. "But it also helps to like the person you're married to. Makes everything else go easier."

Wolf looked over at Hailey again. She was still deep in her conversation. As he watched her, a solid sense of peace spread through him. The emotion settled over him like a whisper.

Yeah, he liked Hailey. No question about it. But his feelings were far more complicated than simple "like." And more significant. If she walked away from him now, if she were hurt or killed, Wolf wasn't sure he'd ever get over losing her.

His fingers curled together, every muscle in his body growing tense as the truth washed over him.

He didn't just like Hailey. He loved her.

She was strong and sweet and the best person he'd ever met. She'd brought him back to life, and then made him desire an existence beyond himself, beyond just going through the motions of the day.

But was he meant to be with her? Could he provide for her and give her the family she deserved? There were a lot of obstacles standing between them—their different pasts, their conflicting goals for the future and the largest obstacle of all, Clay.

There was suddenly too much to think about, too many questions without answers.

Wolf crossed his arms over his chest and cleared his mind.

Eyeing him like a dog on point, Cora Belle wiped her hands on her food-stained apron, slowly, methodically. Then her gaze narrowed even more. "You gonna marry that girl?"

"That was direct."

"Then give me an equally direct answer."

Wolf shut his eyes a moment. The question should have shocked him, should have sent warning bells clanging in his head. Instead, he felt nothing but confusion, mixed with equal parts hope and fear. "I…don't know."

Cora Belle shook her head at him, disappointment pulling her lips into a frown. "Don't take too long to figure it out." She nodded toward Hailey. "That one isn't going to sit on the shelf for long."

Wolf's breath clogged in his throat. Cora Belle spoke the truth. Hailey wouldn't stay single for long. She was meant to have a family, with a husband who treasured her and put her first in his life.

Wolf wanted to be that man. He wanted to be Hailey's family. But could he give her what she deserved? Did he have what it took to make her happy?

Did he even have the right to try?

Wolf was silent on the walk back to Hailey's house. She hadn't noticed at first, probably because she'd been too busy thinking about Sara.

Hailey was in a unique position to help her new friend. Before today, she'd looked at her charity work—especially sitting on all those boards—as a hindrance to her service for the Lord. But she now realized all those years of making contacts in the business community were invaluable.

Hailey had the tools to help Sara. She also had her

own personal experience to better help her understand the woman's loss.

All this time she'd been setting her sights on ministry halfway across the world, which she still firmly believed was her calling, but maybe the Lord was showing her another way to serve in the meantime. *Maybe* it wasn't a matter of all or nothing, but a matter of serving in more than one capacity.

"I understand why you took me to the Mission," she said to Wolf as she unlocked her front door.

He followed her inside, a frown digging a groove across his forehead. "Why's that?"

"You wanted to show me there are people in need right here in my own city, people I'm uniquely qualified to help."

He frowned. "I wasn't trying to manipulate you."

"Sure you were," she said without an ounce of resentment. "But I don't hold it against you. I can be stubborn. The only way to tell me about the need was to *show* me."

"So you aren't upset with me?"

"No." She waited for him to close the front door then slipped her hands up his arms, clasped them behind his neck. "In fact, I want to thank you." She lifted on her toes. "Thank you, Wolf."

Before she connected her lips to his, he lowered his head and did the deed himself.

She sighed against him.

After a few moments, he lifted his head and stared intently in her eyes. "Does this mean you won't be going to the Middle East?"

"No." She blew out a frustrated breath and stepped out of his embrace. "It means I'm willing to serve in Savannah *and* the Middle East. I can do both."

He didn't argue with her, but simply stared at her. And stared. And stared. "Fair enough."

His words sounded so…final. Like he was saying goodbye to her. "You aren't going to fight me on this?"

"Hailey, when I first arrived on your doorstep, I expected to meet a teenager, a girl with one foot in adulthood and the other still in childhood. I expected my task to be easy. A quick conversation and my duty to Clay would be complete."

His duty to Clay. The only reason he'd sought her out. She'd thought they'd come so far from that day, that they'd managed to build a relationship that was solely theirs. But now she wasn't so sure. More frightening still, if Wolf failed to convince her to stay home, if he stopped fighting her about the Middle East, would he walk away for good?

"I was wrong about you on so many levels," he continued. "You're a beautiful, independent woman, capable of taking care of yourself."

Was he letting her go? "Thanks."

He pressed his fingertips to the bridge of his nose. "I'm not trying to insult you." He dropped his hand and looked directly at her. "I'm trying to tell you I think you're wonderful, beautiful, talented and gifted."

If he thought all those things about her, then why did he sound so grim?

"But when it's all said and done," he continued, "I—"

"Still see me as Clay's little sister." The realization ripped at her heart.

"I don't know, Hailey. I don't know where my feelings of guilt and duty end and where my love for you begins. All I know is that I *will* protect you, even if that means going to the Middle East with you."

"Did you just say you love me?" she whispered.

"Yes, I love you." He practically growled the words.

She'd never expected to hear such a sad, pitiful declaration. Not from Wolf.

Didn't he know he was breaking her heart?

She had to ask him the hard question, the one they'd been dancing around for weeks. "But do you love me because I'm me or because I'm Clay's little sister?"

He didn't answer her. Pushing past her, he walked into the kitchen and pulled the picture of her and Clay off the refrigerator.

"He didn't deserve to die," he said in such a low voice she barely caught his words.

"No, he didn't." She stared at the picture, her stomach wrenching over their mutual loss. "But he did die, and now we have to go on. Life is all about loss, Wolf. We either let it cripple us or let it make us stronger."

He didn't respond, but just kept staring at the picture. "Would he approve of us being together?"

Hailey knew the answer, knew it as sure as she knew her own name. "Haven't you ever wondered why he told me so much about you?"

He continued staring at the photograph. "Because we worked closely together. I was always on his mind."

"It was more than that." She touched his arm, certainty filling her. "Clay wanted us to be together."

"No." Wolf shook his head vigorously. "He didn't want any man to have you, especially not a man like me, who knows nothing about family."

"Of course you know. I watched you at the soup kitchen today. You made those people feel comfortable and at home, like they belonged to a large, happy family. I also saw how Cora Belle treated you like her own son, and she's only known you for two days."

He was silent for a long moment, his gaze still glued to the picture in his hand. "You're embellishing the facts."

"I'm speaking the truth. I've seen you in action. You understand family better than most men I know."

"Even if what you say is accurate—" he turned the picture around his palm "—you know where I come from, what my childhood was like. Clay wouldn't have wanted you with someone like me."

"That's just absurd. Clay was never a judgmental jerk." She raised her voice to make her point. "How dare you suggest otherwise."

He snapped his gaze in her direction and the picture dropped to the floor.

Finally, Hailey had his complete attention. "Now you listen to me, Captain Wolfson. Your childhood never mattered to my brother. And it doesn't matter to me."

He blinked at her, his shock evident in his eyes.

Softening her expression, Hailey cupped his face tenderly. "Oh, Wolf, don't you understand? I'm only concerned with your future, and whether or not you have room for me in it."

Sighing heavily, he relaxed into her palm, then reared back.

She let her hand drop to her side, saddened by the internal struggle she saw on his face.

"Hailey, don't look at me like that. I can't think with you touching me. And I *need* to think. It would be too easy to ignore my doubts, to go with my feelings rather than the facts, but that wouldn't be fair to you."

Maybe he was right, but she was afraid to let him walk out of her home with their conversation unresolved, especially knowing that next week she'd be leaving for Haiti.

Trust the Lord. He's already got this worked out. The

thought came to her with such clarity she felt a huge sense of relief flow through her. If she and Wolf were meant to be together, God would make that happen.

She also had to trust that Wolf truly loved her, for her, not out of misguided guilt or loyalty to a fallen friend. That he would ultimately see her as his family and his future.

In the meantime, it couldn't hurt to give him a little nudge in the right direction.

"Wait right here. I have something for you." She turned to go then swung back around. "Don't leave."

"I won't."

She ran to her room, dug the box of Clay's e-mails out from under her bed and then rushed back into the kitchen.

"These are the e-mails Clay sent me from Iraq." She held out the box to Wolf. "I printed them out."

He raised his hands in the air, palms facing forward. "They're private, between you and your brother."

"Please, Wolf, I want you to read them, especially the ones concerning you."

His hands dropped to his sides and a look of confusion blanketed his face. "Why?"

"You'll understand once you do." She pressed her lips to his cheek. "Take your time reading them. I leave for Haiti next week. I think it's best we don't see each other until I get back. We can talk more then."

He didn't argue, which made her think about despairing, but she didn't give in to the emotion. She was going to trust God all the way.

Putting on a brave face, she walked Wolf to the door. "I love you."

Without another word, she kissed him on the lips, gave him a shaky smile then shut the door in his face.

Chapter Sixteen

Ten days, seven hours and twelve minutes after Hailey kicked Wolf out of her home, he paced through his town house.

His steps were jerky and out of sync, not so much because his leg ached but because his heart ached. He shouldn't have honored Hailey's demand to stay away from her until after she returned from Haiti. He shouldn't have let her leave the country with so much unsettled between them.

What if she got hurt while she was away? What if she were kidnapped? The muscles around his heart clenched in helpless agony.

What if she didn't come back at all?

Gritting his teeth, Wolf prowled into the living room and turned on the television. A twenty-four-hour weather report popped onto the screen. For the last six days, Wolf had alternated between this station and various news channels. If anything disastrous happened in Haiti, he would know as soon as it occurred.

Unfortunately, having immediate access to vast

amounts of information only made him feel more uneasy, not less.

This was what came from caring. This dark sense of foreboding. This inability to calm down as he waited anxiously for news from the troubled region.

Though military husbands and wives had to cope with this every day, it took a great amount of courage and love. And wasn't that the bottom line? Wolf loved Hailey enough to suffer through these moments of fear and helplessness.

So what was holding him back from committing his future to hers? His promise to Clay? His brutal childhood? Maybe a combination of both?

He thought back over his last conversation with Hailey. She'd claimed she didn't care where Wolf came from, and had scolded him for suggesting that Clay might have held his past against him.

Wolf smiled at the memory of her fierce reaction. Hailey was quite the little warrior in her own right.

And now, when it might be too late, Wolf realized he wanted to spend the rest of his life with Hailey O'Brien. He wanted to build a family with her, to serve beside her, to grow old with her.

But did he deserve her? Could he make her happy?

Perhaps the answer was in Clay's e-mails, as Hailey had claimed. Wolf glanced over at the box she had given him. It sat on the coffee table, in the same spot he'd left it ten days ago.

The time had come to read Clay's words to his sister.

With a mixture of impatience and dread, Wolf sat on his couch and placed the box on his lap.

Keeping his emotions in check, he took a deep breath and pulled off the lid. Retrieving the large stack of papers, he tossed the box aside and read the first e-mail. Then he read the next one. And the next.

By the fourth, grief clogged in his throat.

Clay was all over these e-mails. His sense of humor and love of life jumped off the pages. The pain that came from remembering his friend was almost too much for Wolf, like someone had slammed a dagger in his gut and twisted.

Releasing a hiss, he leaned his head back against the sofa. A shudder slipped down his spine. Though he didn't want to continue, he had to keep reading. For Hailey. And maybe for his own sake, as well.

He grabbed another page, skimmed the e-mail until he came to Clay's suggestion for Hailey to think bigger than her current charity work.

"There are people all over the world who need the love of Christ," Wolf read aloud. "You could be the one to carry that hope beyond Savannah, Hailey. With your faith in God and your gift with people, you could make a difference in the Middle East. More than I can as a soldier."

Breathing hard, Wolf crushed the paper in his hand. Hailey hadn't misunderstood her brother after all. Clay had encouraged her to go into ministry. In the Middle East.

No wonder she'd been so filled with conviction.

Wolf squeezed his eyes shut and forced his mind back to that fateful day on the Iraqi roadside.

He would never forget his friend's last words. "No… mission work," Clay had said. "Not here. Not by herself."

Not by herself. Clay's change of heart had been about Hailey's safety. He'd wanted to guarantee his sister didn't put herself into unnecessary danger.

Wolf would never let that happen.

If the Lord called Hailey to the Middle East, he wouldn't stop her. He would go with her.

But would Clay approve?

At this point, there was only one way to find out.

Wolf swallowed and read the next e-mail. There was a lot of nothing in this one, mainly gripes about the dry desert heat and having to fill out situation reports that were long overdue.

Wolf chuckled. Clay had always been behind on his paperwork.

Still smiling, Wolf returned his attention to his friend's words. He read his name and everything in him froze.

Wolf is the brother I never had and the best man I know. When you meet him, you'll think so, too.

Wolf flipped through the stack until he found another one about him. *Wolf saved a child today. He jumped in front of a fast-moving car and whipped the kid into his arms. He never hesitated. He'll make a great father. When you meet him, I know you'll agree.*

Wolf read three more e-mails. And then another five. In all the ones where Clay mentioned his name four words showed up, as well.

When you meet him...

Clay had been matchmaking. Almost as if he'd known he wouldn't get the opportunity to introduce them to each other himself. Had he sensed his imminent death?

Wolf's breath hitched in his throat. No matter how many of Clay's e-mails he read, guilt still held its nasty grip on him. Would regret always rule him?

Somehow Wolf had to find a way to surrender this to the Lord. He went in search of his Bible. Something he should have done months ago, but had been too angry at God to bother.

After nearly an hour of searching, he found the weathered book at the bottom of a box he'd yet to unpack.

Hands shaking, he sat back down on the sofa and flipped through the pages at random. He read aloud the first Scripture that caught his eye, one in the book of Acts. "Everyone who believes in Him receives forgiveness of sins through His name."

Wolf looked up to heaven. "Is it really that easy, Lord? Do I simply believe and this terrible feeling goes away?"

If that were true, healing would have already come. He turned a few pages to his left. Still in Acts, he read, "Repent then, and turn to God, so that your sins may be wiped out."

Believe. Repent. There had to be more to it than that.

Wolf flipped the pages in the opposite direction, stopping in First John this time. "This is love; not that we loved God, but that He loved us and sent His Son as an atoning sacrifice for our sins."

Finally, Wolf knew what he had to do to move past his guilt. He had to believe. Repent. And then receive the gift that had already been given to him.

He lowered himself to his knees and buried his face in his hands.

"Lord, thank You for covering my sins with Your sacrifice. Help me to receive Your forgiveness so I can forgive myself."

Lowering his hands, Wolf took a deep breath. A sense of peace spread through him.

Although he knew God still had a lot of work to do in him, Wolf rose to his feet. Smiling.

Hailey headed toward baggage claim, exhausted, filthy and emotionally wrung out. She'd rushed off the plane ahead of her fellow team members, determined to get to Wolf's town house as quickly as possible.

Despite this sense of urgency, there was joy in her heart, too.

She had gone to Port-Au-Prince determined to make at least one personal connection. She'd made several.

Her time in the Haiti slum had changed her. The people at the Savannah People's Mission had changed her.

Wolf had changed her.

She had so much to tell him about her trip, about the children she'd met. And the old man who'd accepted Christ right before he'd succumbed to cancer. But first…

Hailey just wanted to see Wolf, tell him she loved him and have him hold her in his strong arms for a while.

She wanted to be with him, always. No more obstacles. No more uneasiness between them. Just together. They'd work out the rest of the details as they went along.

Eager to get to him, Hailey picked up the pace but stopped in her tracks when she saw his familiar form several yards on the other side of security.

Wolf had come to the airport to meet her.

Relief, joy, pleasure, all three rushed through her, making her heart stutter in her chest.

Since Wolf hadn't noticed her yet, she drank in the sight of him. He wore black pants, a plain white T-shirt and his trademark leather jacket. He looked good. Really good.

He was standing next to J.T., completely caught up in their conversation. They were both broad-shouldered, lean, handsome men. Hard men with soft hearts—not that either one of them would admit to that last part.

Wolf looked up at last. The moment he caught sight

of her, a smile spread across his lips. It was his wolf smile.

Hailey's blood thickened in her veins. Wolf was her man. Her future. Her bold warrior. Hers. Hers. Hers!

So what was she doing standing here staring at him? He gave her a look that asked the same question.

She dropped her carry-on and set out at a dead run. On something between a sob and a laugh, she launched herself into his arms.

He caught her hard against his chest, then buried his face in her hair. "Welcome home, sweetheart."

"Oh, Wolf, I missed you."

"Yeah. Me, too."

They clung to each other, ignoring everyone around them, pretending it didn't matter that the last time they'd seen each other Hailey had kicked him out of her house.

She pulled back, went in for a kiss but froze when J.T. cleared his throat.

Far less embarrassed than she should be, Hailey stepped away from Wolf. But she kept her hand on his arm, half-afraid he might disappear if she gave him the chance. "Hi, J.T. I… I didn't mean to ignore you."

"Sure you did." His eyes gleamed with amusement. "But no offense taken. You had other…" He gave her a knowing grin. "Priorities on your mind."

She let out a little laugh, glancing at Wolf sideways. Their eyes locked and they shared a brief moment of homecoming.

Wolf moved behind her, wrapped his arms around her waist then rested his chin on her head.

Still grinning, J.T. lifted his eyebrows. "Okay. I see you two have a lot of catching up to do. And I have the rest of my team to welcome home."

Wolf pulled Hailey tighter against him. "You're not intruding, J.T." His voice said differently.

"You're not," Hailey agreed halfheartedly. "We just haven't seen each other in a while and we… Oh, my carry-on. I left it…" She shot out of Wolf's arms and looked helplessly around her. "Somewhere."

J.T. chuckled. "It's over there, on this side of security. I'll bring it down to baggage claim for you." He turned in the direction Hailey had just come. "I'll meet you two downstairs in a few minutes."

"Thanks, J.T.," she called after him.

He tossed a wave over his head. "My pleasure."

An uncomfortable silence fell in his wake.

Now that Hailey was alone with Wolf, and the initial pleasure of seeing him had worn off, she felt a flood of uncharacteristic shyness wash over her. Sighing, she twisted her hands together.

When five long seconds passed and Wolf didn't speak, either, she lifted her gaze to his. Relieved at what she saw in his eyes, she relaxed. Wolf loved her. He wanted to be with her.

Everything was going to work out just fine.

Tugging her gently toward him, Wolf lowered his forehead to hers. She clutched at his arms.

"Let's get the rest of your luggage. And then we'll head home." He stepped back and caressed her cheek. "I have a lot to tell to you."

"Oh, Wolf. Me, too." She tipped her face up to his. "I lo—"

"Not here." He pressed his finger tenderly to her lips. "Let's wait until it's just the two of us."

Just the two of us. She liked the sound of that.

A lot.

Chapter Seventeen

Hailey entered her living room with anxious excitement nearly busting out of her. She was home. Wolf was here with her. The rest would work itself out in time.

She moved through the room, turning on lights while Wolf set her bags at the bottom of the stairs.

Once he joined her again, she went to him and wrapped her arms around his waist.

Feeling at peace, she smiled up at him. He was her big, handsome warrior. His blue, blue eyes were filled with genuine tenderness, the kind of look every woman dreamed she'd see in the eyes of the man she loved. "I'm glad you came to the airport to pick me up. I—"

"You're different."

"I am?"

He hesitated, just a little, then ran his hand down her hair, hooking a tendril around his finger. "I mean that in a good way."

There was affection in his eyes, and a deeper emotion. *Love.* He was through fighting the inevitable, through fighting the notion of them being together.

Hailey's stomach fluttered in anticipation of the future that lay ahead of them. But first, they had to deal with the obstacles that still stood in their way. "You look different, too." She angled her head. "More at peace."

"I am. I..." He stepped away from her, giving her the opportunity to read his expression as he spoke. "I'm not drowning in guilt anymore."

She could see the truth of his words, in the way his gaze held hers without faltering, in the way his shoulders remained straight and unflinching.

"Oh, Wolf, you've forgiven yourself." Tears of joy welled in her eyes.

"I don't know if I'd go that far." He ran a hand through his hair. "But I've given it up to God."

She wiped at her cheeks and sighed. "That's the first step."

"I'll always regret what happened to my men." The slight catch in his voice revealed his continued grief. "But I'm done questioning things I can't change. I can't keep looking backward." He shut his eyes a moment, then shook his head and reopened them. "I have to start looking forward."

He was so courageous, so strong. Was there any wonder she was in love with him?

With another sigh she moved forward, and placed her palm on his chest, near his heart.

He covered her hand with his, but didn't speak again. He didn't have to. His eyes said everything. He was right here with her. In the moment. Present and awake. Ready for whatever came next. "Looking forward," she whispered. "I like the sound of that."

He smiled at last. "Tell me about your trip."

She'd give him the details later. For now she wanted

to focus on the lesson she'd learned. "I discovered something very important while I was gone."

He lifted an eyebrow.

"I learned that there are hurting people everywhere, people who need compassion and grace, understanding and mercy. The things I can give them as a servant of Christ."

His hand dropped away from hers. "What are you saying, Hailey?"

"I'm saying…" She let her own hand flutter to her side. "That I don't have to go to the Middle East to do the Lord's work."

"Does that mean you're not going to pursue a posting overseas?" His voice remained neutral, as did his gaze. The only clue to his thoughts came in the slight tightening of his jaw.

Grateful for his subdued reaction, she answered him frankly. "No. It means I'm not going to serve the Lord with blinders on anymore. I'm going to go where He sends me, whether that turns out to be here in Savannah, or a Caribbean island, or the Middle East."

Wolf frowned faintly, shaking his head. "Is this change of heart because of me?"

"Not *because* of you, no. But you did play a role in my decision. You helped me see past my grief over Clay's death to the truth. I don't have to go to the Middle East to honor my brother's life." She walked over to the sofa, then perched a hip on the arm. "I can do that anywhere."

Nodding, he shifted to face her head-on. "I want you to know that *if* you're called to the Middle East," he said, "you won't go alone."

She instantly understood his meaning and loved him

all the more for it. "And who, might I ask, would go with me?"

"Someone who knows the region and the culture." He stepped closer, staring at her with a serious expression on his face. "Someone who understands the enemy, as well as the locals."

"Someone like…oh, say, a United States Army captain?"

He smiled at last. "That would be the ideal choice."

What a generous, selfless man he was. Hailey had found something richer and stronger with Wolf than she'd ever dreamed possible. "But that would mean quitting the Army." She grimaced as the realization sank in. "I would never ask you to sacrifice your future for me."

"*You're* my future, Hailey." He moved closer still, close enough to reach down and cup her cheek. "God has a plan for both of us, together. We'll make our own family, always looking ahead of us and not behind. That might involve me quitting the Army, or it might not."

She closed her eyes a moment and leaned into his hand. "You're sure this is what you want, Wolf? Are you sure you want me? Us? No more worries over whether or not Clay would approve?"

"I read his e-mails." Wolf dropped his hand. "He wanted us together."

She smiled and nodded.

"He also wanted you to go to the Middle East. As long as I keep you as safe as humanly possible, I will have fulfilled my duty."

"No more guilt over his death?"

"I'll always wish things had turned out differently, but I'm learning to accept that there are some things I can't control. Accidents happen."

Hailey had never been more proud of him than in that moment. He'd come so far. "Oh, Wolf, I love you."

"I love you, too, Hailey."

She rose, lifted onto her tiptoes, and then pressed her lips to his in a fleeting kiss that left her mouth tingling when she pulled away.

"I still have a few years of active duty left." He placed his hands on her waist, but then let them drop just as quickly. "I will be deployed again in that time. After all you've been through, all your losses, waiting for me is a lot to ask of you."

She gave him a soft smile. "If there's anything I've learned in the past few years, it's to take whatever joy I can today because there might not be a tomorrow."

He kissed one of her hands and then the other. "You're amazing."

"I want to be with you, Wolf, however long that turns out to be."

"I may never leave the military," he warned.

She wouldn't ask it of him, ever. That was between him and the Heavenly Father. "We'll take each day as it comes."

"I'm thinking about going back to school part-time. I want to take a few seminary classes, see if that's where God is leading me."

"I'll support you, no matter what."

"Even if I become an Army chaplain? Despite what you might think, Hailey, it's a dangerous job, especially in wartime."

"Maybe I haven't made myself clear. I want to be with you, whatever that means, wherever it takes us. You are my family now, and I'm yours. We'll face the future together, as a unit."

"Even knowing our future is uncertain?" he asked, stepping back so he could stare into her eyes.

"No one's future is certain. Whether you're a soldier or a minister, whether I'm called to stay in Savannah or travel to the Middle East, I want us to serve the Lord together."

"So we go where God leads us?" he asked. "No personal agendas, no firm plans, just open minds and open hearts?"

"That sums it up nicely."

He lowered to one knee, and then smiled up at her. "Hailey O'Brien—" he took her hand and kissed her knuckles "—will you marry me?"

"Yes."

Laughing, he drew her into his arms and then lowered his mouth to hers. The kiss was slow, sweet and full of silent promises for their life together.

She couldn't have asked for a better homecoming.

Epilogue

One week later, Hailey's twenty-seventh birthday dawned windy and bone-chilling cold. The frigid air made Wolf's leg ache more than usual, but he was learning to accept the bad with the good. His leg fell under the bad column, but only when the air turned cold and wet.

Under the good column, Wolf had signed up for seminary classes yesterday and, today, he was going to make his engagement to Hailey official.

He'd been awake since 0400, but had decided to be a gentleman and wait until after sunrise to make the drive to Hailey's house.

A rush of joy surged through him as he drew Stella to a stop in the front of her home. All the lights were on.

Hailey was up...waiting for him.

Life was good.

The crate beside him shook, followed by a sad, pathetic whimper.

"Yeah, yeah. All right. You can come out now." Wolf opened the door to a face full of dog drool and crooked teeth.

Grinning down at Hailey's birthday gift, Wolf scratched the puppy's massive head.

"I must be in love," he muttered. "Why else would I buy an ugly mutt like you?"

The dog's sorry excuse for a tail started wagging.

"Hold still," Wolf said to the squirming bundle of bad breath and under-bite. "You're making it impossible to put this ribbon around your neck."

After more struggle, and a little unnecessary rough-housing, Wolf tied the bow. It hung at a cockeyed angle.

"You look ridiculous."

The miniature bulldog shook his head, sending the bow farther off-center.

"Hailey's going to love you."

In answer, the fat tongue went for his chin. Wolf dodged to his left and exited the car, puppy tucked under one arm.

He teetered up to Hailey's front door. "I think you've put on weight since we left the house."

The dog rolled his enormous eyes.

With his hands full, Wolf literally leaned on the doorbell. "Remember to smile."

Hailey swung open the door. "You're early." Her gaze dropped to the squirming puppy in his hands and she gasped. "Oh! Oh, Wolf! You didn't."

He smiled at her, a big loopy grin that probably matched the one on the ugly mutt's face. "Happy Birthday, sweetheart."

"I love him." She lifted misty eyes back to his face. "I love *you*."

"Now that's what I like to hear."

"Get in here." She tugged him forward.

Inside the living room, Wolf set the puppy on the carpet then straightened.

Hailey yanked him against her and kissed him hard on his lips. "Thank you, thank you, thank you."

"You're welcome."

After another kiss, longer and deeper than the first, Hailey dropped to her knees in front of the puppy. "What are we going to name him?" She raised her gaze up to Wolf. "It is a boy, right?"

"It's a boy." Wolf laughed. "To be honest, I'm partial to... Tank."

"Tank." She studied the dog with his broad shoulders, huge head and bowed legs. "I like it." She kissed the puppy on the head. "I dub thee Tank. The newest member of our family."

She and the dog wrestled on the floor for a while.

Wolf simply watched them. He was so happy to see Hailey falling in love with her new puppy he'd completely forgotten the other present he had for her. "Check Tank's bow."

Hailey cocked her head at him.

"Go on," he urged. "There's one more gift attached to the ribbon around his neck."

"Oh. *Oh!*" Reaching out, she began carefully untying the bow. She made it halfway through before her fingers froze.

Tears filled her eyes. "Oh, Wolf." She blinked at the engagement ring. "It's beautiful."

"Take it off the ribbon. Let's see if it fits." A wave of doubt filled him and his stomach rolled. "Unless you're having second thoughts about marrying me."

She twisted her lips at him, clearly insulted by the mere suggestion. "No second thoughts. None whatsoever."

Her quick, heartfelt response loosened the knots in his gut.

She pulled the bow free and held up the ring he'd picked out. The simple square-cut diamond caught the light.

"It's gorgeous," she said.

The knots returned. He hadn't wanted to go too big, just shy of a carat, but maybe he hadn't gone big enough. "You're sure?"

"Absolutely." She thrust it toward him. "Will you put it on me?"

He nodded, slowly. Emotion chocked the breath in his lungs. After two failed attempts, he managed to slide the ring on her finger.

"It's a perfect fit," she said, pressing her cheek to his.

"No, Hailey." He pulled her onto his lap and kissed her soundly on the mouth. *"You're* my perfect fit. In life and in love."

She snuggled deeper into his embrace. "Be careful, soldier. You're on the verge of getting a lifelong commitment out of me."

"That *was* the general idea behind the engagement ring. Ah, Hailey." He tightened his grip around her, "I want you in my life. Forever and always."

"Good thing you feel that way." She turned her face up to his. "Because you're never getting rid of me. Not in this lifetime."

A rush of love filled him.

After years of wandering from house to house, Army post to Army post, Wolf was finally home. And ready to build a family with the beautiful, smart, talented woman of his dreams.

* * * * *

Award-winning author **Mindy Obenhaus** lives on a ranch in Texas with her husband, two sassy pups, and countless cattle and deer. She's passionate about touching readers with biblical truths in an entertaining, and sometimes adventurous, manner. When she's not writing, you'll usually find her in the kitchen, spending time with family or roaming the ranch. She'd love to connect with you via her website, mindyobenhaus.com.

Books by Mindy Obenhaus

Love Inspired

Bliss, Texas

A Father's Promise
A Brother's Promise
A Future to Fight For
Their Yuletide Healing

Rocky Mountain Heroes

Their Ranch Reunion
The Deputy's Holiday Family
Her Colorado Cowboy
Reunited in the Rockies
Her Rocky Mountain Hope

Visit the Author Profile page at LoveInspired.com. for more titles.

FALLING FOR THE
HOMETOWN HERO

Mindy Obenhaus

He heals the brokenhearted
and binds up their wounds.
—*Psalms* 147:3

To all of our wounded warriors.
May God bless you richly.

Acknowledgments

For Your glory, Lord.

To my amazing husband, Richard. I am so blessed to have you in my life. Your support carries me through the toughest of times. Thank you for countless brainstorming lunches and for your desire to help me achieve my goals.

To my guys, Ryan and Michael: y'all endured countless leftovers, pizza and pot pies and had to forego many a homemade treat for this one. Thanks for allowing me to do what I do.

Thanks to Lisa Jordan for stepping in the gap and allowing me the privilege of being your "Rachel."

To Becky Yauger: missed you, girl. So glad you're back.

Thank you Robert and Mary Ellen Bolton, motorcycle couple extraordinaire, for enlightening me on the world of motorcycle travel.

Many thanks to Vanessa Villanueva, LVN, and Yvonne Brefo, RN, for the medical info.

To Brandy Ross for rockin' the pink shirt and putting up with the silliest of questions.

To Ted and Betty Wolfe for your friendship and guidance.

To Noah Galloway: I knew nothing about you when I started this book, but seeing you on *Dancing with the Stars* gave me so much more insight. You are an inspiration to all of us.

Chapter One

His dream had come true.

As a kid growing up in Ouray, Colorado, Kaleb Palmer dreamed of owning a Jeep tour company. Of sharing the history and beauty of the San Juan Mountains with others. That dream had kept him going during the darkest time of his life and, finally, it had become a reality.

The online reviews said Mountain View Tours had terrible service.

The whispered words of a passerby echoed through his mind as he leaned the freshly painted wooden sign that read Under New Ownership beside the entrance. If they only knew. He'd had plenty of experience overcoming adversity.

Returning to the open bay of the garage, Kaleb tugged a shop rag from the back pocket of his jeans and rubbed the smudges of red paint from his fingers.

Excitement coursed through his veins, as it had so many times since purchasing Mountain View Tours a few months ago. It would take time to rebuild the company's tarnished reputation. And with the Jeeping season lasting less than five months, time wasn't exactly on Kaleb's side. There were loans to be paid, and he would not let his investors down. How could he when they'd given him the courage and financial backing to follow his dream?

The late afternoon sun had him rolling up the sleeves of his tan work shirt as he looked out over Main Street, surveying Ouray's colorful Victorian buildings. Now that May had arrived, businesses that had closed for the winter were primping for the upcoming high season. All over town, folks were painting, planting flowers and sprucing up in preparation for the thousands of people who would flock to the Switzerland of America over the next few months.

Out of the corner of his eye, he noticed a black motorcycle easing alongside the curb in front of his business. A potential customer, perhaps. Either way, his pulse kicked up a notch. This wasn't just any motorcycle. It was a sleek BMW K 100 LT, a touring motorcycle that put all other motorcycles to shame in his book.

As a teenager, he yearned for the day he'd own one and had even contemplated purchasing that very model once he left the army. How he'd longed to conquer the Million Dollar Highway that wound its way through the mountains south of town, leaning the machine into every hairpin curve.

Of course, that was back when he had two legs.

Absently rubbing his left thigh, where his stump and prosthetic met, he watched the leather-clad, undeniably female figure dismount the bike that was bigger than her. Was she traveling alone or waiting for someone to join her?

The woman removed her helmet then, allowing her dark hair to tumble halfway down her back.

Kaleb's breath left him. He swallowed hard, the reaction taking him by surprise. He couldn't remember the last time a woman had that kind of effect on him. Especially one he'd never met.

She looked up and down the street, allowing him a glimpse of her face. Much younger than he would have expected. And while he couldn't put his finger on it, there was something about her that intrigued him. The determined square of her shoulders, the confidence in her stance.

Again wiping his hands, he pretended not to notice as she left her helmet on the bike and started in the direction of Mountain View Tours' front office. Maybe this was the day he'd book his first tour.

Leaving his fanciful thoughts in the shop along with his rag, he slid past one of his new tour trucks—bright blue and specially outfitted with open-air seating for nine—opened the office door and went inside.

"Afternoon." He moved behind the crude particleboard reception counter. "Welcome to Mountain View Tours."

"Hi." The woman unzipped her black leather jacket, her smile wide as she took in the front office. "I'm looking for Kaleb Palmer."

A dozen scenarios sprang to his mind as to why a beautiful motorcycle-driving woman would be looking for him. A relative of one of the men who'd been with him that fateful day in the Afghan desert, perhaps?

"I'm Kaleb. What can I do for you?"

She opened her mouth, then closed it without saying a word, her expression seemingly perplexed. Her hazel eyes fell to the concrete floor, before bouncing back to his. "Sorry. I guess I expected someone older."

Pink tinged her cheeks as she held out her hand. "I'm Grace McAllen."

Her firm grip wasn't the only thing that surprised him. Granted, he'd shared only one phone call and a couple of emails with Grace, but with her husky voice, military background and no-nonsense approach to business, he never imagined his new office manager would be so...pretty.

Scratching his head, he glanced at the calendar on the wall. "I must be mixed up on my days. I wasn't expecting you until tomorrow."

"No. You're correct." She took a step back. "I just pulled into town and thought I'd drop by before checking in at the campground."

"You're staying at the campground?" Not something he would have expected from a single woman.

"Why not? I have a camper."

He peered out the window, noting the low-profile trailer hitched to the back of her motorcycle.

"Don't let appearances fool you." She'd obviously caught his stare. "It's a pop-up. Much bigger than it looks."

That was good, because it still looked pretty small to him. However, he was six-three and liked his space.

"Cool." He turned his attention back to Grace. "So would you like to start working tomorrow, then? Or would you prefer a day to familiarize yourself with the town?"

"Tomorrow is fine."

"Good." He rounded the counter to join her in the open space that was flanked by a vintage Coke machine and a particleboard brochure rack that matched the desk. "The faster we can get you up to speed, the better I'll feel. And I figure the best way to start is with a couple of informal tours. I'll give you a firsthand look at what we do and, in turn, better equip you to assist customers."

"Sounds reasonable." She shoved her hands into the back pockets of her jeans and looked him in the eye. "I haven't been to Ouray before, but if the drive up here is any indication, I can hardly wait."

"I like your enthusiasm." Kaleb had prayed long and hard that God would lead him to the right employees. Those who would share his love for this area and pass that zeal on to customers. "Most of the passes are still closed, but we can make a run up to Yankee Boy Basin. Which also happens to be one of the area's most popular destinations."

"What time should I be here?"

"Eight o'clock too early?"

"Not at all."

Nodding, he leaned an elbow against the counter and tried not to stare at his newest employee. The way her silky brown hair spilled over her shoulders and the hint of a dimple in her right cheek.

He cleared his throat. "The front office here is where you'll spend most of your time. That's my office there." He motioned to the small room at his left.

Her brow puckered as she scrutinized the area. "It has promise. A few simple cosmetic changes could brighten this space considerably."

"Cosmetic changes?" What was she talking about? "The place is perfectly fine. A bit rustic, but in some circles, the rustic look is all the rage. I put my money where it really mattered. Upgrading the rental Jeeps and tour trucks."

His former boss, Mountain View Tours' previous owner, had been a notorious cheapskate, barely putting any money into his vehicles and, in turn, ruining the company's once-glowing reputation. A reputation Kaleb was determined to restore.

Grace smiled politely. "Okay, then—"

"I got a lollipop!" The announcement came from Kaleb's four-year-old nephew, Jack, as he barreled through the front door in cowboy boots and shorts, lips bright red from the candy he proudly held in his hand.

"Is that for me?" He scooped the child into his arms before sticky fingers could make contact with anything or anyone.

"No." Jack squirmed and giggled, his brown eyes alight with amusement. "You hafta get a haircut to get one."

"Jackson Kaleb, you are supposed to wait for Mommy." Sami, Kaleb's sister, looked fit to be tied as she strode into the office, fists clenched at her sides, her blond ponytail escaping its confines. "What if there had been a car coming?"

Kaleb glared at his nephew. "Jack…? Did you run across the street by yourself?"

"But I wanted to show you." The sincerity of Jack's words settled into Kaleb's heart.

After falling prey to an IED in Afghanistan, Kaleb had returned to Ouray just before Jack was born. He soon discovered that holding Jack and spending time with him was the best medicine Kaleb could have asked for, taking his focus off of his inabilities and forging a special bond. A bond Kaleb hoped to one day share with a child of his own.

He softened his expression. "Safety first, soldier. You

know that." He regarded his new employee. "Jack, this is Grace. She's going to be working here this summer, so you'll probably see a lot of her."

"Hi, Gwace." Jack popped his lollipop into his mouth.

"How's it going, Jack?" Smiling, she waved and Kaleb saw a spark in her eyes that had him suspecting she liked kids. Yet as quick as it came to life, it was gone.

Suddenly shy, Jack laid his head against Kaleb's shoulder.

"Hi, Grace." His sister extended her hand. "I'm Sami, Kaleb's sister, part-time helper around here and mom to this little mischief maker." She poked a thumb toward Jack.

"Nice to meet you."

"Grace just got into town." Kaleb smoothed a hand across his nephew's back, the sweet smell of strawberry enveloping them both.

"Welcome to Ouray." Sami gave Grace her full attention. "This your first time to visit us?"

"Yes." Grace's eyes drifted to the window. "And it's even prettier than I imagined."

"That it is." Sami let go a contented sigh, before addressing Grace again. "Where are you from?"

"All over." Grace faced his sister. "I grew up a military brat then joined the navy right out of high school."

"Wow!" Sami's dark brown eyes flashed with excitement. For all of her contentment, Kaleb knew his sister longed to travel. "I bet you've been to some exotic places."

"I suppose. But few as beautiful as what I saw driving in today." Grace hesitated, a puzzled expression on her face. "I'm sorry—have I said that already?" She looked from Sami to Kaleb. "It really is true, though."

The conviction in Grace's voice was hard to miss. And precisely what Kaleb needed to set Mountain View Tours on the road to becoming a thriving business once again.

Anticipation flooded through him as he set Jack on the floor. "Grace, you haven't even seen the tip of the iceberg. Just wait till you find out what's in store for you."

Grace, you are such a goober.

Gravel crunched beneath her tires as she backed her bike into the tree-canopied campsite that butted against the jagged sandstone surface of the mountainside.

When she'd talked with Kaleb Palmer on the telephone, his deep voice had her envisioning him to be somewhere upwards of fifty years old, with a moderate paunch around his midsection, wearing an old trucker hat and coveralls. Instead, he was only a few years older than her twenty-eight years, well built, with biceps bigger than her thighs. Not to mention those gray-green eyes that had her gushing like a schoolgirl.

She cringed, recalling how many times she'd used the word *beautiful* or some variation thereof. Even if she had meant it, she probably came across as phony.

Much like her ex-husband. *It's all right, Grace. We've got each other, and that's all we need.* Over the two years that Grace had tried unsuccessfully to conceive, Aaron had uttered those words month after stinking month. She'd even started to believe him. Until he left her for his pregnant girlfriend.

Annoyed that she'd allowed her mind to wander down that depressing path, she killed the engine, dropped the kickstand and got off her motorcycle. After removing her helmet, she surveyed the place that would be her home for the next few months.

The showers weren't too far away, so that was a bonus. Across the way, a large motor home was parked at an angle. Several sites down from her, there was a silver Airstream trailer and a few more RVs dotted the campground. Aside from that, the place was empty. Something she was certain would change as they moved into summer.

Focusing on her own campsite, she noted the picnic table and a small fire pit that doubled as a grill. A water spigot and electrical box. Lifting her gaze, she studied the mountains, many still topped with snow. Definitely something she wasn't used to seeing from the deck of an aircraft carrier. Or from the screened-in porch at her home in Jacksonville, Florida.

She shook away the unwanted memories, dropped her helmet and jacket atop the picnic table then tugged the phone from her back pocket and sent a text to her sister, letting her know she'd arrived safely. Thirty seconds later, the phone rang and Lucy's name appeared on the screen.

Grace should have known her little sister wouldn't be satisfied with a text.

"Hey, Luce."

"I told you to call me when you got there. Not text."

"Just trying to save time." Grace sat down at the table. "I haven't even set up camp yet."

"In that case, I'll cut you some slack. So… What do you think of Ouray?" Excitement laced Lucy's tone.

Her sister and mother had spent the summer after Dad's death up here and Lucy had fallen in love with the town. If only things had been that simple with their mother.

"In a word? Gorgeous. The pictures you showed me didn't even begin to do it justice."

"See? Didn't I tell you?"

"You did." Something she was certain Lucy would never let her forget.

"I think the change of scenery will do wonders for you, Grace. At the end of the summer, you'll feel like a new woman, refreshed and ready to conquer the world."

Conquering the world was exactly what Grace planned to do. Unfortunately, the ship the cruise line had assigned her to was in dry dock, undergoing renovations, and she wouldn't be setting sail as an excursions manager until late September. So, at Lucy's relentless urging, Grace reluctantly accepted a summer job in Ouray.

Using her finger, she traced the heart someone had carved into the wooden tabletop. "I hope so." After her divorce last year, she finished out her enlistment then discharged from the navy, eager to flee Jacksonville and start a new life. A life lived on her terms, not those of a God who'd turned His back on her.

"Have you been to see Mama yet?"

Grace's whole being sagged. That was the one aspect of this summer she was divided on. She knew she needed to reconnect with her mother, at least on some level, before heading out to sea. But seeing her mother meant she would also have to see *him*.

"No. Like I said, I have to set up camp."

"I still don't understand why you won't stay with Mama and Roger."

"You know why."

"Come on, Grace. They've been married for three years. Don't you think it's time you gave Roger a chance?"

"Not particularly." That would be like turning her back on her father.

"He's a good guy, Grace. He makes Mama happy."

"Perhaps." But how her mother could move on only a year after Daddy's death was something Grace would never understand. "Hey, look, I need to get things going here, so I'll talk to you later, Luce."

Grace ended the call, eager to be done with any and all talk of Roger, grabbed work gloves from her saddlebag and unhitched her trailer from her bike. With a firm grip on the tongue of the trailer, she maneuvered it back and to the right, a position that would afford her a nice view, as well as some privacy.

Forty-five minutes later, both her trailer and a separate canopy she'd use as a lounge/kitchen area were ready to go. Sure it was small, but compared to her cramped quarters on the aircraft carrier, it was the Taj Mahal.

She giggled then, remembering that was exactly what her father used to call it. When he was alive, he would take a monthlong road trip on his motorcycle every summer. Sometimes he'd go to bike rallies or visit her if she wasn't at sea. Wherever he went, though, this camper was his home away from home.

A tear spilled onto her cheek and she quickly wiped it away. If only he could be here now. Maybe then she wouldn't feel so alone. So vacant. He'd wrap her in one of his famous bear hugs and help her make sense of her life.

I miss you, Daddy.

She ducked under the canopy and collapsed in her favorite lawn chair, suddenly exhausted. The sun had barely risen when she pulled away from her sister's house in Flagstaff this morning. Lifting the lid on the cooler beside her, she snagged a Diet Dr Pepper and was just about to kick off her riding boots when she noticed the back tire on her motorcycle was flat.

"Are you kidding me?" She groaned, setting the un-opened can on the cooler, and went to investigate. Once she removed the saddlebags, it didn't take her long to find the nail lodged into the tread. Thankfully, it would be an easy repair.

After pulling her hair into a quick ponytail, she opened the first saddlebag and dug through it, search-ing for a plug kit. Coming up empty-handed, she moved on to the next one. "Where are you?" She always car-ried at least two plug kits.

"Aha!" She pulled out the orange box and opened its lid.

Her heart dropped. Everything was there. The tools, the rubber cement… But no plugs.

She looked at her watch. Five thirty. What time did stores close around here anyway? She'd spotted a hard-ware store on her way in. Hopefully, they'd not only be open, but have what she needed, as well.

She tucked her saddlebags inside the tent, then briskly walked the six blocks to the hardware store.

"I'm sorry, but we're temporarily out of both the plugs and plug kits." The clerk's apologetic smile did little to comfort her. "But you could check with one of the Jeep tour places. They might be able to help you."

Seriously? A Jeep place?

Okay, so they had a lot of tires to worry about, but she was only familiar with one Jeep place and the idea of going back there again today didn't settle well. What if Kaleb thought she was one of those women who was merely looking for an excuse to return?

You could check with your mother.

Definitely not. Besides, she was planning to walk to work tomorrow.

What if there's an emergency, and you need your bike?

She blew out a frustrated breath. Logic left so much to be desired.

Trekking across the street, she swallowed her pride and walked into the somewhat dingy office of Mountain View Tours. A gallon or two of paint would do wonders for this place.

Kaleb stood behind the desk, his back to her. "Be right with you." The overhead fluorescent bulbs highlighted a bit of blond in his short sandy-brown hair.

She waited in silence, her anxiety building.

"Grace?" His smile was easy and he appeared almost happy to see her. "What are you doing here?"

"I have a flat on my bike. By any chance do you sell tire plugs?"

"No, we do not."

In that instant, her tire wasn't the only thing that was deflated. Oh, well. At least she was within walking distance of work. She'd just have to wait for the hardware store to replenish their stock. Or check with one of those other Jeep places the clerk had mentioned.

"But I'd be happy to give you one."

Her gaze jerked to Kaleb's. "Really?"

"Mountain View Tours always takes care of their customers."

"I'm not a—"

"And their employees."

"Oh." Her cheeks grew warm and she turned her head to hide the reaction.

"I'll be right back." He rounded the counter and disappeared through the door that led to the garage. A minute later, he reappeared. "Here you go." He handed her a bag with three plugs. "You need any tools?"

"Those I have, so no—" she dared to look at him "—thank you."

"My pleasure." He glanced at the generic round wall clock behind the desk. "I'm about to lock up. I could give you a lift and help with that tire, if you like."

"Oh, that won't be—"

"Grace, a gentleman does not let an unaccompanied female fix her own flat tire."

"But—"

"No matter how capable she might be."

Again she felt herself blush. Totally weird since she couldn't remember the last time she'd blushed. Still, she didn't need or want Kaleb's help. She didn't like to rely on other people. She could take care of herself.

"Look, this wouldn't be the first plug I've done." No, it would be the second. "I can have it fixed—"

"Grace." The look he gave her left no room for question. Much like her commanding officer. "I'm coming to help you, and that's all there is to it."

Great. So her boss thought her a damsel in distress. She'd just have to prove him wrong.

Chapter Two

Kaleb held the passenger door of his Jeep open as Grace, now sporting a ponytail and a plain gray T-shirt, reluctantly climbed inside. Clearly, she was a strong, independent woman, evidenced by the fact that she drove a motorcycle and was staying alone at the campground. Still, he preferred to make sure things were done and done right.

"This really isn't necessary, you know." Grace's tone held a hint of annoyance, which he chose to ignore.

"So you've said." He tossed the door closed, continued around to the driver's side and hopped in. "But given that you're new in town, it's only logical that I should offer my newest employee a hand. People helping people. That's how we are in Ouray."

While she stared out the window, he started the vehicle, crossed Main Street and headed down Seventh Avenue.

Grace jerked her head in his direction. "How do you know which way to go?"

"Easy." He eyed the cross streets for traffic. "There are only two RV parks within walking distance of Main

Street. I saw you coming up Seventh before turning into the hardware store." He shrugged. "Simple process of elimination."

She didn't say anything, but her narrowed eyes told him she wasn't necessarily pleased with his observation. Not that he cared. War had taught him to pay attention to detail.

He made a right onto Oak Street, gravel crunching beneath the Jeep's heavy-duty tires. "I'll have to rely on you to direct me to your campsite, though. Either that or drive around until I see your motorcycle."

"Wouldn't take you long. I'm just a few sites into the campground."

Sure enough. Once they'd passed the office on the right and showers to their left, he spotted her motorcycle and camper.

Grace was halfway out the door before he even brought the Jeep to a stop in front of her campsite. She moved around the vehicle and continued straight on to her tent.

Women. He hoped she wasn't going to be this stubborn about everything.

She had a tire that needed fixing, though, and he intended to do just that.

He stepped out of the Jeep and retrieved his toolbox from the backseat. When he turned around, Grace reappeared—carrying a toolbox.

Uh-oh. *Tread lightly, Palmer.*

"For the record—" he set his toolbox on the ground beside her motorcycle "—I'm not a chauvinist or anything. I just like to make sure things are done correctly."

She set her toolbox down with a thud, then crossed

her arms over her chest. "You don't think I can do it correctly?"

"I didn't say that." He eyeballed the flat tire, spotting the nail right away. "It'll just make me feel better, that's all."

Kneeling on his good knee, he lifted the lid on his toolbox and reached for a pair of pliers. "Do you have a compressor or something to inflate the tire once it's repaired?"

She continued to glare at him. "Wouldn't take a road trip without one."

"Glad to hear it." Using the pliers, he pulled the nail from the tire. "You said you had a plug tool?"

Her brow shot up. "You mean you don't have one?"

He pondered the spitfire staring down at him. "Actually…" He dug through his toolbox until he found his own plug kit tucked in the bottom. "Yep." He held it up.

Threading the thick rubbery plug through the eye of the tool that was best described as a giant needle with a handle, he glanced over his shoulder.

"That's an interesting setup you've got there." Definitely not like the campers he was used to seeing. Instead of the pop-up going up and out on both ends, it went up and then out on one side, making it look like a tent sitting on a wagon.

"Thanks." Arms still crossed, she watched as he jammed the tool into the tire. "It belonged to my dad."

Melancholy wove its way through her last statement, telling him far more than her words.

"I take it he's no longer with us?"

"Cancer." She scraped a booted foot across the gravel. "Four years ago."

Even with the distance of time, her grief was evident.

"He must have been a young man." Kaleb pulled the tool back out then grabbed a pair of cutters to trim the excess plug.

"Fifty-six."

That had to be difficult. Losing someone who, by all counts, was in the prime of their life. He knew what that was like. Tossing his tools back into the box, he stood and looked at her, his annoyance fading. "I'm sorry."

"Don't be. It wasn't your fault." Despite a momentary chink, her armor was back in place. "I'll get that compressor."

She turned and again headed for her tent, but not before he noticed the sadness in her hazel eyes. Beyond the striking mix of green, brown and gold, there lurked something that intrigued him all the more.

For all of Grace's toughness, it seemed her heart was as tender as the wildflowers that blanketed the mountains in late July. Those that endured the harshest of winters only to flourish and grow more beautiful.

Not at all like Gina, his ex-fiancée. She'd wilted as soon as the storm clouds rolled in.

The hum of an electric engine drew his attention. Looking up the road, he spotted Luann Carter zooming toward him in her signature red golf cart, her grin as wide as ever.

She slowed to stop in front of him. "I thought that was you, Kaleb." She hopped out, scurried around the cart and greeted him with a hug. "It's always a joy to see you."

"How's it going?" He released the sixty-some-year-old redhead and peered down at her. Luann was a short one all right. Not even reaching five feet tall. But what she lacked in height, she more than made up for in spirit.

"Just wonderful. And how 'bout yourself? I'm sure you're so busy you're havin' to turn away customers."

"I wish things were that good, Luann. But I'm hoping they'll pick up after Memorial Day."

"That reminds me. " She wagged a finger his way. "Make sure you bring me some brochures. I want to have plenty on hand so I can tell everyone about the *new* Mountain View Tours."

He couldn't help smiling. Seemed the whole town had rallied around him, willing him to bring this fledgling company back from the brink of disaster. He was determined to show that their faith in him wasn't unfounded.

"I'll be sure and do that just as soon as I get them printed." Of course, before he could do that, he had to have someone design them. Add that to the long list of things he had yet to do.

"Well, hello there." Luann's attention shifted to somewhere behind him.

He turned to find Grace, compressor in hand. "Luann, I'd like you to meet my new office manager. Grace McAllen, this is Luann Carter. She and her husband, Bud, own the campground."

"Pleasure to meet you." Grace smiled at the older woman. "I think I met your husband when I checked in."

Luann waved a hand. "Probably. I've been out running errands most of the afternoon." Her assessing gaze skimmed over Grace. "So you'll be working with Kaleb?"

"Yes, ma'am."

"Well, let me tell you, sugar, this is probably one of the finest young men you could ever work for." Luann rested a hand on his arm. "He is kind, generous, respectful…" She hesitated a moment, then forged on. "Ol' Bud and I were having some car trouble back this winter and, well, things were a little tight financially." She gently squeezed his arm. "So Kaleb here fixed it for us and didn't charge us a thing, 'cept for the parts."

Warmth crept up Kaleb's neck as Grace's focus shifted to him.

"Poor fella spent two days in that freezing-cold garage and never asked for anything more than one of my coconut cream pies."

He cleared his throat. "Grace, if you ever have one of Luann's coconut pies, you'll understand that it was a very fair trade."

Luann playfully swatted him, her own cheeks turning pink. "Oh, stop, you."

Grace watched the two of them, a smile lifting the corners of her mouth. "You have a lovely campground, Luann."

"Thank you, sugar." Luann's phone whistled. She tugged it from the clip attached to the pocket of her cargo pants and looked at the screen. "Looks like Bud needs me. Gettin' close to dinnertime, you know." She winked at Kaleb before turning her attention back to Grace. "I hope you enjoy your stay with us. Just let me know if there's anything I can do for you."

Luann hugged both of them before hurrying back to her golf cart. "Catch ya later." She waved as she sped off.

Kaleb looked at Grace and they both cracked up.

"You won't find many people with a bigger heart than Luann," he said.

Grace lifted a shoulder. "According to her, you'll give her a pretty good run for her money."

"Yeah, well. She tends to exaggerate." He toed at the dirt. "Hey, look, about the tire. I'm sorry if I was a little pushy."

"A little?" There went that perfectly arched brow again.

"Okay, so one of the first things you should probably know about me is that I like to be in control."

Her gaze narrowed. "Does that mean you'll constantly be looking over my shoulder at work? Questioning my abilities?"

"Not at all. Your job entails things I won't even pretend to know about. But I do appreciate an attention to detail and, based on our earlier conversations, I think you bring that to the table."

She nodded, her lips pursed. "And just so you'll know, I'm…not usually so stubborn. My mother taught me to play well with others."

He chuckled.

"Speaking of my mother, can you tell me how to get to Fifth Street?"

"Sure." He pointed toward the southeast corner of town. "Simply head up Seventh Avenue and make a right onto Fifth." He faced her again. "Donna and Roger will be happy to see you."

Her smile evaporated, her eyes narrowing. "How do you know who my mother is?"

His stomach muscles tightened. She didn't know. "Uh, Roger. He's one of my guides. Matter of fact, he's the one who convinced me I should buy Mountain View Tours." Even going so far as to provide some financial backing. But she didn't need to know that. Nor did she need to know that, after learning Grace was one of the applicants for the office-manager position, Roger was the one who'd recommended her for the job.

"One of your guides?"

"I'm surprised they didn't say anything to you."

"I'm not." The words were mumbled, so he wasn't sure he heard her correctly.

"What?"

"I mean, they probably thought I already knew." She shifted the compressor to her other hand and proceeded to unroll the electrical cord. "So, it looks like Roger and I will be working together, huh?"

"To a point, yeah. I mean, he's a guide, so it's not like he'll be hanging around the office all day or anything." Lowering his head, he tried to read her expression. "That's not going to be a problem, is it?"

She continued with the cord, seemingly taking forever. When her eyes finally met his, her smile appeared a little too forced. "No. No problem at all."

Then why did he suddenly get the feeling it was going to be a big problem?

With her tire fixed and Kaleb gone, Grace swapped her traveling clothes for a pair of skinny jeans and a long-sleeved tunic top and grabbed a quick bite to eat before heading to her mother's. She hadn't planned to visit until tomorrow evening. However, after learning that Roger worked for Kaleb, she decided she'd better put in an appearance tonight or else face the possibility of an even more awkward scene tomorrow at work.

Why hadn't Mama said something—anything— when Grace told her where she'd be working? Instead, her email said simply, Can't wait to see you.

Now, as Grace plodded up Seventh Avenue, hesitation plagued each step, her roast beef sandwich souring in her stomach. She and her mother had never had the kind of close relationship Grace had shared with her father. No, while her mother and Lucy bonded over clothes and shoes, Grace and her father bonded over motorcycles.

Then, suddenly, Daddy was gone and Mama married someone else. Leaving Grace drifting aimlessly, without a compass or anything to hold on to. Not even her husband.

Seemed she didn't fit in anywhere.

Turning onto Fifth Street, she continued a couple more blocks. Moving past the rows of mostly older homes, some well kept, some not so much, she could feel the weight of anxiety settling in her chest. Then she spotted the slate-blue-and-white Queen Anne style two-story.

Her heart pounded against her rib cage. How could she do this? Set foot inside *his* house? Not her mother's, not one they'd purchased together, but the house Roger had grown up in, according to her mother.

You're simply going to visit your mother.

She drew in a deep breath. That was right. Maybe he wouldn't even be there. She eyed the white wicker chairs and love seat on the porch. Perhaps she wouldn't even have to go inside.

Picking up the pace, she marched up the front walk, climbed the two white wooden steps and rang the doorbell.

A minute later, the door swung open, and Roger stood before her. His silver hair still had that tousled appearance, and the medium blue Henley he wore seemed to match the color of his eyes. If he were anyone else, she'd think him a fairly handsome man.

"Grace!" Though his smile was quick, his brow

puckered in confusion as he pushed open the screen door. "We weren't expecting you until tomorrow. Come on in."

The aroma of lavender and vanilla wafted outside, stirring fond memories of every military house Grace had ever lived in. No matter where in the world they were, Mama's favorite fragrance made it feel like home.

Shaking off the recollection, she kept her feet planted on the porch. "Um…is my mother here?"

"'Fraid not. They're having a VBS planning meeting at the church tonight."

Of course, her mother would be there. She had taken an active role in every vacation Bible school at every church they'd ever attended.

Apparently her love for Grace's father was the only thing that didn't transcend time.

Roger held the door wider. "You're welcome to come in and wait on her, though."

"No. Thank you." Grace squared her shoulders. "I hear you're a guide at Mountain View Tours."

"Going into my fourth year."

She nodded. "And nobody felt the need to share this information with me?"

He moved out onto the porch in his white sock feet. "We weren't trying to deceive you, Grace. We were afraid that if you knew I worked there, too, you might not come. Your mother's looking forward to seeing you."

Looking everywhere but at Roger—the wooden floorboards, the neighbor's house, the hanging flower basket swaying in the breeze—Grace fought to keep her breathing even as the words seeped in. While her knee-jerk reaction was to reject the notion, she knew deep inside that Roger was probably right.

"In that case—" she started down the steps "—I guess I'll see you around. Tell my mother I stopped by."

"I'll do that. And, Grace?"

As much as she hated to, she halted her retreat and turned.

"You're welcome here anytime." His smile was sincere, the lines around his eyes indicating it was something he did a lot.

Maybe Lucy was right. Maybe he wasn't so bad. But Grace wouldn't betray her father.

Her gaze drifted to the ground before bouncing back to Roger. "Good night."

She moved down the street at a much faster pace than when she'd arrived, ready to put this day behind her. Despite her long sleeves, the cool evening air sent chill bumps skittering down her arms, making her wish she'd brought her jacket. All she wanted to do now was get back to her camp, crawl into bed and hope tomorrow wasn't as convoluted as today.

Coming to Ouray was supposed to rejuvenate her. Instead, it felt more like a chore. That cruise ship was sounding better and better all the time.

Rubbing her arms, she surveyed the surrounding mountains. Though the town lay bathed in shadows, the sun's fading rays radiated from behind the western slope. Glancing eastward, her breath caught in her throat. The gray, volcanic-looking mountains that seemed to hug the town were now painted the most beautiful, yet indescribable color. Shades of orange, rose and yellow blended into one harmonious hue that was unlike anything she'd ever seen before.

"Grace?"

Turning, she saw Kaleb coming up the block.

Couldn't she go anywhere in this town without running into him?

Gravel crunched beneath each step as he continued toward her, looking annoyingly handsome. "Enjoying the alpenglow?"

"The what?"

Hands on his hips, he nodded in the direction of the colorful mountain. "Alpenglow. It's a phenomenon that often happens this time of night."

She readily focused on nature's beauty. "What causes it?"

He shrugged. "Something about the sun reflecting off particles in the atmosphere. I tend not to question it. I simply enjoy it."

"I can see why." It had that same captivating quality as a rainbow. A supernatural splendor that commanded one's attention.

"Were you visiting your mom?"

The colors had begun to fade by the time she faced Kaleb. "That was my intention, but she wasn't home. Roger said something about a vacation Bible school meeting."

"Yeah, that was tonight." He dragged the toe of his work boot over the dirt road. "Did you and Roger have a nice visit?"

Visit? They barely conversed. But getting the impression that Kaleb was rather fond of Roger, she said, "I suppose. Yeah."

"He's a good man. A fellow vet, too. But then, I suppose you already knew that."

She did not, but was too exhausted to offer anything more than a nod.

"Hey, I hate to cut this short, but I need to get back

to camp. New job tomorrow." She had to make herself smile. "Gotta get a good night's rest so I can make a good impression on my boss."

"I don't think that'll be a problem." His grin set off a strange and unwanted fluttering in her midsection. "Don't forget to make sure any food you've got at your campsite is secured inside a cooler or something with a latch. Bears like to wander down the mountain at night and help themselves."

She puffed out a laugh. "You're kidding, right?"

His smile evaporated. "Not at all. I'm surprised Bud didn't say something to you when you checked in."

The fluttering morphed into a whirlwind. "Let me get this straight. While I'm asleep, bears are going to be roaming around my campsite?"

"Possibly."

She surveyed the rapidly darkening sky, sweat suddenly beading her brow. "I'll see you tomorrow." Despite the fatigue nipping at her heels, she broke into a jog.

Controlling bosses, working with her stepfather and now bears. With all that on her mind, she'd never get any sleep.

At this rate, Ouray was turning out to be the worst idea her sister ever had.

Chapter Three

Kaleb pulled his Jeep into a parking spot alongside Mountain View Tours shortly after noon the next day. As promised, he'd taken Grace on her first tour to Yankee Boy Basin and, so far, it had been a fantastic day. "My goal is to create a memorable experience for each of our guests. One they'll talk about for the rest of their lives."

And judging by Grace's reaction, he'd achieved just that. The look of unequivocal reverence as she took in the snow-covered peaks that stretched as far as the eye could see was something he'd never forget. Her genuine interest and appreciation for every little thing, from the old mines to the cascading waterfalls to a grosbeak's sweet song, reinforced his belief that he'd made the right decision in hiring her.

Now he shifted the vehicle into Park, glancing toward her in the passenger seat. "Unfortunately, the previous owner didn't feel the same way, so I've got an uphill battle."

"Which is why we need to appeal to folks from the

moment they walk into Mountain View Tours, if not before." She gathered her things and exited the vehicle.

He climbed out, liking the way she used the word *we*, as if they were one, focused on the same common goal. Yes, the sooner he could bring Grace up to speed and put her to work, the better off his business would be. Memorial weekend, the unofficial kickoff of the high season, was only a few weeks away, and there was still much to do.

Meeting her at the front of the Jeep, he stared down at her. "And how do we do that?"

"I have a few ideas, though you may not like them." She wasn't afraid to meet his gaze. As though issuing a challenge.

Like he'd back down from a challenge. "Try me."

"Okay. You said you want to create a memorable experience for your guests."

"Yes."

"What if we added a tagline?" She shifted her weight from one foot to the next. "Something like, 'Mountain View Tours… Memories in the making.'"

He let the phrase tumble through his brain. "Okay. Yeah. I'm kinda liking that. Tells people exactly what our goal is."

"Just like a tagline is supposed to."

"That would look good on my new brochures, too." Rubbing his chin, he took a step back. "Which reminds me. You wouldn't happen to know anything about designing brochures, would you?"

"Sure. I'm pretty good with websites, too."

He couldn't stop smiling. "Grace, you may just be the best thing that ever happened to Mountain View Tours. So what other suggestions have you got?"

Clasping her notepad and camera against her chest, she took a deep breath. "I think you need to consider sprucing up the front office. Something as simple as a fresh coat of—"

"No."

"Why no—"

"We discussed this yesterday. The rustic look stays."

She took a step closer, her gaze narrowing. "For your information, it's industrial, not rustic. And it only works if it's done right." She pointed toward the building. "That's not it."

Hands on his hips, he put himself toe-to-toe with her. "So what? My building, my business, my decor."

After a momentary staredown, she took a step back. "You asked for my input."

Something he'd think twice about next time.

Exasperation mounting, he started toward the building and pushed through the front door, the heels of his work boots hammering against the concrete floor. "Sami, would you please tell Grace the office looks perfectly fine."

Sami glanced up from behind the counter. "Grace, the office looks perfectly fine. *If* you like drab and uninviting."

Behind him, Grace choked back a laugh.

He glared at his sister.

"I'm serious, Kaleb." Sami rounded the counter. "This place is about as lackluster as you can get. I about fell asleep while you were gone. You need to liven things up. Make Mountain View Tours a place people *want* to be."

"Now, where have I heard that before?" Tapping a

finger to her lips, Grace pretended not to look at him. A move that only served to further annoy him.

Sami stepped between them, her dark brown gaze fixed on Kaleb. "Mom and I were talking about this just a little while ago. You know that we all want Mountain View Tours to be a success. However, we also know that you have some huge hurdles to overcome."

He couldn't argue with her so far. No matter how much he might want to.

"Which means you need to do whatever you can to overcome some of those hurdles."

"Like replacing all of the tour trucks and rental fleet? I've already done that."

Sami jammed a fist into her hip. "That's not what I'm talking about." She strode to the counter, spread out a swath of papers then stabbed them with her finger. "This is what I'm talking about. Just look at these before and after photos I found online."

He didn't want to look at them. But curiosity got the best of him.

Easing toward the desk, he cast his sister a wary eye. "Those are some pretty dramatic changes." Not to mention costly.

"Yep. All with little more than paint."

Grace sidled up beside Sami, no doubt pleased to have someone else in her corner. "I like how they incorporated the brick wall into the design of this one." She pointed from the picture to the brick wall behind his reception counter. "With the right color paint, some rustic elements, you could really make that stand out."

"Though they don't look like much right now, Kaleb's got some great pieces around here he could use." Sami turned. "Like that old Coke machine." She pointed across the room. "That thing is too cool to be hidden in a corner."

Grace strolled over to the vintage machine. "It's not often you find a soda machine that offers glass bottles. Does it work?"

"Yes," said Kaleb.

"Sami's right, then." She faced them again. "You need to move this someplace more prominent. Keep it stocked and you've got another source of income."

Kaleb tried to hide his annoyance. Not only due to the bossy women in front of him, but the fact that he hadn't given more consideration to the Coke machine.

"So what do you say, Kaleb?" Sami looked like a kid begging to open just one gift before Christmas. "We're only talking about the cost of materials. Mom and I are both willing to paint."

"Me, too." Grace thrust her arm in the air like a second grader. "It'd be fun. As a matter of fact—" She waved a hand then dropped it to her side. "Ah, never mind." Her narrowed gaze drifted to Kaleb. "I've learned to keep my suggestions to myself."

"Oh, no. You're not getting off that easy." Sami inched toward her. "Out with it, Grace."

Grace looked from him to Sami, as if deliberating whether or not to divulge her secret. "What if you had a grand opening? Something that invited people to come in and check out the new Mountain View Tours."

Sami's eyes grew wide. "That's an outstanding idea." She whirled toward Kaleb. "We could do it Memorial Day weekend. You could have your new trucks on display, offer discounts on tours... We could have cookies, balloons—"

He held up a palm, cutting off his sister. "No. I appreciate the suggestion. However, something like that involves a lot of work. I think we best focus our energies on bringing in business."

"That's exactly what we're trying to do." Returning her fist to her hip, Sami scowled at him. "Besides, wasn't it just the other day I heard you say that you were looking for a way to separate the new Mountain View Tours from the old?"

He hated it when she used his own words against him. "Yes. But a party wasn't exactly what I had in mind."

"Then what did you have in mind?" His sister's smug grin only served to irritate him.

He didn't have a response. All he knew was that painting and parties took time. Time that he didn't have.

"Kaleb," Sami continued, "you've said a million times how important this first season is going to be. Why not do it right?"

Grace cleared her throat. "All you'd really have to do for a grand opening is set up shop outside. Go to the people instead of waiting for them to come to you." She tucked a strand of dark hair behind her ear. "We're talking very little time and effort. However, the payoff could be worth it."

His sister's expression softened. "So what do you say, big brother? You going to go big or go home?"

He definitely didn't want to go home. Not only would he be letting his investors down, he'd be lost. He'd been working toward this goal for years.

Scanning the bare-bones office, he could see where it might seem a little cold.

We need to appeal to folks from the moment they walk into Mountain View Tours, if not before.

Of course, the more appealing things were, the more likely people were to be drawn in.

He eyed his sister. "You and Mom will do all the work?"

"And Grace." Hope lit Sami's dark eyes. "When she's not doing things for you, that is."

"And you'll get the work done quickly?"

"As quick as we can. After all, Memorial Day is right around the corner."

He lowered his arms to his sides. Even though he was ready to say yes, he paused for effect. "Okay, you can redecorate. So long as I approve all ideas and colors first. Got it?"

"Got it." Sami's grin was so big, he thought she might burst. "And what about the grand opening? Scott and I would be happy to help out. I'm sure Mom and Dad would, too."

Honestly, the more he thought about it, the more he liked the idea. Though he didn't have to let his sister or Grace know.

"We can probably work something out."

"Yes!" Sami charged him then and hugged his neck so tight he could barely breathe. "Okay." Letting go, she began her retreat. "I'm going to run over to the hardware store to look at some paint chips." After a final scan of the place, she continued. "I can't wait." She yanked open the door. "Oh! Hello, Donna." She held the door for Grace's mother.

"Hello, Sami." The woman in her late fifties continued inside, looking as well dressed as ever in her tan slacks and flowing blue shirt. "Kaleb, I hope you don't mind me dropping by to see my daughter."

"Not at all." He could use a break. Being ganged up

on by two headstrong women was enough to do any man in. "This'll give me a chance to run and pick us up some lunch before we get down to business."

"It's so good to see you." Donna embraced her daughter. Her short auburn hair was a contrast to Grace's long dark brown. However, they shared the same hazel eyes.

"Hi, Mama." Grace's hug seemed a bit more tentative. Even awkward.

Perhaps because he was there.

"Grace? Burger or sandwich?"

Her mother released her.

"Burger's fine. With everything, please."

"Done." He started for the door. "See you later, Donna." Outside, he crossed the street and headed toward Granny's Kitchen.

Scrubbing a hand over his face, he let go a sigh. Talk of redecorating and a grand opening, while both great ideas, also added to his angst. There was so much to do and so little time in which to do it. Could they really pull it off?

God, I want to get this right.

Honestly, he really liked the ideas Grace and Sami proposed. And if everything went according to plan…

On the flip side—

No. He wasn't going to go there. Because for as much as he hated to admit it, Grace just might be the key to his success.

Grace did not want to do this now.

She hadn't seen her mother since Lucy's wedding last year. Right after Grace had returned from deployment and learned that her own marriage was over. So why on earth would Mama come to Mountain View Tours—

a public place—for their first encounter? What if the place had been filled with customers?

Unless her mother was trying to protect herself, thinking Grace wouldn't call her out if someone else was around. But now that Kaleb was gone...

"Why didn't you tell me Roger worked here?"

Mama squared her shoulders in a defiant manner.

"I'm not trying to pick a fight, Mama. The news just kind of blindsided me, that's all. I wish you would have told me."

Lifting her chin, her mother said, "If I had, though, would you have taken the job?"

"I guess we'll never know, will we?" Though resignation laced Grace's tone, she made sure there was no accusation.

"Grace, you're my daughter. I miss you. And I'd like to have a relationship with you."

"Like you do with Lucy." The two of them were always chatting up a storm about the latest fashion trends, celebrities and such. Things Grace didn't have a clue about. Especially after spending ten months at sea.

Mama shrugged. "It's easier with Lucy. She lets me in."

"I tell you things."

Her mother chuckled. "Only when I ask. Even then, you only give me enough to get me to stop with the questions. Yet you never had any problem talking to your father." Mama looked away. "I always envied that."

Envy? Seriously? Grace's gut churned with the shock of Mama's revelation, leaving any words she might have said stuck inside.

She glanced out the window. "Kaleb will be back

soon." And she didn't know how to continue this conversation with her mother. "We've got a lot of work to do."

"See what I mean. Instead of allowing anyone in, you avoid whatever makes you uncomfortable."

She let Aaron in. And look how that turned out.

"This isn't about being uncomfortable. This is reality. And reality dictates that I have a job, which means I have a boss. A boss who will be back any moment, expecting me to work." She took a deep breath, contemplating her next offer. "I can stop by tonight…if you like."

Mama's expression turned hopeful. "For dinner? I'll make your favorite."

Grace's spirits lifted a notch. "Nonna Gigi's lasagna?"

"Of course."

Grace's mouth watered just thinking about it. Nonna Gigi's lasagna was the ultimate in comfort food. One Grace had not had the pleasure of indulging in for years.

Mama sure knew how to dangle the carrot.

"I don't get off work until six."

"That's all right. We typically don't eat until six thirty or seven."

"One burger with everything." Kaleb blew through the door. "Along with some of the freshest French fries in Ouray."

She caught a whiff of the enticing aroma as he walked past. If they tasted half as good as they smelled…

Her mother eased toward the door. "I'll get out of your hair so you two can get back to work."

Kaleb set the white paper bag on the counter and turned to face them. "Did Grace tell you we're going to be doing some redecorating in here?" He gestured his hand about the office.

"She did not." Mama paused, her hand on the door-knob, a smile at the corners of her mouth.

Evidently, now that he'd had time to think, Kaleb decided the suggestion had been a good one.

"Looks like we'll be doing some painting and who knows what else to get the place in shape."

"Oh, I'd love to help." Having transformed many a bland military house into a warm and inviting home, Mama not only loved, but had lots of experience with decorating.

Working alongside her, though?

Slinking toward the desk and the tantalizing aromas, Grace spotted the local newspaper on the corner of the counter.

"That'd be great, Donna. Like my grandmother always said, many hands make light work."

Try as she might, Grace couldn't share Kaleb's enthusiasm. Too many memories to be objective, she supposed.

"What's Roger up to today?"

"He's substitute teaching at the school."

Talk of Roger had Grace wishing she were already on that cruise ship. She picked up the newspaper and thumbed through the pages. Maybe there was another job in Ouray that she might enjoy. One that didn't involve working with her stepfather.

"Grace?"

"Hmm…?" She looked at Kaleb first, then her mother.

"I'll see you for dinner, then?"

She closed the paper. Folded it. "Just as soon as I get off work."

With her mother gone, Kaleb opened the bags and sorted out the food.

Grace accepted her burger. "Sorry my mother interrupted us like that. I'm sure she won't make a habit of dropping in."

"Don't worry about it. After missing you last night, she was probably eager to see you. I understand." He passed her a small bag of fries. Thin-cut, just the way she liked them. "Pull up a stool." He pointed behind the desk.

While he unwrapped his burger and took a bite, she grabbed the basic wooden stool and sat down, her appetite waning.

"Something wrong with your burger?"

"No. Just thinking about this evening."

Kaleb jerked his head up, a blob of mayo clinging to his bottom lip. "Problem?"

He grabbed a napkin and wiped his mouth.

She picked up a fry, rolling it between her forefinger and thumb. "I just don't know how I'm going to handle spending an entire evening with Roger."

"Why? He's a great guy."

"So people keep telling me. But what kind of guy goes after a woman whose husband has been dead less than a year?"

Kaleb settled his sandwich on top of the flattened bag. "Did you know Roger lost his wife to cancer, too?"

"I knew he was married." But beyond that…

"For thirty-five years." Kaleb wiped his hands. "Everyone around here worried about him after Camille died. My mom said he looked like a dead man walking. Until he met your mother."

Grace tossed the fry she'd been holding back into the bag. "Sometimes life really stinks."

"Yep. The buffet line of life is notorious for throwing stuff on our plates that we don't necessarily like." He shrugged. "Doesn't mean they're not good for us, though. What doesn't kill us makes us stronger, right?"

Staring at her handsome boss, who seemed to have the world at his feet, she puffed out a disbelieving laugh. "What could you possibly know about it?"

He narrowed his gaze on her, as though contemplating his response. "Far more than you might think." He rounded the counter then, his expression intense, and lifted the left leg of his cargo pants.

"What are you—" At the sight of his prosthetic leg, her words and her heart skidded to a halt. "Oh, my." She continued to look at the metal-and-hard-plastic contraption that went all the way above his knee. "I—I never would have guessed."

She looked at him now. "What—"

"IED. Cost me four of my buddies and my leg." He let the pant leg drop. "So don't go acting like you're the only one who's been handed a raw deal. Because, sweetheart, I do know a little something about it."

Chapter Four

❧

Grace would love nothing more than to go back to her campsite and lick her wounds. Next time, she needed to think twice before inviting someone else to her pity party.

In one swift, stealthy strike, her boss had put an end to her sulking. And yes, despite her strong desire to turn tail and run, Kaleb was still her boss. Despite their disagreements, she felt as though she could make a difference at Mountain View Tours.

Of course, that also meant she'd still be working with Roger, so she supposed she should put aside her pre-conceived notions and, at least, give the guy a chance.

Now here she stood in Mama and Roger's cottage-style kitchen, feeling like a bit of a jerk. She hadn't realized he'd lost his wife of thirty-five years. Probably because she never took the time to listen to anything her mother—or anyone else—had to say about him.

"What can I do to help, Mama?" She pushed up the long sleeves of her purple T-shirt and headed toward the farmhouse sink under the window to wash her hands.

"Why don't you set the table while I finish with

this salad." Her mother rested the knife on the marble-topped island and wiped her hands on a dish towel before opening one of the white cupboards behind her.

"Silverware?"

"First drawer on the right." Mama pointed with her elbow while pulling out a stack of plates. She set them on the counter. "We'll eat in the dining room tonight."

"Okay." Eating utensils clasped in one hand, Grace reached for plain white plates with her other. "I think you gave me one too many."

"No, I didn't. The fourth one is for Kaleb. Roger thought it would be nice to invite him for dinner, too."

Grace simply stood there, uncertain what to make of her mother's sudden announcement. After all the head-butting she and Kaleb had done today.

"Oh, and place mats and napkins are in the drawer in the hutch." Mama picked up her knife and continued slicing tomatoes. "Let's go with the turquoise ones. Add a little color."

Good thing Grace's workday had ended on a positive note. Otherwise, seeing Kaleb tonight could prove to be even more awkward.

She moved into the dining room and set the plates and silverware on the table before searching for the linens. Not that it would be difficult. Mama always kept them in the right-hand drawer.

Turning toward the wall at the far end of the room, she vaguely recognized the tall piece of furniture whose glass case held Mama's collection of pastel-colored Depression glass. The style of the piece was similar to the one Grace remembered growing up, except instead of the honey oak finish, this one was white.

She pulled the crystal knob to open the drawer on

the right and gasped. It *was* the same piece. While the outside of the hutch had been painted, the inside of the drawer still bore hers and Lucy's names. Names they'd written in permanent marker along the inside of the drawer. A move that had earned them both a stern scolding and a lengthy time-out.

Stepping back, she stared at the furniture piece, a bittersweet feeling leaching into her heart. She remembered the look of pure delight on her mother's face the Christmas Daddy presented it to her. "You need a special place to display your collection," he'd told her.

Grace thought it was the most beautiful, if not ginormous, thing she'd ever seen. Yet as she stared at it now, the hutch looked prettier than ever. Like a better version of itself.

A noise in the kitchen interrupted her reverie and stole her attention.

"Smells delicious." Roger closed the door behind him, wiping his booted feet on the rug before making his way into the room. His arm snaked around her mother's waist as he set a plastic grocery sack on the counter. He said something, though the words were too soft for Grace to hear. Whatever it was, though, made her mother giggle and had a blush creeping into her cheeks.

"Love words" were what she and Lucy used to call it when Daddy would whisper sweet nothings into Mama's ear. Sometimes she would blush, sometimes not, but either way, Grace and Lucy knew it was an intimate conversation, meant only for Mama and Daddy.

Suddenly uncomfortable, Grace grabbed the place mats and napkins and returned her focus to the table.

"Hello, Grace." Roger stood just on the other side of the doorway between the two rooms. "Glad you could make it." Hands stuffed into the pockets of his jeans, he seemed to look everywhere but at her.

Just like she did when she was uncomfortable.

Could it be that Roger was as nervous about tonight as she was?

"Thank you for having me." Hands shaking, she finished laying out the silverware, realizing she'd forgotten to grab another set. "You have a lovely home."

"Yeah." He moved closer, just enough to admire the dining room and adjoining living room. Both had that same cottage feel, lots of white furniture against dark hardwood floors and pale blue-gray walls. "Your mother's quite the decorator."

He'd let her mother redecorate? But this was his house.

"She managed to fuse our former lives and our new life into something fresh and different."

Much like the old hutch.

All of Lucy's words about Roger being a good guy flooded her memory. Grace had chosen to ignore her sister. Now her emotions warred within.

Perhaps her mother wasn't quite so eager to forget the past after all.

The doorbell rang then.

"That would be Kaleb." Moving along the opposite side of the table, Roger headed toward the door.

Feeling as though she still had egg on her face when it came to her boss, Grace took the opportunity to retrieve that fourth set of utensils.

Inside the kitchen, her mother was removing a large baking dish from the oven. The aromas of meat, cheeses and whatever other secret ingredients made up Nonna Gigi's famous lasagna wafted throughout the room, reminding Grace of simpler times.

She inhaled deeply, wishing she could find a way to capture the scent for those times when life got rough. "That smells amazing."

"Always does." Mama set the pan atop the stainless-steel stove, then grabbed a sheet pan that held a split loaf of French bread spread with garlic butter and sprinkled with cheese. "Now all I have to do is get this garlic bread baked." She set the pan in the oven and adjusted the heat.

Hearing Kaleb's voice in the other room, Grace opened the drawer and took out another knife, fork and spoon. "Mama?"

"Yes, baby." Leaning her hip against the island, she gave Grace her full attention.

Grace pushed the drawer closed. "Did you know Kaleb was injured in the army?" His revelation had stunned, if not shamed, her. Sure she'd noticed that something was a little off in his gait on occasion, but she thought maybe he had a bad knee. Boy, was she wrong.

"Oh, yes. He doesn't hide it. In fact, he's an inspiration to everyone here, sharing his story at area schools and churches. He's our own real-life hero."

A hero whose title had come at a great price. Yet he didn't seem bitter or angry, and she wondered how that could be.

"Good evening, ladies."

Both Grace and her mother turned at the sound of Kaleb's deep voice.

"Hello there, Kaleb." Mama tossed her potholders on the island. "We're so happy you could join us."

"Are you kidding? After hearing Grace talk about her grandmother's lasagna all afternoon, I was thrilled when Roger extended the invitation."

His attention shifted to Grace then, his smile reaching across the room, wrapping around her heart like a warm blanket on a cold night.

She couldn't help noticing that while she'd come directly from work, he'd changed into a pair of dark wash jeans and a tailored red-and-white button-down that hugged his muscular torso. His hair was also damp, indicating he'd likely showered.

Nothing like being shown up by a guy. Especially one who'd suddenly garnered a great deal of her respect.

Making dinner with Mama and Roger seem like a cakewalk compared to spending the evening with a guy whose character and outlook on life had her taking a long, hard look at herself…and not liking what she saw.

Kaleb had hoped for a relaxing evening and, so far, it had been just that. While there was no question that he wanted to support Roger by being here for him, he feared things could be a little tense. After the way he shut Grace down today… And even though they'd patched things up, one never knew how well that patch might hold.

Sitting in Roger and Donna's dining room, next to Grace, no less, Kaleb finished his last bite of lasagna. "Donna, your grandmother's lasagna has a new fan." He set his fork atop his empty plate. "I've never tasted anything like it." It was the perfect balance of meat, cheese and pasta. And those seasonings. Just the right kick, without overpowering the other flavors.

Grace's mother dabbed the corners of her mouth with her cloth napkin. "That's the response this recipe usually gets."

"I only wish she'd make it more often." Roger nudged

his wife's elbow with his own, sending her a playful grin.

Donna blushed, returning her napkin to her lap. "Kaleb, I can't tell you how excited I am about the Hometown Heroes exhibit at the museum."

His chest tightened. The way it always did when his name and the word *hero* were used in the same sentence. He was no hero.

"Hometown heroes? Museum?" Grace spooned another small portion of lasagna onto her plate. Her third helping, if he wasn't mistaken. Where did she put it?

Donna addressed her daughter. "I volunteer at the historical museum here in town. We're planning to have a whole room dedicated to those men and women from Ouray who have served our country. We've received a few items—everything from photos to uniforms to ration cards—dating back to the First and Second World Wars, the Korean War and Vietnam." She smiled at Kaleb. "However, our most recent hero is going to round things out for us. Make the exhibit more personal and real by bringing it into the twenty-first century."

Eager to deflect the unwanted attention, Kaleb motioned toward Roger. "What about Roger? I'm sure he's got lots of items."

"Are you kidding?" Roger draped an arm across the back of his wife's chair. "Donna had me pulling boxes from my Vietnam days out of the attic weeks ago."

"We'll have the ribbon cutting on June twenty-third, a day we're calling Hometown Heroes Day, and Kaleb here has volunteered to give a short speech, along with our other donors."

Volunteered? More like coerced. A bunch of women

ganging up on him like that, plying him with all kinds of baked goods. A fellow didn't stand a chance.

Now he was committed.

"When do you think you'll have your items ready for us?" Donna smiled sweetly.

"I need to finish sorting through everything." Of course, before he could finish, he needed to actually start the process. For now, the untouched boxes were still stacked in one of his spare bedrooms, right where his parents had left them a month ago. He knew he needed to move a lever. Yet every time he thought about it, a sense of dread seemed to settle over him. "It's a little overwhelming."

"I can imagine." Leaning back, Donna folded her hands in her lap. "You were in the army how many years?"

"Eight."

Grace rested her elbow on the table, perched her chin on her palm and stared at him. "How many tours of duty?"

"Three. All in the Middle East."

Donna gasped. "I just had an idea."

Kaleb and Grace collectively turned to her mother.

"Grace, why don't you help Kaleb sort through his things?"

A look of horror flashed across Grace's face. She straightened, lowering her arm. "Mama, I don't think that's really appropriate. There may be some things that Kaleb doesn't want anyone else to see."

Donna laid a hand at the base of her neck. "Yes, I suppose you're right." She met Kaleb's gaze. "I apologize if I was out of line, Kaleb."

"No worries, Donna."

"Well, so long as we have everything by June ninth, we should be okay." Donna pushed away from the table. "Who's interested in dessert?"

Despite his stomach being twisted in knots with guilt, Kaleb managed to down a slice of chocolate cake, another of Grace's purported favorites, before bidding Roger and Donna farewell.

"I'm going to say good-night, too." Grace grabbed her jacket and pack from the closet near the front door. "Thank you for dinner, Mama." She hugged her mother, the gesture appearing more heartfelt than the one they'd shared earlier that day. "The lasagna was even better than I remembered."

Outside, the last vestiges of daylight faded in the western sky. The night air was cool, something he was used to, but he was glad Grace had a jacket.

They strolled along Fifth Street, silent. Was she feeling as sheepish in the wake of this afternoon's events as he was? He struggled to think of something to say, but couldn't.

Finally, "I, uh—" Grace stepped into the void. "I'm sorry for what my mother said. About me helping you. Obviously she's a little out of touch."

"Ah, she's harmless. I know there was no ill intent."

After another pause, Grace continued. "You haven't begun to sort through your stuff, have you?"

Wow. He wasn't expecting that. "You figured that out, huh?"

"Yep." Her gaze remained straight ahead.

For some odd reason, he felt relieved. As if his secret was finally out in the open. "I have every intention of meeting that deadline, you know."

"I know." Hands stuffed in the pockets of her jacket,

she forged on. "But delving into your past makes you uneasy."

.   "How did you know?" He'd known this woman barely twenty-four hours and yet she was able to read him so well.

She shrugged. "We all have pasts."

He followed her around the corner at Seventh Avenue. "It's not like I'm hiding anything."

"I understand. You'd just prefer the past remain in the past."

"Sort of. It's just—"

She stopped in the middle of the street. Looked at him with eyes that seemed to cut right through him. "Just what?"

"Um— My prosthetic. Challenges. You know." Now it was his turn to shrug.

"Memories."

One innocuous word but, boy, did it pack a punch. "Yeah."

Her weak smile said she understood. "They have a way of sneaking up on us, don't they?"

Us? What memories did Grace not want to unearth?

"I can't imagine what you've gone through, Kaleb. But your sacrifice deserves to be honored. People *want* to honor it. Why not let them?"

Because they might see that I'm a fraud. That I'm not worthy of their honor.

They crossed Main Street, the sound of the river growing louder as they approached. Much like the turmoil cutting a swath through him. Why couldn't he go through those boxes? What was he so afraid of?

Perhaps Grace's mother was right. Maybe he did need

help. Someone to give him direction and keep him on task. After all, he had a deadline and he was a man of his word.

But who would he ask? His mother would want him to donate everything. His father was too close to the situation, too. Maybe Roger. He was military and knew how to cut to the chase. Though Kaleb hated to take him away from Donna.

Why his gaze drifted to the woman walking beside him was beyond comprehension. He barely knew her. Still, she was military. So, in a practical sense, she would know what might be best for the museum. And, now that he thought about it, not having any personal attachment to him or anyone else might actually make her the best person for the job.

But there was a lot of stuff in those boxes. Stuff that spanned his life from boyhood to manhood. Did he really want her sifting through every photo and newspaper article? From basic training to the IED that ended his career.

They rounded onto Oak Street and Kaleb realized they were almost to the RV park. He'd been so lost in thought that he not only lost track of time, but location, as well. He hadn't intended to walk Grace home, though he supposed it was the gentlemanly thing to do.

Unfortunately, he didn't believe in accidents. God wanted him to walk Grace home for a reason. And as he continued to ponder the boxes in his spare room, he had a pretty good idea what that reason was.

"Grace?" He stopped in front of the empty campsite just down from hers and turned to look at her. "Would you be interested in helping me dig through my military memorabilia? I realize I'm asking a lot—I mean, you barely even know me—but I need help."

She watched him, seemingly intrigued. "How much stuff are we talking about?"

"At least a dozen boxes."

Her eyes widened. "No wonder you're overwhelmed."

He lifted a shoulder. "My mom insisted I share everything with her, and since I didn't know what was important and what wasn't, I had an ongoing box that I'd toss stuff into. When one got full, I'd send it to her and start on another."

Grace smiled then. "That's actually pretty sweet. Not many guys would be that considerate."

"You obviously haven't met my mother."

Grace snickered.

"So what do you say, Grace? Would you be willing to forfeit your free time to help a poor soul?"

"Give up my free time? Boy, you really know how to sell this."

"What if I throw in dinner?"

"Okay, now you're speaking my language." She crossed her arms over her chest, her gaze narrowing. "So why do you want me to help you?"

He stuffed his hands into the pockets of his jeans. "I don't know. I guess for the same reasons I hired you as my office manager. Military background, attention to detail…"

She nodded, yet remained silent for a moment. "Okay, I'll do it." Lowering her arms, she turned and took two steps toward her campsite before twisting back around. "And just so you'll know, steak is my favorite meal."

Chapter Five

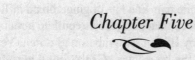

Grace wandered up Seventh Avenue three days later, surprised at how quickly Ouray had begun to take up residence in her heart, granting her a measure of tranquillity she hadn't known in a long time. She never would have thought the fabric of small-town life would feel so good. Yet here she was, savoring every cozy thread.

The laid-back lifestyle was a pleasant change. Much different from the navy. And the cruise ship would likely keep her hopping, too. Day and night. She'd better enjoy this while she had the chance.

Diet Dr Pepper in hand, she eased onto Fourth Street as the sun drifted farther below the town's western slope. After work, she'd gone back to her campsite and changed into a pair of sweatpants and a baggy sweater. If she was going to spend her evening weeding through a bunch of dusty boxes, she was going to be comfortable doing it.

She still wasn't sure why she'd agreed to help Kaleb sort through his army stuff. Didn't they spend enough time together at work? Or was Kaleb one of the reasons she was enjoying her time in Ouray?

Her steps slowed. That had to be the most ludicrous thought she'd ever had. She was about to embark on a high-seas adventure. See places she'd only dreamed of. The last thing she needed was a man in her life.

So why was her stomach fluttering at the sight of Kaleb's single-story bungalow?

Yellow with white trim and lots of gingerbread millwork, the house beckoned passersby to pull up a rocking chair and enjoy life on its wraparound porch. Yet for as inviting as the house was, Grace found herself with a sudden case of nerves.

What was she? Sixteen again? She was there only to help him make a dent in those boxes.

With a bolstering breath, she downed the last of her drink, nudged her anxiety out of the way and continued up the walk onto the porch and rang the bell.

A few moments later, Kaleb appeared behind the screen door wearing the same medium wash jeans and work shirt she'd grown accustomed to seeing him in.

"You're just in time." He pushed the door open, inviting her inside.

"For what?" She slipped past him.

"I was just about to throw a couple of rib eyes on the grill."

Her mouth watered at the mention of steak. "But I thought we were going to—"

"You haven't eaten, have you?"

Following him toward the kitchen, she dared a few peeks at the rest of his house.

For as classic and feminine as the outside of Kaleb's house was, the inside was classically male. The living room had dark brown furniture positioned in front of a large flat-screen television and the dark wood coffee table was littered with game controllers and a laptop.

The next room had likely once been a dining room. Sadly, it was now a gym, complete with a treadmill, weight bench and chin-up bar.

This lovely old home, victimized by a bachelor.

"No. But—"

"I figured, why settle for sandwiches when we could have steak."

But steak was an official meal. Like a— She gulped. A date.

That's what you get for telling him you like steak.

She had done that, hadn't she?

She cringed.

"How do you like yours cooked?" He tossed the words over his shoulder as they entered the kitchen.

"M-medium rare."

He snagged a plate with two thick slabs of meat from the kitchen counter and continued on to the back door. "Care to join me?"

"Sure." Tossing her empty can into the wastebasket as she passed, she followed him outside, admiring the small, though well maintained, backyard. "Anything I can do?"

The meat sizzled as he laid it atop the hot grates.

"Nope." He adjusted the steaks with a pair of tongs. "Baked potatoes are in the oven. Should be ready by the time the steaks are. I've got butter, sour cream, shredded cheese and bacon bits for those. Salad has already been tossed and is in the fridge."

Holy cow. In her world, that was a three-course dinner. "Sounds like you've been busy."

"Not really." He sent her a sheepish grin. "I used bagged salad."

She couldn't help smiling. "That's my favorite way to prepare it."

"I'm curious," he said as they delved into their meal twenty minutes later. "What are you planning to do come September? When you're finished at Mountain View Tours?"

Sitting at a tiny round table tucked in the corner of the living room, she used her knife to slice off another bite of perfectly seasoned meat. "I'll be working as an excursions manager with Crowned Prince Cruise Lines."

He paused, his knife and fork in midair. "Seriously?"

She nodded, attacking her food. "The ship is in dry dock, undergoing renovations. My contract starts September fifteenth." She shrugged. "Hence the reason for temporary employment."

"You're not making this up, are you?" He watched her across the table.

"No." She paused her eating. "Why would I?"

He shook his head. "I've just never known anyone who's wanted to do that before."

"It's the same reason I joined the navy. The open seas. Exotic ports of call."

"But what about a home? Don't you want to settle somewhere?"

Her shoulders sagged. She'd tried that. It didn't work out.

Setting her utensils on her plate, she reached for her water, hoping to convey an air of confidence. "I prefer a more nomadic lifestyle. I mean, growing up, my parents were always moving here and there. It suits me."

He watched her curiously as she took a sip, but didn't say a word.

Uncomfortable with the sudden silence, she picked up her plate. "I think it's time we get started on those boxes."

After putting their dishes in the dishwasher, he led her down a short hallway to a small bedroom filled with boxes.

"This is my storage room."

"I can see that." Kaleb had more stuff in one room than she even owned. "Please tell me this isn't *all* memorabilia."

"No. Just these two stacks right here." He laid his hand atop the two that were just as tall as he was. Bankers boxes, no less. Not the small boxes she'd imagined he'd sent his mother.

"Kaleb, your mother is one blessed woman. But this is going to take us *forever*."

"Now you understand my predicament." He lifted one from the top of the stack and set it on the floor. "Shall we?"

She dropped to her knees and blew out a breath. "We gotta start somewhere."

He lifted the lid. Inside were photos and newspaper articles. He picked up a picture. "This was from basic training." He studied the photo. Touched a finger to it. "Beau LeBlanc."

"What?" She leaned in for a closer look.

"Beau LeBlanc. He was my first friend at camp Benning. We were together every step of the way." Kaleb was silent a moment before clearing his throat. "All the way to the end."

Her heart twisted. No wonder Kaleb didn't want to

go through these boxes. They were littered not only with memories, but painful ones at that. Memories he carried with him every single day in a very real way.

What should she do? Try to change the subject or let him remember?

Kaleb made the decision for her. "Beau was a Southerner to the core. Though not necessarily a gentleman. He had some spicy lingo, that one. Didn't take flak from no one." Kaleb looked at her without ever seeming to see her. "Then he met Vanessa and all that changed. I've never seen a guy mind his p's and q's as quickly as he did. He knew he'd hit pay dirt with her."

"Did they get married?"

"Just as soon as he could talk her into it." Kaleb's gaze fell to the worn hardwood floor. "Vanessa was pregnant when he was killed. Beau never got to see his little girl."

Grace's eyes fell closed. She would not cry in front of this man who was so grieved by the loss of his friends. Turning, she swiped away a couple of wayward tears before looking at Kaleb again.

"They're coming here, you know."

She watched him with curiosity. "Who?"

"The families. After I bought Mountain View Tours, Vanessa and one of the other wives thought it would be good to have a reunion here. So they're all coming to Ouray next month. Wives, kids, parents…"

"I can see that." Grace stretched her legs out in front of her. "They share a common bond."

"I just don't understand why they have to drag me into it." Kaleb stood, dropping the photo back into the box. "Perhaps we should do this another time." He held out a hand to help her up.

Allowing Kaleb to pull her to her feet, Grace was befuddled. Why wouldn't he want to see his friends' families? Their children? Didn't he realize he was their last connection to their loved ones?

She wished she knew the story surrounding the IED attack. But this definitely wasn't the time to ask. For now, she could only surmise that Kaleb was suffering from survivor's guilt.

"Whatever you think is best."

Perhaps next time, she'd suggest she go through the boxes alone and then bring any prospective museum items to him for approval. Seeing the pain swimming in Kaleb's suddenly dark eyes, though, she wondered if there would be a next time.

What was best was to leave the past in the past.

Kaleb had been a fool to think that having someone else with him would make this job any easier.

Standing in his spare room, staring down at Grace, he could only imagine what she must think of him. He recognized the pity in her gaze as she looked up at him. It was the same look his ex-fiancée, Gina, had as she sat with him at Walter Reed Medical Center.

Grace's pity was the last thing he wanted.

"I'll walk you home." He turned for the door.

"That's not necessary." She was on his heels as he started down the hall.

"Yes. It is." He tossed the words over his shoulder as they entered the living room. "It's dark outside." Besides, he needed the fresh air.

"I'm a big girl, Kaleb. I've walked alone in the dark before."

He jerked open the front door. "Yeah, well, not on my watch."

Outside, the night air was cooler than he'd expected. Just what he needed to clear his head and send those haunting memories back where they belonged.

"Thank you for dinner," said Grace as they started up the street. "That was the best steak I've had in a long time."

"You're welcome." The words came out harsher than he'd intended and he could sense Grace pulling away. She didn't deserve that. Not after she'd done so much to help him.

Touching her elbow, he stopped.

She followed suit.

"I appreciate your willingness to help me." He made sure to keep his words soft. "You've been nothing but great. Sorry I turned into such a jerk."

"No apology needed. However—" she shoved her hands into the pockets of her sweatpants "—if you'd like to talk about it, I've got a nice stack of wood just waiting for a campfire."

While steak might be Grace's weakness, campfires were his. The smell alone was the best aromatherapy ever. But she'd also thrown in the word *talk*. As if it was a stipulation. Nothing like driving a hard bargain.

"I may not be very forthcoming." He could at least be truthful.

Under the dim streetlamp, he saw something flicker in her eye. "We'll see about that."

"Is that a challenge?"

"Call it what you want." After a momentary stare-down, she continued on, as though the gauntlet had been thrown down.

He walked beside her, uncertainty plaguing his every step. *Talk about it.*

Grace was practically a stranger. Why would she think he'd talk to her?

You're the one who asked her to help you go through your stuff.

Okay, so maybe Grace understood him better than most people. But only in terms of the military experience. Still, she hadn't suffered the loss of a comrade.

Arriving at her campsite, he spotted the stack of wood in question.

"So, what do you think?" She playfully eyed the small fire pit. "Seems like a nice night for a fire." She picked up a handful of kindling.

Surrounded by the sounds of the night, he studied the area. The camper. The canopy. The lone camp chair. "There's only seating for one."

Pursing her lips, she shook her head. "Nope. I've got a cooler that makes a great seat."

It was almost as though she were daring him to open up. In that case, "Bring it on."

The mischievous light in her eyes had him immediately rethinking things. Yet, before he knew it, an inferno threatened to overtake the tiny fire pit.

"Care for a drink? Water? Diet Dr Pepper?" With the pizzazz of a flight attendant, she smiled at him.

"No. I'm good." He picked up the lone camp chair and moved it from the canopy to the fire pit. For all practical purposes, they were alone. The nearest neighbor a large RV across the way.

He breathed in the aroma of fire and waited for calm to infuse his being. But it never came.

Grace settled beside him, atop the large cooler, a Diet Dr Pepper in hand. "Nice fire, huh?"

"Kinda small, if you ask me."

"Yeah, I'm a bit limited here. You should consider building a big fire pit in your backyard."

He glowered at her. "Maybe I will."

"Might come in handy." Her smug look teased him.

"Okay, what is it you want to know?" He wasn't afraid to call her bluff.

"I don't recall asking anything." She stared at the fire. "Though there's obviously something bothering you."

He leaned forward in his seat, rubbing his hands together. "And what do you think that something might be?"

"Why don't you tell me?" Her sideways glance only served to bug him more. But then, she already knew that.

"You're relentless, you know?"

She took a swig of her diet soda. "I have no idea what you're talking about."

He watched her a moment, his blood pressure rising. He knew what she wanted. The question was, could he give it to her?

A part of him wanted to. The other part wanted to fight tooth and nail.

The odd thing was, he'd told his story to countless people, giving motivational speeches at area schools, churches and service organizations. Too many people had given up on themselves, on life and on God because they were too focused on what they didn't have. He wanted to encourage them to think about what they did have.

Yet talking with Grace about the event seemed, somehow, different. Back at the house, she'd got a glimpse of him at his worst. And he'd found himself on the receiving end of her pity.

He didn't want Grace's pity. He simply wanted her to know.

"Five years ago I was driving a Humvee and hit a trip wire." For as often as he'd shared his story, this time he found himself hesitating. He took a breath and forged ahead. "I don't remember much about the actual event. Just the sound of the explosion and then waking up in an army hospital several days later."

He shifted slightly, adjusting his artificial leg. "Of course, I had no idea what had happened. So my parents filled in the blanks the best they could." He looked over at Grace. "Seems the explosion packed enough punch to send that nine-thousand-pound vehicle flying through the air."

Her smile was a sad one.

"They explained that my jaw had been shattered, I'd been burned and that I'd lost my leg. And that my buddies…" He cleared the emotion that never failed to thicken his throat.

"I can't imagine how difficult that must have been." Illuminated by only the firelight, she twisted to face him. "But why do you blame yourself?"

"Who said that?"

"You did. Though not in so many words."

He searched her face, wondering how this woman could possibly read him so well. "What are you? Some kind of shrink?"

She puffed out a laugh. "Hardly. Just too curious for my own good."

The fire snapped and hissed, sending a shower of sparks into the air.

"Okay, then here you go. I don't like being called a hero and I don't need anybody's pity."

"Why would they pity you?"

"Why don't you tell me?"

Her gaze narrowed. "What are you getting at?"

"I saw the way you looked at me when I was talking about Beau. I don't need you to feel sorry for me, Grace."

"Feel sorry for you?" Setting her soda can down on the cooler, she stood. "I think you'd better get your eyes checked. The only thing I was feeling back there was your pain." She started to pace. "I can't even begin to comprehend the anguish you must feel over the loss of your friends. Or the torture you had to endure as you fought your way back from your injuries. I admire you. So to have you cheapen that by saying I feel sorry for you? I've got news for you, buddy. You're not worthy of my pity."

Chapter Six

Grace lay in her bed the next morning, listening to the rain slap against the waterproof fabric of the camper top, trying to decide who was the bigger fool. Kaleb for believing she felt sorry for him or her for going off on her boss. After all, the Kaleb of last night was not the same Kaleb she'd worked with all week. Last night's was a torn, grieving man, while the Kaleb that was her boss was one of the most positive and encouraging people she'd ever known.

No telling which one she'd face at work today. Assuming she still had a job, after the way she dismissed him last night.

She'd just have to apologize and prove herself worthy of her position with Mountain View Tours. Because there wasn't another job in town that paid as well. And she certainly wasn't going to spend the rest of the summer staying with her mother or Lucy.

Frustrated, she pulled the pillow from beneath her head, covered her face and screamed into the fluffiness.

There. That felt better.

She again tucked the pillow under her head and burrowed deeper under the covers, savoring a few more minutes of nothingness.

A drop of water landed on her cheek. Followed by another.

"What on earth…" She bounded off the bed that sat a couple of feet higher than the floor, eyeing her fabric roof. "Waterproof, my eye." Rubbing her bare arms, she spotted a leak in the ceiling. A tiny hole. Nothing some duct tape wouldn't fix.

She shivered as she opened the storage compartment beneath her mattress and rummaged through everything from extra blankets, to clothes, to her toolbox, but came up empty-handed. Turning her attention to the floor, she dropped to her knees and dug through her saddlebags.

"Where could that—" She snagged her gray navy sweatshirt and tugged it over her tank top as she stood. That was when she saw it.

Her breath. Clouding the frigid morning air.

In May? One should not be able to see their breath in the month of May. That was, unless they lived in Alaska.

Obviously, she'd spent too much time in warmer climates.

Her gaze inadvertently drifted heavenward and she huffed out a cloudy breath.

A few minutes later, she found the tape. It was indeed in her storage compartment, only inside her toolbox, which she'd failed to open the first go-round. By the time she patched the hole, the rain had stopped.

When she emerged from her tent a short time later, dressed in something warmer than her pajamas, gray clouds hovered over the town, obscuring the mountaintops. The air was still, yet damp and cold. She zipped up her jacket, annoyed that neither her sister nor her mother had warned her to bring some warmer clothes.

Fearful of more rain, she hauled a tarp from her storage compartment, along with some rope. Even with the hole patched, an extra layer of protection couldn't hurt. Might mean the difference between climbing into a wet bed or a dry one. Call her crazy, but she preferred her bedding dry.

Outside, she unfolded the blue plastic sheet and looped a rope through each corner. Then, standing on the tongue of the trailer, she attempted to throw one corner over the tent. At five foot seven, she wasn't exactly short, but since the tent peaked somewhere around seven feet, this was going to be a challenge.

"Looks like somebody could use a little help."

Grace jerked around at the sound of Kaleb's deep voice, the rubber sole of her riding boot slipping on the tongue's wet metal. She tried to catch herself, but fell backward, stumbling right into Kaleb.

"I gotcha."

Her heart broke into a thundering gallop as strong hands gently gripped her arms and lifted her straight. Warmth radiated from Kaleb's body, and she found herself longing to be enveloped in his embrace.

Shocked by the notion, she turned to face him, too embarrassed to look him in the eye. "What are you doing here?"

"Uh—hoping to ply you with a peace offering?" His brown insulated jacket looked a lot warmer than her leather number and she found herself coveting the black beanie pulled over his head and ears.

"What?" She pushed the hair out of her face, tucking it behind both ears.

"You had me awake half the night."

She felt both of her eyebrows reaching for the sky.

"Well, not *you*, but what you said."

Chagrin washed over her. She toed at the dirt with her boot. "Yeah, about that—"

"You were right."

Her gaze shot to his. "I was?"

"Yes. I owe you an apology for acting like a self-centered, misguided fool." He moved toward the picnic table. "And, since it's a cold morning, I thought I'd bring you hot coffee and breakfast to help win your forgiveness."

"Wait a minute." She scrubbed her hands over her face. "You have hot coffee?"

"Right here." He gestured to the cardboard carrier that held two cups. "I picked them up on my way over." He grabbed one and handed it to her. "Almost lost them when you fell, though."

"Well, I'm glad you didn't." She took hold of the cup, blessed heat seeping into her frozen fingers.

She took a sip, the hot liquid warming her from the inside out.

"There's some sugar and creamer in case you need it." He pointed to the cup holder.

"No, black is perfect."

"I had a feeling it might be."

She sent him a curious look.

"You were military. We learn to drink our coffee strong and black."

She puffed out a laugh and watched as it hung in the damp air. "And sometimes with chunks."

He nodded. "You won't have to worry about that today. Granny's Kitchen brews a decent cuppa joe, but without chunks." He reached behind him. "Celeste Purcell, the

proprietor, also makes the best cinnamon rolls in town."
He held up a white bag. "Get 'em while they're hot."

Grace couldn't help it. She simply stood there, blinking. A hot breakfast on this cold morning was more than she could have asked for. And far more than she would have managed on her own.

"Hello?" Kaleb waved the bag in her direction.

"Yes. Let's eat." She accepted a large, warm roll and a napkin and promptly picked off an icing-laden chunk. The sweet, gooey goodness practically melted in her mouth, filling her with a sugar-induced wave of delight. "This is *so* good."

"Does that mean I'm forgiven?"

Considering she had planned on apologizing to him… "Definitely."

Smiling, Kaleb eyed her tarp that now lay on the ground. "What were you trying to do up there?"

She held a hand in front of her mouth and spoke around her second bite. "There's a leak in my woof." She swallowed before continuing. "I patched it with duct tape, but looking at these clouds, I thought it might be a good idea to add an extra layer of protection."

"Do you have a heater in this thing?" He pointed to her camper.

Savoring another bite, she shook her head.

"Is that your only coat?"

She eyed her leather jacket. "Mmm-hmm."

Frowning, he said, "I'll be right back." He walked past her, gravel crunching beneath every booted step, and continued on to his Jeep, retrieved something from the backseat and returned. "It might be a little big, but it's warm." He handed her an insulated jacket, similar to the one he wore, only tan.

Grace was taken aback by the gesture. "Oh, I don't—"

"Yes, you do. Can. However, you were planning to object."

This was the Kaleb she'd experienced all week. The one who put others above himself. Suddenly she wondered if that wasn't what he was doing with his buddies who died. They were his heroes. And he'd let them down.

Which made the hero label people affixed to him feel as scratchy as woolen undergarments.

"Thank you." She spread the coat he gave her over her legs, humbled to realize that Kaleb hadn't just picked up coffee and breakfast. He'd actually put some thought into his actions.

It had been a long time since someone had anticipated her needs. Certainly no one on the ship. Even Aaron had grown accustomed to letting her take care of herself.

Hands perched low on his hips, Kaleb moved to the front of the trailer and studied her roof. Then he picked up the tarp and, with one strategic toss, sent it sailing. A few seconds later, the entire tarp covered her camper.

"You sure made that look easy." She stuffed the last bite of roll in her mouth and wiped her hands before hurrying to secure each corner with a stake.

"Height had its advantages."

He definitely had plenty of advantage, then.

"Everything secure?" He watched her as she finished hammering in the last stake.

"Yep." She approached him, hammer in hand, her stomach filled with that peculiar fluttering again. "Thank you for breakfast."

"My pleasure." He stared down at her, making her feel more petite than tall.

"I really should get ready for work."

"I'm sure your boss will understand if you're late."

Yes! She still had a job.

"Perhaps. But I'm not one to push the envelope."

He quirked a brow. "I don't know about that."

Her gaze lowered. "Yeah..."

Laying a finger to her chin, he tilted her head to look at him. "Thank you for holding me accountable."

Her mouth went dry. "I—uh..."

The corners of his mouth lifted. "What are you planning to work on today?"

"Well, I..." *The website, you idiot.* "The website. Now that the brochures are off to the printer, I'm hoping to finish the website."

"I'm still in awe of your talents, Grace." He dropped his hand and she found herself missing his touch. "Seems wherever I'm lacking, you know just how to pick up the slack." He turned and waved as he started for his Jeep. "See you at the office."

Grace watched him walk away, feeling a little disconcerted. For someone who wasn't comfortable with the hero tag, Kaleb had waltzed in here and saved her entire morning. And while looking after one's creature comforts might not seem very superheroesque, it meant everything to her. Not to mention, spoke volumes about the man behind it.

She started for her tent. Fortunately for her, she wasn't looking for a hero.

Kaleb stared at the computer screen, unable to contain the wide grin that spread across his face. A new tagline, new brochures and, now, a new website. Was there anything Grace couldn't do? In only a few days, she'd single-handedly changed the face of Mountain View Tours.

So, as the sun rose on a new week, it seemed only fitting they start revamping the front office, too. He'd picked up the paint from the hardware store this morning and his mom and sister, along with Grace's mother, were scheduled to be there at ten.

Excitement welled inside him. He could hardly wait for Memorial weekend and the grand opening of the *new* Mountain View Tours.

"Good morning." Grace breezed into the room, holding a can of Diet Dr Pepper, wearing torn, faded jeans, flip-flops and her leather jacket. Her long dark hair was pulled back in a ponytail and covered with a well-worn navy ball cap. Not her usual work attire, but then, he didn't make a habit of wearing holey cargos and a T-shirt left over from basic training either.

"Morning." He sipped his coffee. "And how was your Mother's Day?"

"It was quite nice actually." She paused at the counter. "After church, Roger took Mama and me out to dinner in Montrose and then we all went to the hot springs pool."

"That's weird. I saw Donna and Roger at church. How'd I miss you?"

"I…" Her gaze lowered momentarily before bouncing back to his. "Was taking advantage of my one and only day to sleep in."

Why did he get the feeling that Grace wasn't giving him the whole truth?

"What did you do yesterday?" Obviously eager to shift the conversation.

"Dad, Scott and I fixed dinner while Mom and Sami lost themselves in far too much HGTV."

"Where was Jack?"

"With us guys, of course."

"Ah, I see you got the paint." She eyed the three cans stacked against the wall.

"Yep. We're all set." He turned back to the computer. "Come here a minute. I need your opinion on something."

"Sure." She took a sip of her soda before joining him behind the counter. "What's up?"

"This." He pointed to the screen.

Setting her drink on the counter, she looked from the image back to him. "What am I looking at?"

"Carpet tiles." He reached for the mouse. "Let me show you a better picture." He clicked on the image of a carpeted room.

She leaned in for a closer look. "Those are carpet tiles?"

"Yep."

"Wow. They look really nice." She straightened. "Are they for your house?"

"No. They're for the office." He pointed to the unadorned floor.

"Really?" Her eyes were as big as her smile. "You mean no more cold concrete?"

"That's right."

She perched a hand on her hip. "All right, who are you and what have you done with Kaleb?"

"Very funny." He shifted his attention back to the computer screen, hoping she couldn't see the heat he felt creeping up his neck. "Let's just say I'm starting to see the wisdom in what you and Sami have been saying."

"What was that?" She leaned closer. "I didn't quite hear you." Grace was enjoying this way too much.

"You were right, okay. Are you happy now?"

Her satisfied grin said it all. "Ecstatic."

"I have to say—" he leaned against the low bookcase behind the desk, crossing his arms over his chest "—I'm pretty stoked about this makeover. Not to mention the grand opening."

"Me, too." She shrugged out of her jacket, revealing a paint-splattered United States Navy T-shirt. "I'm glad I get to be part of it."

Moving to the opposite corner, she tossed her jacket onto a limb of the coat tree. "Have you given any thought to this counter?" Smoothing a hand along the finished wood top, she made her way around to the other side. "We can work with the top, maybe sand and restain it, but this particleboard on the front doesn't hold much potential."

"I thought you were planning to keep any more suggestions to yourself?" He followed her, liking the way she took such an interest in Mountain View Tours. As though it were important to her.

She lifted a shoulder. "I changed my mind." Still pondering the face of the reception desk, she said, "What if we covered it with some beadboard paneling, then painted it the same red as the trim."

"Hmm…" He rubbed his chin, trying to visualize the red.

The door opened then and a bearded man entered, carrying what appeared to be a file folder.

"Welcome to Mountain View Tours." Kaleb offered his hand.

The man took it. "Are you the owner?"

"Yes, sir. Kaleb Palmer."

"I'm Barry Swanson with the Bureau of Land Management." Since when did government agencies make personal visits?

Kaleb studied the man, who was slightly shorter than himself and wore wire-rimmed glasses. "What can I do for you, Mr. Swanson?"

"Barry, please." Still holding the folder, he crossed his hands in front of him. "As I'm sure you're aware, Jeep tour companies need permits from the BLM in order to operate on land owned by the forest service."

"Yes, I am aware of that."

"How long have you owned Mountain View Tours, Mr. Palmer?"

"Kaleb. Since the end of February." He assumed his at-ease stance, feet apart, hands clasped behind his back.

Barry opened the file folder. "I'm sorry, Kaleb, but we have no record of your request for permits."

"Mr. Chapman, the previous owner, said he had taken care of them. That even though the business had changed owners, the permits would carry over."

Barry shook his head. "I'm afraid Mr. Chapman was mistaken. Not only did we not receive his paperwork, permits are not grandfathered in based on a change of ownership."

Kaleb's throat constricted. "I see. When is the paperwork due?"

Barry closed the file. "They were due in March."

Kaleb felt as if the air had been sucked out his lungs. All of his plans. The grand opening. He could almost hear the door slamming on his dreams.

Why hadn't he followed up on those permits and made sure they were taken care of? Instead, he was focused on trucks and Jeeps.

Panic wormed its way through his being. A feeling he knew well and despised.

"Mr. Swanson, I'm Grace McAllen, Mr. Palmer's office manager." She shook his hand. "I'm curious. Suppose Kaleb hadn't purchased the business until April or even this month. Would he still have been allowed to apply for the permits?"

"Yes, ma'am." The field officer tapped the file against his leg. "As I said, the permits do not carry over, so a new one would have to be issued, and then every subsequent year, the paperwork would be due in March."

Kaleb wasn't sure what Grace was up to, but she seemed to have a better mind for business than he did. So when she met his gaze, he issued a quick nod, urging her to continue.

Her attention returned to Mr. Swanson. "Since Kaleb was led to believe that the permits had not only been granted, but grandfathered in, is it possible you could extend him a little grace?"

The field officer appeared to mull over her request. He studied Kaleb first, then the antiquated office. "Back when Dale Hannon owned this place, it ranked among the best tour companies in town."

Clearing his throat, Kaleb straightened, hands at his sides as though he were still in the army. "Yes, sir. And I intend to do everything in my power to show guests we're worthy of that distinction once again."

Lips pursed until his mouth disappeared behind his brownish-red beard, Barry nodded, still studying the space. Did he think it was a hopeless cause or was he recalling Mountain View Tours' former glory?

Finally, just when Kaleb thought he couldn't take it anymore, Barry opened the folder, pulled out a small stack of papers and handed them to Kaleb.

"You'll need to fill these out and provide all of the

information listed there on the first page. Paperwork and fees will be due ASAP."

Relief washed over Kaleb, like air-conditioning on a steamy day.

"This is Monday…" said Grace. "What if we got them to you by, say, next Monday?"

Good plan. That would give them the weekend to work on things.

The man looked at Kaleb. "Do you have your general liability insurance?"

Kaleb nodded. "Yes, sir."

"Then let's shoot for Friday. Preferably by noon."

"This Friday?" For the first time, the despair Kaleb felt sparked in Grace's hazel eyes.

"Yes, ma'am."

What had they got themselves into? Neither he nor Grace knew anything about the paperwork Barry tasked them to do. And if there was one thing Kaleb knew about government agencies, it was that their paperwork was never easy.

He examined the documents in his hand, noting what all they required. "Any recommendations on how I come up with these estimates of land use?"

"Most people go back to their drivers' logs from previous years and base it off those numbers. Fees are based on the numbers you give. I know this is your first season, but you'll need to be as accurate as possible."

Accurate? How could they expect him to be accurate when he'd never done this before? And he didn't have a clue as to where the drivers' logs were, if there were even any here. Still…

"I understand." He shook the man's hand. "Thank you, sir."

As Mr. Swanson departed, Kaleb's gaze remained fixed on Grace. Not only had she gone to bat for him, as far as he was concerned, she'd hit a grand slam.

She shifted her weight from one foot to the other. Crossed her arms over her chest, looking everywhere but at him. "Okay, I know—I overstepped my boundaries and stuck my nose somewhere it didn't belong."

"You saved us, Grace." He raked a hand through his hair. "I was afraid he might shut us down on the spot. But you stepped up to the plate and saved Mountain View Tours. Thank you."

"You've worked hard, Kaleb. You don't deserve to have curveballs like that thrown at you." She cleared her throat. "So what do we have to do to get these permits?" She pointed to the papers.

He set them on top of the counter. "Let's see. Aside from a usage estimate, an operating plan, map of the areas we intend to access, copy of my current brochure…"

"Maps and brochures are easy enough. But the rest is going to take a while."

"No kidding. And we've only got four days." He drew in a frustrated breath. "I sure hope we can find those drivers' logs. In the meantime, it looks like we'll have to postpone the painting."

"Postpone? Are you crazy?"

No, but she might have a screw loose. "Priorities, Grace. We have to start looking for the logs right away."

"We will. But you've got three people coming to paint. Let them paint while we work on the estimates. Because we will meet that deadline."

Chapter Seven

Grace ached for Kaleb. Why hadn't the forest service come to him sooner? Why did they wait until he was open for business?

It was what it was, though, and Grace was determined to see to it Kaleb met that deadline. Even if she wasn't quite sure how.

For two full days, they had been going through the previous owner's files, yet they'd located only about half of the drivers' logs. They'd searched the office and the shop. Drawers, cupboards, boxes. Kaleb had even gone so far as to call the former owner, who was confident all of the logs had been put into boxes and stowed in the shop.

Yet it was as if the other half had just disappeared. And from what Kaleb had told her about his former boss, they very well could have.

Still, they had to keep trying.

Kaleb was doing his best to remain positive, but failing miserably. The dark circles under his eyes told her he hadn't slept, and she had a feeling eating wasn't at the top of his priority list either. His frustration was almost palpable. And mounting with every hour that passed.

Paint fumes still hung in the air as Grace glanced from the computer to the door that separated the office from the garage. She imagined Kaleb pacing through the shop, raking a hand through his hair as he scoured for more boxes, despite having gone through the place multiple times.

She jumped when Kaleb burst through the door and moved into the freshly painted office. His booted feet thudded against the concrete floor, the carpet tiles she was so looking forward to having been put on hold.

"I found another box. In the rafters, no less." Hoisting it onto the counter, he blew the dust off the top.

She hoped this one contained what they needed.

"Let's see what we've got." Behind the counter, Grace coughed, fanned the airborne particles with her hand and lifted the flaps. She pulled out a stack of papers and leafed through them.

Credit-card receipts from four years ago, followed by a wad of old rental agreements.

Peering inside the box, Kaleb grabbed another stack and sifted through them. "There doesn't seem to be any rhyme or reason to any of this." Bills marked with payment dates and check numbers, a to-go menu from some restaurant and gas receipts. "Ross was a worse businessman than I thought." He tossed the pile aside, the lines on his face growing more pronounced.

"But you're not." She rummaged through what was left inside the cardboard container. "You're conscientious and, unlike him, you care about your customers." She stopped her search, her spirits dipping another notch as she looked at Kaleb.

"No logs?"

She shook her head. "Sorry."

He shoved the box aside and started toward the shop. "I'm going to check the rafters again. See if I missed anything."

Moving around the counter, she stepped in front of him. "I think our time would be better spent if we stopped looking and started actually working on the estimates."

Hands on his hips, he glared down at her. "And how are we supposed to do that without the logs?"

"I don't know. But we're both smart people and you've been a guide for a long time. I'm sure we can figure something out."

Still staring at her, he pondered her suggestion. "I don't know." He scrubbed a hand over his face.

"Look, why don't we take a break? Maybe grab a bite to eat." Grace looked at the clock. "It's after one. I don't know about you, but I'm fading."

"I can't think about eating with this deadline hanging over my head. This is my life, Grace."

"I know it is. However, if you don't get some sustenance, you might not have a life to worry about." Moving back behind the counter, she grabbed her pack and unzipped it. "I think some food will revive us both. What are you in the mood for?" She pulled out her wallet. "Burgers or a sandwich?"

"You go on." He started toward the garage. "I've got to keep looking."

"And just how effective do you think you're going to be?"

He shot an annoyed glance over his shoulder.

Unwilling to be deterred, she again moved toward him. "You're exhausted, Kaleb. Both mentally and physically. You need food. Not to mention some fresh air to clear your head."

"I hired you to manage my office. Not me."

Instinct had her narrowing her eyes, though she quickly caught herself. "A good lunch will also improve your disposition. Now come on. We won't be gone that long."

Hunger audibly rumbled in his gut and she shot him a satisfied grin.

"All right." Changing directions, he aimed for the front door. "But just long enough to grab a quick bite."

Outside, she squinted against the midday sun, wishing she'd thought to grab her sunglasses. Temps were beyond perfect. Not too hot, not too cold. The kind of day no one wanted to be cooped up inside.

"So what'll it be?" Grace faced him, shielding her eyes with her hand.

"This way." He headed north at a pretty good clip. Despite his artificial leg, she practically had to double-step to keep up.

"What's the rush?"

Pausing, he whirled toward her, his fiery gaze boring into her. "Don't you get it? If I don't find those logs, I lose everything. Which means you'll be out of a job."

"That's not true and you know it." She wagged a finger in front of his face. "We can figure this out. But you need to chill."

With a growl, he started again, crossing Eighth Avenue at a brisk pace. "I'll relax once I get those permits."

"And how is Mountain View Tours' newest owner doing?" A cute strawberry blonde smiled up at Kaleb with a baby on her hip. "Whoa. You don't look so good, Kaleb."

"Thank you," Grace said behind him.

"Blakely, this is Grace, my office manager." He glanced her way. "Blakely owns Adventures in Pink over there on Seventh Avenue."

Ah, another Jeep tour place. "Blue building, right?"

"That's right." Blakely smiled, adjusting the adorable child, who was chewing on a set of toy keys. "It's nice to meet you."

Try as she might, Grace couldn't ignore the baby. "And who's this little cutie?"

"This is Katelynn." Blakely took hold of her daughter's arm and tried to make her wave. "Say 'Hi, Grace.'"

Katelynn was interested in only the keys.

Smoothing a hand across her daughter's back, Blakely again turned her attention to Kaleb. "So what's up? I've never seen you so downcast."

Grace looked from Blakely to Kaleb, suspecting Blakely more friend than foe. If that were the case, she might be able to advise Kaleb on how to come up with usage estimates. That was, if he were willing to ask.

"We're just busy gearing up for the season." He scratched a hand through his hair.

Perhaps Grace ought to stick her neck out and ask for him. Or at least prod him a bit. Of course, she might only succeed in irritating him even more. Though if it helped, it would definitely be worth it.

Grace held up a hand above her eyes to shield them from the sun. "How long have you been in the Jeep tour business, Blakely?"

Shifting the babe to her other hip, she said, "It was my grandfather's place, so practically all my life. This is my third year as owner, though."

"Wow. I bet you've got things down to a science, then. Like all the paperwork and things like permits?"

Blakely chuckled. "It took me a while, but I'm finally getting the hang of it. How are things going with you guys?"

Grace dared a glance at Kaleb. To her surprise, he actually appeared interested in the conversation. *Ask her, ask her...*

He drew in a deep breath.

Go on. Do it.

"You know the permits we have to get from the BLM?"

Grace mentally fist-pumped the air.

"Yes."

He hesitated a moment, seemingly surveying the mountains. "Any suggestions on how to come up with usage estimates?"

"I usually use the previous year's drivers' logs."

Kaleb looked at Blakely. "What if you didn't have them?"

"Oh." She thought for a moment. "Well, do you have any logs at all?"

"Less than half."

"Okay." Blakely nodded. "Did you happen to keep your own logs when you worked for Ross?"

"The last couple of years, yeah."

"So pull together everything you've got, your personal logs and whatever you have from the other drivers and come up with an average."

Grace couldn't help herself. "What a great idea."

"I guess that would work." Kaleb shrugged, but Grace could see the wheels turning.

Katelynn began to fuss.

Blakely stroked the child's dark hair. "Looks like somebody's ready for their nap." She faced Kaleb again. "I'd better run. But if you have any problems, please, don't hesitate to give me a call. I know how challenging it can be to get a grasp on some of this stuff."

"I will." He almost smiled as she walked away. "Thanks."

Arms crossed over her chest, Grace welcomed the breeze that skittered over her face as she stared up at her boss. "So, looks like there is another way to get those numbers."

Looking a little chagrined, he scraped his boot across the sidewalk. "I guess I should have listened to you."

"I want Mountain View Tours to succeed every bit as much as you do, you know."

"I fully believe that, Grace." He watched her with an intensity she'd never seen before. "I apologize for giving you such a hard time."

Knowing she'd pushed the envelope enough for today, she lowered her arms. "Ah, don't worry about it. But I do have a question."

"What's that?"

"Do you know where *your* logs are?"

"Remember that room full of boxes?"

"Yeah." She cringed just thinking about it.

The corners of his mouth twitched. "There's a file cabinet tucked in the back. Everything is sorted by month and year."

This time she really did fist-pump the air. "Let's grab some lunch. Then we'll head to your house to get those files so we can start working on those estimates?"

"Sounds like a plan. But, Grace?" His smile evaporated.

"What?" She searched his gaze, fearful that she might have crossed another line by broaching the subject with Blakely.

He stared down at her, the light returning to his gray-green eyes. "Thank you for believing in me. And Mountain View Tours."

By the close of business Saturday, Kaleb was ready to celebrate. Not only had he and Grace met the designated BLM deadline yesterday, thanks to a temporary permit, they'd capped it off today with not only one, but two official tours.

Standing outside The Outlaw restaurant, Grace shot him a wary glance. "I thought we were going to work through some of your memorabilia tonight."

"We will. Right after we eat." That was, unless he could think of a way to get out of it. "But considering the week we've had, we deserve a little splurge."

"If you say so."

They moved past the clusters of people gathered outside and into the small, rustic restaurant that always bustled with activity.

Kaleb caught the eye of his friend Neil, the manager of The Outlaw, and held up two fingers.

After a quick perusal of the restaurant, Neil pointed to a corner table.

Kaleb waved his thanks.

As he and Grace moved toward their seats, he touched her elbow, urging her closer. "You like John Wayne?"

"I like steak more."

Did the woman know how to coerce a smile out of him or what? "Well, in case you're interested—" he pointed across the room "—there's his hat."

"Ooh…" Though her eyes were wide with feigned interest, she barely glanced at the well-worn cowboy hat on the wall.

Surrounded by the din of other patrons and ragtime music, they settled in at their table.

Grace picked up a menu, while Kaleb scanned the restaurant. He'd been here so many times he knew the menu by heart.

"I've always loved this place. Even as a kid."

Grace laid her menu down, her attention shifting to Kaleb. "What was it like growing up in Ouray?"

He shrugged, not giving it much thought. "Not so different from growing up anyplace else, I suppose. We just got into different kinds of trouble. And when we did, you could be certain that anyone who saw you not only knew who you were, but knew your parents, too." Resting his forearms on the table, he leaned forward. "I remember this one time—I guess I was about seven—my friend Max and I were trying to climb the rocks at Cascade Falls—"

"That's near town, right? I've seen the sign."

He blinked. "Wait a minute. You've been here for almost two weeks and you haven't been to Cascade Falls? How is that even possible? I mean, for most people, it's one of their first stops."

Looking a tad sheepish, she leaned back in her chair. "I'm working all the time."

He sent her a perturbed look. "No, you're not."

Apparently out of excuses, she remained silent.

"Okay, we need to hurry up and order. Because we're going to Cascade Falls."

"Tonight?"

"Yes."

An hour later, after Grace had tackled every last scrap of her New York strip like a Broncos linebacker, they exited the restaurant into the mild evening air.

Main Street was alive with shoppers, onlookers and those happily enjoying ice cream on one of the town's many benches as they took in the scenery. He and Grace headed north, dodging young and old alike, as well as the occasional four-legged canine friend. Though Memorial Day weekend was still a week away, the town's population had already begun to swell. Only a precursor of what was to come as they headed into the high season.

With Grace at his side, they turned onto Eighth Avenue and continued east, the rocky road growing steeper with every step. Behind them, the sun slid below the mountains and, while it was still daylight, shadows had begun to fall over Ouray.

"Perhaps we should do this another time. Earlier in the day." Grace sounded a bit winded. "I mean, what about the stuff for the museum?"

"Sorry, Grace, but I cannot let another day pass without you experiencing Cascade Falls."

"Why?" She stopped.

So did he. "Because it's very important to me."

She let go a sigh. "Lead on, then."

Before long, the sound of rushing water touched their ears.

"Are we getting close?" Her expression was hopeful.

"Yep. Keep walking."

"Just so you'll know—" she huffed and puffed "—my muscles are burning. Doesn't this climb bother your leg?"

"Nah. I'm used to it." He slowed his pace so she could catch up. "This was my first stop after returning home." He loved this place. Always had. But even more so since the IED.

Excitement coursed through him as the falls came into view. He couldn't wait to see Grace's reaction. Stepping out of the way, he glimpsed the slow smile that overtook her face.

"Oh, Kaleb."

The sight of silvery-white water as it plummeted over some ten stories of craggy rocks never ceased to move him. And the roar of the falls, coupled with the gentle breeze that carried the songs of sparrows, filled him with a peace he longed to share with Grace. Because for all of her business smarts, all her plans, something was amiss. At times, he'd detect a deep sadness, an emptiness. If only he could find out what it was.

"Let's get closer." He nudged her across the wooden bridge and onto a narrow path. When they emerged, they were on the other side of the stream, mere feet from the falls.

The gentle mist touched their skin.

Grace rubbed her arms. "This is...stunning." Closing her eyes, she inhaled deeply. When she opened them, she peered up at him through thick lashes. "Thank you for urging me to come up here."

As daylight faded into night, he looked down at her. "You can't simply be in Ouray, Grace. You've got to experience it." Whether it was the faith she had in him or her genuine desire to make Mountain View Tours a success, Grace stirred something in him that had been long dormant. Something he'd do well to ignore since she'd be leaving at the end of the summer.

"You said this was the first place you came after coming home. Why is it so special to you?"

Taking a step back, he shoved his hands in the pockets of his jeans and took in the familiar surroundings. "It never changes." He had to raise his voice to be heard over the falls. "Sure it might appear different throughout the seasons, and nature sometimes has a way of relandscaping—" he gestured to the boulders and logs that littered the valley floor "—but the falls, the mountain... They're unchanging." He turned toward her now. "They remind me that while that IED may have changed my body, the God that lives inside me never changes. And regardless of what I've lost, He's promised me so much more."

With the slightest tilt of her head, she watched him, her gaze probing. "You really believe that, don't you?"

"With all my heart. The way I see it, when the going gets tough, we can either cling to God or run away." He shook his head. "But it's impossible to outrun God."

Her brow lifted. "I think your faith may have faltered a bit this week. When you were freaking out over the drivers' logs."

Chagrined, he lowered his head. God had brought him through far worse, and yet, instead of reflecting on God's faithfulness, Kaleb worried. *Forgive my unbelief, Lord.*

His gaze met Grace's. "You're right. Instead of trusting in God to provide, I trusted in myself. And I failed. I'm just glad God didn't."

Nodding, she toed a rock. "I'm curious, then. What was your reaction when you found out you'd lost your leg?"

The evening air stirred then, sending a shiver up his spine.

"Mind if we sit down?" He gestured toward a massive boulder that sat several feet away.

As daylight faded, they eased onto the rock, close enough that they wouldn't have to yell to hear each other over the rushing water.

Grace wrapped her arms around herself.

"Are you cold?"

"Cool, but I'll be okay."

He drew in a deep breath. "To answer your question, when I first heard about my leg, I wished I'd died with my buddies." He saw Grace's body sag. "For six months, I merely existed in that hospital, doing whatever they told me to do. But deep inside—" he pointed to his chest "—I'd given up. I'd lost my leg, my fiancée and, as far as I was concerned, my life."

She straightened. "You were engaged?"

"Her name was Gina. She was tough as nails. Or so I thought. But as soon as the going got tough, she bailed. I'm just thankful I discovered that little character flaw before we said 'I do.'"

Grace's gaze drifted to the turbulent stream in the distance. "Sometimes people profess to love without ever really knowing what it truly means."

The remark caught him off guard. Somehow, he didn't think she was talking about Gina.

Looking at him again, she said, "What brought you back around?"

"Sami."

Grace's eyes widened. "Really? What did she do?"

"She showed me a picture."

"Of what?"

"Jack. Of course, we didn't know it was Jack yet."

Grace appeared confused.

"It was Jack's first sonogram. Kind of looked like a gerbil to me—"

Her soft chuckle eased the inevitable, albeit momentary, grief that usually accompanied his story.

"While I pretended not to listen, Sami went on about how she'd always looked up to me and how she wanted her baby to do the same. She told me to stop feeling sorry for myself. To stop focusing on what I'd lost and thank God for everything I still had. Then she taped that picture where I'd be sure to see it."

"What did you do?"

"Continued to sulk. But the more I looked at that picture, something grabbed hold of my heart. Not only did I want to meet my niece or nephew, I wanted to be part of his or her life. To teach them all those things Sami and I used to do when we were kids. Suddenly, Jack became my reason to live."

"That explains why you're so close to him now."

"Yeah. I couldn't love that kid any more if he were my own."

"He's lucky to have you."

"I don't know about that. I tend to look at it the other way around."

Hands clasped in her lap, Grace studied them for a moment. "I can't imagine how difficult it was to learn about your buddies."

He stared at the falls, nodded, his throat too thick to respond.

"But I don't understand why you don't want to see their families. I mean, you were the last one to see their loved ones alive. You're their last connection."

The words slammed into his chest, burrowing their way into that dark part of him he refused to let anybody see. Yet somehow it rose to the surface.

"I'm the reason my friends are dead." He cringed the moment the words left his mouth.

"Wha—"

He stood, refusing to discuss it anymore. "It's dark. I'll walk you home."

Chapter Eight

The aroma of fresh-popped popcorn filled the air in front of Mountain View Tours on Memorial Day. Inside, the front office had been completely transformed. From the carpet tiles to the freshly painted walls, everything had been revived.

Finally, with all of the obstacles behind him, Kaleb could relax and enjoy the grand-opening festivities. He felt as though this entire weekend had been one big party. The weather was perfect, every tour was full and the number of people sharing in the fun was beyond anything he'd imagined.

God had knocked this one out of the ballpark.

And to think, Grace almost kept the idea to herself. Boy, was he glad Sami had coaxed it out of her. This weekend had been exactly the kind of kickoff he'd dreamed about, yet had no clue how to execute. Thanks to Grace, though, that dream was now a reality and the *new* Mountain View Tours was on its way to reclaiming its once-glowing reputation. Something that was bound to bring in more business.

Wearing a pair of denim capris and a sleeveless white

blouse, Grace filled another batch of red-white-and-blue helium balloons at the table just outside the entrance. Times like this, he wondered where he'd be without her. Despite a somewhat rocky start, she had quickly exceeded his expectations for an office manager. And so much more.

Grace seemed to know him inside and out. At times she'd push hard, though she also knew when to back off. Like last weekend, when he'd blurted out something that was better left unsaid. She hadn't brought it up since.

A patriotic song echoed from the docking station behind Grace, sending Kaleb's gaze to the four American flags swaying in the breeze along the front of the building. One for each of the four men who were with him that day in Afghanistan.

His gut churned as regret and sorrow flooded his inner being. If only he'd seen that trip wire. Swallowing around the sudden lump in his throat, he tilted his face heavenward. *God, I don't know why You chose to spare me, but I pledge myself to You once again and ask that You would use me in whatever manner You see fit.*

He took a deep breath. *Thank You, God, for the privilege of knowing each of those men and I ask a special blessing upon their families.*

Their families. In just a little under a month those families would be coming to Ouray, expecting to see him and spend time with him and, no doubt, wanting to talk about their loved ones. Grace was right. He was their last connection. Wives and parents were probably curious about their last days.

Early on, after he settled back in Ouray, he'd spoken to a couple of them on the phone. But that was different. He didn't have to look them in the eye.

Returning his focus to the flags, he knew that Memorial Day would never be the same for him. He'd fought alongside men who gave their lives for this country. They were his friends and he would not let them be forgotten.

A tapping against his thigh had him looking down. Jack stared up at him through his star-shaped sunglasses. The innocence on his nephew's face chased away Kaleb's morose.

"What's up, Jack?" He lifted the child into his arms.

"I wanna dwive."

The kid loved it when Kaleb let him play in the trucks. "You want to drive, huh?"

Jack nodded emphatically.

"We need to see what your folks have to say about that one, buddy." Kaleb strode toward the table where Sami and her husband, Scott, were tying long ribbons on the freshly inflated balloons.

"Somebody wants to do some driving." He nodded to the bright blue rental Jeep he had on display in front of the building. Not only was it for people to have a look-see, they'd had kids hopping in and out all weekend for photo ops. "Told him we'd have to check with you."

"Sure. But, Jack—" Sami sent her son that motherly warning look "—I want you to sit on your bottom. No standing, you hear me?"

"Yes, ma'am." Jack turned his attention to Grace. "Wanna wide wif me, Gwace?" The kid had really taken a liking to her.

Kaleb couldn't say that he blamed him. He'd kind of taken a liking to her, too.

"I'd love to, Jack, but I need to help your uncle Kaleb. Can I take a rain check?"

Jack's expression turned serious. "It's not waining, Gwace."

She smiled. "You're right. It's not. Silly me."

"Maybe Grace can ride with you later." Kaleb moved toward the vehicle, opened the door and deposited Jack in the driver's seat. He moved the seat as far forward as it would go. "What's the first thing we do when we get into a vehicle?"

"Seat belt!"

"That's right." Kaleb grabbed the restraint and reached across his nephew to secure it. "You're ready to roll, soldier."

"Close the doow."

He pushed the door closed, taking a moment to listen to the vrooming noises coming from Jack. Chuckling to himself, he turned to rejoin the other adults.

An older couple stood at the table, looking over a brochure as Grace spoke with them.

"Yes, we do still have some openings on our tours for tomorrow. Were you looking at morning or afternoon?" She eyed him as he approached. "Kaleb, this is Mr. and Mrs. Russell." Her focus returned to the couple. "Kaleb is the owner of Mountain View Tours."

"Good to meet you, son." Mr. Russell held out his hand.

Kaleb accepted, noticing the Desert Storm Veteran insignia on the man's ball cap. "What branch of the military were you in?"

"Army. Second Armored Division."

Kaleb smiled. "Hundred and First Airborne Division. Operation Enduring Freedom."

"A man who knows what Memorial Day is truly about." Mr. Russell gestured to the decorations.

"Yes, sir." Far better than he cared to.

Someone screamed and Kaleb instinctively scanned the area, his heart leaping into his throat.

Jack!

The Jeep was rolling down Mountain View Tours' drive, aimed for the street. Sweat beaded his forehead as he rushed toward it.

People scrambled to get out of the way. One man attempted to reach the passenger door, but missed.

With a final lunge, Kaleb grabbed hold of the driver's door and flung it open. His pulse and the Jeep were the only things that seemed to be moving quickly. People had moved into the street, waving their arms to stop oncoming traffic.

Holding tight to the door, Kaleb lifted himself enough to get his right foot inside and on the brake pedal. The Jeep jerked to a stop.

Glancing at the line of cars now stopped in the northbound lane, he breathed a sigh of relief.

Then the applause started. Just a couple of people at first, and then more joined in until it thundered around him.

"That was fun." Jack cheered.

Kaleb released the buckle. "Scoot over, Jack." His nephew climbed over the center console and Kaleb hopped in. And that was when he saw it.

The emergency brake wasn't set. And the gearshift was in Neutral.

He could have killed Jack. Why hadn't he double-checked the brake when he put Jack in the Jeep?

He quickly returned the vehicle to its original position, regret beating like a woodpecker against his rib cage. Once again, he'd allowed himself to become distracted, risking the lives of those around him.

Sami snagged her son from the passenger side, pressing his little body against hers as she held him close. "Oh, thank God, you're okay, baby." She kissed his face, but Jack was oblivious to all the commotion.

"I was dwiving, Mama."

"You sure were, son." Scott reached for the boy. "But that's enough for one day."

Sami met Kaleb as he stepped out of the Jeep. "Once a hero, always a hero." Slipping her arms around him, she fell against him in a powerful hug. "Thank you, big brother."

He was no hero. Not now, not ever.

He grabbed his sister by the arms, breaking her hold, and stepped back. "The parking brake was off."

Her liquid eyes searched his.

Raking a disgusted hand through his hair, he tried unsuccessfully to quell the storm raging inside him. "It was my fault that the Jeep rolled into the street."

Sami shook her head. "But you saved him."

He glared at her now. "It shouldn't have happened in the first place." Walking past his sister, he ignored the crowd that had gathered and continued into the deepest corner of the garage. The smell of petroleum and rubber hung heavy in the air.

Tilting his head up, he blinked away the tears that blurred his vision. *God, thank You for protecting Jack. Forgive me for not paying closer attention.*

So much for restoring the company's reputation.

"You okay?" He should have known Grace would follow him.

He turned away, not wanting her to see him like this. "Yeah."

"I heard what you said to Sami."

Great. Now she knew just how incompetent he was.

"You're wrong, though."

He sensed her moving closer.

"Danny was the one who parked that Jeep. If anyone—"

Unwilling to listen to any of her excuses, he whirled to face her. "I'm the owner. I should have checked the parking brake."

"It was an accident, Kaleb. No one *meant* for it to happen."

"It did happen, though."

"And you saved the day. Jack is safe because of you. In my book, that's a hero."

He blew out a disbelieving laugh. "Heroes don't allow things to happen in the first place."

"No, because no one can control everything."

Touché.

Locked in a staredown with his office manager, he drew in a deep breath, willing his pulse to a normal rate. "In here—" he pointed to his head "—I know you're right. But my heart has a hard time accepting that what happened to my buddies, what happened to Jack, wasn't my fault. If I'd have done just one thing differently, like check the parking brake, or not allowed myself to become distracted, I could have changed the outcome."

Taking a step closer, Grace laid a hand on his forearm, sending a wave of awareness through him. "Kaleb, we all second-guess ourselves." She cocked her head, making her appear more thoughtful. "Do you believe in God's providence? That He has a plan and a purpose for everything?"

"Yes."

"Then why are you trying to put yourself above God by second-guessing what He allowed to happen?"

Was that what he'd been doing?

He stood there, paralyzed, as conviction rained down on him. "Is that what you think I've been doing?"

Grace didn't say a word, simply lifted a brow as if to say, "What do you think?"

My ways are not your ways.

"I think you've just opened my eyes, Grace." He laid his hand atop hers. "Thank you for the perspective."

"You're welcome." She pulled her hand away then.

"I didn't realize you'd spent so much time in God's word."

"I did a lot of Bible studies while I was deployed." Rubbing her arms, she took a step back.

"That's great." He stepped toward her, thrilled with the knowledge that Grace was a woman of faith. "I know I need my daily dose of the Bible every morning. Maybe we—"

"I'd better get back outside."

Grace had fallen in love with Ouray. The beauty, the history, the sense of community... Though there were days when she wished she were aboard that cruise ship, away from the lure of what-ifs and what-could-have-beens.

This was one of those days.

Still frustrated over her conversation with Kaleb yesterday, she unlocked the post office box and peered inside. She welcomed the opportunity, no matter how small it might be, to get out of the office and enjoy a little fresh air, away from her increasingly handsome boss.

Oftentimes, when she was at sea, she'd sneak away from the engine room and make her way topside to fill her lungs with something besides jet fuel vapors and soak up a little vitamin D.

It was also where she would talk to God, keeping Him as her anchor when she was half a world away from those she loved.

A lot of good that did her.

Unlike Kaleb, she wasn't second-guessing what God allowed to happen.

God had failed her. He took her dad, made her unable to conceive and then allowed her husband to fall into the arms of another woman who was able to give him a child. Grace was better off on her own, not trusting in a God who seemed eager to knock her down at every turn.

So who was she to go spouting off spiritual truths? Leading Kaleb to believe she was some faith-filled woman when her faith had died right along with her dreams of a family.

Shaking off the depressing thoughts, she retrieved the short stack of mail and locked the box before making her way back through the glass double doors onto Main Street.

Kaleb was the kind of man Grace had once dreamed of finding. A man who did his best to live out his faith in word and deed. A man who would never be interested in a woman whose faith was on the skids. And yet her sleep was plagued with dreams of him.

The subconscious mind could be so annoying.

Strolling down the sidewalk, she paused in front of

one of the gift shops to study their window display. She'd been wanting to pick up a T-shirt or two, but was having a hard time deciding which ones she liked best.

Unfortunately, she didn't dare waste too much time. Over the past few days, business at Mountain View Tours had shifted into high gear. This morning alone, they'd had six tours, half a dozen phone inquiries and at least twice that many from the website. And the season had barely begun. At this rate, she'd never keep up.

Kaleb was beyond ecstatic and she was happy for him. He'd worked hard, putting his heart and soul into this business, and deserved to be rewarded.

Still undecided about the T-shirts, she gave up and proceeded on to the deli to pick up a couple of sandwiches for her and Kaleb.

Lunch in hand, she made her way back to the office, pausing to admire one of the gorgeous flower baskets that hung from every lamppost along Main Street. Ouray was the kind of charming little town she used to envision calling home. The picture of Americana, complete with white picket fences, colorful old buildings and purple mountains' majesty. A place that made her want to put down roots.

She blew out a frustrated breath and moved on, approaching Mountain View Tours as one of their morning tours returned. Kaleb was outside, greeting everyone and asking if they'd enjoyed their tour. As if he couldn't tell from the smiles on their faces. Perhaps once they heard the news that Corkscrew and Engineer Pass had opened ahead of schedule, they'd be ready to sign up for another outing tomorrow.

Which meant she'd better get inside.

Her cell phone rang. With the bag containing their

lunch dangling from her left hand, she tucked the mail under the same arm and retrieved the phone from her back pocket.

One glance at the screen sent her heart into a tailspin.

Why would Aaron be calling her?

A hundred scenarios clamored through her brain, none of them making any sense. Once upon a time, she'd prayed that he would call, telling her he'd made a mistake and begging her to take him back. That call never came. And even if this was it, she'd tell him in no uncertain terms that she had no interest in reconciliation. Something she couldn't have said a year ago.

The phone continued to ring, her angst building with each jingle. She could simply let it go to voice mail and see if he left a message. But if he didn't, she'd be left wondering why he called.

With a shaky breath, she touched the accept icon and put the phone to her ear.

"Hello."

"Grace. Hey, it's Aaron." As if she didn't already know that.

Keep it light. Upbeat. "Hey, Aaron. How's it going?" Ugh. Nothing like trying too hard.

"Pretty good. Just busy. AJ is crawling now." He chuckled. "The kid's into everything."

As if she wanted to hear that tidbit of information.

"But, hey, that's not why I'm calling."

No "How are you?" or "How's it going?" In typical Aaron fashion, he forged right ahead with his agenda, never even bothering to ask where she was or what she'd been up to.

"Tessa and I have found a house we want to buy."

Funny, last time Grace checked, he had a house. A house he'd once shared with her.

"Which is why I'm calling. In your rush to leave Jacksonville, you failed to sign the quitclaim deed."

Rush to leave? He'd turned her world upside down. Left her for another woman, one who happened to be carrying his child. Something Grace wasn't able to give him. Aaron had practically deemed her worthless, in front of God and everybody. Why on earth would she want to hang around any longer than she had to?

Dropping onto a nearby bench, she allowed her gaze to roam the mountaintops, finding the strength to temper her flailing emotions. "What's a quitclaim deed?"

"A form that basically states you no longer have an interest in the house and removes your name from the deed, freeing me up to sell it."

No interest? The house where she'd spent countless hours stripping wallpaper, painting and tearing out flooring. Where she'd learned to tile bathrooms and backsplashes and lay hardwood floors. All in an effort to call it her own. The house that was supposed to be her haven. A place she could finally call home. Where she'd settle down and raise a family.

How could she possibly have no interest? Even though he did pay her half of what little equity they had in the house.

"We need to move quickly on this other house, Grace. So would it be all right if I overnighted you the form?"

The final piece of her once-seemingly-happy life was being ripped from her already-bloodied hands. Just like every other dream she'd had.

A tempestuous storm arose in her gut, churning with fury. How could she have loved someone so heartless?

Perhaps she should refuse to sign the form. Tell him she wasn't interested in selling.

But that was Aaron's style, not hers.

Her body sagging, she dropped her head in her hand and stared at the sidewalk. "Yeah. Send it on."

"Awesome. I just need your address."

Knowing she'd be at work, she gave the address for Mountain View Tours.

"Thanks, Grace."

Ending the call, she glared at the screen, feeling as though she might be sick.

"Everything all right?"

She jerked her head up to find Kaleb standing over her.

"Yeah." She forced herself to smile and pushed to her feet. "Why wouldn't it be?"

"I don't know." Kaleb's gray-green gaze narrowed. "But whoever you were talking to, you didn't look too happy."

"Oh, that." She returned the phone to her back pocket, determined not to let Kaleb see what a mess she was inside. "It was nothing."

Arms crossed over his chest, he continued to scrutinize her. "You know—" his deeper-than-usual voice didn't bode well "—over these past few weeks you've gotten to know me pretty well. You've pushed and prodded, getting me to tell you things I've never told anyone else. But there's not a whole lot I know about you."

Which was how she preferred it. Because if she let someone like Kaleb in, her heart might never survive.

"Sure there is." Looking everywhere but at him, she adjusted the bag on her arm. "I hope you're hungry. I picked up your favorite sandwich from the deli. Not to mention some of those homemade kettle chips."

"Grace…"

She hated it when he said her name like that. So comforting and inviting. Yet edged with warning.

Quickly herding her scattered emotions, she forced herself to look him in the eye. "Yes?"

His smile was slow as his arms fell to his sides. Shaking his head, he took the bag from her hand. "Let's go eat."

She followed him into the office, breathing a sigh of relief. As wound up as she was, if Kaleb had pressed her, she might have lost it right there on Main Street. And that was so not her.

However, with Aaron's request hanging over her head, her nerves would remain as frayed as that worn-out pair of jeans she kept in the bottom of her footlocker. If Kaleb decided to push her the way she'd pushed him…

She couldn't let that happen. Wouldn't let that happen. Because she'd never let anyone past her defenses again.

Chapter Nine

Kaleb wanted nothing more than to help Grace. As was typical of his office manager, though, she tried to act as though all was well. But from the moment he saw her sitting on that bench yesterday, he knew she was hurting. The pain in her eyes when she looked up at him only confirmed his suspicions.

Now, standing at the top of Engineer Pass, hands jammed in the pockets of his jeans, he looked out over the surrounding peaks. Despite a mild winter and an early spring, patches of grass still battled snow for ownership of the gray, barren rock below, while pale gray clouds blanketed much of the sky.

He wished Grace would have come. Perhaps the change of scenery would have taken her mind off whatever troubled her. Yet even though Sami had offered to fill in, Grace had declined his invitation, claiming she had too much paperwork to do.

Turning, he watched his guests as they took pictures atop the rocky peak, hoping to capture the beauty around them. Memories they'd carry home to share with family and friends.

He was in his element, doing what he loved. Helping others experience things they otherwise might never see. Memories in the making.

So why did he feel so lousy?

Grace.

In the few weeks that he'd known her, she'd challenged him in ways no one ever had. She pushed him to look within himself and find the strength to overcome the torment he still harbored inside. And while he had a long way to go, he wished he could do the same for her.

"Excuse me, Kaleb?" He turned to see two of his guests—Mr. and Mrs. Higgins, as he recalled—a couple close to his parents' age.

Mrs. Higgins held out a camera. "Would you mind taking our picture?"

He couldn't help smiling. "That's what I'm here for."

The couple wrapped their arms around each other, fitting together as if each were designed specifically for the other.

"We're celebrating our thirtieth wedding anniversary," said Mr. Higgins.

"Congratulations." Kaleb aimed the camera. "Let's make this a good one, then."

The couple's smiles were filled with joy, their love evident by the glint in their eyes.

Kaleb took two shots for good measure, then handed the camera back, a sudden loneliness leaching into his heart.

He longed to find that kind of love. That one person God created just for him. Who loved him despite his flaws and that he couldn't imagine living without.

Shaking away the thought, he addressed the seven

people he'd had the pleasure of taking on a tour today. "Okay, folks. Time to wrap things up."

A few rushed to take some last-minute photos, while others climbed back onto the tour truck.

Once everyone was loaded and accounted for, Kaleb began their descent down the mountain. Sharp, jagged rocks littered the road, meaning he had to move at a snail's pace or risk jostling his guests right out of the vehicle. They didn't seem to mind, though. Instead, they were mesmerized by the fourteen-foot snowbanks that lined both sides of the narrow road.

When they arrived back in Ouray a couple of hours later, Kaleb assisted his guests as they exited the truck, taking the time to thank each of them for choosing Mountain View Tours. Without them, there wouldn't be a Mountain View Tours.

"We were thinking about renting one of your Jeeps for tomorrow," said Mr. Higgins. "Do you think that would be possible?"

Beside him, his wife clung to his arm, anticipation evident in her eager smile.

"Absolutely. And it would give you two the opportunity to do some exploring on your own."

The man glanced at his wife. "That's what we were thinking."

"Well, if you'd like to come inside, we'll get you all set up."

They followed him through the front door.

"Grace, Mr. and Mrs. Higgins would like to rent a Jeep."

Behind the desk, she jerked her head up, her smile a little too forced, failing to reach her eyes. "Sure." She hopped off the stool and grabbed a clipboard with the paperwork. "I'll just need you to fill these out."

"Grace will get you squared away. If you have any questions or problems, though, don't hesitate to let me know."

"Great. Thank you, Kaleb." The man waved as Kaleb headed back outside.

After removing the cooler and blankets from the truck, along with any trash, he pulled out the hose and sprayed the vehicle down, his thoughts repeatedly drifting to Grace. Something troubled her. Was she unhappy in Ouray? Was there a problem with her mother or Roger?

The cell phone attached to the clip on his belt vibrated.

Releasing the sprayer to stop the flow of water, he retrieved the phone and looked at the screen.

Vanessa.

His body tensed. Why was she calling him now? Had something happened? Had they decided not to come to Ouray after all?

Wishful thinking.

Dropping the hose, he pressed the accept icon. "Hey, Vanessa. How's it going?" The words came out with far more enthusiasm than he felt.

"Wonderful."

He scratched a hand through his hair. "How's Hannah?"

"She's good. And very much looking forward to our trip to Ouray."

"Glad to hear it." He often worried about Beau's little girl. Growing up without a dad was never easy.

"How's that new business of yours?"

"Great." He eyed the steady stream of vehicles easing their way up Main Street, grateful for the small talk. "We had our grand opening this weekend."

"Congratulations. I know how much this means to you, Kaleb. Beau used to share your stories about Jeeping and the mountains and say that we had to make plans to go to Ouray one day."

Kaleb's chest constricted. What he wouldn't give to make that happen.

"That reminds me. I was looking around the Ouray website the other day and saw that there's going to be some ribbon-cutting ceremony while we're there and that you're one of the guests."

He cleared his throat. "At the museum. Yes."

"That's fantastic. Why didn't you tell us?"

The knot in his stomach twisted. He shouldn't have agreed to speak. Especially not when he knew his friends' families were going to be here.

"Sorry, guess it slipped my mind. You know, with business and all."

"I understand."

He breathed a sigh of relief.

"Okay, so I just wanted to go over a few details, make sure we're all on the same page." Vanessa rattled off arrival dates, who all was coming and where they'd be staying.

"Sounds good." He watched an express delivery truck as it pulled alongside the curb. "We'll see you on June twenty-first, then."

"And, Kaleb?"

"Yes?"

"You will take us on one of your tours, right?"

For Beau's sake—"Absolutely."

While Kaleb clipped the phone back on his belt, the driver of the delivery truck emerged, carrying a large envelope. Spotting Kaleb, his pace quickened. "I've got a delivery for a—" he eyed the address label "—Grace McAllen."

Who would be sending Grace an express package?

Curiosity got the best of him, so rather than directing the driver inside, Kaleb said, "I'll make sure she gets it."

"Just sign here." The driver held out his device and Kaleb jotted his signature on the screen. "Thanks. Have a good one."

Kaleb allowed his gaze to fall to the return address. *Aaron McAllen. Jacksonville, Florida.*

A brother, perhaps?

Hmm… He'd heard mention of a sister, but no brother.

He knew Jacksonville had been her last assignment, but not necessarily her home.

Unless… His heart sank.

Grace was married.

But wouldn't she have said something? Or worn a ring?

A car horn jolted him back to reality.

Grace's marital status was none of his business.

He lowered the envelope and started toward the office, wishing he'd directed the driver inside after all. Maybe then he wouldn't have this sudden ache in his chest.

He pushed open the door, noting that she was alone. "Grace."

She looked across the desk, strands of her long hair escaping the clip that was supposed to be holding it up. "Yes."

"A package came for you." He approached, laying the envelope on the counter.

She glanced at it, then at him, just long enough for him to glimpse the sorrow swimming in her eyes.

"You okay?"

With a quick shake of her head, she grabbed the package and turned away. "Yeah. Everything's great."

Definite overkill on the cheerfulness. Meaning things weren't as great as she claimed.

He didn't like to see her hurting and found himself wishing he could take her into his arms and make whatever was troubling her go away. But he knew Grace well enough to know that she'd only push him away. She wasn't the type to share her burdens. No matter how much she might want to.

If only he could make her understand that she could trust him. That he was here for her and wanted to be her friend.

For whatever reason, though, trust didn't come easy to Grace. Now he could only wonder if Aaron McAllen wasn't part of the reason why.

Grace locked the front door of Mountain View Tours and flipped the sign from Open to Closed, feeling like a can of soda that had been tossed around and was ready to spew. Aaron's phone call had hung over her like a dark cloud all last night and into today.

Now the final piece of her shattered dreams had arrived in the form of a quitclaim deed, with a note that read "Thanks, Grace. You're the best."

Obviously she wasn't the best or Aaron wouldn't have betrayed her in the first place.

She needed to get out of here, find someplace to vent. Someplace safe where she could rant about her troubles and no one would know. Perhaps a long ride on her motorcycle.

She grabbed her pack from beneath the counter, tucked the express envelope inside then went into the garage to let Kaleb know she was leaving.

Amid the smells of various petroleum products, he

stood at the long workbench, sorting through tools and putting them away.

She slipped her pack over her shoulder. "I'm heading out."

He turned, his easy smile replaced by a look of concern. "I know I already asked you, but are you sure you're all right, Grace?"

No getting anything past Mr. Perceptive. Yet for as much as she longed to pour her heart out to him, she didn't trust herself. He was the kind of guy who would listen attentively and do his best to comfort her. And the comforting was what worried her. It would be so easy to fall into his strong arms and believe that all was right with the world.

So, for her boss's sake as much as her own, she'd just have to fake it. "Yeah. I'm just a little tired, that's all."

"I hope you're not getting sick." He moved toward her, his concern mounting.

"I'm fine. I just…" *Tell him. Give the guy a chance.* "I didn't sleep well last night." No fibbing there.

Wiping his hands on a shop rag, he continued to study her. "That would explain the bags under your eyes."

Did he just— "Bags? What do you mean—"

He laughed. "There's the spitfire we all know and love."

Love?

Still laughing, he lowered his arms, closed the distance between them and gave her a hug. "Sleep well, Grace." He smelled of fresh air and masculinity. A toxic mix for someone in her pathetic state. And she missed him as soon as he stepped away. "And remember, I'm always here if you need me." The sincerity in those gray-green depths nearly had her spilling everything right there in the garage.

Yet, somehow, she managed to hold herself together. "I appreciate that. But I'll be fine."

Outside, she waited at the corner for traffic to clear, wishing for the millionth time that her father was still alive. He'd know exactly what to say to make her feel better.

Hands shoved in her pockets, she crossed the street, continuing aimlessly onto the sidewalk. After all this time, after what he did, Aaron still expected her to jump through hoops for him. The gall of that—

"Grace?"

She looked up to see her mother standing in front of the hardware store, holding a plastic bag in each hand, worry lines creasing her brow.

"Mama." A morsel of peace that hadn't been there a moment ago settled in Grace's heart.

"What's wrong, baby?"

Tears sprang to Grace's eyes and she had to work double time to blink them away.

Shifting both bags to one hand, Mama wrapped her free arm around Grace. "Come on. Let's go back to the house so we can talk."

Grace simply nodded, knowing that if she tried to speak, the tears she was desperately trying to fend off would overtake her right there. And that was a sight nobody wanted to see. Especially her.

By the time they arrived at Mama and Roger's house, Grace had regained her composure. Now in the living room of the quiet two-story, she and her mother sat on the white-slipcovered sofa, shoes off, legs tucked under them as they faced each other.

"Where's Roger?"

"Bowling at the Elks Lodge."

"There's a bowling alley at the Elks Lodge?" The historic brick building didn't look that big.

"A two-lane bowling alley."

"Two lanes?"

Mama nodded. "The whole setup is an antique. We'll have to take you over there sometime." She reached for Grace's hand. "Now tell me, what's got you so down?"

Grace drew in a shaky breath. "I didn't think it possible for Aaron to hurt me any more than he already has." She shrugged as tears again sprang to her eyes. "But I guess I was wrong."

"Oh, baby." Mama scooted closer and wrapped Grace in her arms. "I'm so sorry."

Whether unable or unwilling to resist, Grace melted against her mother, her tears falling freely, perhaps for the first time, as she grieved for everything she'd lost. Clinging to Mama, Grace poured out every hurt, every disappointment.

All the while, Mama held her close, stroking her hair, her back. A comforting touch Grace hadn't felt in a long time.

"I tried to be a good wife."

"I know." Mama's voice was soothing.

Grace hiccuped. "I really wanted to have a baby."

"Of course you did."

Sometime later, when the tears finally subsided, Grace lifted her head and looked at her mother in a new light. She hadn't given the woman enough credit. Mama really did love her.

Cupping Grace's tear-streaked cheeks, Mama said, "What did that ex-son-in-law of mine do this time?"

"He wants to sell our house."

"But you don't want to?"

"It's not that I don't want to." She sniffed, accepting the tissue Mama handed her. "I mean, I have no need for it anymore. It's just—" The turmoil that had been smoldering inside her ever since Aaron's call burst into flame.

Fists balled, she shot to her feet, rounded the solid wood coffee table and started to pace. "That was supposed to be my house." She poked a finger at her chest. "The place where I'd spend the rest of my days, where we'd raise our kids and welcome our grandkids." She faced her mother. "Now he expects me to sign some stupid piece of paper so he and wife 2.0 can buy a new house." Tears threatened again and her cheeks burned. "It's *not* fair."

Her mother sat calmly on the sofa, shaking her head. "No. It's not fair. But, baby, it doesn't do us any good to be angry about it either." Standing, she moved toward Grace. "We have to make a conscious choice to put it behind us and move on."

"I thought I'd done that."

"Are you sure?"

She looked curiously at her mother. "What are you getting at?"

Mama slipped an arm around Grace's waist, pulling her against her hip. "There's a difference between moving on and running away. Grace, don't let Aaron's actions rob you of the happiness you deserve. Someday Mr. Right will come along and—"

Grace pulled away. "Don't go there, Mama. Please. Even if there was a Mr. Right, I will never be Mrs. Right."

"Now, why would you say that? You're young, beautiful—"

"And broken." She flopped back down on the sofa. "No man wants a woman who can't give him children."

Mama's gaze narrowed as she returned to the couch. "Did a doctor tell you that you can't conceive?"

"No. But after trying unsuccessfully for two years, it's pretty obvious that God doesn't want me to have children."

"First of all—" her mother's expression softened "—even if you weren't able to conceive, that doesn't mean you can't have a family. And second, perhaps God simply didn't want you to have children with Aaron."

Grace snagged the pale blue throw pillow beside her and fiddled with the fringe. "Why would God not want me to have children with my husband? The man I vowed to love, honor and cherish until we were parted by death."

"God knows everything about us, Grace. You, me… Aaron." Conviction sparkled in Mama's hazel eyes. "Have you ever stopped to think that maybe He was protecting you?"

"Protecting me from what?"

Mama looked away briefly, as though she were afraid to say what was really on her mind. "I shouldn't try to speak for God. However, I can tell you this. I know what it is to feel broken. And even though I tried to run away, God still met me in my deepest pain."

"When Daddy died?"

Mama nodded. "I felt as though I'd died, too." Her eyes shimmered with unshed tears. "All the hopes and plans for our future were gone. I was all alone. And I was *so* angry." She reached for a tissue on the side table. Dabbed the tears that now streamed down her cheeks.

Grace watched her mother, wanting to comfort her, but unsure how. Finally, she laid a hand on Mama's knee.

Mama covered it with her own. "I tried to carry on. Went through the motions of day-to-day life, but it always felt as though there was this…tremendous weight on my shoulders."

Grace knew all too well what that felt like.

"One day, I couldn't take it anymore. I'd had enough. I went into my bedroom, dropped to my knees and gave God a piece of my mind."

"Really? What did you say?"

"Through gritted teeth, I said, *I* can't *do this. I don't* want *to do this*." Tilting her head, her mother seemed to ponder the memory. Then the corners of her mouth lifted. "And you know what?"

"What?"

"In that still moment, I realized that wasn't what God was asking of me at all. Instead, He was holding out His hands, waiting for me to give it to Him. My pain, my worries and fears…" Mama shrugged. "So I did. Which is what I should have done in the first place."

She made it sound so simple.

"And did He take away the pain?"

"Not right away. I still had to walk that road, but I wasn't alone. And just like any wound, it healed over time."

She took both of Grace's hands in hers. "My precious daughter, I've loved you your whole life. But God loves you so much more than either your father or I ever could. And I promise you, God's got more in store for you than you could ever imagine. But you have to let go of your anger. Give it to God and just see what He can do."

She appreciated what Mama was saying. But Grace had been running for so long and allowed the chasm between her and God to grow so deep… "I don't know if I can."

Chapter Ten

Dusk had fallen over Ouray by the time Grace was ready to leave her mother's. Talking things over with Mama had been easier than she'd imagined and she was glad they'd crossed paths. In her heart, Grace knew it was no coincidence, but she wasn't willing to acknowledge it as anything else just yet.

"You're sure you don't want to stay here tonight?" Mama followed her out onto the porch.

"I'm sure."

"I could drive or walk you back to your campsite."

"No, thanks, Mama. I have a lot I need to sort out, so it might be best if I'm alone."

"Will you check in with me tomorrow? Let me know how you're doing?"

Grace adjusted the pack on her shoulder. "I will. Thank you." She hugged her mother. "You were just what I needed tonight."

Tears filled Mama's eyes when they parted. She cupped Grace's cheek. "You don't know how much it pleases me to hear you say that."

Grace turned away before she started crying herself. "Night, Mama. I love you."

"I love you, too, Grace."

With the glow of the porch light fading behind her, Grace dabbed her eyes, trying to remember the last time she'd told her mother she loved her. And even when it had come, in phone calls or such, Mama was always the initiator. But she'd learned a lot about her mother since coming to Ouray. Enough to realize that, perhaps, they weren't so different after all.

Between Fifth and Sixth Avenues, Grace heard noises behind her. The crunching of gravel. Footfalls. Rapid footfalls. Though some sounded slightly different than the others.

At the sound of heavy breathing, she quickened her pace, daring a glance behind her.

A tall figure jogged along the street. Her momentary angst eased as she took in the basketball shorts, sleeveless T-shirt and—prosthetic?

"Grace?" Kaleb continued toward her, stopping in front of her. "What are you doing here? I thought you'd be fast asleep by now."

"Uh—" It wasn't just his question that gave her pause. Instead it was the rapid rise and fall of his muscular chest and that sweaty gray T that not only exposed his massive biceps, but the burn scars that spread up his left arm. Lowering her gaze, she eyed the bladelike prosthetic. "You run?"

Hands on his hips, his smile was slow. "And ski and just about everything else I did before the accident." He moved closer, his smile evaporating as he studied her face. "Have you been crying?"

She immediately turned away. She could only imagine what she must look like. Red-rimmed eyes, tear-streaked cheeks...

Drawing closer yet, he said, "Talk to me, Grace. Something's been bothering you for a couple days now. I don't like to see you hurting."

Hurting? How did he know she was hurting?

The concern in his eyes had her looking everywhere but at him. While she was fine with getting him to talk about his issues and pointing out in no uncertain terms where he was wrong, she was used to keeping things to herself. Why bother sharing when the person doing the asking really didn't care?

But Kaleb wasn't Aaron. He genuinely cared about people. Including her.

And, she supposed, there was one thing she needed to set the record straight on.

"Remember Memorial Day, when I followed you into the garage after the incident with Jack?"

He nodded, his gaze still boring into her.

"I led you to believe that I was some strong Christian woman when, actually, I'm kind of on the outs with God right now."

His brow shot up. "You're on the outs with Him or He's on the outs with you?"

She let go a sigh. "Probably the latter."

After examining her for another moment or two, he crossed his arms over his hulking chest. "So why are you mad at God?"

How did he come up with that? "Did I say I was mad at Him?"

"No. I inferred it."

"Oh." Taking a sudden interest in the dim streetlight overhead, she struggled for a response.

"Are you mad at Him?"

She dared to look at him again. "Let's just say He allowed a lot of things to happen in my life that I'm not real crazy about."

Kaleb chuckled as he hiked up the left leg of his shorts. "Are you sure you want to go there with me?"

She narrowed her gaze. "My wounds may not have been physical, but I have plenty of scars."

"I'm sorry. That was rather callous of me." He hesitated a moment. "Don't suppose you'd care to share, would you?"

"Not particularly." Her gaze fell. She wasn't good at sharing.

"You sure?" He scanned the stars that illuminated the night sky. "Nice night for a campfire."

She smiled, recalling that night they'd first started going through his military stuff. She'd pushed him relentlessly until he finally told her what his problem was. And then she went off on him and stormed away.

Yet it was Kaleb who'd apologized the next day, because he finally understood what she had been trying to make him see.

"Throw in a Diet Dr Pepper and you've got a deal."

A short time later, flames danced in the small fire pit at her campsite.

Night sounds echoed around them as she popped the top on her soda. She sat beside Kaleb at the picnic table, grateful that the campsites on either side of her were still empty. "That package that came for me today. It was from my ex-husband."

Something flashed in Kaleb's eyes, though she wasn't about to guess what it was. "I wasn't aware that you were married."

"A little over four years."

"So what happened?" With his back against the table, he stretched his legs out in front of him, as though settling in for a long story.

She took a deep breath, wondering where to start and just how much to say.

"Of course, you don't have to tell me, if you don't want to."

The fact that Kaleb was willing to let her off the hook encouraged her to continue. "Aaron and I tried for two years to have a baby." She fingered the water droplets on the outside of the soda can she'd set atop the table. "But I couldn't get pregnant. So, while I was out to sea, my husband went looking for someone who could."

Watching Kaleb, she saw his left eye twitch. His jaw squaring as the muscles tensed.

"Nothing like coming home from a ten-month deployment to news that your husband wants a divorce because his girlfriend is pregnant." She couldn't have stopped the sarcasm in her tone if she tried.

"That's rough." Raking a hand through his still-damp hair, he blew out a long, slow breath. "Sounds like your ex-husband was a real piece of work."

That wasn't exactly how she'd put it. "I'm just ashamed that it took me so long to realize it."

He turned, brushing the stray hairs away from her face. "Grace, you have nothing to be ashamed of. After what he did, Aaron is the one who ought to be ashamed."

"I know. But I still heard the whispers, saw the sympathetic stares."

"Believe me, I know all about those."

She contemplated him for a moment. "Yeah, I'm sure you do."

He took hold of her hand, as if offering his strength. "Mind if I ask what was in the package?"

She told him about the house and the document her ex needed her to sign.

Kaleb shook his head. "For the life of me, I don't understand how some people can be so heartless. You didn't deserve to be treated like that, Grace. Especially by your husband. He vowed to love, honor and cherish you." His gray-green eyes bored into hers. "You deserve to be cherished, Grace."

The intensity of both his words and his gaze had her pushing to her feet to stand beside the fire. "Now you know all about me and my baggage. However, after venting to my mother tonight, I am happy to say that I have signed the document without the least bit of remorse and am eager to move on with my life."

Kaleb stood. "And what about God? Is He still on the outs?"

Her shoulders sagged. "I haven't decided yet. Right now, He seems pretty distant."

"He hasn't moved, Grace. He's right where He's always been, waiting with open arms for you to return."

"I know. I'm sure I'll find my way back eventually. I'm just too weary, perhaps embarrassed, to make that journey right now."

"I understand. I've been there." Touching a finger to her chin, he forced her to look at him. "And I can tell you from experience that no matter how tough the journey may be, it's all worth it." He caressed her cheek, sending chill bumps down her spine. "What Aaron did was wrong. But don't let him steal your joy. You deserve to be happy, Grace."

Seeing the depth of sincerity in Kaleb's eyes, she real-

ized that he was the kind of man who could do just that.
A thought that was as comforting as it was disconcerting.

Good thing she was leaving at the end of the summer.

Or maybe not.

By early Saturday evening, Kaleb wasn't any more
enthusiastic about gathering things for the museum than
he was before. However, he was determined. He'd made
a promise and he prided himself on being a man of his
word. No matter how difficult it might be.

At least Grace would be there to help him.

"You ready to go?" He smiled at her across the office.

Behind the counter, she hoisted her pack onto her
shoulder. "Yep. Pizza's ordered, so I think we're good
to go."

Just the thought of spending time with her brought
a smile to his face.

In the few weeks that they'd known each other they'd
learned more than most people would over the course of
months. It was as though there was some unseen connection between him and Grace. They simply got each
other in a way no one else could. Something he found
heartening and terrifying at the same time.

And after hearing what her ex had put her through,
Kaleb's desire to protect her had grown even stronger.

"Better batten down your hatches." He opened the
front door to an onslaught of wind and rain. "Go, go,
go." He rushed Grace out the door and toward his Jeep
as he locked the office behind him.

He hurried after her, throwing himself behind the steering wheel. "This is nuts. Reminds me of monsoon season."

"Monsoon season?" She eyed him across the center console.

"It's a weather pattern we usually go through from July to September."

She continued to stare at him. "A monsoon? In southwest Colorado?"

"Sounds crazy, I know." He fired up the engine before glancing her way. "You still want to help me tonight?"

"Better than weathering this out in my camper." She turned toward him, the corners of her mouth tilted upward. "However, I wouldn't mind checking on it."

He turned on the windshield wipers and shifted the Jeep into gear. "I hear you loud and clear."

Arriving at Grace's campsite, they saw that the tarp he'd helped her with a couple of weeks ago had come loose on one side and was flapping wildly in the wind. They quickly got out and attacked the problem, cinching the rope until everything was secure.

After retrieving the insulated jacket he'd loaned her from her camper, Grace dived into the Jeep alongside him, slamming the door behind her. "Monsoons, huh? Does this mean you're prone to hurricanes, too?" She shoved her arms into the sleeves of the coat.

"Not that I'm aware of." He adjusted the air from cool to heat and turned on the defroster to remove the fog from the windows. "Sure is raining enough, though."

"I'll say." She leaned back against the seat as he again hit the road.

After stopping to pick up their pizza, he headed straight for his house. Times like this he hated not having a garage. "Looks like we're going to have to make a run for it."

She lifted her pack over her head. "I'm ready."

"Isn't your computer in there?"

"Yes. But it's a waterproof bag."

He held up the pizza. "And what about this?"

She reached for the door handle. "Guard it with your life, soldier." Bailing from the vehicle, she sprinted for the front porch.

Donning a raincoat he found tucked in the backseat, he followed her at a brisk pace. "I usually use the back door."

A grin carved that dimple into her right cheek. "But there's no cover there." She eyed the roof that stretched the expanse of the porch.

"Good point." He opened the screen, shoved his key into the lock and held the door open for her.

Inside, he tossed the raincoat aside and set the pizza on the coffee table. "I'll be right back." He made his way down the hall to the linen closet and grabbed two towels. "Here you go." He pitched one her way when he returned to the living room.

"Thanks." She toweled her face first, then her hair before shrugging out of his old coat.

Continuing on into the kitchen, he grabbed a roll of paper towels. "What would you like to drink?"

"Got any Diet Dr—"

He'd meant to buy some. "Sorry. How about water?"

"That'll work."

By the time he returned, she was digging through one of the boxes he'd hauled into the living room and attempted to tackle the other night. Only to leave it untouched beside the coffee table.

"This would be great for the exhibit." She held up a zip-topped bag of Middle Eastern currency.

"I hadn't thought about it, but I guess you're right." He handed her a bottle of water.

With the water in one hand, she turned the bag with the other for a better look. "I know I'm right. People love this sort of stuff." She laid it on the table then twisted off the lid of the water bottle to take a drink.

He offered up a quick prayer before taking his favorite spot on the sofa and lifting the lid on the pizza box. He picked up a slice and was just about to take a bite when Grace cleared her throat.

He looked up at her. "Yes?"

"Don't get too comfortable. We still have work to do." She grabbed her own slice while rummaging through the box with her free hand.

Several slices later, both boxes sat empty.

Grace rolled up the sleeves of her plaid button-down shirt. "One down, a dozen or so to go." The spunk in her hazel eyes when she glanced at him made him feel as though he were on a carnival ride. One that dipped, twisted and turned at warp speed. "You ready?"

"Ready as I'll ever be." He pushed himself off the couch. "Sounds like the winds might be dying down." He flipped on the light in the hall as they continued.

"Yeah, it does." She fell in line beside him. "That'll make my sleep experience a better one."

Reaching around the corner into the spare bedroom-turned-storage room, he located the light switch and flipped it on.

"What's that sound?" Grace looked at him curiously.

"I don't know."

Grace's sharp intake of breath echoed his own. "What happened?"

Something that looked like a pile of dirt sat just inside the door while water rained down from a two-by-three-foot hole in the ceiling.

Stepping into the room, he studied what could only be described as a disaster. He eyed the wet Sheetrock as he peered into the attic. Only then did he realize that what he thought was dirt was actually insulation.

"Oh, no. The boxes." Without a second thought, Grace charged into the room and scooped the nearest box into her arms.

Somewhat dazed, he watched as she scurried down the hall and deposited it in the living room before moving toward him again.

"Don't just stand there." She sent him her fiercest look. "Grab a box."

"Oh. Yeah." He rushed in behind her and armed himself with two containers. He passed Grace in the hall. She was carrying the towels they'd used earlier. "What are those for?"

"The floor," she hollered over her shoulder. "Those old hardwoods don't take kindly to water."

More than an hour later, they collapsed, breathless, onto the sofa.

"Well…that was not how I'd planned to spend this evening." He absently massaged his left thigh where his stump and prosthetic met. It ached from all the back and forth.

"Me either." Grace huffed and puffed beside him.

He eyed the stack of boxes now in the corner of his living room. "We make a pretty good team."

Rolling her head to face him, she sent him an incredulous look. "You're just now figuring that out?"

"No. I'm just now stating it."

"Oh."

They sat in silence for a time, collecting their thoughts as well as catching their breath.

"Kaleb?" With one arm draped across her stomach, she stared at the ceiling.

"What?"

"You hear that?"

"Hear what?" He didn't hear anything.

"I think it stopped raining."

Standing, he moved to the front door. Opened it. "You're right." He stepped onto the porch, the rain-cooled air chilling his sweat-dampened skin.

Grace joined him, rubbing her arms. "It smells so clean out here. Earthy."

He leaned against the railing. "Thank you for helping me tonight. Sorry it didn't turn out the way we'd planned."

"I'm just glad we were here to discover what had happened. And that that pile of…whatever landed on the floor and not the boxes."

"Insulation."

"What?" She looked at him as if he were crazy.

"That pile. I'm pretty sure it was insulation."

"But it was black."

He shrugged. "Somehow the rain got into the attic, soaking the insulation, which, in turn, soaked the drywall, weakening it, and then the weight of the wet insulation caused it to cave in."

"I thought insulation was pink."

"Not in a hundred-year-old home."

"Eww." She looked so cute the way she scrunched up her nose.

He couldn't help laughing. "I'll call my insurance agent tomorrow."

"On a Sunday?"

"Good point. I'll just talk to him at church." He pushed away from the railing. "I'm sorry I wasted your time tonight, Grace."

"Wasted my time? Oh, you mean as opposed to me hanging out inside my camper all night to escape the rain?"

"In that case, I'm glad I could provide a little excitement." His boot scuffed against the wooden porch planks. "Still, we didn't accomplish much."

"We have one item."

He jerked his gaze to hers. "We do?"

"The money?"

"Oh, yeah. I forgot about that." He was procrastinating now. For whatever reason, he didn't want Grace to leave. Standing in front of her, he continued. "Thank you for helping me, Grace. You pitched right in. You were a real trooper."

Even in the dim lighting he could see the blush that crept into her cheeks as she looked up at him. "Nah, just a reformed petty officer. When water is involved, my instincts kick in."

"Either way, I appreciate it."

"You're welcome."

He stared down at her, wanting nothing more than to take her into his arms and hold her close. To run his fingers through her hair and feel its softness. To taste the sweetness of her lips.

Raking a hand through his hair, he turned away. "It's time to get you home."

A while later, as he watched her disappear into her camper, he pondered what it would be like to have someone like Grace at his side all the time. A partner. A helper. Someone he could walk through life with, knowing that if he stumbled, they wouldn't let him fall.

Grace was that kind of woman. But, come September, she'd be gone. And he didn't have a clue what he'd do without her.

Chapter Eleven

A shopping trip in Montrose with Mama Sunday afternoon was an unexpected treat. And considering Grace's all-too-basic wardrobe, one she intended to take full advantage of.

"What about this one?" Mama held up a silky turquoise tank top. "It would look beautiful on you."

Grace fingered the delicate material. "You don't think it's too dressy?"

"Not at all. This would go great with jeans, shorts, a skirt…just about anything."

Since Grace didn't have a lot of fashion sense, she appreciated her mother's flair for style. "Okay, I'll try it."

Grace continued to peruse a rack of shirts, amazed at how much lighter she felt since talking with her mother and Kaleb a few days ago. It was as though a burden the size of an aircraft carrier had been lifted from her shoulders.

A part of her wondered if by not signing over her portion of the house before she left Jacksonville, it allowed Aaron some invisible hold over her. But in her heart, she knew it was because she had finally acknowledged her bitterness toward God. And while she still had a long road back to a fully restored relationship, she was at least talking to Him again, if only to voice her displeasure.

"This is cute." She showed her mother a deep burgundy T-shirt with black and silver embellishments, grateful that God had reconciled them. After Daddy died, Grace was so wrapped up in her own grief that she failed to consider how much Mama must have been hurting. For that, she was ashamed. Mama had lost her best friend and the only man she'd ever loved. And Mama had stayed by his side until the very end.

"Oh, yes. Very nice."

After Daddy's funeral, Grace went back to Florida and Lucy returned to school, leaving Mama to pick up the pieces of her broken heart all by herself. The realization had Grace thanking God for bringing Roger and Mama together. From now on, she would judge Roger for the man he was, not the man she believed him to be.

Standing on opposite sides of the rack, they continued to flip through hangers.

"So have you and Kaleb made much headway for the museum?"

"A little." Grace slid one shirt after another from right to left. "But that leak in his roof kind of stopped us in our tracks."

"Has it been difficult for him? Going through all those memories."

"Yeah." Grace picked up a tangerine tunic, then put it back. "The first night was really tough on him."

"Oh, I hate that this is causing him pain. We want this event to be touching, but we also want it to be uplifting."

"I know that. And I think he knows that." She contemplated what Kaleb had said about blaming himself, but wasn't about to share something so personal. "Still, there's a lot of stuff in there that puts him face-to-face with the friends he lost." She approached her mother, who was holding an armload of clothes. "Okay. I think I'm ready to try—"

Mama grimaced momentarily, holding a hand to her chest.

"Are you okay?" Grace stepped closer.

"Yeah." Mama waved her off. "Just a little indigestion, that's all."

"Are you sure? Do you need anything?"

"I'm fine, baby." She handed the clothing to Grace. "You go try these on. And don't forget to come out and model for me." Just like when Grace was little. But she didn't mind. Matter of fact, she was actually kind of enjoying shopping for a change.

"I'll be out in a sec." Inside the dressing room, she tried on the red-and-black T first. Yuck. The colors were fine, but the style did not fit her at all. Better let Mama have the last word, though.

She strolled out of the dressing room.

"It's…okay." Her mother cocked her head this way and that.

"No worries, Mama. I don't like it either."

The woman looked relieved. "Okay, good."

Next one. The turquoise tank. She slipped it over her head. Looked in the mirror. Yep, this one was a keeper.

Again, she headed into the store. "Mama?" Her mother was slumped against the wall, seemingly struggling for each breath. Grace rushed to her side. "Tell me what's wrong, Mama."

"I—I—" She gasped for air. "My chest. Hard to—"

Tugging the cell phone from her back pocket, Grace dialed 911.

"9-1-1, please state your emergency."

"It's my mom. I think she's having a heart attack." Grace swallowed the lump in her throat. She'd already lost one parent. She was too young to lose another. Not now. Especially not now. She and Mama were finally forming a bond. "We're at Avery's Style Mart. Hurry. Please."

By the time the paramedics arrived, Mama was whiter than Grace had ever seen her. Grace clung to the woman's hand. "I'm right here, Mama. I'm right here."

Roger.

He'd taken out a tour today. She glanced at her watch. Three o'clock. He probably wouldn't be back for another hour.

While the paramedics evaluated her mother, she dialed his cell phone. No answer.

Not knowing what to do, she dialed Kaleb. "I need your help."

"What's going on?"

"I don't know, but I think Mama might be having a heart attack. I need to let Roger know."

"Where are you?"

"We're in Montrose. I don't know. Do they have a hospital here?"

"Yeah. A good one, too. She'll be in good hands."

She could feel tears stinging the backs of her eyes. "Tell Roger to hurry."

"Grace?"

"Yes?"

"God's got this, all right. I'm praying for both

Donna and you. You just stay calm and be there for your mama."

A sob caught in her throat as they loaded Mama onto the gurney. "I will."

Grabbing her mother's purse, she followed as they wheeled Mama to the ambulance.

"Miss? Oh, miss."

Grace turned to see a clerk trotting behind her.

"The shirt. I'm sorry, but you'll have to pay for it."

She glanced at the price tag, grabbed a wad of bills from the back pocket of her jeans and handed a twenty and ten to the clerk. "Keep the change."

"Will you be following us?" The female paramedic looked back at her as they loaded Mama into the ambulance.

"No." Still holding her mother's red cross-body purse, she climbed up behind them. "I'm coming with you."

With sirens wailing, they set off for the hospital.

Inside the ambulance, they started an IV on her mother, as well as an EKG. Before they could do any more, they arrived at the hospital.

Grace couldn't remember her heart ever beating so wildly.

As they opened the back doors of the ambulance, her mother looked at her. Behind the oxygen mask, Grace saw a look of fear. One that seemed to say, "Don't leave me."

She was pretty scared herself. But she had to stay strong. "I'm still here, Mama." She reached for her hand. The woman grabbed hold and Grace squeezed.

Then they pulled the gurney from the vehicle, breaking the connection.

Grace followed as they rushed through the automatic doors, into the emergency room.

"Female, age fifty-nine," one paramedic rattled off. "Possible heart attack."

She looked down at her mother. Though she didn't think it possible, her mother had grown even more ashen. "We're here, Mama. We're at the hospital. They're going to take good care of you."

They rushed through another set of doors, then made a quick left into a triage room.

Fluorescent lights glared overhead as they transferred Mama to the hospital bed. Nurses pulled on blue exam gloves and hurried to connect monitors.

"BP is one-sixty over ninety," said another paramedic. "Heart rate one-ten."

The flurry of activity had Grace pressing her back against the wall. She didn't like feeling so helpless. But what could she do?

Pray.

Pray? That was something she hadn't done in a long time. Okay, so she was talking to God again. But praying? That involved faith. Believing that God might actually do what you were asking.

There was a time when she believed God heard her prayers. That He interceded on her behalf. But now? Did she trust God to help Mama?

A tiny spark somewhere deep inside her told her that she could. But she'd have to choose to believe.

God, I know You're there. And I know that You know what's going on down here. Please be with Mama. Comfort her and protect her. She drew in a shaky breath. *God, I can't lose her. I wasted so many years being angry with her.* She swallowed hard. *And You. Forgive me. Please.*

Lucy. Grace needed to call her. No, she'd wait until she had some news. And then face her sister's wrath. Lucy would have a cow if she knew Grace hadn't called her immediately.

Pulling out her phone, she moved just outside the door where she could still see and hear everything that was going on.

"Hey, Grace. What's going on?"

"I'm in the emergency room. With Mama."

"Oh, no! What's wrong?"

"We just got here, so I don't have any details, but she might have had a heart attack."

"A heart attack? Mama?" Lucy's voice quivered. "This can't be happening." Grace imagined her sister shoving her fingers through her long blond hair. "We can't lose her, too, Grace."

"I'm not about to let that happen, Luce. I need to go now, but I promise I'll call you back just as soon as I know something."

"Okay. Thanks, Grace."

"Mrs. Hamilton, do you have any allergies?" she heard one of the nurses ask as she reentered Mama's room.

Did Grace even know the answer to that?

The nurse punched the information into a computer.

"Do you have a DNR?" Why did the nurse continue to badger her mother? Couldn't they see she was struggling just to breathe, let alone talk?

"Thank you." The nurse returned to her computer.

Grace resumed her post at the wall. Watching her mother, a woman so full of life, suddenly forced to fight for it, shook Grace to the core. She battled the tears that begged to be unleashed. But she would not give in. At least not when her mother could see her. She had to stay strong. Something she should be good at by now. Instead, she felt as though she could crumble at any moment.

God, I'll do whatever You want. Just, please, don't take Mama.

Roger was visibly shaken when Kaleb gave him the news about Donna. So there was no way Kaleb was going to let him drive all the way to Montrose. Better to close a couple of hours early than risk his friend's life.

Besides, he wanted to be there for Grace. When he'd talked with her on the phone, he could tell she was struggling. And given that she'd been the calm in more than a few of his storms lately, it was time to return the favor.

By the time he and Roger arrived at the hospital, doctors had determined that Donna had not had a heart attack. Unfortunately, they feared she may have a blockage, and she was undergoing a heart catheterization when they finally located Grace in the waiting room.

She stood, her expression hovering between worry and relief. Enduring something like this was never easy, but it was even tougher when you had to face it alone. "Glad you guys finally made it."

"Me, too," said Roger. "Any word?"

"No." Her arms were crossed over her chest. "They said someone would be out to talk to us once the procedure is over."

"Guess all we can do is wait, then." Roger raked a hand through his gray hair, leaving it standing on end.

Kaleb could only imagine what was going through his head. After all, he'd already buried one wife. Donna was his second chance. And Roger loved her with every fiber of his being, just as he had Camille.

While Roger paced, Kaleb kept his focus on Grace. He could see the fear in the depth of her hazel eyes. "How are you doing?"

She shrugged. "As well as can be expected, I guess." The nonchalance of her response gave him pause.

He'd heard the angst in her voice when she called him earlier. The fear of losing another parent had threaded every word.

Now she was shutting him out. Closing the door on her emotions and mentally retreating to that place where no one or nothing could hurt her.

And it stung. He'd revealed so much to Grace. Taking her to some of his darkest places. And yet she still refused to trust him.

A man dressed in blue scrubs pushed through the door then.

Roger and Kaleb flanked Grace as the doctor continued toward them.

His gaze traveled to Roger. "Are you Mr. Hamilton?"

"Yes, sir."

"Dr. Griffith." The man shook Roger's hand before addressing them collectively. "Mrs. Hamilton had significant blockages in her coronary arteries. We were, however, able to insert stents into both, so she should be ready to go home by tomorrow."

Grace and Roger both let go a sigh of relief.

"When can we see her?" Roger watched the other man intently.

"Only one of you will be able to join her in recovery. The nurse will let you know when they're ready for you."

As the doctor left, Grace turned to Roger. "Mama will be eager to see you."

Roger let go a sigh, shoving his hands into the pockets of his jeans. "I'm pretty eager to see her myself."

"I know you are." Grace squared her shoulders. "I can see her later."

She was putting on quite the act. But Kaleb had glimpsed behind the mask. He knew the tender heart that lay behind the tough facade. So for now, let her walk that tightrope. However, he'd also make sure that he was there to catch her when she fell.

"Kaleb?" Roger looked past Grace. "Would you mind running Grace to pick up Donna's SUV?"

"Not at all."

When he and Grace exited the hospital thirty minutes later, the sun hovered over the western horizon.

She walked through the parking lot in silence, her arms wrapped around her middle as though she were fighting to keep her emotions from escaping.

Placing his hand against the small of her back, he urged her around to the passenger side of his Jeep. For a moment, he felt her trembling. Before she jerked away.

"Grace?" He stepped in front of her, hoping she might relax and let down her guard. But when she refused to look at him, he continued. "Where are we going?"

"Avery's something."

"Ah, Avery's Style Mart." He opened the door. "Hop in."

The round-trip took all of twenty minutes. And though she tried to evade him, parking on the opposite side of the parking lot, he caught up to her on their way into the hospital.

"What are your plans for tonight?" He followed her

through the automatic door. "Are you going to stay here or do you want me to take you back to Ouray?"

She continued across the shiny tile. "I think it's best if I stay here with Mama."

Why did he get the feeling she'd been rehearsing her response. "I'm sure Roger will want to stay, too."

She pushed the up button on the elevator. "Then I'll sleep in the waiting room if I have to." Stubbornness squared her shoulders.

How much longer could she go on like this? At some point, she was going to break.

Nonetheless, he said, "Whatever you like."

He waited with Roger while Grace went in to see her mother. "How was Donna?"

"She's resting comfortably." Forearms on his thighs, his friend rubbed his hands together. "Boy, you talk about a sight for sore eyes."

Roger was a blessed man. To find love twice. Kaleb had yet to have a relationship that even resembled that kind of love. Though he wasn't about to give up hope.

When Grace rejoined them, Roger presented her with a set of keys. "Could I get you to check on the house for us?"

The conflicted expression on Grace's face had Kaleb biting back a laugh. So much for staying at the hospital.

"Oh." She tentatively took hold of the keys. "Um… sure."

"You don't mind driving her back to Ouray, do you, Kaleb?"

"No, of course not." Though he could guarantee that Grace wasn't too excited about the prospect.

"I appreciate it." Roger smiled at Grace. "You're welcome to stay there, if you like."

"Uh, yeah… Thank you." Her gaze fell to the tan carpet.

Though Kaleb had no doubt that Grace wanted to be with her mother, he also knew she'd be better off getting a good night's rest. Something that was not easily accomplished in a hospital. Besides, Roger would call if anything were to happen.

Kaleb touched her elbow. "It'll be dark soon, so we should get going."

She reluctantly acquiesced.

"Shall we grab a bite to eat?" He motioned to a fast-food place on their way out of Montrose.

"I'm not hungry." Grace stared out the window, continuing to do so until they pulled up in front of Roger and Donna's darkened house thirty minutes later.

She quickly jumped out.

Kaleb killed the engine and followed her. "Looks like everything's off to me."

"I'd better make sure." Grace continued up the front steps.

She unlocked the door and went inside. Once she'd turned on a lamp or two, Kaleb stepped just inside the front door. "Check the kitchen."

A moment later, she returned. "It's fine. I'll check upstairs." She disappeared for a short time and he heard floorboards creaking overhead. Then she made her way back down the steps. "Everything's fine."

If only that were true.

"Okay, good." But Grace was far from fine. He watched her as she hesitated at the foot of the stairs. "What's going on, Grace? Why are you shutting down on me?"

She immediately crossed her arms over her chest,

her feet riveted to the hardwood floor. "Shutting down? What do you mean?"

He moved closer. "Let it go, Grace. We both know you're hurting."

Though she refused to look at him, he saw her bottom lip quiver. She was fighting hard to keep it together.

"You're not as tough as you pretend to be." He continued toward her. "You're afraid of losing the only parent you have left." The words sounded harsh, even to his own ears. But he had to get through to her.

Her liquid eyes looked everywhere but at him. Her shoulders drooped.

Erasing what little space remained between them, he pulled her to him and enveloped her in his embrace.

Instead of objecting, she wrapped her arms around him, sobs racking her body.

He caressed her hair. "It's okay, Grace. You're safe. Let it go." He would hold her forever if she needed him to.

She fisted his shirt. "I was—" she hiccuped "—so scared. I can't lose her, too. I can't." Her words were muffled against his chest.

"I know. And you did great. You got your mom the help she needed." He tightened his hold and simply allowed her to cry.

When she finished, she looked up at him, her eyes still shimmering with unshed tears. "Do you think she's going to be okay?"

"Yes, Grace, I believe your mother is going to be okay. But what about you?"

"I've been, um—" her gaze drifted to the ceiling and she blinked rapidly "—praying. A lot."

"That's good. Matter of fact, that's real good."

"How did Roger take it?" She tried to swipe away her tears. "When you told him."

"Not too well." He stroked her hair. "Like you, he's lost someone he loved very much. So a lot of those fears you had were going on inside of him, too. And the fact that he wasn't there only exacerbated things."

With his arms still around her, she nodded, her eyes never leaving his. The gold and green flecks that had diminished earlier were back. And more stunning than ever.

His heart pounded. He needed to get out of here. Take Grace back to her campsite before he did something he'd regret.

He released her. Took a step back. "We need to go."

"I was, um, thinking I'd stay here tonight."

Conflicted, he stared down at her. "Do you need to go get some clothes or anything?"

"No, I'll be all right."

"And what about tomorrow? You're welcome to take the day off, if you like."

She took a step closer. "I'll probably come in early and then go from there."

"That's fine."

For the longest while, they continued to stare at each other. His mouth went dry, his pulse racing like crazy.

"Grace?"

Her eyes were wide as she stared up at him. "Yes?"

Try as he might, he couldn't make himself look away. He didn't want to. All he wanted was to taste her lips.

Reaching for her, he lowered his head and did just that, as though it were the most natural thing in the world.

Best of all, she kissed him back. And he'd never tasted anything so sweet.

Wrapping both arms around her waist, he pulled her closer, deepening their kiss.

Grace threaded her fingers through the back of his hair. She smelled amazing. Like flowers and sunshine.

Then she tensed and pulled away, her eyes wide. "You should go."

His breathing was ragged. "I think you're right."

He turned for the door, raking a disgusted hand through his hair. What had he been thinking? Kissing her when she was at her most vulnerable.

She kissed you back.

Yeah, because she needed to be comforted. Not taken advantage of.

Hand on the storm door, he glanced over his shoulder. She remained where he'd left her, fingers pressed to her lips.

"Sleep well, Grace." Heart heavy, he stepped into the night. Though the timing of his kiss may have been off, there was one thing he now knew for certain.

He'd fallen for Grace.

Chapter Twelve

Grace downed her second cup of coffee the next morning, then reached for a Diet Dr Pepper. After tossing and turning all night, she'd need all the caffeine she could get her hands on just to make it through the day.

After showering at Mama's, she'd come back to her campsite to change and get ready for work. Despite having a comfortable bed for a change, sleep was elusive. Worries about Mama had plagued her brain. She was beyond grateful that God had spared her mother. But she also prayed that they could have more time together.

And then there was that kiss.

Even now, her lips tingled at the thought. The warmth of Kaleb's embrace made her feel special and wanted. Yeah, she'd enjoyed it all right. Until she realized what a huge mistake she was making.

Inside her camper, she picked up a brush and ran it through her still-damp hair. She was only in Ouray for the summer. Kaleb knew that; she knew that. So kissing him was like playing with fire. And she'd be the one getting burned.

Her cell phone rang.

She tossed the brush aside and grabbed the phone from its charger.

Lucy. Probably looking for an update on Mama.

Grace had called her last night before turning in. Unfortunately, she hadn't spoken with Roger yet this morning, so she didn't have any more news.

"Hey, Luce."

"Any word on Mama?"

"Not yet." Holding the phone between her ear and shoulder, Grace pulled her hair back, gave it a couple of twists and affixed it to the back of her head with a claw clip.

"I figured, since I hadn't heard from you. Anyway, the main reason I'm calling is to let you know that I'm coming to Ouray."

She again took hold of the phone. "When?"

"I'm already on the road. Should be in sometime this afternoon."

"Mama will be glad to see you." However, she had to admit that she'd kind of enjoyed having her mother to herself. When Mama and Lucy were together, Grace couldn't seem to find a way to fit in.

"Ditto. I just wish it was under better circumstances. I'm so glad you were there for her, though. I mean, what if you'd been out on that cruise ship? How would we have gotten ahold of you?"

"I'm sure they have ways for you to contact me in case of emergency. How long are you planning to stay?" She glanced at her watch, then picked up her blush and swiped each cheekbone a couple of times.

"A few days. A week. Whatever it takes to help her get settled in once she comes home."

"If all goes according to plan, that should be today."

She glanced at herself in a hand mirror. Rough, but it would have to do. "Hey, I'm late for work, Luce. I'll call you if I learn anything."

Ending the call, she took a deep breath. This was definitely going to be one of *those* days. Starting with having to face Kaleb. *God, please help me keep it together.*

Grabbing her pack, she set off for work, hoping to hear from Roger soon. With Mama coming home today, there was no point in Grace going to the hospital. If that changed, she'd catch a ride with Lucy later today.

Gravel crunched beneath her übercomfortable, though not-so-cute, sandals as she hiked up Seventh Avenue. The day had already been chaotic. And it was only a little past seven.

What if you'd been out on that cruise ship? Lucy's words replayed in her mind.

What if Mama hadn't been in Montrose when her breathing failed? She was only there because of Grace. If she'd been in Ouray, they'd have lost at least thirty minutes of valuable time.

And what if Grace were at sea? Did the cruise line have a plan for getting the crew home in case of emergencies? Surely they did. Though it would likely involve their next port of call. By then, it could be too late.

Arriving at Mountain View Tours, she shoved her thoughts aside and drew in a long, bolstering breath before going inside. *Nothing has changed, so just act normal.*

She hurried through the garage, offering a quick "Good morning" to Kaleb and five of his guides before moving inside. After dropping her pack behind the counter, she trashed her empty soda can, snagged a fresh one from the mini fridge and pulled the clipboards for this morning's tours before unlocking the front door.

Fortunately for her, Kaleb had volunteered to cover Roger's tours. That meant she wouldn't have to worry about being alone with him. It would also give her time to further rein in her flailing emotions, tie them in a tidy little bow and stuff them so deep they'd never have a chance to surface again.

The front door pushed open then and a young family entered, led by two energetic boys she remembered from Saturday. Somewhere around six and eight years old, both held small action figures and readily provided sound effects as the figures zoomed through the air, guided by the boys' small fingers.

A loud "Shooooom..." echoed through the air, followed by an explosive sound as one of the action figures careened toward the newly carpeted floor.

"Boys..." The father's warning went unheeded.

The garage door flew open then and Kaleb stepped inside. His commanding presence seemed to stop the boys in their tracks.

Buzz-cut heads tilted all the way back; mouths agape, they stared up at Kaleb.

"Looks like you fellas are having fun." Kaleb smiled down at them. "Are you ready to do some exploring today?"

The boys nodded as if in awe.

"All right. Well, you just hang tight for just a couple minutes." He shook both parents' hands. "Good to see you again."

He joined Grace behind the desk, glancing over the clipboards as he approached. "Lane's going to be taking Roger's tours."

Her gut tightened, her emotions fighting against the flimsy restraint she'd halfheartedly cinched around them. "So you'll—"

"Be here. Yes." He didn't sound any happier about the prospect than she was. And he had yet to look her in the eye. Obviously she wasn't the only one with regrets about last night. So how come his bugged her?

Once the tours departed, Grace didn't see hide or hair of Kaleb. She had no doubt that he was hiding from her, trying to avoid any discussion about what had taken place last night.

Fine by her. She'd rather forget the whole incident. Or at least that was what she told herself. Yet images still crept into the forefront of her mind and she'd find herself wondering what it would be like to have the love of a man like Kaleb. A man who loved through actions and not just words. A man who knew what love really meant.

Shaking them away, she heard the garage door open. That could only mean—

"Grace, I think we need to talk."

She turned away from the computer and, for the first time today, allowed herself to look into Kaleb's handsome face. "About?"

"I think you know." Still standing a few feet from the counter, he removed his camo army ball cap and scratched a hand through his short hair before tugging the cap back into place. "I shouldn't have kissed you last night."

She lowered her gaze, not wanting to feel the stab of pain his words inflicted on her heart. Of course he shouldn't have kissed her. Now that he'd had time to think, he probably realized the error of his ways. After all, what man would want a woman who couldn't bear him children?

"Though I can't say that I'm sorry about it either. Just the timing. You were vulnerable, and I took advantage of that."

He thought she was vulnerable? When she'd wanted, practically initiated, that kiss?

She lifted her head as he moved closer.

"I like you, Grace." His smile was bashful and boyish, which only added to his charm. "I like you a lot. And, given the opportunity, I'd like to see where things could lead with us."

Us? What us? There was no *us*. She was leaving in September.

But he wants there to be.

She swallowed the sudden lump in her throat, not sure how she felt about what he'd just said. The part of her that could fall for Kaleb in a heartbeat wanted to run with the prospect. But the practical, been-burned-before part of her told her to keep her distance.

"I—uh…"

He lifted a palm to stop her. "It's okay. You don't have to say anything." Shoving his hands in the pockets of his medium wash jeans, he started toward the garage. "I just wanted to acknowledge the elephant in the room and let you know how I feel." With that, he shoved through the door and was gone.

So much for taking control of her emotions. They'd now broken loose and were running rampant. Some wanted to fist-pump the air, while others were ready to run and hide.

She'd never felt more conflicted. Imagining herself

with Kaleb was so easy. But she'd been down that road before and the results were disastrous.

Besides, she had other commitments. Commitments that took her far away from Ouray.

Her gaze drifted to the window, taking in all that was small-town life. The flags that lined Main Street waving in the breeze, the old buildings painted in an array of colors and people stopping to chat on the street.

Oh, but Ouray wasn't just any small town. The mountains that enveloped it, along with their rich history, were the very essence of Ouray. Her focus lifted to the evergreen-blanketed slopes at the town's edge. The pioneering spirit may not have been born in Ouray, but it still thrived. In the month that she'd been here, she'd met person after person who had given up their homes, jobs and 401(k) plans in exchange for something more meaningful. Something fulfilling. No matter how hard they had to work.

Her phone rang, stirring her from her thoughts.

"Hey, Roger. How's Mama?" Little by little she was growing more comfortable with him. In no way, shape or form was he the opportunistic man she'd once imagined him to be.

"Better than expected. Her color is back to normal, she's breathing freely…"

Grace's heart swelled. "That is good news. Is she coming home today?"

"Yes."

"Oh, I'm so glad to hear it. Tell Mama that Lucy called and she's on her way up here for a few days."

"Donna will be happy about that. But, Grace, I was hoping… Well, would you reconsider staying with your mother and me for the rest of your time here in Ouray?"

A smile started somewhere in her heart, quickly moving to her face. She opened her mouth, but the words refused to come.

"You'll have your own bedroom, your own bathroom. You can come and go as you please. It would mean a lot to both of us."

Her bottom lip quivered as unbidden tears trailed down her cheeks. Despite all her rebellion and ornery antics, God had given her the desire of her heart.

"Thank you." She sniffed, feeling rather humbled. "I think I'd like that very much."

Wednesday evening, Kaleb could feel panic closing in. He eyed the boxes still stacked in his living room, his gut churning. He'd never make it by Saturday. At least not on his own. If he intended to get his stuff to the museum in time, he needed Grace's help.

He hated to ask her, though. She was dealing with her own stuff. Her mother, moving… Not to mention what a fool he was for kissing her.

Still…

He at least had to give it a shot. If she said no, well, he'd figure that out if and when the time came.

Grabbing his car keys, he hurried outside, fired up his Jeep and headed the few blocks to Roger and Donna's.

What if Grace said no? Sure, things had been fine between them at work, but this wasn't work. He was selfishly asking her to do something out of the goodness of her heart. Not much different than that night he took advantage of her kiss.

But he wasn't taking advantage of Grace. At least,

he didn't think so. He liked being with her. Valued her input. Trusted her enough to share his darkest secrets.

Shadows covered Ouray as he parked alongside the road and made his way up the front steps, glancing at the unfamiliar car in the drive. Must belong to Grace's sister.

The window was open on the storm door, so he could hear voices and the television through the screen.

With his heart beating erratically, he pressed the bell.

"Hey, buddy." Roger pushed open the door. "What's up?"

"Is Grace here?"

"No, she went over to her campsite to shut things down and bring her trailer back here." The older man stepped out onto the porch, wearing cargo shorts and a T-shirt. "I offered to go with her, but she insisted she could take care of it herself."

"That sounds like Grace." He thought back to that day she first arrived, when she had a flat tire. She was good at refusing help. Although he suspected it had more to do with looking after her mother this time than accepting help. "Don't worry, Roger. I'll head on over there. See if I can't give her a hand." And, hopefully, vice versa.

Windows open, he took off across town. This week had brought them some fantastic weather with above-normal temps, which was good for business. Lord willing, the warm weather would also speed up the snowmelt in the higher elevations, allowing the county to get some of the passes there open earlier than usual.

Easing up to Grace's campsite, he saw that her camper was once again a tiny trailer and hitched to the back of her bike. He took a minute to admire it. Another time, another place…

Dressed in jeans and a gray United States Navy T-shirt, Grace lifted a footlocker onto the trailer's tongue.

He got out of the Jeep and started toward her. "Need some help?"

She blew at a stray hair that had escaped her clip to dangle in front of her face. "Little late, don't you think?"

He picked up the cooler. "I would have been happy to help, if somebody would have told me what they had planned."

"Yeah, yeah." She took hold of the cooler. "There are some bungee cords in my right saddlebag. Mind grabbing them for me?"

He did and handed them to her.

"Thanks." While she secured the items, he scanned the now vacant campsite, feeling a bit melancholy that she was leaving. Well, moving, anyway.

"Looks like you've got everything."

"Yep." She slipped her hands into her back pockets. "I'll settle up with Bud and Luann in the morning."

His gaze drifted to the fire pit, thinking about how integral it had been to their relationship. "I see you've got a few pieces of wood left." He glanced at Grace. "Shame to let it go to waste."

Eyes narrowing, she perched her hands on her hips. "You can't be serious."

"What? You know I love campfires."

She gestured to the three split logs. "There isn't enough wood to make a big fire."

"Who said anything about big?" He simply wanted to have her to himself for a little longer.

Shaking her head, she chuckled. "You're incorrigible."

"I've been called worse things." He gathered some twigs, tossed them into the pit. "So what do you say? I'll still make sure we get your trailer back."

"We?" She crossed her arms over her chest.

"Yes, we. I came with the intention of helping you and I intend to do just that. No matter how late I might be."

"How did you—"

"Would you mind handing me your lighter?" He'd seen it in her saddlebag.

Digging through his pockets, he pulled out a couple of receipts and tucked them beneath the kindling. "Have a seat." He gestured to the picnic table. "I'll be right with you."

She puffed out a laugh. "You're a mess, you know that?" She plopped down on the bench.

"That's me. An incorrigible mess." He lit the papers. Waited a few moments before blowing on the flame. "We've had some interesting conversations around this fire pit." As the flames spread, he added the larger twigs. "This'll be our last hurrah."

"Let's see." She touched a finger to her chin. "It was here that I pushed you to reveal your baggage and it's also where you pushed me to tell you mine. So what are we going to discuss this time?"

He laid the split logs on the fire before joining her. They sparked and flared to life. "I don't know. What baggage have you got left?"

Her genuine laughter was like rain on parched soil.

"I need your help, Grace. Saturday is the deadline to get my items to the museum. Yet, whenever I look at those boxes—"

"You're overwhelmed."

"Exactly." He let go a sigh. "Look, I know you've got your own life to deal with…"

"That's true. However, do you know how upset my mother would be if you failed to meet that deadline? She's convinced that your memorabilia is what's going to make this exhibit."

He stared at Grace. Donna upset? That was hard to imagine. Disappointed maybe. "We definitely can't have that."

"After what she's been through, no, we cannot. So, we've got to hit it and hit it hard. Tomorrow night, Friday night, even Saturday morning, if need be."

"Um…" Dumbfounded, he scratched his head. "Okay. Yeah. I'm willing to put forth whatever it takes."

"That means no more distractions, you got that?" She was beginning to sound like a drill instructor.

"You think I planned to have a leaky roof?"

"No. But no more steak dinners. Pizza is fine. Sandwiches. Anything we can eat with one hand."

"Works for me."

As daylight faded, he kept his focus on the flames, but held out his hand. "How are things going? I mean, with your sister here and all?"

Grace actually took hold. "Not too bad, I guess."

He sensed her hesitating. "But?"

She took a deep breath. Blew it out. "Tonight, at dinner, Lucy announced she was pregnant."

Ouch. "How do you feel about that?"

"I'm happy for her, of course. But she's only been married a little over a year." Grace lifted a shoulder. "It stings a little that she was able to achieve something I couldn't."

"Did Lucy know you had been trying to get pregnant?"

"No." Grace shook her head, then laid it against his arm. A move so subtle, yet one that seemed to validate his feelings.

"Grace?"

"Yeah."

"Just for the record, when I kissed you, I wasn't trying to take advantage of you."

Lifting her head, she looked at him as if he were crazy. "I know that." Her gaze seemed to search his. "In case you couldn't tell, I wanted you to kiss me."

"You did?" Hmm... Apparently his sensors were out of whack.

"I did." She let go of his hand. "And then I realized how selfish that was. I mean, I'm leaving in September. It's not like we could have any kind of long-term relationship or anything."

He halfway smiled. "I had the same thoughts." Although, it didn't stop him from wishing. And praying. "But we could definitely stay in contact. Through email and such."

"Absolutely."

The wind rustled the leaves overhead, filling the void.

He scanned the darkening sky. "I suppose we should get you back to your folks." Eyeing the water spigot, he stood, knowing he'd need to douse the fire.

"Yeah." She pushed to her feet. "And then tomorrow night—"

"We hit the boxes and work to make your mama happy."

Chapter Thirteen

Grace grabbed another box Friday night and pulled open the flaps. They'd made a lot of progress last night, coming up with a few items. Though they still hadn't come across anything significant for the museum display. And at this rate, they might not.

On the other side of Kaleb's living room, he stood near the sofa sorting through stacks of photos. She was proud of him for his stick-to-itiveness. For pushing past whatever emotions he might be battling to get the job done. Because tomorrow they would be handing off whatever they came up with.

Peering into her box, she saw layers of wadded packing paper, unlike the others where stuff had just been tossed inside. She removed the paper to find another slightly smaller box with a lid.

"Any idea what might be in here?" She pulled out the smaller box and set it on top of another box.

"Not a clue." He was beside her now. "Shall we find out?"

She watched as he lifted the lid, realizing it was a hatbox of some sort.

Kaleb pulled out the tissue paper. "It's my helmet."

No doubt about that. Except this helmet had a pretty hefty dent in it and the pixelated camo cover was torn in multiple spots, as though it had been pelted repeatedly.

That was when it hit her. "Is this the helmet you were wearing when the IED went off?"

"Sure is." He pulled it from the box. "This thing probably saved my life." He fingered the dent.

Judging by the size and location of the spot… "I'm certain it did." A shudder ran through her. Though she'd heard the extent of Kaleb's injuries, this visual made her realize just how close he'd come to dying. And even though he was alive and well and standing beside her now, the thought still made her sad.

"Guess you didn't have to wear these in the navy." He looked from the helmet to her.

"Nope." She eyed the tattered piece. "I'm kind of glad, too. Looks a little cumbersome."

"You get used to it." He shrugged. "Here." He placed the helmet on her head. "How does that feel?"

"It's not near as heavy as I would have expected." Since it was too big, she reached a hand to steady it.

He stood back and smiled. "You look awful cute. But then, you always look cute."

The wink that accompanied his comment had a wave of heat creeping into her cheeks. Removing the helmet, she turned so he wouldn't see. Cleared her throat. "That's the sort of thing that would be perfect for the exhibit. That is, if you're okay with it."

"No, I think it's a great idea." He set it back in the box, adding the tissue paper and lid before picking it up. "I'll set it over here with the other items." The adjacent dining room-turned-home gym was the designated drop zone for all potential museum items.

Grace moved over to the box he'd been working on. Retrieved a stack of photos. "Have you considered loaning them one of your uniforms?"

Now standing at the end of the sofa, hands resting low on his hips, he shook his head. "I can't believe I didn't think of that. I mean, I've got an entire closet full of uniforms."

"Looks like we just came up with another item."

"Which uniform, though?"

Continuing to shuffle through pictures, she said, "If you still have one of your combat uniforms that would be good. Especially since Mama talked about you bringing things into the twenty-first century." She glanced his way, shrugging. "The Universal Camouflage Pattern does just that."

"Okay." He moved beside her, picking up the photos he'd been working on before. "I'll grab it later. Just don't let me forget."

"Are these pictures of you in Afghanistan?" She fanned out three images. One of him in full gear, standing near a Humvee, another of him with a series of tents in the background and yet another of him in the desert.

He leaned closer. Close enough for her to feel the warmth radiating from his bare arms. "Yep. Those were from my second tour."

"I'm sure they could scan these, maybe blow them up to use in the display."

"We can always offer."

"Do you have an envelope or a zip-top bag I could put them in so they won't get lost?"

"Sure. Just give me one second."

While she waited, she continued to sift through the plethora of photos. "You know, at some point, you should consider sorting all these out and putting them in albums."

He reappeared, holding a plastic Baggie. "That sounds about as much fun as watching paint dry."

Without thinking, she elbowed him in the side. "I'm serious." She snatched the bag.

He flinched then rubbed his ribs as though she'd hurt him. "I know you are. Let's just say it's not high on my priority list right now."

She dropped the photos into the bag. "Well, you should at least think about it."

Continuing to look at snapshots, she came across one of Kaleb looking very handsome in his dress uniform with his arms around the waist of a pretty blonde.

"Who's this?" A strange sensation fluttered through her as she showed him the picture.

"That's Gina."

"Your fiancée."

"*Ex*-fiancée." He looked at Grace, a mischievous grin on his face. "Why? Are you jealous?"

She cast him an incredulous look. "No." To be jealous would mean she had feelings for Kaleb. Feelings that went beyond friendship.

So why is your stomach churning?

Besides, she'd never been the jealous type. At least not until she found out her then-husband had a girlfriend.

"I'm just teasing you, Grace."

Two could play at that game. "What would you do if I were jealous?"

"Hmm…" He rubbed his chin, pondering. "Well, first I'd be flattered."

"Pfft." She waved a hand. "Typical male."

"And then—" he moved closer, slipping his arms around her waist "—I'd do everything I could to prove that you had no reason to worry."

Looking into his smoldering eyes, her heart stopped. She could easily believe that any woman fortunate enough to have a man like Kaleb would never have cause for alarm. But she certainly did. His lips were mere inches from hers. All she had to do was push up onto her tiptoes—

"Easy, soldier." She pressed a hand to his chest. "We have work to do."

He hesitated a moment, his smile as teasing as it was tempting, before finally moving away. "Can I get you something to drink? Diet Dr Pepper, perhaps?"

Considering how warm it had suddenly got— "Since when do you have Diet Dr Pepper?"

He started toward the kitchen. "Since I picked some up at the store the other day."

She eased onto the sofa, her legs feeling a bit wobbly. Not only did he know her favorite drink, he actually made the effort to go out and get it.

"Here you go." He handed her a cold can.

"Thanks." Sinking back into the overstuffed cushions, she surreptitiously watched him as he moved across the hardwood floor and opened another box. *A man who loves through actions, not words.*

"Hey, I forgot all about this." He reached inside the box and pulled out a uniform shirt. But it wasn't like the others. "This came from my Afghan friend Akram." He held up the desert camo shirt. "He was one of our trans-lators. He gave me this in exchange for a pair of Nikes."

"Really?" She scooted to the edge of her seat, but still didn't trust herself to stand.

"He was a pretty cool guy." Kaleb turned the uni-form this way and that. "Think they'd like to have this at the museum?"

"They might. I mean, it's definitely not something people see every day." She popped the top on her drink. Took a sip. "Add it to the pile and let them decide."

After setting her soda on the side table, she grabbed another wad of pictures from the box in front of her. The guy had enough photos to fill a hundred albums.

She shuffled through them. Desert. Desert. Armored vehicle. Hmph. The next image was of Kaleb in full combat uniform, playing soccer with a group of chil-dren. She thumbed to the next one. Kaleb sitting with a dog and three little boys, his grin as big as the sun. Another was of him holding a smiling little girl. And yet another of him cradling an infant.

"Whatcha got there?"

She hadn't realized he was beside her. "More pic-tures." She handed them to him, her heart twisting as a smile bloomed on his face.

"Oh, yeah." His head bobbed up and down as he studied the images. "The kids were great. To see their smiling faces in the midst of such chaos always did wonders for our battle-scarred souls. And they loved to play soccer." His thoughtful gaze drifted from the pictures to her. "It never ceased to amaze me that, even though they were surrounded by death and destruction, they were always ready with a smile."

She reached for her soda can, trying to ignore the

ache that leached into her chest. "From what I've heard, kids can be pretty resilient."

He gestured to the photos. "This is living proof."

Though she already knew the answer, she asked anyway. "You really like kids, don't you?"

"Are you kidding? Kids are great." Grinning, he tossed the pictures on the table. "But you'll find that out soon enough, *Aunt Grace*."

As Kaleb returned to the other side of the room, a tempest of unwanted emotions whirled inside her. Somewhere along the way, no matter how hard she'd tried to fight it or told herself they were just friends, she'd foolishly opened her heart to Kaleb. Allowing him to take up residence in those areas she'd deemed off-limits.

Now she'd pay the price.

Thankfully, she was leaving. Because if she were to stay in Ouray, she'd only grow more attached. And seeing the look on his face just now as he spoke about the kids, one thing came through loud and clear.

She could never be the woman for him.

He had to check out that sway bar link. Whenever a rental vehicle was down, it meant a loss of income. Yet Sami insisted she needed his help.

Forgoing his internet search for replacement bolts, he dropped his smartphone on the office counter and looked at the computer screen.

"I've got a customer on hold. I'm trying to deduct their coupon, but the computer won't let me. It keeps showing the original price."

This was so not his forte. Vehicles he knew. Computers, not so much.

He studied the monitor, glancing at the time stamp

in the corner, wondering how much longer before Grace would be back. Since Roger was scheduled for a tour, she'd taken her mother to Montrose for a follow-up with the cardiologist.

"Did you click on Apply Coupon?"

Sami sent him a look. "Kaleb, I am not an idiot. Of course I clicked Apply Coupon."

"Okay, okay." He contemplated the issue awhile longer. "You'll just have to tell the people we'll get back to them with their total and then let Grace handle it." Technology. It was great when it worked the way it was supposed to, stank when it didn't. "I'll be in the garage if you need me."

He quickly moved back into the shop, the smells of rubber and petroleum products doing little to calm him. Even he didn't understand why he was so stressed. After all, his deadline with the museum had been met, business was great and the sway bar could be as simple as tightening a couple of bolts. So why was he wound up tighter than a two-dollar watch?

Easy. Because the families would be arriving next week and he was supposed to be giving some speech about being a hero at the museum ribbon cutting.

Regardless of what Grace had said about God's providence, he still wasn't comfortable being labeled a hero. He'd relived that night in the Humvee over and over in his dreams, both waking and not, and in every one of them, he was laughing and joking with his buddies right before the explosion.

Those were not the actions of a hero.

Continuing under the lift, he stared up into the carriage of the Jeep Wrangler. This he understood. With the help of an impact wrench, he removed the lug nuts and pulled off the front tires to give him a better look at the issue.

Wait a minute. He was going to order some extra replacement bolts to have on hand.

He reached for the phone on his belt, but it wasn't there. Where had…?

He groaned. He'd left his phone inside. However, the last thing he wanted was to get drawn into another one of Sami's computer issues. He shook his head.

The phone could wait.

After successfully tightening one bolt and replacing another, he reattached the wheels and lowered the vehicle. He'd need to take it for a test drive before renting it again. Didn't want customers having any problems. Especially when they could have been avoided in the first place.

He again made his way into the office, praying Sami wasn't having more computer issues. "Mom, what are you doing here?" He continued toward the desk and gave her a one-armed hug.

She held a finger to her lips. "Shh. Sami's talking to Vanessa."

"Vanessa?" Beau's Vanessa?

He jerked his gaze to his sister, mortified to see that she was using his phone.

"A cookout is an excellent idea. And forget about the park—my parents would be thrilled to have all of you over."

"Cookout? What?"

Sami waved him off like a madwoman. "You are not imposing at all. My mother was just mentioning that we needed to have some sort of get-together that first night, so I guess great minds think alike."

Seemed everyone and his sister was excited about the families' upcoming visit. Everyone except him, that was.

"Aw, I'm looking forward to meeting you, too, Vanessa. See you soon." Sami ended the call.

"What are you doing?" He strode behind the desk and grabbed his phone.

"You left your phone in here. It rang. I saw Vanessa's name and figured I'd answer."

"Yeah, well, you figured wrong."

"Kaleb, that is no way to talk to your sister. She was simply trying to help."

He looked at his mother. "Sorry, Mom, but that was my business to handle, not Sami's."

"What's got you in such a bad mood?" Sami glared at him.

"You." He slammed the phone onto its clip and started for the door. "I've gotta test-drive that Jeep. I'll be back later."

"How much lat—" The slamming door cut Sami off.

He knew he should feel bad, but he was too agitated to care. He was worried enough about coming face-to-face with his friends' family members as it was. Now they were planning some big shindig at his parents'? Without asking him? Out of the question.

But how could he retract the offer now?

He climbed into the bright blue Jeep. Maybe he wouldn't have to show up.

Under a clear blue sky, he headed north out of town, turning off at County Road 14, the road to Lake Lenore and the old Bachelor-Syracuse Mine. Of course, he bypassed both destinations and continued farther up, onto rockier terrain. That should give the vehicle a sufficient workout. It wasn't uncommon for these bumpy mountain roads to sometimes vibrate the bolts loose.

His grip tightened on the steering wheel as he maneuvered onto a tree-lined trail. Why did Grace have to be gone today? She wouldn't have answered his personal phone. Even if she had, she wouldn't have made plans for him. Now he was committed to something he'd never agreed to in the first place.

He needed to talk to Grace. Since handing his stuff over to the museum on Saturday, he hadn't seen her as much. Well, at least not after hours. He couldn't blame her for wanting to spend time with her mother, but he missed the teasing and playful banter. Even the probing conversations.

Yeah, Grace could help him sort through all of this.

Convinced that everything was in perfect working order, he turned around and drove back into town, going straight to Roger and Donna's. Perhaps he could catch Grace before she went back to the office.

He pulled up in front of the house only to discover that no one was home.

Sitting inside the Jeep with the windows rolled down, he drew in a deep breath and allowed himself to get lost in the mountain views. *Lord, help me.*

At the sound of gravel crunching behind him, he looked in his rearview mirror to see Grace and her mother pulling up in Donna's SUV.

He could feel himself relax a notch as they eased into the drive.

He exited the Jeep and went to assist Donna.

He opened the passenger door and offered his hand. "How did the appointment go?" His own issues paled in comparison to what Donna, Grace and Roger had gone through.

Looking as lovely as ever, Donna took hold and gracefully stepped onto the gravel drive. "He said I was doing great."

Grace exited the driver's side, tossing the door closed behind her. "He also said that she needed to continue to take things easy and come back in two more weeks."

"Ack." Donna waved a hand, looking much like her daughter. "Details."

He laid her hand in the crook of his elbow. "When we're talking about your heart, though, those details can be kind of important."

"Yes, I suppose you're right." She guided him toward the back door. "Would you care to join us for lunch?"

"No, Mama. Kaleb and I have to get back to work. You need to rest. This has been the most activity you've had since you got out of the hospital."

Donna let go a sigh. "Yes, dear."

Once Grace had her mother settled, she shooed Kaleb out the door, following on his heels. "What are you doing here?"

They continued down the back steps and around the side of the house.

"Oh, I blew up at Sami."

"What happened?"

A pair of broad-tailed hummingbirds whizzed past them, aiming for the feeder hanging from Donna's porch.

"Vanessa, the wife of my buddy Beau I told you about? She called."

Hands shoved in the pockets of her denim skirt,

Grace squinted against the sun. "What does that have to do with Sami?"

"I made the mistake of leaving my cell phone in the office, so my sister took the liberty of answering it. My mom was there, too. Next thing I know, they're planning to have some big cookout the night the families arrive."

They paused beside the Jeep.

Grace's gaze narrowed. "And the problem with that is what?"

"You know my fears about seeing the families. And just thinking about that speech they want me to give at the ribbon cutting has me so stressed out I'm likely to snap at any moment. Which is pretty much what I did with Sami." He scraped his boot across the gravel, shrugged. "You always seem to know how to cut to the chase and help me sort things out. How am I going to do this?"

Crossing her arms over her chest, Grace eyed the leaves on the trees, the neighbor's dog in the yard next door and the grass before turning her focus back to him. "You want to know what you should do."

"Please."

She took a step closer. "Get over yourself." She jammed a finger into his chest. "Those families have spent five years dealing with their own stuff and all you can think about is you. Well, guess what, Kaleb? It's not all about you."

Chapter Fourteen

Grace sat on Mama and Roger's front porch Saturday evening, knees clutched to her chest, her heart heavy. She couldn't go on like this. But what choice did she have?

Memories of her conversation with Kaleb Thursday afternoon had plagued her brain. Even now, they made her cringe.

After realizing just how strong her feelings had grown for him, she'd purposely worked to put some distance between them. Completing the task for the museum definitely made that easier. But after a rough morning with Mama, dealing with her fears of life never being the same, Grace snapped, sounding absolutely horrid, even to her own ears.

Wearing the most comfy pair of shorts she could find, she stretched her legs out on the white wicker love seat. The evening air was still, the temperature hovering somewhere around perfect. The sun had dropped behind Ouray's western slope, though there was still plenty of daylight. Maybe, if she kept watching, there'd be an alpenglow.

She felt bad that she hadn't apologized to Kaleb for her behavior. But it was probably for the best. That was, if she truly wanted to keep her distance.

Which she did. Most of the time. Deep inside, though, she missed him. Missed the way he took such pleasure in the simple things, like campfires and Cascade Falls. The way he seemed to know just what she needed exactly when she needed it. Most of all, she missed the comfort of his embrace and how he made her feel special. Wanted.

The sound of shifting gravel stirred her from her musing.

Peering over the side of the porch, she spotted a jogger. Every muscle in her body tensed.

Basketball shorts, a sweaty tank top and a prosthetic. Kaleb.

She tried to disappear into the brightly colored floral cushions of the love seat, but it was too late.

Still a house away, he came to a complete stop. His eyes riveted to her. Hands on his hips, he watched her for what seemed like an eternity. His scrutiny was unnerving to say the least, but, try as she might, she couldn't make herself move to go inside.

Finally, he started again.

She released the breath she'd been holding, closing her eyes for a moment.

"You okay?"

Her eyes flew wide.

Kaleb was standing at the bottom of the steps.

She straightened in her seat, swinging her bare feet over the side. "Fine. Yeah." She tucked her hair behind her ear. "I'm good."

"Glad to hear it." Using the handrail for support, he climbed the wooden steps and continued toward her, the blade he used for running making a gentle thump against the white floorboards.

While her pulse set off for parts unknown, a plethora of monarchs took flight in her midsection.

"Mind if I sit?" He gestured to one of the wicker chairs.

"No. Go ahead." She grabbed the throw pillow from behind her and clutched it in front of her. "Out for your nightly run?"

Sitting, he rested his elbows on his thighs, clasped his hands together and looked her square in the eye. "Yes, but I also wanted to see you. I owe you an apology, Grace."

Seriously? Hadn't they been through this before? Obviously he was much better at apologizing than she'd ever be. And while the first time he apologized had been justified, this time, she wasn't so sure.

"I thought about what you said and realize I came on a little strong the other day, forcing my problems onto you. I had no right to do that."

No right? Weren't they supposed to be friends? Of course, he had a right to expect his friend to listen. That was the kind of thing friends did.

Except she shut him down.

So what was she going to do now?

"I thought that voice sounded far too deep for Grace." Roger pushed through the screen door. "I didn't know you guys had plans tonight." His gaze moved between her and Kaleb.

"We don't." Kaleb ran a hand through his sweat-dampened hair. "I was just out for my run and thought I'd stop and say hi."

Always the gentleman. Making her feel like an even bigger jerk.

"Nice night, that's for sure." Hands buried in the

pockets of his cargo shorts, Roger looked out over the neighborhood. "Probably one of the best ones we've had so far this year."

She glanced at Kaleb. Caught him watching her.

She quickly looked away, heat creeping into her cheeks as she pretended to be enthralled in the colorful flower basket hanging overhead.

"It has been an interesting year." Though she refused to look, she knew Kaleb's eyes hadn't left her.

"Roger?" Mama pushed the door open. "Why, hello, Kaleb." A smile lit her face. Even though it had been only two days since they went to the doctor, she seemed to be feeling a lot better, which, in turn, had improved her outlook on everything else.

Kaleb stood and went to greet her. "We were just enjoying this perfect weather. Care to join us?" He motioned to the chair he'd vacated.

"It is lovely out here, isn't it?" Mama breathed deep, gazing out over the yard as though seeing it for the first time. "I do believe I've been cooped up in that house for too long."

Roger took hold of her arm. "Come on. Let's sit." He escorted her to the chair closest to the love seat before taking the seat beside her.

"Have a seat, Kaleb, so we can discuss the exhibit."

A look of panic flitted across his handsome, though sweaty, features. Considering the only seat available was on the love seat, next to Grace…

She scooted over, getting as close to the arm as possible before patting the cushion beside her. "I promise not to bite."

Mama leaned back in her chair and addressed Kaleb. "I spoke with Delores Whitley today. She is absolutely thrilled with your donations and says the exhibit is coming together even better than they'd hoped."

Kaleb was on the edge of his seat, as though ready to flee at any moment. "Good. Though I can't take much credit. It's Grace we have to thank. Without her, I'm afraid I wouldn't have been much help at all."

Grace's gaze slid sideways. *Oh, just rake the knife of guilt over my heart, why don't you.*

"I know what you mean." Mama reached for her hand. Gave it a quick squeeze. "Without her, I might not even be here."

How many times had she heard that since moving in. "Mama…"

The woman leaned back again. "So, how's your speech for the ribbon cutting coming along? It's only a week away."

If it was possible, even more sweat beaded Kaleb's brow. "I'm still mulling over what I want to say."

Grace dared to face him this time. Mulling, her eye. If anything, he was trying to figure out how to get out of it.

"Really? Well, I wouldn't take too long. It'll be here before you know it and you want to be prepared."

No doubt about it, Mama was definitely feeling more like her old self.

"Yes, ma'am."

Grace actually felt sorry for Kaleb. Poor guy came to apologize and ended up being grilled.

"Oh, goodness." Mama covered a yawn with her hand. "I guess all of this fresh air is getting to me." Gripping the arms of her chair, she pushed to her feet. "I should think about getting to bed."

Roger was already standing, offering his arm. "I'm right behind you, dear."

They turned for the door.

Mama waved. "You kids have a good night."

"Good night," they said in unison.

As Roger and Mama disappeared into the house, Grace wrestled with how to respond to Kaleb's apology. If she coldly accepted it then they'd carry on, with every interaction being as awkward as they'd been these past few days. Or she could apologize to him and enjoy one of the greatest friendships she'd ever had. But doing that also meant putting her heart on the line. Was that something she was willing to risk?

Kaleb stood. "I should—"

"Wait." Tossing the pillow aside, she jumped to her feet. "You don't owe me anything, Kaleb, least of all an apology. I was having a bad day Thursday and I took it out on you."

"Yeah, but I shouldn't have—"

She held up a hand to cut him off. "We've shared a lot over these last several weeks. Of course, you would have expected you could vent without fear of having your head bit off. But I did just that. And I had no right. So I apologize."

Hands on his hips, he stared at the painted floor. "Here's the problem, though."

Her heart sank. She'd blown it. Kaleb was one of the sweetest, most genuine people she'd ever known and she'd stomped all over his feelings.

He looked at her now. "You were right. It's not all about me. Yet I keep trying to make it that way."

As daylight faded and night sounds filled the air, she breathed a sigh of relief and smiled up at her friend. "I don't have a campfire, but if you'd care to sit and talk, perhaps we could figure out that speech of yours."

The corners of his mouth lifted. "That'd be great." He hesitated a few seconds. Scratched his head. "Okay, this might be pushing it, but how would you feel about accompanying me to a cookout Thursday? Strictly for moral support."

She knew how anxious he was about seeing his friends' families. Though she believed his worry unfounded. Still, they were very real to him and she wanted to help.

"What's on the menu?"

"Meat."

She couldn't help grinning. "Then it looks like you've got yourself a date, my friend."

Any other time, Kaleb would have been over the moon to be in the company of such a gorgeous woman. Yet while Grace was beyond stunning in a long turquoise sundress and strappy sandals, he simply wanted to make it through tonight.

"Kaleb?"

They paused in the street.

She took hold of his hands and stared deeply into his eyes. "I'm here for you." She gently squeezed. "It's going to be fine. I promise."

He appreciated her reassurance, though it did little to bolster him. Still, he was beyond grateful to have her with him. Since that night on Roger and Donna's porch, they'd spent a lot of time together, both at work and after hours. And while they hadn't acknowledged their feelings, it was as though they'd both accepted them, becoming comfortable with the occasional touch or embrace. Though he had yet to kiss her again.

"Are you ready?"

Standing in front of his parents' two-story folk-style home, he blew out a breath. One. Two. *Lord, please give me the words to say to these people. And don't let them hate me.*

With one hand in Grace's and the other tucked inside the pocket of his khaki cargo shorts, he said, "Okay. Let's go."

The aroma of grilled meat filled the air as they moved across the lush green yard, aiming for the oversized wooden deck on the home's south side.

"Here they are now." His mother, Bev, strolled across the deck, meeting them at the steps. She and Grace must have compared notes, because she also wore a long sundress, her chin-length blond hair pulled up in a clip.

"Sorry we're late." Addressing the large group of people that milled about, he tamped down his panic and forced a smile. "Had to finish up some things at the shop."

Vanessa approached him, her sable hair pulled back into a ponytail, her dark eyes swimming with tears. "It's so good to see you again." Her hug was fierce, full of warmth and welcome.

When they finally released, a young girl came near him. She was beautiful, looking so much like Beau with her blond curls, carrying a small bouquet of flowers. "These are for you, Mr. Kaleb." She curtsied as though he were some kind of royalty.

Overcome with emotion, he dropped to his knee and hugged the child for all he was worth. Beau would be so proud of his daughter.

As he stood, a man came closer, stopping beside Vanessa.

"This is my fiancé, Brandon," she said.

The dark-haired man, somewhere close to Kaleb's age, extended his hand. "It's an honor. I've heard a lot about you."

Vanessa grabbed hold of Brandon's arm. "We're getting married next week."

Married? How could that be? Had she forgotten about Beau?

Before he had time to think further, another woman moved toward him. "I'm Shannon White. Jason Meador was my husband." Tears spilled onto her round cheeks as she motioned another man forward.

"Ron White." He shook Kaleb's hand. "It's good to finally meet you."

Kaleb's throat thickened. Vanessa was about to get married. Jason's wife had already remarried.

He felt a hand on his shoulder. Turning, he saw Grace smiling.

She leaned toward him. "Remember, it's been five long years for them."

He simply stared at her, understanding dawning. "Thanks for the reminder." Because in many ways, it seemed like only yesterday.

How did she know what he was thinking?

A slightly older man and woman made their way to him.

The man reached out his hand. "Ron and Michelle Squires, Stephen's parents." The man's voice broke.

Before Kaleb could respond, the man pulled him close, sobbing.

Tears welled in Kaleb's eyes. He'd been ready for them to hate him, but he hadn't counted on this.

When the Squires finally retreated, another couple moved closer.

Again, the man held out his hand. "Kurt and Abigail Kowalski. Dayton's folks."

Kaleb couldn't contain himself any longer. Dayton had been the youngest among them. Barely making it to his twentieth birthday. Gulping for air, he hugged the couple. His body shook as he gave in to his emotions, not only with grief for what these people had lost, but for the love they'd shown him.

When the Kowalskis had also retreated, Kaleb was beside himself. Overwhelmed and shocked beyond words. He'd come in here on the defensive and found himself surrounded by people who genuinely cared.

He felt an arm around his shoulders.

Without even looking, he knew it was Grace.

She handed him a napkin. "I think I speak for Kaleb and the rest of his family when I say that we are blessed to have each and every one of you here. We look forward to hearing your stories, so, please, enjoy yourselves."

He dried his eyes, watching her step aside.

Grace was exactly what he'd been looking for when he began his search for an office manager. Someone who could easily handle those things that didn't come naturally to him. Someone who shared his vision and whose skill set complemented his own. In Grace, he'd found the perfect partner. Except tonight, those thoughts had nothing to do with business.

Where he was weak, she was strong. She wasn't afraid to step in and lift him up. He only prayed he could do the same for her.

"Is everybody ready to eat?" His father, Tom, stood beside the grill, spatula raised in the air.

His query was met with a resounding "Yes!"

"All right, then. If everyone would join hands, I'd like to offer a blessing."

Everyone did as he'd requested, quickly forming a crude circle.

Kaleb took hold of Grace's hand, giving it a gentle squeeze of thanks.

She glanced at him and smiled.

"If you'd bow your heads, please." Dad began. "Father God, we thank You for this day and for these people who've traveled far to be with us. I ask a special blessing on each and every one of them. Lord, we ask that You would bless this food to the nourishment of our bodies, in Jesus's name, amen."

"Amen."

Sometime later, after he'd relaxed enough to allow himself to grab a burger, he stood at the edge of the deck, watching Beau's daughter, Hannah, and Vanessa's fiancé playing soccer in the yard. It still broke his heart that his friend had never got the chance to meet his little girl. That she'd had to grow up without her father.

He looked intently at Vanessa's fiancé, Brandon. Did he always play with Hannah or was this interaction just for show?

"He's a good man."

Kaleb startled at Vanessa's voice. Had she really known what he was thinking?

"He seems okay."

"We met when Hannah was three." Arms folded across her chest, she watched her daughter and fiancé. "It's taken me a long time to find someone who could hold a candle to Beau." She smiled. "But I finally found him."

Spotting them, Brandon waved and jogged toward

them. "I can't believe this place. There are mountains everywhere I look."

Kaleb couldn't help but grin, eyeing the peaks around them. "Yeah, nestled in a bowl like this makes Ouray pretty special."

"When Vanessa told me where we were going, I had no idea. But this is incredible."

Hannah trotted toward them then. "Daddy, come on." She motioned for Brandon to join her.

"Sorry. Duty calls." Brandon hurried off.

Kaleb's heart skidded to a stop. Daddy? That was a title that should have been reserved for Beau.

But you wanted Hannah to have a father.

"Brandon is planning to adopt Hannah."

He faced Vanessa. "I think Beau would approve."

Her eyes welled with tears. "I think so, too."

"Kaleb."

He turned to see the Kowalskis headed toward him.

Vanessa touched his arm. "I'll catch up with you later." She made her way down the steps to join Brandon and Hannah.

"Hope you all are enjoying yourselves." He leaned against the deck rail.

"Beautiful town you have here." Kurt lifted his gaze.

"Wait until we take you on one of our tours. You'll get to see a whole lot more."

Abigail seemed to bubble with excitement. "I can't wait."

Kurt's expression turned more somber then. "Our Dayton thought very highly of you."

Kaleb swallowed hard. "He was a good kid. A fine soldier. I was proud to know him."

"He admired you a great deal," said Abigail. "Used to talk about you all the time."

Kurt pulled a paper from his shirt pocket. "He sent this email shortly before he died. We thought you might like to have it." He handed it to Kaleb.

He opened the paper, noting that one section had been highlighted.

I can't say where, but we were in a firefight the other day. And out in the middle was this woman and her kid. Next thing I know, Sgt. Palmer yells for us to cover him. Crazy fool ran right into the cross fire, grabbed the kid and shielded the woman until they were safely behind us. Talk about selfless. That's the kind of hero I hope I can be.

"Wow." It was all he could manage.

"You were a good example for those young men out there." Kurt sniffed. "You should be proud."

"Thank you, sir."

As the Kowalskis walked away, Grace moved alongside him. "Tough night in some ways, uplifting in others."

"You got that right." He reached for her hand. "And I realized something."

"What's that?"

He scanned the faces that had traveled to be with him. "They've all moved on." He looked at Grace now. "The past is a part of them, but it doesn't define them."

She laid a hand against his chest. "Perhaps we could both learn from that."

Chapter Fifteen

The sun was shining brightly when Kaleb and Grace arrived at the museum early Saturday afternoon. Flags swayed in the breeze, as did the red-white-and-blue banner over the museum door that read Welcome to Our Hometown Heroes.

People had already begun to gather. He recognized many of them as townspeople; however, there were just as many folks that he didn't recognize.

"There's my handsome son." His mom emerged from the small crowd, phone in hand, dodging a couple of people in the process.

"You're looking pretty good yourself, Mom." Her favorite white dress was accented by a pair of glitzy sandals.

As usual, Dad brought up the rear. "Son." He held out his hand. When Kaleb took hold, his father reeled him in for a hug. "I'm proud of you."

Even though it wasn't the first time he'd heard those words from his father, his throat still thickened.

"Get in the shade so I can take your picture." His mother pointed to a grassy spot.

Grace let go of his arm and stepped away.

"No, no, Grace." Mom waved her back toward him. "I want you in the picture."

Considering she was wearing a dress for the second time this week, he wanted her in it, too.

He slid his arm around her waist, inhaling the sweet floral fragrance he'd come to recognize as uniquely her. He liked having her with him. If only he could convince her that Ouray was where she belonged. With her family. With him.

Likewise, Grace slipped her arm around him. "I'm glad my mom suggested you wear your uniform." She smiled up at him. "You make that thing look good, soldier."

The comment sent a strange sensation whirling inside him. One that had nothing to do with his speech.

"Smile." Mom held up her phone. A second later, she stared at the screen. "Cute couple."

"Let me see." Coming from behind them, Donna slowly sidled up to his mom and studied the shot. "Aww... You'll have to send that one to me."

He pulled Grace against him. "Hear that? We make a cute couple."

"Yeah, I heard." A blush crept into her cheeks as she eased out of his grip.

"Sorry, but I need to borrow Kaleb for a minute." Donna took him by the arm and led him along the front of the stone building that had once been a hospital. A podium adorned with red-white-and-blue bunting had been positioned to the right of the main entrance.

"We'll have all of our donors lined up along here." She gestured to the sidewalk. "You're welcome to hold the microphone or leave it on the podium, whatever you're comfortable with. By the way, you're going to be the last one to speak."

Yes, let's just prolong the agony.

"Where's Roger?"

"Right here."

Kaleb turned to see his friend sporting a blue garrison cap with the VFW emblem. He choked back a laugh. "Nice hat."

Roger smirked. "Hey, I'm not the one wearing a beret."

Beyond his friend, he saw Grace talking with Vanessa and the other families. "Excuse me, please."

He wove his way toward the group. Seeing them no longer filled him with dread. Instead, they gave him hope for the future.

Yesterday, he'd taken everyone on a Jeep tour over Imogene Pass. What a great group of people. They had so much fun. There had even been talk of making this reunion an annual event. Maybe next time he'd suggest they come for an old-fashioned Ouray Fourth of July.

"Afternoon, everyone."

"Afternoon!" They responded in unison.

"If you wouldn't mind, I'd like to get a group picture with all of you." He handed Grace his phone. "Do you mind?"

"Of course not. Why don't you all get up on the steps there so we can get everyone in the shot."

They huddled together, Kaleb in the middle at the bottom.

"Cheese."

A few minutes later, Roger tapped him on the shoulder. "They're ready for us."

"Okay." He turned to Grace.

"You'll do fine." She ran a hand along the breast of his jacket.

"As long as I know you're here."

She smiled. "So what are you waiting for?"

Kaleb lined up to the side of the podium with the five other men. He knew Phil Purcell, the father of his friend Gage, who'd served in the Marines, and Clay Musgrove, caretaker of the Bachelor-Syracuse Mine, who, like Roger, had served in Vietnam. The other two, one a Korean War vet, the other Desert Storm, Kaleb wasn't familiar with.

Delores Whitley, the museum's director, took the podium to welcome everyone. "Today, we are here to honor our hometown heroes. Those who have served our country, never to be forgotten." She briefly explained what the exhibit was about and what folks might find there.

The Korean War vet was the first to speak, followed by Roger, Clay, Phil and the Desert Storm guy. Some shared stories, while others spoke about what it meant to them to serve their country.

Finally, it was Kaleb's turn. He set his notes on the podium, electing to leave the microphone right where it was. Then he stared out at the hundred or so faces before him, scanning them until he found Vanessa, Shannon White, the Squires and the Kowalskis.

Suddenly, he had the clarity he had been hoping for all along. He knew exactly what he was supposed to say. And it came from the heart.

He shoved his notes aside. "The theme for this exhibit is hometown heroes. However, not one of us standing up here today is a hero. We're just ordinary people who were put in extraordinary circumstances and forced to step out of our comfort zones."

He cleared his throat. "As some of you may know, while serving in the Middle East, I was injured by an IED. But the four men with me that day perished. They paid the ultimate price for our freedom. They are the true heroes."

Applause filled the air. Only this time, he didn't mind it so much. Because it wasn't for him. It was for those who rightfully deserved it.

When the noise wound down, he continued. "Thank you for coming today. And I hope you enjoy the exhibit."

Stepping away from the podium, he sought out Grace. Just the sight of her made him smile. No matter what she said or did, his heart refused to be derailed.

She was clapping along with everyone else, but the wink she sent was just for him and he knew he'd made her proud.

In that moment, he knew he couldn't let her go. And before this day was out, he had to tell her how he felt.

While cake was served to those in attendance, Kaleb and the other five donors, along with a photographer from the local newspaper, were led inside the museum for the official ribbon cutting at the room holding the display.

Later, he and Grace and the families made their way inside.

Looking at everything from photos to uniforms to World War I weaponry, he had to admit that he was impressed. They'd managed to span every era from World War I to today.

"There's my daddy!" Hannah pointed to a photo of Beau, Jason, Stephen, Dayton and Kaleb standing in front of their Humvee.

He turned to Grace. "Was that in my stuff?"

She nodded. "We had it blown up for the exhibit.Along with a few extra copies. There's an eight-by-ten for each of you."

While the families enjoyed the entire museum, Kaleb whisked Grace outside and, with Donna's permission, into the log cabin that sat to the side of the main building.

"What are you doing?"

Envisioning a future with Grace had become second nature. The way they seemed to work toward the common goal of building a successful business reminded him of his parents.

He'd never forget the day they opened the Palmer Realty office. Seeing their dedication to each other, their family, as well as their business. He wanted that. A partner. A helpmate.

Grace was all of that. And so much more. She understood things he couldn't even put into words.

"This." Slipping an arm around her waist, he pulled her to him and kissed her.

Her arms wound around his neck, filling him with hope.

When the kiss ended, he watched her, waiting to see if she had any regrets.

Instead, she gave him a shy smile. "What took you so long?"

He laughed, tucking her head under his chin as he held her close. He caressed her silky hair, noting how perfectly they fit together. As though they were made for each other.

When she lifted her head, he combed his fingers

through her hair. "I don't want you to leave, Grace. I love you. Please, stay in Ouray."

Her stunned eyes searched his. "Y-you love me?"

"With all of my heart." Then he lowered his head and claimed her lips in a kiss that would erase any doubt. Grace was his future. And even though she was supposed to leave, he was trusting God to work out the details. Because living without her was not an option.

Grace was on the front porch Sunday evening, putting on a pair of strappy sandals, when she saw Kaleb walk up. He was wearing shorts again. Denim this time, along with a deep maroon polo shirt that hugged those massive biceps.

She liked a man who was comfortable in his own skin.

The families had left today, promising to extend their visit next time. She'd really enjoyed her time with them. It was because of them that Kaleb had grown. Learning to accept the past and move forward.

"Wow!" Kaleb's appreciative smile when he spotted her set her insides to bubbling. She felt as though she were at a junior high school dance. And just as petrified.

She had yet to respond to his declaration of love or his request that she stay in Ouray. Interestingly enough, she'd received an email from the cruise line just this morning, saying that, due to unforeseeable circumstances, the ship's renovations would be delayed and that they would not be able to set sail until November. Making her contract null and void, unless she was to sign an amendment.

"I'm glad you approve." At the last second, she'd chosen to wear the turquoise tank she'd accidentally bought in Montrose the day Mama fell ill, along with a pair of white shorts.

"Grace, you'd look great no matter what you wore."

Her cheeks warmed, though it had nothing to do with the heat. "I think we'd better go."

Sami had invited the family for dinner tonight and she didn't want to be late.

As she descended the steps, Kaleb offered his arm. With him, chivalry was not dead. Things with Kaleb were easy. Comfortable. She still found it hard to believe that he actually loved her.

But did she love him?

She could easily see herself loving him. But fear was a powerful emotion. What if he stopped loving her like Aaron had?

Gravel crunched beneath their feet as they meandered from one street to the next, talking about the weekend's events. The slightest hint of a breeze stirred the evening air as two broad-tailed hummingbirds zipped past them. Their playful cricket-like chirps still amazed her, since every hummingbird she'd ever seen was silent.

He stopped and kissed her. Every nerve ending in her body went on high alert. Kaleb made her feel cherished. And more alive than she had in a very long time.

Resting her head against his chest, she sighed and listened to the pounding of his heart. She savored the strength of his embrace and the protection it offered. He was the kind of man she had always dreamed of. Was it possible that her dreams had finally come true? Was there really a hope and a future for them?

They started walking again, stopping a few blocks later.

"And here we are." Kaleb paused in front of a cute

single-story house that she suspected was new construction, yet had the charm of an older home. "You smell that, Grace?"

She sniffed the air. "Meat." On the grill, of course. Smiling, she closed her eyes and inhaled deeper. "Ribs... Chicken... Burgers..." Opening her eyes, she glanced up at Kaleb. "Smells like the three basic food groups to me."

His grin was priceless. "You're my kind of woman."

That comment, coupled with the protective feel of his hand against the small of her back as he urged her up the walkway, robbed her of all rational thought. And had her wondering if, just maybe, she really could entrust her heart to someone again.

Holding her hand, Kaleb rang the bell.

Sami swung open the door. "About time you two got here."

"Hey, it's not like we have a business to run or anything." Kaleb pushed past his sister, bringing Grace with him.

Grace couldn't help noticing how he used the plural sense. As if Mountain View Tours belonged to both of them.

Jack charged toward Kaleb. "I'm a monster twuck."

Kaleb intercepted him, flipping him end over end until he rested on Kaleb's shoulder. "You're a monster all right."

Jack giggled when Kaleb tickled his belly.

While Kaleb set Jack on the floor, Sami gave Grace a quick hug before leading them to the back of the house, where Scott was grilling on the patio.

Tom and Bev relaxed in the glider, though Bev quickly stood.

Grace liked her. Liked all of Kaleb's family, for that matter.

Jack charged ahead of them.

"Sorry we're late." Grace continued toward Bev, who was awaiting a hug.

"Uncle Kaleb, I got bubbles." As if to emphasize his claim, Jack dipped the wand into the small red bottle of liquid he held in his other hand, pressed it against his lips and blew. Naturally, the bubble burst without ever making it into the air.

Kaleb crouched to his nephew's level. "Don't touch it to your mouth, soldier. You gotta hold it in front of your mouth, then blow."

Jack dipped the wand again and blew. This time a stream of bubbles took flight, swirling around them. "Yay! I did it."

"You sure did." Kaleb ruffled the boy's curly brown hair, his smile filled with pride.

"Grace, what can I get you to drink?" Sami stood at a table near the French doors that led into the house. "Water? Lemonade? Soda?"

"You don't even have to ask, sister dear," said Kaleb. "Just hand her a Diet Dr Pepper and move on down the road."

"Oh, so I'm that predictable, am I?" Her fist planted firmly on her hip, Grace only pretended to glare at him. "I was actually thinking some lemonade might be nice." She winked at Sami.

A short time later, Sami handed both Grace and Kaleb their drinks. "Now that everyone's here, there's something Scott and I would like to share with all of you."

Tom moved into the circle as Scott slipped an arm around his wife's waist.

Sami peered lovingly up at her husband before addressing everyone else. "We're going to have another baby."

A collective gasp filled the air, followed by a round of cheers.

Bev let go a squeal as she hugged her daughter. "When?"

"January."

Kaleb nabbed his nephew and threw him in the air. "You hear that, Jack? You're going to be a big brother. Just like me."

Tom shook Scott's hand before embracing his daughter. "'Bout time. Your mother's been chomping at the bit for another little one."

"Oh, I have not." Bev dabbed her eyes.

"Congratulations to both of you." While Grace's wishes were sincere, she was helpless to stop the sadness that leached into her heart. What she wouldn't give to be able to make an announcement like that. To be surrounded by excited family members and have a loving husband by her side.

But if past experience was any indication, Grace would likely never experience that same pleasure.

Perhaps God simply didn't want you to have children with Aaron.

Her gaze drifted to Kaleb. With Jack perched on his shoulder, he hugged Sami, his smile explosive. How much greater would his reaction be if the child were his own?

Suddenly chilled, she rubbed at her arms. Kaleb longed for a family. He deserved a family. But, with her, he might never have that joy.

What had she been thinking? She'd allowed herself to get caught up in emotions and had begun to think that, maybe, someone could love her, regardless. That maybe Kaleb was that guy.

Watching the ongoing celebration, she wished she could escape. But she wasn't about to ruin everyone else's good time. She'd put on a happy face and, somehow, make it through the night.

When she and Kaleb finally left, he wrapped his arm around her. "I'm sorry you had to endure that. I could tell you were struggling."

She lifted her face to look at him, trying to pretend all was right in her world. "And why would I be struggling?"

"Because of Sami's announcement." He held her close. "The light in your eyes fades when you're hurting."

"Oh." Could he really read her that well? She drew in a deep breath. "So apparently there's something in the water and everyone's getting pregnant. Your sister, my sister… I'm happy for them."

He tugged her closer. "I know you are. Just remember, you get to be the cool aunt."

She appreciated his attempts to make her feel better. But she cared about him too much to allow him to settle for a what-if.

She'd already decided it would be better for everyone if she just left Ouray. Away from the close-knit community that made her want to call it home. Away from the man who stirred her heart like no one before. And away from the dreams that had dared to take root.

Chapter Sixteen

❧

What a weekend.

Kaleb's time with the families had surpassed all of his expectations. So much so that even an out-of-commission Jeep couldn't bring him down on this rainy, gloomy Monday.

In the span of just a few short days, his outlook on life had done a complete one-eighty. Instead of regret holding him captive to the past, he was now free to contemplate the future. A future he prayed would include Grace.

Since his guides had yet to arrive, the shop was quiet. Kaleb liked it that way. Liked hearing the sound of rain on the tin roof.

Standing beneath the rental Jeep in question, he stared up at a leaky rear differential. Likely the result of being dragged across a rock. It shouldn't take too long to fix. However, due to the weather, it wasn't as if his rentals would be in high demand.

He seated a drain pan to catch the fluid, then grabbed a socket wrench from the rolling tool chest beside him. Telling Grace he loved her had been the right thing to do. Everything was finally out in the open, erasing any doubts she might have had regarding his feelings for her. Now they could concentrate on their future.

He chuckled to himself. The word still seemed foreign to him. Suddenly the future wasn't just about him or his business. Grace was his future. And while they hadn't discussed marriage, it was only logical that that would be the next step. When the time was right, that was. Spring, perhaps. Before the high season set in, limiting their time.

Okay, so maybe he was getting ahead of himself. Because even though he'd told Grace he loved her, she had yet to say she loved him. There was also that issue of her contract with the cruise line.

He removed the first bolt, each turn of the socket wrench making a zip, zip, zip sound. Last night at Sami's, Kaleb couldn't help noticing how well Grace fit in with his family. Grace and his sister had chatted half the night, Sami picking Grace's brain about the places she'd been, while Jack practically wore him out playing ball.

If only his sister's announcement hadn't affected Grace so negatively. He didn't like to see her hurting. He understood her desire to have children and that her ex-husband had done her wrong. However, he wasn't her ex-husband and was determined to do whatever it took to earn her trust.

"Yo, Kaleb."

Glancing over his shoulder, he saw Roger wandering into the garage.

His friend paused beside the tool chest. "Grace said to tell you she was running late. Said she'd be in around nine."

That was odd. Grace was never late. "Is she feeling bad?"

"This is just a guess, but I don't think she got much sleep last night."

"Hmm…" Kaleb couldn't help wondering if it had something to do with the previous evening.

"Problem?" Roger nodded in the direction of the vehicle on the lift.

"Rear dif."

"Fun." He took a step closer to inspect the damage. "So what did you think about Saturday?"

"For all my reservations, I thought it was great."

Roger looked at him now. "Your speech brought the house down."

"Better than having a hundred deadpan faces staring at you."

"You mean like they did with me and the other fellas?"

They both laughed.

Stepping out from beneath the vehicle, Roger continued. "Donna mentioned something about you sneaking Grace out to the log cabin." He toed at something on the concrete. "You two sure have been spending a lot of time together lately."

"You're not going to give me some fatherly warning about your daughter, are you?"

"No. You've sure got Donna's hopes up, though. She likes having Grace here."

Realizing he'd need to open up the office, Kaleb followed his friend. "I know their relationship was a bit strained when Grace first arrived. I'm glad they're doing better." He set his wrench atop the tool chest and picked up a rag.

"Me, too."

"Hey, I pulled your tour truck in." He pointed to the far bay.

"Thanks. Guess I'd better get it dried off and put on the canopy."

"Yeah, and I'd better get inside and unlock the door."

Kaleb stopped at the sink to wash his hands before making his way into the office. He hoped Grace wasn't still bothered about Sami and was half tempted to give her a call and see how she was doing. Then again, if she was trying to get ready for work, he'd just be interrupting. He'd simply have to shove his impatience aside and wait until she got here.

Fortunately, Grace was very thorough, so the clipboards for this morning's tours were already laid out on the counter. Two to Yankee Boy Basin, one to Imogene Pass and the other to Corkscrew. And even though it was raining, the tours would go on.

Once the tours had departed, Kaleb returned to the shop, eager to knock out that differential. Before he even got started, though, the telephone rang, echoing throughout the garage.

Changing directions, he made his way to the tool bench.

"Mountain View Tours, this is Kaleb." He fielded questions from a potential customer and was still on the call when he heard the office door open.

Glancing across the garage, he motioned to Grace. After a slight hesitation, she slowly continued in his direction, looking much the way she had the day she first arrived at Mountain View Tours. Hands tucked in the pockets of her riding jacket, there seemed to be an air of uneasiness about her. But why? Maybe she wasn't feeling well.

"Yes, all of our tours are listed on our website. However, if you have any questions, don't hesitate to give us a call." Ending the call, he met Grace halfway. "Good morning."

He hugged her, though it was kind of like hugging a pole.

When he stepped back, he saw her looking everywhere but at him. Meaning she was uncomfortable about something.

"Grace?" He tilted her chin to look at him. "What's going on?"

Pulling her hand from her pocket, she held out a piece of paper.

"What's this?" Anxiety settled in his gut as he unfolded what looked like a letter and started to read. "You're resigning?" He kept reading, his breaths coming quicker with each word. "Effective immediately?" He looked at her now, his blood roaring in his ears. "Is this supposed to be some kind of joke?" He motioned to the paper.

She lifted her chin. "It's not a joke."

"I don't get it, then. Why would you resign?"

Squaring her shoulders, she said, "Because I'm leaving."

"Leaving? But—I thought we had this all figured out." Panic roiled within him. This couldn't be happening. He couldn't lose her. Not now. Not ever.

"I've been talking with the cruise line. Seems there's been a change in plans."

"I don't believe you." Confusion muddled his brain as he sifted through every conversation they'd had in recent days, looking for any hint that she was considering leaving early. But all he could think about was the way she'd kissed him. No hesitation. No fear. No—

Wait a minute.

"It's because I told you I love you, isn't it? I'm a big boy, Grace. If you don't love me, just tell me." Noting the way she refused to look at him, he stepped closer. "But I don't think that's it. I think you're afraid."

She assumed her toughest stance. "What would I have to be afraid of?"

"Of being hurt again. And your instincts are telling you to run, aren't they?"

"You don't know what you're talking about." She turned to walk away, but he stopped her, turning her to face him.

"Oh, yes, I do. And I've got news for you, Grace. You can run, but you can't hide. Love has a way of taking up residence in your heart, even when you don't want it to. I know that you love me, Grace. You can try to deny it all you want, but I know the truth."

"How could you possibly know what I'm feeling?"

"I lost my leg, but I'm not blind." He stopped, the bitter taste of bile burning the back of his throat as memories of Gina surfaced. "Or is that the problem? That I'm not whole?"

"No!" The word echoed off the concrete floor and walls. "It's because I'm not."

Confusion riddled his mind. "What?"

"I can't have children, Kaleb. You know that."

"So?"

"So, I've seen you with Jack. The smile on your face as you played with him last night. Someday you're going to want kids. You deserve kids." The unshed tears glistening in her eyes made him want to pull her into his arms and will her to believe him. Sure, he'd always dreamed of having his own kids. But more than that, he wanted a life with Grace. With or without kids.

"Then we'll adopt."

Her lip curled. Nostrils flared. "Aaron said the same thing. And we both know how that turned out."

The words hit him like a stun gun. And before he had sense enough to respond, she was gone.

Should-haves and what-ifs pelted his brain. His heart felt as if it might explode. Frustration pulsed through his veins.

Turning, he crumpled the paper in his fist and slammed it into the red tool chest with a guttural roar even he didn't recognize.

The chest toppled with an explosive crash. One by one, drawers fell open, emptying their metal contents onto the concrete floor with a deafening cacophony that brought back memories of that fateful night in the desert.

Pain racked his body. Leaning against a nearby post, he willed the fury to subside.

He stared at his bloodied knuckles through a blur of tears, knowing the damage to his heart was far worse.

How dare she compare him to that lowlife she was once married to. Then again, it wasn't as if he was unfamiliar with the distrust caused by past hurts. Otherwise, he wouldn't have accused her of believing him half a man.

Helplessness washed over him like the rain outside the window. It was a feeling he knew well and had vowed he'd never feel again. Right now, though, it was all he had.

Why had Grace let Mama talk her into staying until tomorrow? It was only a little rain.

Lightning flashed and thunder boomed just then, rattling the windows on Roger's garage.

Okay, maybe Mama had a point.

Grace unhooked the bungee cord that secured her footlocker to the tongue of her trailer. She set the trunk on the concrete floor and lifted the lid so she could add a few last-minute items.

It wasn't as if she wanted to leave Mama so soon. Matter of fact, given her heart problems, Grace would just as soon stay. But what choice did she have? Even if she wasn't working for Kaleb anymore, Ouray was tiny. She was bound to run into him. Not to mention that just about every place in town would remind her of him.

Thoughts of the pained expression on his face when she turned in her resignation this morning had her dinner feeling more like a lead weight in her belly. There was no doubt in her mind that he did indeed love her. But that was now. What about later? What if he changed his mind? She couldn't go through that again.

Thunder cracked overhead.

Grace shot to her feet, wrapping her arms around her stomach. Why had she allowed herself to fall in love? This gut-wrenching ache was exactly why she'd promised herself she'd never open her heart again. Yet she did it anyway. Allowing Kaleb to sneak past her defenses.

The side door opened then and Roger stepped inside. Pushing back the hood of his jacket, he shut the door behind him. "'Tain't a fit night out there for man or beast."

She grinned, thinking about her father. He used to say the same thing. "Sounds like it's getting worse."

"I believe you're right." Shoving his hands into the pockets of his faded jeans, he stepped into the one-car space that had housed her motorcycle and trailer while she stayed with them. "Thought I should check on you. Make sure everything was okay."

"I'm fine." She glanced down at the open footlocker. "Just making sure I'm all set for tomorrow." The cruise line had agreed to look at the possibility of assigning her to another ship. Something that sailed sooner. Even though she might have to take a different job. In the meantime, she'd decided to stay with Lucy in Flagstaff.

He nodded. "I'm sorry you have to leave so soon. I've enjoyed getting to know you."

"Likewise." Embarrassment had her tucking her hands in her back pockets. "It certainly took me long enough."

"Ah, don't worry about it." He hesitated a moment. As though carefully choosing his words. "You know, my, uh, first wife and I didn't have any kids of our own. But if I'd had a daughter, I'd like to think that we would've been as close as you and your father were."

Tears pricked the backs of her eyes, though she quickly blinked them away. "I know this is none of my business, but why did you and Camille choose not to have children?"

"It wasn't our choice." He moved to the small workbench on the far wall, grabbed two stools that were tucked underneath and set them near the trailer. "Have a seat."

Raindrops pelted the window as they sat.

"We tried for years to have a baby. For the longest time, Camille felt as though she'd failed me as a wife."

Grace could definitely relate to that.

"However, nothing could have been further from the truth."

She studied the silver-haired man before her, waiting for him to continue.

"I married Camille because I loved *her* and wanted

to share my life with her." Hands clasped in his lap, he continued. "Kids simply would have been an extension of that love. But it never changed."

"Unconditional." Something she'd always heard of, but had never experienced outside of familial relationships. The longer they were married, the more she realized that Aaron's love always seemed to hinge on something. How she dressed or who her friends were or how many toys she'd let him buy. *You want me to be happy, don't you, Grace?*

"That's right. Real love is steadfast. Just like all these mountains." He gestured toward the window that spanned the wide garage door.

"And Cascade Falls." Their steadfastness was what made them so special to Kaleb.

"Exactly."

Roger's wife had been a lucky woman. "Was Camille ever able to accept that you loved her regardless?"

"Over time. God showed her that He had other plans for her life. Like teaching young girls. Mentoring them. By the time she passed away, she had more kids than she'd ever dreamed of."

Grace couldn't help smiling. "I wish I could have known her."

Roger cleared his throat, his expression serious. "Grace, don't let what Aaron did define you. Or any man God might place in your path. We're not all jerks."

She puffed out a laugh.

"God has a plan for you, Grace. Just follow His lead." If she had a nickel for every time she'd heard that…

"That would be easier to do if fear didn't have me in a choke hold."

"I hear ya. However, I know for a fact that God is

bigger than our fears. He's chased away more of mine than I care to count."

Another streak of lightning, followed by a loud bang. The lights flickered.

Roger stood. "I think we'd best be getting inside."

She watched the trees dancing wildly on the other side of the window. "I think you're right." She rose and handed him her stool, thinking how much her father would have liked Roger. "Thank you, for being patient with me and for telling me Camille's story."

"You're welcome." The sincerity in his blue eyes made her wonder what had been wrong with her all those years, why she'd refused to accept him.

"And just for the record, I'm really glad Mama married you." Fighting back tears, she wrapped her arms around his waist and hugged him. And he hugged her back.

Later that night, after the rain had passed, Grace lay in her bed, tucked beneath her grandmother's quilt, thoughts of Kaleb drifting through her mind. Conflicted thoughts. If only he were here. He'd be able to help her sort through them.

Even though that wasn't possible, she still longed for the strength of his embrace and the protection it offered. He was a good man. A godly man. A man who could be trusted. Like Roger.

She replayed his and Camille's story in her mind. What a lucky woman Camille had been to have such a wonderful husband. And Grace couldn't help wondering—

Dear God, is there someone out there who could love me unconditionally?

She closed her eyes, sending tears trailing into her ears. *Someone like Kaleb.*

I do love him, God, and I hate that I've hurt him. But I'm so afraid.

God is bigger than our fears. Roger's words echoed in her mind.

I'm such a mess. God, I've been an idiot to think I could handle life without You. Forgive me. Help me, God. Save me from myself. Right now, I choose to trust You. Remove the fears that have blinded me and show me what it is You would have me do with my life. Whether in Ouray or somewhere else, I want to live the life You would have me live, be the woman You want me to be. Please, God. In Jesus's name.

Opening her eyes, she stared into the blackness. Yet inside, the part of her that had been hollowed out by grief and despair was filled with an incredible light that brightened the darkest corners of her being. She felt alive and whole, for the first time in years.

And it felt amazing.

Chapter Seventeen

Kaleb couldn't sleep. Restless, he'd finally got up and paced his living room for so long he was surprised he hadn't worn a trail in the hardwood. He didn't care, though. He was too busy kicking himself for being so stupid. Instead of telling Grace he wanted her to stay in Ouray, he should have proposed. Reassured her that he loved her, whether they were able to have children or not.

He had to go after her. That was all there was to it. And once he found her, he'd do everything in his power to keep her from leaving again.

Problem was, he had no idea where she'd gone.

Roughing a hand over the stubble that lined his jaw, he glanced at the clock on the wall. Five thirty. Would Roger be up by now, or should he wait until six?

Ah, who cared. He'd waited long enough. Maybe some fresh air would help him piece together his thoughts so he wouldn't sound like a bumbling fool.

Outside, the morning air was still, the streets empty as he hoofed his way to Roger and Donna's. Kaleb couldn't remember ever feeling so torn up inside. Not after his accident, not even when Gina left.

But Grace wasn't Gina. She was the rose to his thorns. The face he looked forward to seeing every morning at work. The one who was his voice of reason, able to talk him down off the ledge. He couldn't imagine life without her.

But what if he couldn't find her? No, she'd tell her mother where she was.

He raked a frustrated hand through his hair. Grace had mentioned something about a change of plans with the cruise line. He thought it was just an excuse. But what if they wanted her to come early? Was she headed there now? If so, where was there?

Groaning, he stopped. Hands on his hips, he looked to the sky. Though still dark for the most part, to the east light was trying to make itself known.

Lord, I need Your help here. Show me what I'm supposed to do.

When he finally made it to Roger's, he noticed there were lights on inside. Good. They were up.

Grabbing hold of the handrail, he made his way onto the wooden porch. Suddenly he found himself hesitating. He'd better knock quietly in case Donna was still asleep.

He rapped on the door, noting the scabs on his knuckles. It had taken him hours yesterday to sort through his tools and put them back into their rightful places inside the tool chest. Served him right for reacting the way he did. Though it had seemed like a good idea at the time.

"Come on." He raised his fist to knock again when the door opened.

"Kaleb?" Roger pushed open the screen door. "What are you doing here? And so early?"

He let go a sigh. "I could really use a friend."

Concern morphed into a smile as Roger stepped out of the way and said, "How about a cup of coffee?"

"How about an entire pot?" Kaleb shoved the door closed behind him, then followed his friend into the mostly white kitchen.

While Roger poured the coffee, Kaleb slumped into one of the four wooden chairs around the kitchen table. "Donna still asleep?"

"Yeah. Since coming home from the hospital, she's taken to sleeping a bit longer." The man handed him a large, steaming mug.

Kaleb inhaled the aroma and took a sip.

Roger settled in the chair across from him. "You look terrible, by the way."

He hadn't looked in the mirror, but— "No doubt."

"So what's going on?"

Kaleb rested his forearms on the table. "I didn't tell you, but Grace quit yesterday. Though, seeing as how she's left town, I'm sure you know that by now."

Roger leaned back in his chair. "Any idea why?"

"She said something about the cruise line having a change of plans, but that may have been just fluff. Because, ultimately, she admitted it was because she couldn't have kids and that I deserved them."

"I see." Roger eyed him over the rim of his cup.

"I told her it didn't matter, that we could adopt."

"And?"

Kaleb's heart twisted. "She said her ex told her the same thing."

Roger leaned forward now. "I understand what you're

feeling, Kaleb. I mean, while there wasn't a third party involved, Camille often expressed her regret that she couldn't give me a child." He clasped his hands. "Society tells them that's what they're supposed to do. So when they aren't able to live up to those expectations, they feel as though they've let us down."

"Yeah, well, Grace's ex didn't do me any favors." He took another drink. "Why can't they just believe that they're enough? I didn't say, 'I love you *if* we have kids.' I told her I loved her."

"Do you?"

"Are you kidding? Everything within me is crying out for her. I gotta find her, Roger. Please tell me you know where she's gone."

Something sparked in his friend's gaze and he slowly grinned. "I don't think you'll have to go far."

"What?"

Roger nodded toward the door.

Kaleb whirled around to see Grace standing behind him. He was in such a hurry to stand, he almost toppled his chair. "Grace." He simply stared at her, his breathing ragged.

Grabbing his coffee cup, Roger pushed to his sock feet. "I think I'll leave you two alone."

Still staring, Kaleb wasn't sure whether to hug Grace, kiss her or simply ask her to sit down. Finally, he held out his hand.

Hope flooded through him when she took hold.

He pulled out the chair beside him and she sat down. Without ever letting go of her, he sat, too. "How long were you standing there?"

She smiled then. "Long enough."

He raked his free hand through his hair. A move

he'd done so often, it was probably standing on end like Roger's. But he didn't care. Grace was all that mattered. "How come you're still here?"

"Mama wanted me to wait until the rain passed." She shrugged. "And I needed a little more time with her."

He wasn't sure he wanted to know the answer to his next question, but he'd ask it anyway. "Are you still planning to leave?"

Her beautiful hazel eyes bored into him. "I don't know. Is there a reason for me to stay?"

He brushed his thumb over her knuckles. "I didn't know what my life was missing until you walked into it. And now I don't want to live without you." Scooting to the edge of his seat, he eased down onto his good knee. "I guess what I'm trying to say is, I want to marry you, Grace. And spend forever with you." Looking up at her, he took hold of her other hand, clasping them between both of his. "Grace McAllen, will you marry me?"

Tears welled in her eyes. "Yes." Pulling her hands free, she cupped his cheeks. "You have shown me the true meaning of love, Kaleb Palmer. You taught me to trust again. In God, in love. In you. I love you and I would be proud to be your wife."

Standing, he took her into his arms and kissed her. Best of all, she kissed him back. Without fear or reservation.

When they finally parted, he couldn't stop smiling. Until he remembered— "What about the cruise line? Your contract?"

She laid a hand against his chest. "As I said yesterday, there's been a change in plans."

"I thought you were just saying that."

She shook her head. "No. I got an email Sunday.

They said that, due to unforeseeable circumstances, they were going to have to push our sail date into November. Making my contract null and void, unless I signed an amendment."

"Did you?"

"Not yet."

He nearly choked. "You mean you're still considering it?"

"Not really. Because now I'm thinking that November might be a good time for a wedding."

"Sweetheart, if you're talking about you and me, I'm ready whenever you are."

Epilogue

Grace could hardly believe her ears. Sure, she hadn't felt good since shortly after she and Kaleb returned from their honeymoon in Cancún in November, but she figured it was because she drank the water. Throw in the hubbub of the holidays and anyone would feel a little off-kilter. But this…

"Say that again, Doctor."

He looked at her with a quirky grin. "Mrs. Palmer, not only are you pregnant, the sonogram showed two heartbeats. You're having twins."

"Trent, you need to do me a favor and keep this to yourself, while I figure out a creative way to deliver this news to my husband."

Dr. Lockridge, husband of Kaleb's friend Blakely, laughed. "No worries, Grace. However, I expect to see him with you during your next visit."

Grace practically fell into her new SUV, disbelief still swirling around her. She laid a hand against her belly. She was actually pregnant. With twins!

Kaleb was going to be beside himself. But this wasn't the kind of news she could blurt out in a single statement. This was the kind of thing that needed to be savored a little bit at a time.

And if it involved a little fun on her part, at her husband's expense, so be it.

Okay, first she'd need to make a couple of stops on the way home. Then project baby bomb was under way.

First stop, the market, where she picked up a few items. Then it was on to the hardware store.

Kaleb was so perceptive, though. She was going to be hard-pressed to keep this from him. Not that she planned on waiting forever. After all, a girl could only keep a secret from her husband for so long.

She pulled into the drive, excitement and anticipation vying for center stage. Drawing in a deep breath, she grabbed her bags and headed inside.

"Hey, sweetheart." Kaleb met her at the door and gave her a quick kiss. "What did the doctor have to say?"

"Um, he said I've been drinking too much water."

"Too much water? I didn't think that was possible."

"Apparently it is." She turned to hide her smile. "So what are you working on?"

"Same thing I was when you left. Stripping the wallpaper in the dining room." He slinked out of the kitchen, still not thrilled about giving up his home gym. Fortunately, a gift certificate from his parents to the gym at the hot springs seemed to help soften the blow.

She grabbed her bag from the market, pulled out two pears and gave them a quick rinse. "Hey."

He turned back around.

"How 'bout a snack." She tossed one his way before taking a bite of her own.

He glanced at it. "What's this?"

"A pear, silly. We should start thinking in pairs."

Confusion marred his handsome features. "Are you sure you're okay?"

"Couldn't be better."

A while later, she called him back into the bedroom that still contained all those boxes of memorabilia. "What do you think about one of these colors for this room?" She fanned out several pastel paint chips.

"Grace, I thought we were going to hold off on this room until we finished the others?"

She shrugged. "I know. I just wondered what colors you might like."

To his credit, he studied them. "They don't really go with what we have planned for the rest of the house."

"I know, but I thought we could have a little fun with this space."

He rubbed the back of his neck. "If you say so."

Grace wanted so badly to spill the beans, but forced herself to wait a little longer.

In the spirit of celebration, she prepared seared steak for dinner.

"Kaleb, honey, would you check the oven for me, please?" She really did appreciate the fact that he insisted on helping with meals.

"What's this?"

He held up a hamburger bun.

She had to bite her tongue to keep from laughing. "Looks like somebody put a bun in our oven."

"A bun with steak? That's the most—"

She could almost see the lightbulb flicker to life.

His mouth fell open. "Grace? Did you? Do we?"

Unable to contain her secret anymore, she nodded, her grin from ear to ear. "You are going to be a daddy, my love." She threw her arms around his neck as he lifted her off the floor.

"So that's what these weird things you've been saying were all about."

"Uh-huh."

He spun her around the kitchen. "We're going to have a baby. We're going to have a baby!"

She couldn't resist just one more opportunity to mess with him. "Sort of."

He set her on the floor. "What do you mean, sort of? We're not going to have, like, puppies or something, are we?"

"Not that I'm aware of. However, I was wondering— how many car seats do you think we can fit in the back of the Jeep?"

The countless reactions that crossed his face were absolutely priceless. "Grace?" That deep voice meant it was time for her to come clean.

"According to the doctor, I am pregnant. With twins."

Those same reactions she'd seen just a moment ago returned with a vengeance. His hand fell to her belly. "Twins?"

"Yep." She slipped out of his embrace and snagged her purse from the counter. Then she pulled out the picture of the sonogram and handed it to Kaleb. "Baby A and baby B." She pointed.

He ran a hand through his hair as he exited the kitchen, still staring at the picture, and headed toward the living room. "Two babies?" He dropped onto their new, slipcovered sofa. "This is amazing."

Grace curled up beside him. "Trust me, I was every bit as stunned as you are."

He wrapped an arm around her and pulled her to him. "So when are you—"

"August. Which means we'll need to make plans for the shop. Perhaps we could get Mama and Roger to fill in for a while."

"I have a feeling that won't be a problem." He pulled her into his lap. "I love you, Grace. And just when I think I can't love you any more, you blow me out of the water."

Her hand caressed his cheek. "I guess God had something bigger in store for us."

"Even if he hadn't, I'd still love you with everything I have. These babies are just an extension of that love."

Tears sprang to her eyes as she remembered what Roger had told her about Camille that night in his garage. Camille was a blessed woman. And so was Grace.

God had a plan for her. All she had to do was entrust Him with that plan. And even if children hadn't been a part of it, He had brought her into a new life. One filled with happiness and love and the hope of brighter tomorrows.

* * * * *

LOVE INSPIRED

Stories to uplift and inspire

Fall in love with Love Inspired—
inspirational and uplifting stories of faith
and hope. Find strength and comfort in
the bonds of friendship and community.
Revel in the warmth of possibility and the
promise of new beginnings.

Sign up for the Love Inspired newsletter
at **LoveInspired.com** to be the first
to find out about upcoming titles,
special promotions and exclusive content.

CONNECT WITH US AT:

 Facebook.com/LoveInspiredBooks

Twitter.com/LoveInspiredBks

Get 4 FREE REWARDS!

We'll send you 2 FREE Books plus 2 FREE Mystery Gifts.

FREE
Value Over
$20

Both the **Love Inspired®** and **Love Inspired® Suspense** series feature compelling novels filled with inspirational romance, faith, forgiveness, and hope.

YES! Please send me 2 FREE novels from the Love Inspired or Love Inspired Suspense series and my 2 FREE gifts (gifts are worth about $10 retail). After receiving them, if I don't wish to receive any more books, I can return the shipping statement marked "cancel." If I don't cancel, I will receive 6 brand-new Love Inspired Larger-Print books or Love Inspired Suspense Larger-Print books every month and be billed just $5.99 each in the U.S. or $6.24 each in Canada. That is a savings of at least 17% off the cover price. It's quite a bargain! Shipping and handling is just 50¢ per book in the U.S. and $1.25 per book in Canada.* I understand that accepting the 2 free books and gifts places me under no obligation to buy anything. I can always return a shipment and cancel at any time. The free books and gifts are mine to keep no matter what I decide.

Choose one: ☐ **Love Inspired**
Larger-Print
(122/322 IDN GNWC)

☐ **Love Inspired Suspense**
Larger-Print
(107/307 IDN GNWN)

Name (please print)

Address   Apt. #

City   State/Province   Zip/Postal Code

Email: Please check this box ☐ if you would like to receive newsletters and promotional emails from Harlequin Enterprises ULC and its affiliates. You can unsubscribe anytime.

Mail to the Harlequin Reader Service:
IN U.S.A.: P.O. Box 1341, Buffalo, NY 14240-8531
IN CANADA: P.O. Box 603, Fort Erie, Ontario L2A 5X3

Want to try 2 free books from another series! Call 1-800-873-8635 or visit www.ReaderService.com.

---

*Terms and prices subject to change without notice. Prices do not include sales taxes, which will be charged (if applicable) based on your state or country of residence. Canadian residents will be charged applicable taxes. Offer not valid in Quebec. This offer is limited to one order per household. Books received may not be as shown. Not valid for current subscribers to the Love Inspired or Love Inspired Suspense series. All orders subject to approval. Credit or debit balances in a customer's account(s) may be offset by any other outstanding balance owed by or to the customer. Please allow 4 to 6 weeks for delivery. Offer available while quantities last.

Your Privacy—Your information is being collected by Harlequin Enterprises ULC, operating as Harlequin Reader Service. For a complete summary of the information we collect, how we use this information and to whom it is disclosed, please visit our privacy notice located at corporate.harlequin.com/privacy-notice. From time to time we may also exchange your personal information with reputable third parties. If you wish to opt out of this sharing of your personal information, please visit readerservice.com/consumerschoice or call 1-800-873-8635. **Notice to California Residents**—Under California law, you have specific rights to control and access your data. For more information on these rights and how to exercise them, visit corporate.harlequin.com/california-privacy.

LIRLIS22

Someone was shooting at them!

Liam hit the gas and Shauna braced herself for the
worst. Her body began to shake uncontrollably as the
SUV sped up and jerked from side to side as Liam
attempted to escape.

They were shooting at her this time. Not just attempting
to run her off the road.

These people, whoever they were, wanted her *dead*.

Just like her mother.

Why? She couldn't seem to grasp why she'd suddenly
become a target. It just didn't make any sense. Tears
pricked her eyes, but she held them back.

After what seemed like eons but was likely only fifteen
minutes, the vehicle slowed to a normal rate of speed.

"Are you okay?" Liam asked tersely.

She hesitantly lifted her head, scanning the area. "I—Yes. You?"

"Fine. Thankfully the shooter missed us. I wish I knew exactly where the gunfire came from." He sounded frustrated. "This is my fault. I knew you were in danger, but I didn't expect anyone to fire at us in broad daylight."

"At me." Her voice was soft but firm. "Not you, Liam. This is all about me."

He glanced sharply at her. "They could have easily shot me, too, Shauna. Thankfully, they missed, but that was too close. And you still don't know why these people have come after you?" He hesitated, then added, "Or why they killed your mother?"

"No." She shrugged helplessly. "I'm not lying. There is no reason I can come up with that would cause this sort of action. No one hated either of us this much."

"Revenge?" He divided his attention between her and the road. She didn't recognize the highway they were on, but then again, she didn't know much of anything about Green Lake.

Other than she'd brought danger to the quaint tourist town.

Don't miss
Hiding in Plain Sight *by Laura Scott,*
available September 2022 wherever
Love Inspired Suspense books and ebooks are sold.

LoveInspired.com